PRAISE FOR THE AUTHORS

JENNIFER BLAKE

"Jennifer Blake touches the hearts of
her audience..."
–*Rendezvous*

Jennifer Blake will "thoroughly please."
–*Publishers Weekly*

"Blake...consistently produces
compelling stories..."
–*Library Journal*

EMILIE RICHARDS

Iron Lace is "a gripping novel of
shattering intensity from a storyteller
of outstanding merit."
–*Romantic Times*

Iron Lace "is intricate, seductive and a
darned good read."
–*Publishers Weekly*

Rising Tides "features a multilayered
plot, vivid descriptions, and a keen sense
of time and place."
–*Library Journal*

JENNIFER BLAKE
AND
ÉMILIE RICHARDS

Southern
GENTLEMEN

MIRA

ISBN 1-55166-419-4

SOUTHERN GENTLEMEN
Copyright © 1998 by MIRA Books.

JOHN "RIP" PETERSON
Copyright © 1998 by Patricia Maxwell.

BILLY RAY WAINWRIGHT
Copyright © 1998 by Emilie Richards McGee.

CONTENTS

JOHN "RIP" PETERSON
by Jennifer Blake

1

"I want *you.*"

The bald declaration echoed against the crumbling plaster walls of the old parlor. John "Rip" Peterson let it stand for its shock value, but also because it was the exact truth.

The woman who faced him paled but did not look away. Rip had to admire her valiant self-possession even as he damned it. He didn't scare Anna Montrose one bit. And he wanted to, needed to, or he might as well call it quits.

Backing off was not in the plan. If it had ever been an option, he wouldn't be here at the historic plantation house known as Blest, would have no purpose in confronting Anna. He certainly wouldn't be laying his needs and desires on the line.

"You expect me to—sleep with you?" she asked with disbelief. Her eyes darkened to storm-cloud gray as she waited for his answer.

What would she do if he said yes? The need to find out pounded in Rip's veins, throbbed in the lower part of his body with every hard beat of his heart. Would she allow him to take her if he reached out for her? Or would she slap him down?

The answer would have to wait. He had too much at stake to play that game. At least for now.

"That's a quaint way to put it, also highly inaccurate," he said with a short laugh as he shoved his hands deep into his pants pockets. "Sleep would be the last thing I'd expect—if that kind of payment was what I had in mind. But, no. What I expect from you is something you and your family have always had without question. I want respectability."

Her features went blank for an instant, during which it was almost possible to see her mentally switch gears. The pale tint of her skin flared to a wild rose shade. She moistened her lips—a movement that Rip followed with intense interest and also a drawing sensation in his chest.

When she spoke again, her voice was husky. "I don't think I understand."

No, she wouldn't.

Anna Montrose had never understood him. Not when she was a child, dressed as a Christmas angel with gold-tinsel-edged wings and long, shining blond curls, while he was shanty trash from across the river in ragged denim and broken-down shoes, watching her in awestruck adoration. Not when she was the teenage daughter of the town's most prominent family, zipping around in her fancy convertible while he drove the rusty pickup he'd rescued from a junkyard and put back together with his own greasy hands. Not when he had made a friend of her brother Tom for the sake of being near her, and always claimed he wasn't hungry when invited to eat because they had such perfect table manners while he had none.

Anna would not recognize the low cunning that had made him wait until she heard the rumors he was back, saw his bulldozers on Blest's lawn and finally came to him. She could have no idea that he had planned this meeting so she faced him in the dim room with the light from the high windows falling across her face while his back was to it.

Anna Montrose hadn't changed. She still had the classic features, wide-spaced eyes and shining hair that people thought lovely. She was still perfect while she made him feel like the boy he had once been—big, dark and awkward, hiding his tender feelings under sullen bravado.

He wasn't the same at all. Prison did that to a man.

"It's simple," he answered in caustic explanation. "I want what this town took away from me sixteen long years ago. I intend to begin where I left off, to have my old life back, only better."

"And you think I can arrange that for you?" The question carried wonder beneath its disbelief. He also heard relief, which did nothing for his ego.

Voice soft, gaze lethally straight, he said, "I know you can."

"If I don't, or can't deliver, then you're going to raze Blest."

She drew a deep breath, as if she could not get enough air. The movement lifted her breasts under the cream silk of the short-sleeved suit she wore against the summer heat. She was well aware of where his attention strayed, it seemed, for she crossed her arms over her chest. Her voice was sharp when she spoke.

"You would actually do that, tear down one of the most famous old houses in Louisiana, for the sake of a bunch of retirement condos around a golf course?"

An ironic smile curled his lips. "Is that what the gossip says?"

"Do you deny it?"

"Oh, hell, no," he drawled. "When did it ever do me any good to deny anything in Montrose?"

She hesitated, as if attentive to something in his voice or face. When she spoke again, it was a single, expressionless word. "Why?"

"Business," he said, and stared at her, daring her to contradict him.

She lifted her chin. "I don't think so. I think it's revenge."

"Do you?" he asked. At least she was thinking, which meant he had her full attention.

"You're striking back at the people around here for daring to send you to prison, and at my family for the testimony that helped put you there."

"And what about you? Don't you think I have anything against you?"

She made a small, despairing movement of her head that caused the light from the dusty windows to dance across the wild honey waves of her hair. "I never did anything to you."

Rip's fingers tingled with the need to reach out and shake her, or else smooth his hands over the satin fineness of her skin, the gentle curves under her suit. At the same time, he had a flash of the old, disturbing feeling that his touch might sully her.

As he stared at her, however, he saw she was not quite as he had pictured her so often in his mind. She was taller, and her face had lost its youthful fullness so that the skin conformed more closely to the fine symmetry of the bone structure. Her eyes were more secretive, yet oddly more vulnerable. Just looking at her made his throat tighten and his chest swell.

"Maybe it was what you didn't do," he answered finally, though the suggestion carried an undertone of derision directed, for the most part, at himself.

Her lips tightened and she looked away. It was a hint that she remembered, as well as he did, the hot, delirious summer afternoon when they had almost become lovers.

For an instant he was there again in that far-off moment. He could feel the tender shape of her beneath him, the warm sun between his shoulder blades, the grass tickling his forearms braced on either side of her. He remembered the haunting fragrance of her skin and hair, the quick thuds of her heart beating against his chest. She had been so sweet, all yielding grace and innocence. He had been clumsy with disbelief and fear that he might hurt her. And with terror that it wouldn't, couldn't, last.

How right he had been.

"I don't think this has anything to do with me at all," she said finally. "I think you've come back here with fistfuls of money and a king-size chip on your shoulder. You want to prove to everyone that you made good in spite of them, regardless of what happened. You've looked for a way to hurt Montrose and my family, and destroying Blest seems a good place to start."

"It would be, wouldn't it?" The words were pensive as he watched the agitation and distress mirrored on her features.

"Oh, no doubt! If anybody knows how to hurt us, it's you. You understand how much this house means, has always meant. You heard my mother and father talk about the old days here a thousand times. You were there when Tom and I used to scheme about buying it back, restoring it to the way it was before my grandfather lost it during the Depression.''

She was right. Having no dreams of his own, Rip had latched on to theirs, Anna's and Tom's. He had grown to love the old West Indies house with its long galleries like sheltering arms, spacious rooms, intricate woodwork and huge, ghostlike murals. He had even loved the name: Blest, blessed place, home of the blessed.

He had loved it, coveted it. Now it was his, to do with as he pleased.

''I know how you feel about it,'' he said after a moment, ''how Tom felt.''

''You and Tom were…''

''Good friends,'' he supplied as she faltered, then stopped.

She gave him a straight look. ''He never came back.''

''I know.''

''Who told you?''

''I made it my business to stay informed,'' he said evasively.

''My mother always thought you knew something, had some idea where he might have gone.'' The words were taut with suspicion.

''She was wrong. Tom never contacted me.''

Anna gave no answer, only looked away again, shielding her dark gray gaze with lashes that made faint shadow patterns against the fragile skin under her eyes.

''Neither Tom nor any of the rest of it has anything to do with what I want from you,'' Rip said, as much for the distraction as to return to their original discussion. He didn't like seeing her in pain, even if he was the one who had caused it. Especially if he'd caused it.

"Oh, certainly not," she said in sarcastic disbelief as her head came up. "Respectability, I think you said. I suppose you want to be a gentleman farmer, maybe president of the chamber of commerce or even deacon—"

"No!" He stopped her with a chopping gesture of one hand. "Social position, public office—they mean nothing to me. I just want to be a part of this community."

"You don't need me for that."

"Oh, but I do," he said quietly. "I need someone to show me how to dress, how to act, which fork to use—all the things I never knew and haven't had time to learn in the last few years. That someone is you."

"If I agree, you're willing to forget the retirement complex, leave Blest alone. Just like that?"

"Not quite," he said, holding his gaze steady. "If you undertake to turn me into a gentleman, I plan to restore the house and live here."

A puzzled frown pleated her brow. "But you could learn the things you need from anyone."

"You're the key, the only way it will work," he corrected her. "It's not enough to turn myself into the kind of man who might live here. I also need to be seen with you to show that my company's acceptable. That means going out to dinner together, showing up wherever a man and woman might go for entertainment these days. I would expect you to introduce me to your friends and include me in any invitations that might come your way in the next few weeks."

"You have it all worked out."

"I believe in having an alternative plan," he said in answer to the suspicion in her voice. "This was always a possibility."

Anna studied him an instant, as if trying to read his face. "You know most of my friends. We all went to school together."

"That doesn't mean they'll give me the time of day unless you vouch for me."

"You underestimate them, I think," she answered. "But I still don't understand. You've made it big in a world where small town folk like us can't even compete. Why do you care what anyone thinks?"

"Maybe I have something to prove."

"And you'll use me to do it."

"You can always refuse." The words were reasonable enough, but he allowed no hint of compromise to shade his voice.

She moved away a few restless steps. Glancing over her shoulder, she said, "You're certain that's all you expect?"

"It's a start. Of course, if I keep the house I'll have to renovate, make it livable. I'll need you to show me how things once were, help choose colors and furnish the rooms. It could turn into quite a job, but I'm sure we can work out an acceptable financial arrangement."

She stopped, turned to face him. "You're offering to pay me?"

"It's a normal exchange, services for cash."

"I don't want your money."

"You don't have to make it sound as if I'm trying to turn you into a call girl," he said tightly. "Unless you'd prefer it that way."

"No!" As if to soften that rejection, she said again in a lower tone, "No."

His laugh was short. "I thought not."

Anna felt drained, as if she were fighting a losing battle. The man who faced her in the shadowed, high-ceilinged room had a reputation as a hard business opponent, a demon at negotiation and an expert at manipulation to achieve his goals. She could believe it. He was using her doubts and suspicions to make her do exactly as he wanted.

She didn't know Rip Peterson anymore, couldn't begin to guess what was going on in his mind. The man who stood before her was a stranger, powerfully built, attractive in a harsh, intense fashion, but frightening in his assurance and inflexible purpose. Only his midnight black hair, coppery skin and the high cheekbones which proclaimed the Spanish and Indian "Red Bone" blood inherited from his mother's family were any indication he was the same boy she had known.

Blest, her Blest, belonged to Rip Peterson, town bad boy turned electronic mogul, who had confounded them all by beating the odds. He had bought the place from behind the protection of a faceless corporation, so the gossips said, claimed it before anyone could guess what he was doing. It was his and he was holding it to ransom.

Would he really destroy the fine old house if she refused his request? Staring at his hard features across the dusty width of the parlor floor with its threadbare Aubusson carpet, Anna thought he might easily tear Blest down board by board out of sheer malice. Or for no more than a vindictive whim.

Blindly, she turned away from him, moving toward

the open doorway and into the long hallway that cut through the house from front to back. She paused, her gaze on the mural that stretched along the entire length of the north wall.

It showed Blest as it had been in another time, a grand showplace set like a gem against the white velvet of cotton fields in full bloom. Small black figures toiled along the cotton rows while gentlemen in tailcoats and ladies in wide skirts took their leisure on the upper gallery. Still, the scene was misty and ephemeral, as if based on a myth without substance, a false celluloid dream of how life in the south had once been.

The real focal point, however, was the three young people who picnicked under a tree on the front lawn. It was Anna, Tom and Rip in modern clothing, two of them blond and tan, the other dark and slightly apart. All three appeared to be relaxed and contemplative in the summer heat, intent on their own dreams. They were a part of the past yet separate from it; they looked forward, not back.

This particular composition had been done by Blest's caretaker, Papa Vidal, using ordinary house paint, during one of the long-ago summers when Anna, Tom and Rip had first found their way into the big, deserted house. The two old ladies who had bought Blest in the late thirties had just died and the niece from California who had inherited couldn't be bothered to look after it, much less live in it. The niece had let Papa Vidal stay on in the small cottage on the grounds that had been his home all his life.

The elderly black man was a local legend. Even sixteen years ago, he had been of venerable age and quite a character, with white hair like crinkled spiderwebs, patchwork vests he quilted himself, and a Silky chicken named Henrietta that he carried in a deep pocket. He hadn't minded the three teenagers coming around. He knew they weren't apt to bother anything, knew the family history and the fact that half the old furniture in the place were Montrose family heirlooms sold with the estate.

Papa Vidal enjoyed their company. He told them many stories, about the young bride who ran screeching from the house on her wedding night in the 1840s, the sharecropper who hanged himself in the toolshed during the 1880s, the famous author who hid out in a back bedroom in the 1950s and handed manuscript pages through the door in exchange for glasses of whiskey. He told, too, of how he started to paint using brushes left behind by some artistic visitor, and of the yearly art festival that had evolved from the display of some of his canvases downtown on the courthouse square.

The times the three of them spent with Papa Vidal had been balmy, endless days. But they were long gone.

Over her shoulder, Anna said to Rip, "Things have changed since you left. For one thing, my dad died."

"A heart attack, wasn't it?"

His voice came from much closer than she expected. He had followed her, moving with the powerful, silent grace she remembered so well.

"He never really got over Tom's disappearance. He left a fair-size insurance policy but not a lot more. My mother and I had to cut back, move into a smaller house. I couldn't manage college so I went to trade school. Afterward, I took a job as a legal assistant—"

"And married your boss," he said, the words without expression.

She turned to lean against the chair rail under the mural. "If you know that, then you probably know it lasted less than three years, so the job and the husband terminated at the same time. Now I work at the courthouse. What I'm trying to say is, I don't have the influence you seem to think, not anymore."

"I hear you went back to your maiden name, that you're a Montrose again."

"For what good it does. Nobody cares about things like that."

He gave a short laugh. "Don't kid yourself."

"Times are different. Montrose isn't quite the insular backwater it used to be. New people, new businesses have moved in so the old order is almost gone. Anyway, I still don't know why you care. You've moved on, put what happened behind you and become somebody. Peterson Systems is a giant player in cyberspace. You've lived in Dallas, on the West Coast—"

"Was a player," he interrupted. "I've sold out."

She'd heard the rumor but couldn't bring herself to believe it, especially with the millions said to be involved. "Why would you do that?"

"It wasn't fun anymore," he answered, with a moody shrug. "Besides, I had other things to do."

"But you could do them anyplace. Why come back here?"

"What happened here was important to me," he answered, his gaze challenging. "It changed my life, took away a lot of hopes, a lot of plans. I want them back. More than that, I want compensation."

A quick frown pleated her brows. "Compensation? What do you mean?"

"I didn't do it, Anna." His eyes were dark coffee

brown as they held hers. "I didn't rob anybody, and you should know it."

"What? But—"

"Tell me something," he interrupted. "Is the old Bon Vivant Club still around?"

"Yes, certainly," she answered, trying to follow his fast change of subject. What a men's club like the Bon Vivants—with their fish fries on the lake and venison cookouts at the hunting camp—had to do with anything, she couldn't imagine.

"Good. I'd like membership."

"What on earth for?"

"A matter of principle."

Anna thought about it even as she noted the taut muscle in his jaw, the lines that radiated from the corners of his eyes, the width of his shoulders that strained his polo shirt. Finally, she said, "I don't know if it's possible. You'd have to be proposed and approved. It's the kind of thing a man does for his son, his nephew, his wife's brother or maybe an old friend."

"Exactly. It's the Louisiana version of an old boy's club, where the important things get decided, such as who's going to run for state representative or who leases out space for government offices." He paused. "I want it."

"Surely you don't care about any of those things," she protested.

"Call it a symbol," he countered with grim determination. "When I'm in, a paid-up member, I'll know I've made it in Montrose. That's when your job will be over and done."

She could see his point, but there were problems. "You'll need the backing of someone important."

"So persuade one of your cousins to do it."

"I'm not sure it would help."

"You mean considering my criminal record? Or is the problem my Red Bone blood? Those things are what make it a challenge. It would be too easy, otherwise."

"What if it doesn't happen? Isn't there something else that would serve the same purpose?"

He watched her for a long instant, his face shadowed. Then a brief smile flickered across the firmly molded contours of his mouth. With a voice rough yet beguiling in its rich depth, he said, "There is, now that you mention it."

The glint in his eyes warned her; the fleeting expression caused her heart to slam against the wall of her chest. "Yes?"

He smiled again as he answered with precision, "You could marry me."

2

"**Y**ou can't be serious."

Rip watched Anna's eyes widen as she spoke, the pupils growing large and dark. Still, she didn't look particularly shocked or angry. A prickle of wariness crawled down the back of his neck.

"You'd be surprised how serious I can be about that subject," he said quietly.

She looked away. "Even marriage might not bring the acceptance you seem to think it will."

"I'll take my chances." There was something going on behind her smooth, even features, Rip thought. It seemed she could actually be considering his proposition.

"Let me be certain I have this straight," she said, her voice not quite even as she turned back to him. "Either I help you become a respected citizen of Montrose or you'll bulldoze Blest to the ground. As proof of success, you require membership in the Bon Vivant Club. If that fails, you expect me to—become your wife."

"That's about the size of it. Except for one last thing."

"And that is?"

Anna wasn't quite as calm as she appeared, for her lips trembled at the corners before she tightened them. With satisfaction, Rip said, "There's a deadline. One month. You have until the Bon Vivant's midsummer dance."

"That isn't much time!"

"It's all I intend to give it. Anyway, it's enough if it can be done."

She didn't appear convinced. "When would you want an answer?"

"Now would be good."

"You can't expect me to decide so soon. There's a lot at stake. I need time to think." She swallowed hard as she waited for his answer.

Rip dragged his gaze away from that small, convulsive movement, firmly squelching the need to press his lips to her slender throat. "I'll be having dinner tomorrow night at the old steak house on Jimerson Road. If you show up, I'll know we're on. If not, I bring in the demolition crew."

Disdain rose in the fathoms-deep gray of her eyes. "Just like that? You really are a bastard, aren't you."

"I always was." His laugh was hollow as he discovered that the truth still had the power to hurt. "But there's one difference. I know what I want now, and I go for it."

She flinched as she absorbed the threat. For an instant, Rip thought she would answer it. Then she compressed her lips and swung away from him, striding down the long hall. She was silhouetted for an instant against the sunlight beyond the open front door, then she was gone.

* * *

The early summer heat struck Anna like a blow as she descended the front steps. It reflected off the worn treads where the paint had flaked away from the wood, eddied up from the uneven brick sidewalk. The sun's glare was so brilliant that stepping into the deep shade of the old oak where she had parked her car was like entering a cool, dark pool.

Something shifted in front of her. She stopped abruptly.

"Afternoon, Miss Anna."

Relief washed through her at that familiar greeting. Moving forward more slowly, she said, "Papa Vidal. I didn't see you."

"Reckon I'm so old I'm 'bout a ghost," he said, chuckling. "'Course, you were studyin' on other things, important things."

She made a wry grimace. "You could say that."

"Only natural, considerin'. Been thinkin' a lot my own self lately." He gave her an intent look before he wagged his head. "I'm getting on, you know. Be ninety-four, come August."

It was hard to believe, since he never seemed to change. Still, as Anna looked closer, she could see his face was like a wizened brown apple, and his clothes sagged on his frail, bony frame. She smiled with affection as she touched his arm. "Your ninety-fourth birthday! That's fantastic."

"Don't like to think of leavin' Blest. Always expected I'd see a hundred here. It's my home."

"Your work is here, too. It breaks my heart to think of it being destroyed."

"'Preciate that, Miss Anna," he said, ducking his head. "I know it's just a lot of cheap paint slopped over the walls, hardly worth botherin' about a-tall, but the big paintings are my best. The house goes, they go.''

The big murals would never survive removal; Papa Vidal was right about that. The paint was so fragile it would crumble away at any attempt. Pieces might be cut out and preserved, but that would be a sacrilege, since a large part of their impact depended on size and position in the rooms.

But Papa Vidal was far too modest about the value of his work. There was not another African-American painter of his stature in the country, especially not one who had been painting for so long. From his earlier, more primitive paintings done in Blest's outbuildings to the softer, idealized scenes in the big house, his mural series was an invaluable record of how things had been and how he had seen them, as well as a monument to his vision and talent.

The elderly man reached into the gaping pocket of his vest and pulled out his Silky chicken with its feathers like strings of fretted white satin. Cradling it in the crook of his arm, he smoothed the chicken as if to comfort it, while the little hen closed its eyes in bliss. The Silky was the same one he had raised from a chick the summer everything went wrong, Anna thought.

Reaching out to touch the little hen's satiny back, she asked, ''How is Henrietta?''

''Tolerable,'' the old man allowed, ''but gettin' old, like me. She won't like leavin' Blest, either.''

''I know.'' Anna sighed. ''It's so hard to believe Rip would actually destroy it.''

''Mist' Rip, now, he's not a bad man,'' Papa Vidal said, cocking his head. ''He's just kinda lost and hurtin' inside. Reckon he has been for a long time.''

''That's no excuse for destroying Blest.''

"That's so. But he won't do it, not if you don't let him."

Papa Vidal obviously knew something of what Rip had in mind. He could have overheard a snatch of her exchange with the new owner of Blest, or Rip might even have discussed it with him. The two of them must have had ample opportunity to talk since Rip had taken possession.

"Did he send you to tell me that?" she asked, her voice taut with suspicion.

Papa Vidal raised his white brows. "Mist' Rip? He don't bother me none and I don't bother him."

"You're sure? He spent a lot of time hanging around here with you at one time."

"Didn't have nowhere else to go, not after his mama died and his daddy turned snake mean, took to knockin' him around. He was a good boy, used to hold my ladder while I climbed up to paint my skies."

"Yes, I—remember."

Looking away, she followed the swooping flight of a brown thrasher that landed on the sagging, wrought-iron fence of the old family cemetery located on the far side of the drive. The thrasher flitted into a tangle of Muscatine vines and briars under the cedar trees that shaded the graves.

Anna, Rip and Tom had spent long days, years ago, playing among the tall monuments and white marble sofas of the above-ground tombs that lay inside the old fence. It had been their special, quiet place where no one else ever came.

She had given Rip his nickname there one summer after he fell asleep while lying on the weathered slab covering her great-grandfather's grave. It had seemed natural, since his dark head had been pillowed on the ancient, etched initials RIP—Rest in Peace. She had been only, what? Twelve, thirteen? Even so, she'd sat watching him a long time, letting him sleep because she knew his father often staggered home drunk at night and dragged Rip from bed to punish him for some imagined misdeed.

Rip's father had drowned while fishing on the lake near town during a thunderstorm. Evidence indicated he'd been too drunk at the time to seek safety. Rip, then at Angola prison, had not attended the funeral.

"I know Mist' Rip wouldn't do anything against me," Papa Vidal said, reclaiming her attention, "not if he could help it. But if he can't have what he wants, then he'll pull down the whole shebang, get rid of the reminders. Then he'll go away and never come back. Reckon old Papa Vidal will have to head on over to the nursin' home on the east side then."

"Autumn Manor? They say it's nice. You might like it."

"It's not bad, no, ma'am, just won't be home. And ain't no place there for Henrietta."

Papa Vidal, crafty old soul that he was, had an oblique way of getting at things, Anna knew. He would never come right out and plead his case, since that would make her feel bad if she had to decline and cause him the embarrassment of being refused. Regardless, he was asking for her help. He thought he had that right, given that once, generations ago, her ancestors and his had lived and worked together at Blest. The ancient obligation was unspoken, possibly even unrecognized, yet went deep.

She said quietly, "I'll do my best to see that everything turns out right."

His wise old face settled into lines of fatalistic ac-

ceptance as he reached to open her car door and hold
it for her. "That's all a body can do, ain't it? Their
best."

The words remained with Anna as she drove on to
work, and then as she tried to concentrate on her job.
The things Rip had said tumbled through her mind as
well, along with old images of him, Tom and herself
at Blest, images that she had thought long forgotten.
She could almost see the three of them: roasting hot
dogs over a fire in the old smokehouse in winter; playing dress-up with ancient clothes dragged from an attic
trunk; spending a whole week one spring gluing a broken china plate back together. That day, they had used
a piece of the plate to cut their wrists before mingling
their blood and swearing to always protect and be true
to each other.

Papa Vidal had been a part of that time. He was
always there, always looking out for them. She was
troubled by his plea, and by the feeling that she must
not fail him.

There was one other thing that haunted her. It was
the possibility Rip knew more about Tom's disappearance than he was telling. That she might be able
to discover just how much he knew had occurred to
her in the parlor at Blest.

She wasn't sure it would work; still, she had to try.
To do that, she had to agree to what Rip wanted from
her, for there was no other way. But there was a major
problem. First she had to convince her mother that
trying to reestablish Rip Peterson was not only feasible
but reasonable.

Matilda Montrose could be depended on to go off
the deep end when she discovered Anna had talked to
Rip. She had never liked him, never approved of her

son's friendship with him, much less Anna's, so she had always made things extremely uncomfortable when he was around. After the robbery and Tom's failure to come home following Rip's arrest, Anna's mother had become almost unhinged in her hatred. Far from feeling any regret or compassion that he'd wound up in prison at only eighteen, she told everyone who would listen that he got exactly what he deserved. Anna would have to choose her words carefully to make Matilda listen to what she had in mind.

She never got the chance.

"What in the name of heaven were you doing at Blest with that man?" Matilda Montrose demanded as she met Anna at the door of their plain, ranch-style home when Anna returned from work. "I couldn't believe my ears when Carolyn Bates told me she passed by and saw your car. How could you be so stupid? There's no telling what he might have done to you!"

Her mother had been drinking; Anna could smell it on her breath, hear it in her voice. It had become the answer to everything for the older woman, an escape from memories she couldn't bear, refuge from the changes in her life she despised. In weary irritation, Anna said, "Rip didn't do a thing. In fact, he was a perfect gentleman."

"As if that were possible. Well, he won't get another chance because you won't be going anywhere near him. You hear me?"

"How can I help but hear since you're yelling." Moving past her mother, Anna put her purse down on the catchall table in the entrance and walked on toward her bedroom at the far end.

"I'm telling you how it's going to be," the older

woman insisted as she followed her. "I won't have you taking up with your brother's murderer."

"You don't know that Tom's dead," Anna said wearily. "And you certainly don't know if Rip killed him."

"But I do! I feel it here, in my heart." Matilda Montrose clenched a fist and pressed it to her ample bosom.

It was an old claim. Anna felt she should have more patience with it, and with her mother's anguish, but found it hard to sympathize with someone so determined to be miserable. She said with careful logic, "That isn't proof."

"We've had no word in all these years. How much more do you need?"

"I don't know... Something more substantial." She kicked off her plain leather pumps and began to unbutton the jacket of her suit. Her fingers weren't quite as deft as normal—the only sign of her disturbance. Anna took after her father's family, calm in a crisis and stoic in the face of pain. She was slender and of medium height where her mother was stout and short, fair where Matilda was dark. It seemed the two of them were never more different than when things went wrong.

"He's gone, you just won't admit it," the older woman insisted. "But never mind. I want to know what possessed you to stop at Blest knowing that man was there."

Anna explained the meeting in a few succinct sentences, omitting only the details concerning a possible marriage. There was no point in upsetting her mother over something so unlikely to take place.

The diplomacy was wasted. Matilda Montrose went

into hysterics, crying and screaming until she made herself sick. Anna helped her to the bathroom and held her head, then wet a cloth for her face. With her arm around her plump, shaking shoulders, she said, "Don't cry, Mother, please don't cry. It's going to be all right."

"How can you say that? Nothing will ever be the same. Blest has stood there so many years while other big houses rotted or were dynamited out of existence. It's not even my family home and I can't bear it. For you to act as if it doesn't matter—I just don't understand!"

That was true enough, Anna knew. Her mother never could understand or believe in grief that was held inside. She never realized it hurt just as much, maybe more. "Blest doesn't have to be destroyed."

"No, but the alternative is unthinkable! Days, even weeks, spent with that convict? Being seen with him, having people believe— No, no, no!"

"Ex-convict, and long ago at that. He only served three years. Anyway, it wouldn't be so bad, not really."

The older woman held her washcloth to her mouth, giving Anna a look of reproach. "You and Tom always had a blind spot where that boy was concerned. I tried to tell you, but I think you positively enjoyed defying me. You had a stupid schoolgirl crush on that Red Bone trash. I know you did."

"I felt...sorry for him," she answered. Catching sight of herself in the bathroom mirror, she noticed that her eyes were dark with the memories.

"Wasted effort! I remember his mother, a slut if ever there was one. No wonder she got herself pregnant. No surprise his father never married her, either."

"What does that have to do with Rip?"

"Blood will tell. I'm sure that boy deserved every whipping he got."

"You don't know—"

"And don't want to!"

Anna held on to her temper with a supreme effort. "Rip was a real friend to Tom and to me, not that it makes any difference. The important thing now is saving Blest."

"I don't know about that," her mother said, lowering the washcloth and folding it over and over in her hands. "It will be terrible to see it torn down, but it's not the first old house to go, after all, and won't be the last. I can't stand the thought of you and that man together, can't bear my friends to see it. No, it would be too humiliating."

Anna studied the mottled red in her mother's face while determination rose inside her. "Suppose," she said in tentative tones, "just suppose I could learn something about Tom, about what happened that night to cause him to leave?"

Her mother stiffened. Lifting her head, she stared hard at Anna's reflection. "I thought you were sure Rip had nothing to do with it."

"I didn't say that. I just prefer to think there's some explanation, something that doesn't mean Tom is..."

"*Dead* is the word you're looking for" came the acid rejoinder. "Do you really suppose Rip will tell you anything?"

"I don't know," Anna answered. "There may be nothing to tell. But isn't it worth a try?"

The other woman looked away, her eyes unfocused. "You'd have to pretend you like him, pretend to believe any fantastic lie he decides to tell you about that awful evening.''

"Yes." Anna paused a moment before she added, ''Did you ever let yourself think, even for a minute, that he might not be guilty?''

"Never!" The single word was spoken with loathing.

"Has it ever occurred to you how very odd it was for him to smash a window and break into the service station where he worked, when the owner had trusted him with a key so he could come and go as he pleased?''

"He just wanted to make it look like somebody else did it, that's all.''

"Really? When the money was taken from a safe only someone familiar with the place should have known about? You've accused Rip of a lot of things, Mother, but I've never heard you call him stupid.''

"Too smart for his own good is more like it. It's unnatural.''

"Considering where he came from? Shanty trash—isn't that the label you gave him?''

"Exactly.''

"That's what I thought,'' Anna said with a twist of her lips.

To exonerate Rip would mean her mother must find other reasons for the money showing up in his possession later, perhaps even rethink his involvement in her son's disappearance. She might have to look closer to home for motives that would make Tom leave, and that was something she could never do. Tom had been her flawless, darling son who loved his family above all. Nothing must interfere with that vision she held in her mind.

"Rip Peterson was convicted in a court of law," her mother insisted.

"So he was. He was sentenced and he served his time. But why didn't he testify in his own defense?"

"Because it would have been too incriminating!"

"Even a lie would have been better than refusing to say a word."

"That was his way, never opening his mouth for so much as hello or goodbye, always hanging around, coming and going with Tom. Reminded me of some stray dog sneaking in and out."

"Afraid of being run off the premises?" Anna suggested.

"Watching for a handout or a chance to steal something, I always thought! I couldn't stand him around me."

"He knew."

"I should think so, since I didn't bother to hide it. The last thing I wanted was to encourage him. The way he used to follow you around, watching you, made my skin crawl."

"Me?" Anna couldn't keep the startled interest from her voice.

"From the time you were a little girl. I caught him playing with your hair one time when you were only eight or nine. You were just sitting in his lap, letting him do it."

"I remember," Anna said slowly. "You made such a fuss."

"You were between his legs, leaning back against him with your hand on his knee. It was disgusting!"

"I was a child," Anna said in annoyance at the innuendo. "Rip couldn't have been more than eleven or twelve himself."

"Old enough to know what he was doing," her mother insisted.

"And that was?"

"Touching you, taking advantage in the most nasty..." Matilda Montrose shuddered, leaving that damning word hanging.

"I don't remember it that way."

However, Anna had a disturbing flash of warmth as she recalled sleepy pleasure and a feeling of being enclosed by the safe strength of Rip's arms while he wound her hair around his fingers as though he loved the feel of it. The two of them had been so attuned to each other that they breathed with the same deep cadence while their hearts beat to an identical steady rhythm.

Another incident sprang to mind as she stood there. "Speaking of dogs, I don't recall you objecting to Rip being around the day that rabid foxhound came into the backyard."

"He was older and bigger. It was natural for him to step between you and that beast!"

"Tom was older, too, but he ran away," Anna pointed out.

"To get help! Anyway, no one knew it was a mad dog."

Anna gave her mother a straight look. "Rip knew. He told me when he picked me up and put me in the swing, said to stay there and I'd be safe. He didn't run, even when the dog attacked. Afterward, he had to take all those antirabies shots in the stomach."

"Injections your father paid for," her mother replied in righteous indignation.

"You drove him to the clinic."

"Only because you and Tom made such a fuss about being there to hold his hand."

"But Rip never cried, never made a sound," Anna said, remembering out loud.

"Day after day I carted that boy back and forth, but did he speak a word of thanks? No, indeed!"

Anna shook her head. "Why should Rip have been grateful? He fought that dog for me. If he hadn't been there, I might have been killed. Did *you* thank him for that?"

"You and Tom said everything necessary at the time. You actually threw your arms around that Red Bone boy and cried. His blood was all over you, even in your hair. So sickening! Of course, I was never sure that awful mongrel didn't follow him from across the river in the first place."

"Mother!"

"Anyway, it was our duty to see after his injuries and we did it," she continued, flushing as she avoided her daughter's gaze. "If we hadn't, his drunken father probably would have sued because the boy was hurt on our property."

Anna wondered if her mother had any idea how she sounded. It seemed doubtful. It was also unlikely that anything Anna said would bring her self-serving attitude home to her. "It's also my duty, as I see it, to cooperate with Rip. I owe it to Tom."

Matilda Montrose clenched her hands together on the washcloth she still held. "Rip Peterson is dangerous! He's come back here to settle old scores, and won't care who he hurts while he's doing it."

"He spoke of compensation, not vengeance." At least, Anna thought, he had never admitted to the last.

"It doesn't matter. He hates us, hates the whole

town, for what was done to him. You can't forget that, not for a second.'' Her mother stopped abruptly, putting a hand to her trembling lips.

"No, I won't forget. I'll be extremely careful,'' Anna said. She knew very well how dangerous Rip could be to her. No one knew it better.

"No, really, Anna. You're to have nothing to do with him, do you hear me?''

Anna didn't answer.

3

Rip waited for Anna at a corner table. A long-necked beer sat in front of him, and he stripped its label with his thumbnail, watching the operation with concentration. He tried to appear relaxed as he leaned back in his chair, his long legs in black jeans stretched out to one side. It was a pose, however, for the shoulders beneath his open-necked white shirt were stiff with tension, and the free hand that rested on his thigh was curled into a fist.

No one was paying him the slightest attention. In fact, the other patrons in the steak house carefully avoided looking in his direction. He didn't think it was deliberate ostracism, rather that no one wanted to be caught staring. The net effect was to leave him set apart, alone.

He knew the instant Anna arrived. She stood just inside the doorway, looking as if she had half a mind to turn and run. To give her that chance, he returned his gaze to the beer label he'd been mangling.

She didn't leave, after all, but moved forward, threading her way through the tables. A faint smile curved her lips as he turned his head and met her gaze.

"Sorry I'm late," she said, her voice clear and only a little breathless. "I hope you haven't been waiting long."

Not long at all, only a couple dozen lifetimes, Rip thought wryly as he got to his feet and pulled out a chair for her. But he was light-headed with relief that she was here at all. If a flash of triumph came with it, that was his secret. Her presence meant she would do as he asked. The first round was over and he had won.

He made an offhand answer as he seated her, then returned to his chair. Grasping at some kind of normality, he asked if she would like a drink, then caught the attention of a waitress and ordered the iced tea requested. He sat for a moment, then, enjoying the picture Anna made in a sleeveless dress of leaf green cinched by a wide straw belt, with peridot earrings gleaming in her ears. Her makeup was minimal; her lipstick a fresh coral just bright enough to make her lips softly enticing. Her hair was drawn back from the clear lines of her face by a pair of gold barrettes.

As he watched her, a stray impression ran through his mind. He spoke before he thought. "Your hair used to be lighter."

"I suppose so," she said, lifting a self-conscious hand to the soft wave at her temple. "It was sun-bleached back then. Most blondes turn darker as they get older unless they give Mother Nature a helping hand."

"But you don't bother."

"Too much trouble," she agreed, meeting his gaze without evasion.

"I like it natural, makes you look more..."

"Mature?" The word was said in dry suggestion.

"Ladylike," he corrected her, and watched with a feeling of loss as the humor faded from her face.

"That kind of lady went out with bustles and high-button shoes," Anna said. "I'm just an ordinary woman trying to make a decent living while looking after the things that matter to me."

"Such as Blest and an old black man?" His gaze was watchful as he took a deep swallow of his beer.

"You could say that."

"That doesn't strike you as being out of the ordinary?"

"Why should it?"

"Trust me, it is. You're the genuine article," he said with conviction.

"Oh, I don't think—"

Rip shook his head, a smile tugging one corner of his mouth. Setting his beer aside, he spread the fingers of his left hand to count off his points with his right forefinger. "You know who your great-grandfathers were, and their great-grandfathers. You can trace your ancestors back to the Flood. You can set a formal table with the right glasses, spoons and forks in the proper places. You could plan a meal for a political banquet, and have no problem deciding what to make for a church picnic. You are probably able to read a menu in French or Spanish, and you know what somebody means when they refer to an opera or book title. Your handwriting is like elegant script, and you not only have the right phrases for thank-you notes at your fingertips, but actually write the things." He spread his hands and leaned back. "If you're not a bona fide lady, then you're close enough for me."

She stared at him, her gaze wide. Then she laughed with a short, winded sound as she sat back. "Well.

I'm not sure what to say, though I don't know that I'm half as accomplished as you seem to think."

So Anna thought he was guessing? That was good, because Rip knew he'd said too much. The back of his neck burned as he realized how much he'd revealed. But if he was lucky, she'd be so bowled over by his argument that she wouldn't begin to wonder at the extent of his knowledge about her, wouldn't recognize how closely he'd monitored her life-style over the years in order to come by it.

"You can say we're on," he answered, his voice gruff. "Say you'll take me in hand and turn me into the kind of gentleman who might match a lady like you."

Silvery glints appeared in the gray of her eyes. She drew a quick breath before she spoke. "I could be wrong, but I don't think a crash course in how to write thank-you notes is going to be of much benefit to you. What is it exactly that you want to learn?"

"Manners," he said promptly. "Which fork to use. How to order a meal in a fancy restaurant. How to talk to people without making an idiot of myself."

"There's nothing wrong with your manners that I can see. As a matter of fact, not many of the men I know stand up when a woman enters a room anymore."

"Your dad did it," he said simply.

"Well, yes."

"I used to watch him. And Tom."

The light faded from her face. Quietly she said, "Then you couldn't have chosen better examples."

Rip was aware of that, just as he understood he had made a mistake by mentioning the men of her family. To distract her, he nodded toward another table. "On that subject, look at the guy over there still wearing his hat. Even I recognize there's something wrong there. What happened to the rule about taking off headgear before you eat?''

A faint grin twitched her lips, shaded with what might have been gratitude for the change of subject. ''That rule started about because everything was so dusty in the old days that dirt collected on hat brims. A man sitting down to eat with his hat on could dump dirt on the table the minute he bowed his head to say grace.''

''The rule no longer applies now that streets are paved?''

''I wouldn't say that. But so few men wear hats that places like restaurants don't have hat racks anymore. A Stetson sitting on a table is not only in the way but likely to catch food splatters. If it's placed in a chair, somebody may sit on it. Neither one is going to improve a hat, and Stetsons are expensive.''

''Too expensive to leave on a hat rack if one was provided, come to think of it. Somebody could walk off with it.''

''And police today might frown on shooting a man for stealing a hat. The point is, there are reasons for manners. Once the rule makes sense, then it's easy to remember.''

Rip was silent a moment, enjoying the lively interest in her face. ''So do I get a history lesson with every pointer on how to be a gentleman?''

''Probably,'' she answered.

''When do we start?''

''We just did.''

His frown was skeptical. ''In that case, do I take off my hat or not, supposing I have one?''

"Whatever makes you feel better about yourself."

"I'd rather," he said deliberately, "do what makes a woman like you think better of me."

She flushed a little and opened her mouth to answer, but he was given no chance to hear what she meant to say. The waitress arrived with Anna's iced tea, then took out a pad and pen. In the process of ordering their meal, the subject was abandoned.

Anna sat back in her chair, watching the exchange between Rip and their server. He spoke with quiet competence and no sign of uneasiness or the rudeness some men used to cover social awkwardness. He was decisive, yet so pleasant that the young woman showed a tendency to linger, offering him every possible garnish for his steak except the key to her apartment. Her smile as she finally departed was an open invitation, though Rip didn't seem to notice.

"If that was an example of how you go about ordering in a restaurant," Anna said a little dryly as she reached for her glass, "I see nothing wrong with it."

Rip grinned. "I was doing my best to impress you. Actually, I can handle places where they roll up the forks and knives in napkins. Where I have trouble is in restaurants where guys in tuxes hover at your elbow and the food comes sprinkled with holy water."

A surprised laugh caught in Anna's throat, which was unfortunate since she had just taken a sip of iced tea. She choked. Tears sprang into her eyes as she put down her glass and snatched a napkin, spilling silverware from it. She covered her mouth just before succumbing to an urgent need to cough. Behind the paper square, she cleared her breathing passages, then emerged with a rueful smile.

"See," Rip said as leaned back in his chair. "What did I tell you? No sputtering or spilled tea, even if you were choking to death. If that isn't a lady, what is?"

"Don't be ridiculous."

"Never again," he answered enigmatically. Without giving her time to answer, he reached for her eating utensils, then flipped his own out onto the table. "All right. Show me what you'd do with these things if we were having lobster or pheasant under glass."

"You really mean it?"

"I mean it," he said, his gaze steady.

Anna lined up the silverware, substituting the extra dinner forks and knives for the missing salad fork, soup spoon, dessert spoon and so forth. As she worked, she explained the Victorian origins of the system based on types of foods served in a particular order. She was just getting to the simple logic of starting with the utensil on the outside and moving inward when something occurred to her.

"Wait a minute! You can't need this," she accused him as she pointed the tines of a fork at his chest. "You must have been wining and dining clients in the best restaurants for years. How have you been getting by, if you can't tell an iced tea spoon from a sugar shell?"

He propped his elbows on the table, supporting his chin with his hands as he answered. "By letting the clients begin first then copying them."

"But as host, you're supposed to begin and let *them* follow. What happens if nobody makes a move?"

His lips twitched. "In that case, I pick out the most elegant older woman I see nearby, and hope she knows what she's doing."

"For heaven's sake, why not just buy a book?"

"I worked eighteen-hour days, seven days a week, to make a go of Peterson Systems," he said with precision. "The proper fork just wasn't important enough."

"Now it is," she said, her gaze steady on his face.

"Now it is," he agreed.

A warning bell went off in Anna's mind like a signal for retreat as she saw the warmth in the depths of his eyes. The waitress wasn't the only female susceptible to his decisive manner or the self-deprecating charm he could display on command. The realization was a reminder that she was not there for pleasure, or even from curiosity.

Carefully aligning the utensils on the table, she said, "You know, I'm glad we have this opportunity to talk. There are so many things I've wanted to ask you. I wrote to you, but you never answered."

"Didn't I?"

"You know you didn't. I used to think maybe you had nothing to say." She could hear the undercurrent of hurt in her words. Funny—she thought she'd put that pain behind her.

"There was that. It also seemed better to cut all ties and let you get on with your life."

The explanation was so simple it might really be true. Or maybe she only wanted to believe it.

Selecting her next words with care, she said, "The thing that bothers me most, I think, is that I never had a clear picture of what happened that night Tom disappeared. There was no indication of just how much or how little he was involved in the robbery. I wish you would tell me—"

"What purpose is it going to serve to rake it up again?" he asked with trenchant reason. "It's over."

"No, it isn't. I need to know if you saw Tom at all. Did you speak to him? Was he with you?"

"No, we weren't together then."

She seized on the telling word. "*Then,* you said. Does that mean you saw him later?"

"For a few minutes. Anna, don't do this."

"Did he mention anything at all about leaving, say anything that might give some clue as to where he was going?"

Rip shook his head impatiently. "He'd been drinking, but there was nothing unusual about that. Several of the guys in the crowd he ran with that summer stayed lit up like the Fourth of July."

"I know, drugs as well as alcohol. But you didn't."

"I couldn't afford it. Besides, I had to go to work everyday. Anna—"

"Was anyone with him, friends, a woman?"

"Stop it, please," he said, reaching across the table to take her hands. "I can't help you. If I could, I'd have done it long ago."

Finality rang in the words. She heard it, knew she had to accept it, no matter how hard it might be. At least for now.

Removing her hands from his, she said in cool tones, "You have your elbows on the table."

"What?"

"You wanted your manners corrected, didn't you? Well, don't put your elbows on the table. The most you should do is rest your wrist on the edge."

"Right," he said, his face set in grim lines as he straightened. Clasping his fingers loosely together, he propped his forearms on the table rim. "How's this?"

"Better," she answered grudgingly.

The pose was easy, collected, lending an impression

that was almost cosmopolitan. It emphasized the strong molding of his hands and wrists with their dusting of crisp dark hair. His hands reminded her briefly of a drawing by Michelangelo, long-fingered, square-palmed hands that were graceful in a masculine fashion, having more to do with inherent power than artistic purpose. At the same time, old scars made small white lines here and there across their bronzed backs and along the fingers, and one knuckle was a little crooked, as if it had been broken.

They were the hands of a man who was not afraid of work. He had used them to build something substantial, something that had probably meant as much as Blest did to her. Anna was forced to respect that, just as she was forced to accept his position on what had happened to Tom.

Reluctant admiration moved through her as she watched him. There was such pride about him, such dogged refusal to accept the estimation of others. He had come so far from what he had been. She had to applaud whatever it was inside him that had driven him to make it.

At the same time, she couldn't prevent the odd sensation in her chest as she noticed a jagged white line that ended in a purplish depression, like a tooth mark, on the back of one forearm. Rip had that scar because of her, because he had saved her from being savaged by a rabid dog. She owed him something for that mark, and she always paid her debts. More than that, it was a reminder of the long relationship between them made up of mutual memories, mutual feelings.

Reminders like the sensation of his touch, hot against her skin on a summer's day, his hands in careful exploration, as if she were made of spun glass.

Thinking of it as she sat there brought virulent curiosity about the way he might touch and hold a woman now, after all he had been through. She wondered if his caresses would be as strong and tender as she imagined. Or as she remembered.

"Anna?" Her name had a tentative yet vibrant sound in his deep voice.

She lifted her gaze to find him watching. Hot color rose into her face, but she could not look away. His dark eyes had a soft sheen, like golden brown cut velvet. Such steady understanding lingered there that she was afraid he might understand exactly what was going through her mind, afraid that he might be planning to use it against her.

The salads they had ordered were crisp and fresh, spiced with arugula leaves and a hint of garlic. Their steaks arrived perfectly done, crisp and brown on the outside, tender and pink on the inside. Regardless, Anna could hardly force the food down her throat. She jumped when the waitress reached from behind her to light the candle in the center of their table. Anna's hand shook when she picked up her knife or water glass. She was hyperaware of the man across from her, and also of the whispers that circulated through the room and the glances cast in their direction.

As the meal progressed, however, she recognized that it wasn't nervousness alone that sizzled along her veins. No, it was also the champagne-like intoxication of excitement.

How long had it been since she'd felt so alive? How long since she'd stepped out of her staid routine and ventured everything for something she believed in? It must have been years. There had been few such opportunities in her life, even if she had been inclined to take chances. She thought she might have missed a great deal while encased in her safe little world.

The peculiar task she had been set was a challenge that fired her brain and set her pulse to racing. Being with Rip Peterson was disturbing and fascinating. He was so familiar yet incredibly different. There were lines in his face put there by experiences she could not begin to guess at, shadings in his voice that suggested complicated emotions she had no way of unraveling. The urge to discover exactly who and what he had become burned in her mind like a caustic, cleansing acid.

At the same time, she knew she had to be careful. So much was at stake that failure was unthinkable. She could not afford to become too involved.

Not that she thought Rip would really force her to marry him. It was a threat to make her fall into line, that was all. Marriage was far too intimate, far too drastic a step to be used as a mere bargaining chip.

Unless, of course, he expected her to fail, expected to marry her as part of his so-called compensation. She shivered a little as the thought skittered through her mind.

"Something wrong?" Rip asked.

She shook her head, not quite meeting his black gaze. Her throat was so tight she wasn't sure she could swallow. Putting down her fork, she reached toward her glass.

Before she could touch it, he caught her wrist, closing his fingers loosely around it. "Relax, Anna," he said evenly. "This isn't a matter of life and death. I would never do anything to hurt you."

A nebulous, disoriented sensation shifted inside her. Her wrist tingled where he held it, setting off a delicate vibration that she felt to the center of her being. Her stomach muscles tightened and she drew a short, constricted breath. At that small sound, she saw his pupils darken, widen, catch twin flames as they reflected the candlelight. The noises of the other diners receded, fading into silence.

The quiet was real, Anna saw after a strained instant, and had nothing to do with her and Rip. There was something going on at the restaurant entrance. As she turned her head, she saw her mother step inside. There was a man following close on her heels, a man who was obviously her escort.

It was Judge Amos Benson, the man who had sentenced Rip to prison.

The judge was an old family friend, a former hunting and fishing buddy of Anna's father. His wife had died of cancer two years ago, and Matilda Montrose had invited him to dinner a few months back. The two of them had gone out a few times since. Their pairing tonight was not unusual. Still, the sight of them together sent dread pounding through Anna's veins. It was, she thought, no accident.

4

Rip sat perfectly still as he followed Anna's sight line to the woman who stood in the door. It had been long years since he'd seen her, but he recognized her without difficulty.

His grasp on Anna's slender wrist tightened an instant before he realized what he was doing. Then he released her and sat straighter in his chair. He hadn't expected this kind of confrontation, not yet, not tonight. But if it was coming at him, he was ready.

Matilda Montrose had aged since he last saw her, growing haggard and stout. Diamonds glittered at her throat and ears, and the black silk dress that covered her ample form seemed too upscale for Montrose's country steak house. She scanned the sitting area, nodding at an acquaintance or two. Then her eyes locked on him where he sat with her daughter. Matilda's features hardened. The restaurant hostess who bustled up to them at that moment was ignored as if she didn't exist. With the judge in tow, Anna's mother started toward him.

"What a surprise," the woman said in glacially superior accents as she came nearer.

Rip got to his feet, partially from habit but also because he was reluctant to be caught at a disadvantage of having to look up at her. The back of his neck felt hot as he tried to ignore the stares and whispers around them. It had been a long time since he felt so crude and out of place. Anna's mother had always had that effect on him. The old despair of ever being accepted for what he was caught him in its grip. Before he could recover, Anna spoke.

"I see nothing surprising about it, Mother. You knew perfectly well we might be here."

Her bored, slightly patronizing tone was perfectly done, cutting through her mother's pretense like a well-honed knife. That she had come to his defense, ranging herself on his side, made Rip's heart swell in his chest. It also put him on his mettle.

"Won't you and the judge join us, Mrs. Montrose," he said, his smile pleasant as he issued the invitation. At the same time, he offered his hand to Judge Benson, though not at all sure the older man would take it.

"Wouldn't think of horning in," the judge said before Anna's mother could answer. His handshake was firm and without hesitation as he met Rip's clasp. White-haired and dignified of bearing, he was shorter than Rip remembered, but his appraisal was still keen. He continued. "I'm glad of the chance to say hello, nevertheless. It's not often a young man who passes through my court turns around and makes something of himself. You beat the odds, son, and you did it on your own. I'm proud to know you."

"Thank you, sir." Rip kept the words steady with an effort. The judge was one of the few people who had any real understanding of what it had taken to throw off the prison stigma and try for something better. His praise meant a lot.

"Why, Amos," Matilda Montrose said in arch tones, "how very civilized of you. Under the circumstances."

"Not at all." The judge frowned as he glanced at her.

"Well, it seems so to me."

"Mother," Anna said in low warning.

"But then—" the older woman went on as if her daughter hadn't spoken "—I'm only the mother of Rip's friend who disappeared while Rip was embarking on his criminal career. No doubt that gives me a different view of the situation."

On closer view, Rip could see the red-rimmed eyes and slack lines of Matilda's face, could smell the medicinal scent of the mouthwash she had used to disguise the fact that she had been drinking. His voice was a shade softer as he said, "I'm sorry, Mrs. Montrose, more sorry than I can say. But there's nothing I can do about it."

"Perhaps not. Now." Her face twisted as if she was near tears.

"Nor was there anything I could have done then."

"You could at least tell me where he's buried. You've served your time, after all." She paused while a murmur of comment swept through the restaurant like a rising wind. Then she added, "Oh, but years served for robbery wouldn't count against a charge of murder, now would they?"

"Mother!" Anna cried.

Rip reached out to touch Anna's arm. Voice threaded with pain beneath its firmness, he said, "I didn't kill Tom."

"So you claim, and old man Vidal, too, for what good that does." Tears spilled from Matilda Montrose's eyes, making her mascara run. "My Tom's gone, and you're still alive."

Anna withdrew her arm from Rip's grasp, moving around the table. "That's enough, Mother."

"More than enough," Judge Benson said grimly. Putting an arm around the older woman, he turned from the table. She resisted an instant before she wilted, allowing herself to be led away.

The other diners craned their necks, talking among themselves in a low hum of conjecture. Anna, left alone with Rip, could feel their avid regard, but refused to glance around to see. She was suffocating with embarrassment for her mother's attempt to degrade Rip. She could not help wondering if this was the way it had been for him all those years ago, when he had stood up in court with the townspeople of Montrose staring at him, judging him.

Her voice husky, not quite even, she said, "I apologize for what just happened. My mother isn't—hasn't been herself lately."

"Since she heard I was back, you mean."

She couldn't deny that, so made no reply.

His face tightened another notch. There was a white line around his mouth that might have been from rage as easily as from humiliation. Reaching for his wallet, he extracted several bills and dropped them on the table. In taut command, he said, "Let's get out of here."

She didn't hesitate, but moved ahead of him toward the door. He was on her heels, keeping his hand at the small of her back in a gesture that felt oddly possessive rather than helpful. They looked neither left nor right until they were outside in the fresh, warm night air.

Anna's car was there in the parking lot, but she didn't protest as he led her toward his silver BMW and put her in the passenger seat. After the scene inside, she thought she owed him her company if he still wanted it. Moreover, there was unfinished business between them.

As he swung out of the parking lot and onto the highway, she glanced at him. The expression on his face, highlighted by the greenish light from the dashboard, was impenetrable. She faced forward again without asking where they were going.

He drove fast and well. The road ahead of them unfurled like a black carpet rolling into the night. Anna thought once or twice of saying something, anything, to relieve the tension. Nothing came to mind that wasn't trite beyond words. She considered turning on the radio to fill the silence, but wasn't sure she could bear the noise.

A turn appeared ahead of them, and Rip slowed to make it. As he swung the heavy vehicle onto the side road that led away from town and out into the country, Anna knew, abruptly, just where they were heading.

Blest appeared in ghostly splendor at the end of its drive as they pulled up before it. Rip lowered the windows, then turned the key to kill the engine. Silence descended. A few seconds later the automatic headlights clicked off and they were left in darkness.

Night sounds filtered to them—the peeping of frogs, the music of a cricket hidden in the thick, waving grass, the lonely call of a night bird. As their eyes adjusted to the darkness, the shape of the house emerged more clearly, looming massive and dark in front of them. A quarter moon hung just above the tops of the oaks behind the ancient slates of the roof, a sickle of silver almost tangled in the branches. Its pale light washed down the walls, cut black angles under the galleries and lay in cool, shining pools along their floors. It glossed over the imperfections of rot, mildew and sagging wood, searching out and finding the hidden beauty of form and proportion.

Rip pushed his car seat farther back, stretching out his long legs. Leaning his head against the upright, he stared at the old mansion. After a long moment, he said, "It's so quiet out here. I used to think it was the most peaceful place on earth."

"So did I," she said in low agreement. "Like an escape into another world."

He turned his head. "Escape from what?"

"Chores, duties, manners." Her smile had a wry edge as she propped her elbow on the window frame. "All the endless things my mother thought I should have on my mind instead of following you and Tom around."

"You were good at sneaking off when she wasn't looking."

"I was, wasn't I? Especially when you ran interference."

"All I did was knock on the front door and ask if Tom could come out."

"While I scooted down the back steps, then crept around, hiding behind trees until I was sure I couldn't be seen from the house windows. At which point, I ran like a rabbit."

"You sure did," he said, laughing quietly. "I hadn't thought of that in years."

"It's been a long time since I did anything like that."

"Why? What happened?"

"I lost my partners in crime." As she realized what she'd said, she turned swiftly. "I didn't mean—"

"I know what you meant," he said, his voice even. "You don't have to watch every word you say around me, Anna."

The sound of her name in his deep, warm baritone set off vibrations in the pit of her stomach. "I know," she said, "but the last thing I want is to—"

"Hurt my feelings? Believe me, it isn't easy."

The words were like iron, but she wasn't sure they were true. "It was a stupid thing to say, anyway, because that isn't what happened. The truth is I just…grew up."

"And here I am again, asking you to do something you shouldn't, enticing you from the straight and narrow into my wicked way of life."

"Put like that, it sounds almost inviting."

"Does it, now?" he drawled.

She didn't answer, couldn't have if her life depended on it. Her flippant comment, she discovered, was more accurate than she'd intended.

They watched each other in silence. Then he shifted in his seat, resting his arm on the steering wheel as he turned more to face her. "Why not, really? Why did you stay here? Why didn't you get away?"

"Go somewhere and make something of myself?" Anna's words were cool.

"Wasn't there anything you wanted to do? Anything you dreamed of being?"

"I used to think I'd like to be a cruise director and sail around the world. I wanted to be like Jane Digby and have scandalous affairs, then go and live with the Bedouin. I thought I might take flying lessons, be a pilot for some tycoon who alternated between London, Paris, Rome and an island in the Caribbean. Wild, silly dreams like that."

"Not so wild. If I buy a private jet, will you fly it for me?"

"Of course." He didn't mean it any more than she did. Then as she searched his face, she lost some of her certainty.

"So why didn't you do any of those things?" Rip asked quietly.

"My mother wasn't well. She needed me. I had to get a job, make a living."

"She didn't keep you from getting married."

"Would that she had," Anna answered on a short laugh. "But I was still nearby, even as Chad's wife, still available, the dutiful daughter performing as expected." She turned her gaze toward the house again.

"Except that you got divorced."

"Not quite so dutiful, after all." She heard the defiance in her voice but couldn't help it.

"What happened, if you don't mind telling me?" The question was tentative.

She said nothing for a long moment, then she sighed. "You called me perfect back there at the restaurant, and God knows I thought I was supposed to be. I tried really hard. But perfect people can be pretty boring, I guess. Chad found himself someone more interesting."

"Or maybe he found someone who wasn't so hard to live up to. I can see his problem."

"Thank you very much."

He gave her a crooked smile for the dry rejoinder.

"I said I recognize it, not that I share it. Remember, I knew Chad. He always did have a hard time being second best."

"If you're saying I act superior—"

"I'm saying I don't give a damn anymore about status or class, where you came from or where I've been, who's on top and who's not—in any situation. No man likes to play second fiddle, but when two perfectly tuned violins are making sweet harmony, it's a duet, not a competition."

She stared at him with her mouth open for a second before she said, "Nice, very nice."

"So are you going to play? Is Blest worth it?"

"It is to me," Anna answered.

He tipped his head. "No matter what?"

"You mean—"

"I mean the stares, the whispers, and especially the kind of scorn your mother was dishing out back there. She obviously didn't take kindly to seeing you with me. Are you willing to go against her?"

"I—must be, since I'm here."

His eyes were black in the dark car, and his voice was without warmth or softness. "Be sure. If you're going to back out, you had better do it now, before you're in too far."

"I'm not backing out." Anna was amazed at the firmness of that statement but had no intention of withdrawing it.

He watched her a moment longer, sitting perfectly still, then he sighed and looked away. "It won't be easy."

"I know."

"And our deal is really on? You're going to stand by me?"

She thought about it, sitting there surrounded by the scents of leather upholstery, a drifting hint of honeysuckle on the night wind, the smells of ironed broadcloth, expensive aftershave and clean, healthy male. There could be only one answer.

"It's on. I promise."

"If I get rid of the bulldozers tomorrow, call in the architect and carpenters, you're not going to change your mind?"

"Tomorrow?" She couldn't keep the amazement from her voice.

"No reason to delay that I can see. It appears I'll be living in the house, win or lose."

"But I thought—"

"What?" Rip returned his attention to her.

"I know you mentioned that, but is it truly what you want?"

"You expected me to turn the place over to some foundation for an art museum, maybe?"

"I don't know," she said with a vague gesture. "I suppose I thought you'd prefer something modern on a golf course somewhere."

He shook his head. "Because of the rumors? Oh, Anna, you really don't know me, do you?"

She didn't, but was beginning to have an inkling. "You mean to take over Blest so you can rub our noses in the fact that it will never belong to the Montrose family again."

"I don't know about that. It could wind up in the hands of our children, Montroses by blood if not by name."

Their children. If she wrangled the Bon Vivant invitation, he would be set. If she failed, she must marry him and they would live there together. Win or lose, he'd said. She wondered which he considered marriage to her to be.

Glancing past him at the night beyond his open window, she said, "I've been thinking. We could start easing you back into things the day after tomorrow, if you like. I have an invitation from Sally Jo Holmes for a barbecue at her house on the lake that evening. Then the day after, on Friday, is the monthly civic club luncheon. It would be a good way for you to meet the businesspeople in town, and several of the male members are Bon Vivants."

"You're talking about Sally Jo Donaldson, used to go with Billy Holmes?" The question was tentative, as if his thoughts were busy elsewhere.

"They're married and have two kids now, a boy and a girl. Billy's a vet, took over old Doc Graham's practice when he retired a few years back."

"Hard to imagine," Rip commented with a wry shake of his head.

"It's been—"

"A lot of years. I know."

There was a grim note under his even tone, a reminder of his days in prison. Uncertain how he might react to sympathy, she said, instead, "So what do you think? Do you want to go to Sally Jo's? It's supposed to be a small gathering, just Sally Jo and Billy, another couple, and the two of us."

"Sounds like a good place to start."

"I'll call in the morning to let her know, though she said I could bring someone, if I liked."

His gaze narrowed. "And did you like? I mean, was there someone you were going to ask before I came along and ruined your plans?"

"I'm not going out with anyone special, if that's what you mean."

"It can't be from lack of opportunity."

"Thank you for that, but I just haven't been interested." She turned her attention to the moon glow beyond the windshield.

"No? Why is that?"

"I enjoy being by myself. I like going where I want, when I want, eating what I please, when I please."

"I thought you were living with your mother?" The words were dry.

"Well, yes, but the idea's the same."

"Too bad. You don't strike me as the kind of woman who should be alone."

She gave him a straight look. "You think I can't take care of myself, is that it? That I desperately need some man to do it for me?"

"I think some man desperately needs you." He didn't wait for a reply, but went on quickly. "You're really going through with it, then. You'll marry me if that turns out to be the only solution?"

Anna moistened her lips, knowing she was cornered. Decision time. Which was it to be?

Abruptly she tipped her head in agreement. "You have my word."

"Word of a Montrose," he marveled, watching her. Then he straightened, extending his hand. "It doesn't get much better than that."

Anna leaned over the car's console to put her own hand in his warm grasp. He held it a long moment, his gaze meeting hers in the moonlit dimness. Vital awareness connected them, shivered through them. Around them, the summer night sang.

With a whispered exclamation, he drew her toward

him, threading the fingers of his free hand into her hair to tilt her face. He hesitated, searching her still features, lingering on the dark pools of her eyes. Then he fastened his attention on her mouth and slowly, deliberately, lowered his head.

Sweet and warm, his lips brushed hers, discovering the tender surfaces, testing their resilience and texture, before tasting her with a light, delicate flick of his tongue. Heat sprang from somewhere deep in her lower body. It flowed upward to speed her heartbeat and flood her senses with its life-giving warmth. The urge to open to him, to reach out and draw him closer, was so strong, yet impossible to accept, that a small moan of distress left her.

Shocked into awareness by the sound, she jerked away. On a swift drawn breath, she demanded, "What are you doing?"

A corner of his mouth tugged upward as he settled back into his seat. "Sealing our bargain with a kiss."

"I hardly think that's necessary."

"Not even to make it more binding?"

"For whom? As far as I can see, you're bound by nothing." The protest was as much a defensive gesture as anything else.

"Wrong," he answered, his amusement turning grim. "Only I've been wearing my bonds so long they are a perfect fit. I thought for a while I was rid of them, but know now I'd be lost without them."

He meant the shackles of his past imprisonment, she thought, the pressure of abrupt empathy crowding her chest. Quietly she said, "One day you'll be free."

"I doubt it." His reply was followed by a quiet laugh, a phantom sound.

Anna met his shadowed regard there in the darkness. It was implacable, and so blackly intent she felt a tremor of fearful premonition along the surface of her skin. He noticed that small movement, for his lips tightened.

A moment later, he straightened, reaching for the key to start the engine. They pulled away from Blest, leaving it, silent and pensive, behind them.

5

The storm came up after midnight. Thunder jarred Anna awake. She lay for a moment, listening to the rumbling and the sighing wind. Then she flung back the covers and padded from her bedroom and down the hall. Her mother hated storms and usually wanted company until they were over.

The older woman was heavily asleep, lying with her arms outstretched, her face puffy from drink and tears. Her mouth was open, and she snored with every breath. As Anna stepped into the connecting bathroom with its night-light, she saw what she expected—a bottle of prescription sedatives sitting on the counter. Anna closed her eyes for a despairing moment. The combination of alcohol and sleeping pills could be lethal. Matilda Montrose knew it, but didn't seem to care.

Returning to the bed, Anna seated herself on the side and reached for her mother's flaccid wrist. Her pulse was steady and strong, her color was pasty—but no more than usual—and her breathing seemed unrestricted. She could go on hating Rip, and fearing him, for some time to come. Anna sat a little longer, then she replaced her mother's arm on the bed, smoothed it an instant and returned to her own bedroom.

She moved to the window and pushed the curtain aside to look out. Beyond the glass, wind whipped the trees and lightning cracked open the night sky like a giant eggshell. The elemental fury made her feel restless, as if she was waiting for something. She knew what she craved, knew that need had been set off by Rip's kiss as much as by the storm. But the combination of Rip and desire was as deadly for her as alcohol and drugs were for her mother.

She had always been attracted to him. Something in his rough, almost wild upbringing had stirred her imagination and her sympathy as they grew up together. He had seemed so free, coming and going when he pleased, defying authority when it suited him, and never whimpering when the consequences caught up with him. He didn't toe the line like her brother, didn't dress like him, act like him, think like him. Rip's defiance was natural, a part of his personality, not something brought on by a need for petty rebellion.

Regardless, Rip had been different when around her in those early years, often showing a rare gentleness beneath his hard, untamed exterior. The contrast made her feel special, as if she held a place in his life he shared with no other, as if he allowed her to see a part of his nature he exposed to no one else. She had been passionately attached to him in an innocent fashion. Or perhaps not quite so innocent toward the end.

She was, she knew, deeply sensual behind her calm facade. Sometimes she thought her marriage had foundered on this secret snag beneath its surface, that deep in her ex-husband's constricted soul he had been shocked that his brief and inept attentions in bed were never quite enough, that he always left her needing more. More what, she was never entirely sure. Not just more sex, but rather greater tenderness, wider imagination, a slower, deeper exploration of erotic experience. Once or twice he'd tried, but it was beyond him. Finally, he found someone who expected less of him.

The rain began at last, tapping in a wet staccato against the window glass. Anna dropped the curtain and climbed back into bed. Rolling to her side, she rested her head on her bent arm as she watched the lightning flicker around the curtains, listening to the falling rain.

She enjoyed storms, especially when she could watch them while lying safe and warm. She supposed that, like most women, she preferred her excitement to be without violence or unacceptable risk. Of course, nothing about the pact she had made with Rip could be called safe.

Stand by me...

The words he had spoken lingered in her mind like a haunting reminder of times gone by. He had stood firm when the rabid dog had come at her that day. And there had been other times, such as the day he and Tom were in eighth grade. Their English teacher had accused Rip of copying Tom's homework essay, based on a minor spelling error that appeared in both papers. It was Tom who had copied Rip's paper, but her brother had been too paralyzed to confess, afraid of the scene it would cause if their mother and father found out. So he had kept quiet, and Rip wouldn't speak up, refusing to rat on him.

Anna, so much younger than the two boys, had heard distant echoes of the incident on the bus home the day it happened. She'd heard how Rip swore he didn't care and claimed his shame in front of his classmates, and even the paddling he got from the school principal didn't matter. She had been with the two boys later when Tom cried as he tried to make it up to Rip, saying how sorry he was and offering to admit his guilt.

But the bigger boy only gave a moody shrug, and said to forget it, that what was done, was done. Tom had been relieved; even Anna had seen that. She'd also seen that Rip was pretending, saying what he knew his friend wanted to hear.

Later, when Rip went away and sat by himself behind the garage, Anna had followed. Dropping to the ground beside him, she'd drawn her knees up and let her arms dangle across them, imitating him. She had wanted to touch him, hug him, say she was sorry he felt so bad, but she didn't think he would let her.

After a while, she'd done the only thing she could think of, which was to pull from her pocket the chocolate candy bar that she had been saving for a special time. Taking Rip's grubby hand, she pressed the candy into it and curled his fingers carefully around it.

He had looked at her, then, and tried to smile, but the tears he refused to shed had crowded his eyes. It hurt Anna even now to think about it.

It also pained her to remember how she had gone to the jail when he was arrested for robbing the service station. He hadn't wanted to see her, had refused to leave his cell. He only sent word that she was to go home, go away and forget about him. He hadn't wanted anybody to stand by him, not then.

It was just as well, since no one had. Not Tom, who was nowhere to be found. Not Rip's own father, who'd

gone around town cursing and swearing Rip was no
son of his. Not Anna's mother, who declared Rip had
always been a bad influence on her boy, or her father
who reluctantly agreed. Even Papa Vidal had little to
say on Rip's behalf, though his testimony had been
beneficial.

The elderly black man had sworn in court that he'd
seen Tom Montrose driving "hell-for-leather" past
Blest late on the night of the robbery. He'd hemmed
and hawed on the witness stand, but finally placed the
time at least an hour after Rip was arrested with the
service station money in his possession. That had been
enough to remove the suspicion that Rip had harmed
Tom—at least for the jury, Judge Benson and even
Tom's father. Nothing, it seemed, would ever satisfy
Tom's mother on that point.

It was also Papa Vidal who put forth the idea that
Rip, when caught, had been returning the money he'd
stolen. That assumption, and the fact that no weapon
was involved in the robbery and that there had been
no injuries, had caused his sentence to be reduced and
made him eligible for parole after three years.

Anna closed her eyes, trying to relax as she let the
sound of the rain ease her strained nerves. Instead, she
saw Rip in her mind's eye as he had stood in court
that last day. He had been sullen and insolent, with
his long hair flopping into his face and his worn shirt
stretched tight across shoulders that were hard-
muscled from his job in the service station's body
shop. He had appeared tough, with a mutinous tilt to
his head and disdain in his copper-bronze face.

Regardless, when he met Anna's gaze across the
width of the courtroom, such pain had shone in his
eyes that she felt her heart would break. She had wept

for days after he was sentenced, shedding endless silent tears alone in her room. That was until her mother found her crying and slapped her, accusing her of disloyalty to her family and her brother's memory.

Those angry words had sounded strange to Anna then and still did, as if her mother had given Tom up long before anyone was certain that he wasn't coming back. Anna refused to accept that. She couldn't think of him as gone forever, not her brother who shared her love of books and funny movies, got a huge kick out of silly practical jokes and enjoyed the simple things like picnics and walks in the woods. Her brother and best friend who choked up while singing "The Star-Spangled Banner," but had a picture of Confederate General Robert E. Lee on his bedroom wall. The boy who liked to watch deer play in the woods, and was so tenderhearted that he made himself sick by drinking too much the nights before he was supposed to go hunting. She missed him so much, couldn't believe she might never see him again.

She had not managed to ask Rip the right questions about Tom the evening before, but she must. She would do it the first chance she got, perhaps at Sally Jo's barbecue. If she could only figure out how to go about it.

The dawn broke bright, hot and extra humid due to the rain in the night. Anna went to work as usual and had been at her desk less than an hour when Rip called. He wanted her to go shopping with him when she got off. The mall an hour away stayed open until ten o'clock, he said; they would have plenty of time.

She could hardly refuse in light of their agreement. Besides, she had her own agenda.

For all the good she did the rest of the day, she might as well have left work the instant Rip hung up. She couldn't concentrate, was jumpy or else sat staring as if in a trance. The two women who worked with her in the Clerk of Court's office teased her unmercifully about the deeds she filed in the wrong place and land abstracts she copied in error. It was a relief when Rip finally picked her up outside the courthouse.

They rode for several minutes in silence. Anna was aware of everything about him, from how he sat to the way his hair grew over his ears. In an effort to distract herself and establish some kind of normalcy, she said, "So, what kind of shopping did you have in mind?"

"Clothes," he answered with a glancing smile. "Plus a few other things."

"What sort of clothes?"

"Up to you. Whatever I need."

"Jeans?" she suggested, since it seemed necessary to narrow the selection somewhat.

"Jeans I've got," he said. "My business was the kind of Silicon Valley place with a casual dress code that included just about anything *except* a three-piece suit."

"You must have had suits for business meetings or dinners?" Exasperation for his lack of helpfulness was strong in her voice.

"One. Navy blue. I was in a hurry, so I took the first thing that fit. The salesman picked out a shirt and tie."

"And you let him?"

"His taste was bound to be better than mine." His smile was spare.

"Not necessarily," she protested, and meant it. Rip wore jeans again today, though these were faded almost white. His shirt was white also, this one western cut with mother-of-pearl snaps. Its tapered shape, wide at the shoulders and narrowing at the waist and hips, fit his torso with absolute fidelity while its pristine brightness made his skin look like burnished bronze. His rugged body shape and angular bone structure were the kind that rocketed male models to fame and fortune; anything he cared to put on would look great. At the same time, he had a simple style of his own that would be hard to improve.

When he made no answer, she went on, "What will you be doing now that you've sold your company? I mean, will it affect the clothes you need?"

"Probably not that much." He tipped his head in consideration. "I'll be working at home once I get a permanent place and have it wired for a computer. I have a few ideas I intend to develop."

"I thought you sold your operation for enough to put you among the idle rich?"

"A man has to do something to keep busy."

"Then jeans ought to see you through just fine. I don't see why you need me." She crossed her arms over her chest as she stared straight ahead.

"I've got a barbecue to attend tomorrow night, if you recall, and a civic club luncheon the day after. That means I need a few things more upscale, okay. What I buy is entirely in your hands, since you know what it will take for me to fit in. Afterward, I thought we might go look at paint and wallpaper."

The last suggestion was meant to steer the conversation away from the subject of his clothes and his expectations. Anna was just as happy to allow it. "Paint and wallpaper for Blest? But you're months away from needing them."

"Months, huh?" His lashes shielded his eyes.

"At least."

"What if I told you I intend to fix up one of the outbuildings for a place to live, something that can be turned into a guest house later?"

She studied him a moment before she said, "I'd say you think big these days."

"What's wrong with that?"

"Nothing that I can see. It's just—surprising."

His smile faded and his lips set in a grim line. "Considering where I came from, you mean?"

"I didn't mean that at all," she said sharply. "Or at least, I only meant surprising for someone from Montrose, not for, well…"

"Shanty trash from across the river." The words were icy.

"You said it, I didn't."

"To save you the search for a substitute. I'd rather you just came out with it."

"And I'd rather you turned around and drove me home if you're going to be so prickly," she declared, incensed. "I can't test every word before I say it, Rip. I'm not responsible for where you came from or what happened to you, or what you've done or not done since you left here. And I refuse to feel guilty because—" She stopped, turning sharply from him and clamping her lips together. After a moment she said in ragged distress, "I'm sorry."

A strained silence fell. Then he reached out to put his hand over her clenched fists in her lap. "Don't apologize," he said in low tones. "It's my fault. I guess I am touchy. And you have no reason to feel guilty. You've never done a thing to me that I didn't ask for—though I often wished you would."

She swung her head, holding his dark gaze a long moment. His expression was shaded with wry humor, but it was also bold and open. He meant exactly what he said and didn't care if she knew it.

"Rip..." she began uncertainly.

"Forget it," he said, withdrawing his hand, putting it back on the steering wheel. "Let's start again, all right? What kind of wallpaper would you say I need for the building that used to be the schoolhouse?"

She considered the question as best she was able while she waited for the shivery pleasure of his touch to fade from her skin. At last, she said, "Something with an educational theme, maybe. Books? World globes? No, wait. I think I saw a border with Greek scholars and scrolls in sepia tones. It was at the best decorator's showroom in town, though. The shop will be closed by the time we can get to it."

"No problem," he answered. "I made an appointment at a decorator's that may be the place you have in mind, since it came highly recommended. The guy specializes in restorations, and sells antiques and reproduction furniture. He agreed to have take-out food delivered so we can eat while we look. The choice was Italian or Chinese. I told him both because I didn't know what you would like."

"Both. Either," she said a shade incoherently as she struggled to hide her amazement. She was really going to have to stop underestimating John "Rip" Peterson. Before she found herself in real trouble.

6

Rip thought Anna enjoyed making him over once she got into it. He certainly got a charge out of letting her. It was a great boost for his ego, hearing her point out his good points to the guy at the men's shop. Having her step up to smooth a lapel down his chest or check the fit of a pair of pants at the waist gave him a blast, too, more of one than was strictly comfortable. Thankfully, she didn't seem to notice, which made him wonder about the man she had married.

Of course, standing there dressed in whatever she had handed him, while she looked him over like a prize bull, was uncomfortable in other ways. He figured he'd asked for it, though, so he endured it as best he could. To distract himself, he wondered exactly what she was seeing and feeling. And just what it would take to make her appraisal a bit less impersonal.

The insane impulse to stop hiking back and forth to the dressing room and change right there in front of her occupied him for several minutes. He even unbuttoned one of the shirts to the waist and left it open while he worked on the French cuffs. She noticed, too, because he caught her staring. But her vulnerable expression and the wash of color across her cheekbones were a lot harder on him than acting like a male model. He didn't try that again.

The lady had taste. He had known that, of course, had been counting on it. Not that his own was as bad as he'd made out. Anna's choice and his were so often the same he stopped placing mental bets on what she'd decide because it was no longer a challenge. They left the store with more clothes than he'd ever owned in his life, but now his wardrobe was set up for whatever might come along.

At the decorator shop, the owner had called in reinforcements in the form of a sleek blond assistant. It felt a bit like two against one to Rip, since the guy was gay, the assistant single and available, and both were not only predatory in a caressing, ultra-agreeable fashion, but seemed to consider him along for the ride. He was about ready to call the evening a washout, until he noticed that Anna didn't especially like the way the blonde kept touching him with her red talons.

While Anna was preoccupied, he took control. Before the others realized what was happening, he had chosen the earth tones he preferred for his bedroom, and pushed through Anna's suggestion of a French monotone assemblage in taupe for the sitting room. Then he shoved the wallpaper and drapery books out of the way to get to the food that had been ordered.

Later, with half a fortune cookie still in his hand, he left the others discussing techniques for restoring floors while he moved on to the furniture showroom in the back. The others followed soon after.

"What do you think about this for a bed?" he called to Anna, in part because he wanted to know, but also to entice her away from an antique mahogany monster that would take four men to move and required curtains on the sides.

"It's Empire style, a fine reproduction piece," the blond assistant said in authoritative tones as she cut Anna off by sauntering over to wrap her hands around his arm. She tipped her head, giving him a sly glance. "Very Napoleonic and masculine, though the time line is earlier than we've been discussing for your house."

"It's going in a guest cottage," Rip replied curtly. "We'll pretend Great-grandma moved the thing out of her bedroom to make way for something more grand." He held out his hand to Anna in appeal. "Honey? Will it work?"

"Perfectly, darling," she drawled, moving in close enough to take his other arm. "Only you've got a real one like it in the attic at Blest."

He untangled himself from the blonde to give Anna his full attention. If his relief at the rescue showed, he didn't care. "Really? Then maybe we should see what else might be up there before going any further."

"Good idea," she said in dry agreement.

He could have kissed her. And needed to desperately as he felt the brush of her hip and thigh against his leg, caught the jasmine scent of her perfume.

He didn't get the chance. For one thing, it was late by the time they got back to Montrose, too late to do anything except take her straight home. For another, Anna seemed wary and on edge, sitting as far as possible from him and jumping from the car the minute it came to a halt. He unfolded his long frame and got out, walking around to see her to the door.

"About tomorrow," he began as they stopped on the front porch.

"If you've had second thoughts, I certainly understand."

He paused, startled. "Do you now?"

"It's bound to be uncomfortable for you—facing old friends."

"Your old friends. They were never more than acquaintances of mine."

"All the more reason to wait a bit before plunging into the social swing."

"I don't want to wait. In fact, the sooner the better. I'd like to get out as much as possible."

The glance she gave him was unhappy before she looked away. "You can't expect to take up every minute of my time."

"We had an agreement," he reminded her, his voice even.

"What do you want from me?" she demanded, her eyes flashing in the dim light. "I'm doing the best I can."

"I think I made that clear enough. But if you need a reminder..."

"No," she said hastily.

"You've decided you don't want to be seen with me, after all?"

"Don't be ridiculous!"

"It isn't ridiculous! You'd be surprised how many women have discovered that being with me in public is one thing, but seeing me privately is something else again. Or vice versa."

"I'm not other women! I just—don't want you to get hurt."

She had said something similar before. The idea that she might really be concerned made his heart swell until it crowded his chest. "Don't worry, I'm tougher than I look."

The glance she gave him was scathing. "Then you must be positively armor-plated."

"Practically. Look, what is this? Is it about what was going on tonight at the decorator's?"

Her chin came up. "If you think I'm jealous because that woman was rubbing all over you like a cat in heat, you can think again."

"What I thought," he said, keeping his face straight to hide his triumph, "is that you might have objected to being called 'honey.'"

"Oh. Well, I knew you didn't mean it."

Didn't he, now? "I also thought," he continued while he was ahead, "that you might come over Saturday morning and help me find Napoleon's bed."

"Napoleonic era bed," she corrected him while staring distractedly over his shoulder. "He never slept in it."

"Well, I intend to. If I can find it." He waited for her response.

"I don't see what good having me there is going to serve, since nobody will be around to see us."

"You're supposed to be helping me restore Blest, and my bedroom is where I aim to start. Clear?"

"Saturday morning, then, all right," she agreed without enthusiasm.

"Good. About tomorrow night, what time shall I pick you up?"

"The barbecue starts at seven, but you don't have to do that. I can—"

"I want to do it. Be ready at a quarter till." He made it an order. He was pushing, but it was important she realize he meant business.

The look she gave him should have singed his five o'clock shadow. He didn't mind, since he recognized it as a signal of defeat. When she turned on her heel and went into the house, he let her go without protest. He stayed where he was until he saw a light come on, then turned back toward his car. As he walked, he stuck his hands in his pockets and whistled softly to himself.

"You used to be quite a ball player in the old days, Rip. It's a shame you never got the chance to go professional. You might have made a success at it, earned some real money."

Anna looked around as Kingsly "King" Beecroft spoke. The words he'd used were innocent enough— even complimentary taken by themselves—but his smile was superior and his tone patronizing. King, who's name had been shortened in grammar school, was top man at a local cotton-seed mill, a position that gave him considerable standing in town. A former jock and football All-American from an old Montrose family, he was self-satisfied to the point of arrogance.

If Anna had known the other couple invited to Sally Jo's barbecue was King and Patty, she'd never have accepted the invitation for herself, much less Rip.

The contrast between him and Rip was striking. King was going to seed, his hair thinning, his body thickening, the lines of his face becoming fleshy and without definition, while Rip was as fit as ever, and conceded only a few lines and the bolder stamp of his features to maturity. King appeared full of his own importance, which only served to point up Rip's quiet confidence.

Their old schoolmate had as good as insulted Rip

with his crass comment. Now he had the nerve to sit there smiling while he waited to see what Rip would do about it.

Rip laughed, saying easily, "Sports were never a big deal for me. I doubt I'd have lasted long."

Did he know, Anna wondered, that King had not made the grade in professional football. If so, his answer was a neat return for King's dig while still keeping the gathering civilized. From the way King was turning red, however, it looked as if he might upset Sally Jo's party. Anna wasn't averse to running interference.

Her gaze steady on the blond man's face, she asked, "Real money, King? I wonder just how you define that?"

"Lots of athletes walk away with several million," he said with barely a glance in her direction, as if he resented Anna joining what had been, until that moment, a strictly male discussion.

"Limp away, you mean," she returned in dry disparagement. "Rip, on the other hand, realized that kind of profit from his company in California without a single bone broken."

A stunned look appeared on King's face. Swinging to face Rip he demanded, "That right? You pocketed millions?"

"I'd rather not talk money, if you don't mind," Rip said with a flashing glance in Anna's direction. "Bad manners, you know."

Was it a rebuke, or was he laughing at her for rushing to his defense? She didn't know. Still, she tried to send the subject in a different direction. "High school seems so long ago, doesn't it?"

"Longer for some than others, I'd imagine," King answered, "depending on how they spent the time."

"If you're talking about me," Rip said, his gaze level, "then you're right."

Sally Jo, petite, vivacious and a nervous type, jumped up from where she sat next to Anna. Her voice edgy, she said, "I think I'd better go check on the meat. Why don't you freshen everyone's drinks, Billy."

"I'll do that," her husband said heartily. "Another long one for you, Rip?"

Rip declined with thanks. Anna accepted more ice, but that was all. King and Patty, a buxom blonde who helped Mother Nature with artful streaks, allowed themselves to be persuaded, which seemed to be a relief to Billy Holmes as it gave him something to do.

They were seated on the patio—a free-form stretch of concrete with an incised design of concentric shell-like circles resembling some of Europe's cobblestone squares. The open space was set with large pots of ferns and impatiens, while a glossy-leafed gardenia nearby sent its fragrance drifting on the warm evening air, competing with the rich aroma of grilling ribs and sausage. At the opposite end, a glass-topped table was set with brightly colored dinnerware and linens, and Italian pottery bowls held citronella candles that had been lit to keep flies and mosquitoes at bay.

A green swath of lawn swept from the patio down to the lake's edge where a gazebo sat out over the water. The soft breeze off the water stirred the somnolent air, cooling it a few degrees. The surface of the lake rippled, reflecting the last salmon-gold light of the setting sun with the look of hammered copper.

The lake lay on the edge of town, in an area that had once been a swampy wilderness of duckweed, cattails and willows. Developers had moved in some ten years before, draining the swamp, shrinking the lake and creating housing with high price tags because of the water view. The town had slowly taken in the area until it had completely lost its wild aspect and become another manicured community development with all the personality and excitement of a millpond.

Patty Beecroft, shaking the ice in her drink to chill it, said, "I hear you're going to redo Blest, Rip. That's a mighty big project for a bachelor."

"Which is why I called in expert help," he said, and smiled at Anna.

"Oh, I see. That makes sense."

"Sounds to me as if you'll need every dollar you earned," King said sourly. "How'd you do it, anyway? Steal a computer chip copyright, or something?"

"King!" his wife exclaimed in horror.

"Now hold on here." That came at the same time from Billy, who stood in front of the portable minibar with a highball in his hand. A tall man with a hangdog face and knobby knees exposed by walking shorts, he'd always seemed to Anna an odd match for Sally Jo.

The suggestion indicated plainly that King had been aware of the source of Rip's success, if not his method of achieving it. It also showed that he was spoiling for a fight. That Rip realized this was plain from the stiffness of his shoulders and the deliberate way he faced him.

"If you have a problem with me being here," he said quietly to King, "then you'd better spit it out."

The other man sat forward in his chair, a pugnacious

twist to his face. "My problem is with you being any-where within a hundred miles. Tom was a friend of mine."

"He was my friend, too."

"But he's gone because of you."

"Now, King..." Billy began.

Rip ignored his host. "That's a guess," he said in hard tones. "No one knows where he went, or why."

"We can be pretty sure, though, about who was behind it."

"King!" Patty cried. A flush mantled her face that had nothing to do with the drink in her hand.

Rip set his long-necked beer on a side table. "Then you know more than I do. It makes me wonder why you didn't stop him, didn't help him when he got into drugs."

"No one could." King breathed harder through his nose while his face turned a darker shade of red.

"Exactly. Anyway, I did my time and now I'm starting over, if people in Montrose will let me."

"You started over in California. You should have stayed there." The words were more rude than bellig-erent.

"This is my home, the place I intend to spend the rest of my days. Whether you like it or not."

Sally Jo came hurrying up then, her dark hair on end and her piquant face crumpled as if she were go-ing to cry. Looking from one man to the other, she said, "Dinner's ready."

For an instant it appeared that King might decline to share a table with Rip, then he got to his feet and moved to help his wife out of her chair. Anna rose and took Rip's arm, and they all moved toward the feast laid out for them.

It was the most uncomfortable meal Anna had endured in some time. She barely tasted the succulent spareribs or the German potato salad, the molasses-baked beans or the poppy seed coleslaw. The dessert of fresh peach sorbet was delectable, but wasted since she could barely manage three bites. All her concentration was on helping Sally Jo keep the small talk flowing while making small asides to keep Rip apprised of who they were talking about, or what new development in town was involved.

At one point, Sally Jo brought up Little League ball, which was in full swing. Her son was on a winning team, it appeared, and his grandmother had taken him and his sister to a fast-food place that evening to celebrate his recent home run. In the middle of the general congratulations, King said to Rip, "You never played Little League, did you?"

"Couldn't afford it," Rip answered as he pushed his half-full sorbet dish aside.

"I thought Tom's old man bought you a uniform."

Rip sighed as he looked up finally. "My dad made me take it back. He didn't like the idea of accepting charity."

"That didn't keep him from sponging drinks at every dive for miles around, though, did it?"

Anna had had enough. "What is it with you, King?" she asked, her voice sharp. "What are you trying to prove?"

"Nothing...except I don't intend to suck up to anybody for the sake of a few cheap murals and a rat-infested firetrap of an old house. It takes more than fistfuls of money to make a man acceptable in this town."

"What does it take, then, tell me that?" she demanded. "Incredible discourtesy and a fine opinion of yourself? Total lack of concern for how other people feel, including your hostess? Where do you get off, appointing yourself as mouthpiece for people here?"

"It's better than turning into some other kind of piece for a jailbird!"

Rip surged to his feet. He dropped his napkin on the table and braced his hands on either side of it as he leaned toward King. "Listen to me, because I don't intend to repeat myself. You can say anything you like about me and it will make no difference. I've heard it all before from business competitors and yellow journalists far better at name-calling and innuendo than you'll ever be. But say a single word more about the lady with me, and I'll knock your teeth out and shove them down your throat one by one. Have you got that?"

King licked his lips, running his tongue over his teeth. He glanced around at the set faces of the others. Finally, he ducked his head in a stiff nod.

"Good." Rip turned to Sally Jo. "My apologies for ruining your barbecue. That wasn't my intention. Perhaps you'll let me make it up to you once Blest is ready for company."

"We're the ones who are sorry that you had to be insulted in our house," she said with a glance at her husband. "Aren't we, Billy?"

"That we are," he mumbled, though he was clearly uncomfortable at being caught in the middle of the blowup.

"No problem," Rip said as he straightened. "It wasn't your fault." Turning toward Anna, he lifted a brow.

She was already on her feet. Her appreciation for

his self-control and innate dignity could not have been greater. Where he had learned it, she didn't know, but it made the other men look puny and ineffectual by contrast.

"I'm ready," she said.

Sally Jo went with them to the front drive where Rip's BMW was parked. "Please," she said, putting her hand on Rip's arm, "don't think everyone in Montrose is like King, because they aren't. I didn't know he would...well, anyway, I'm going to tell people you're as nice a person as I've met in a long time, and they should let what's past stay in the past."

"I couldn't ask for more," he said with a slow smile. Turning away, he moved around to help Anna into the car, then he got in and drove away.

Anna leaned back in her seat with a long sigh. "That wasn't one of my better ideas."

"Don't you start apologizing," Rip said shortly. "King always was a minor pain in the backside. It's no surprise he's turned into a major one."

"If I'd known he was going to be there—"

"Let it go. Just forget it. Please."

It was a relief to comply. They were both quiet while Rip negotiated the narrow and twisting road that followed the shoreline of the lake. Then abruptly he slowed and took a sharp turn. A few seconds later, he pulled up at a public boat dock, parking within a few feet of where the surrounding woods came down to the water's edge.

The wide, blacktop parking area was deserted, lighted only by a series of mercury lamps around the outer edges. Its concrete boat ramp slanted down toward the water, fading into the darkness. Beyond the circle of light, the lake shone placid and unchanging, gilded with the light of the rising moon.

Rip got out of the car and walked toward the boat ramp to stand staring out over the water with his hands thrust into his pockets. After a moment, Anna opened her door and followed him. He seemed to pay no attention to her, didn't turn as she came closer. He spoke in quiet tones as she stopped beside him.

"This used to be the swimming hole."

She made a sound of agreement. "They dredged it out and built the ramp maybe five years ago."

"Seems a shame."

"A beach was left over there." She nodded toward the manufactured stretch of sand farther along from where they stood.

He made no answer for long moments, then he said, "I want to thank you for speaking up for me back there."

She shrugged a little without answering.

"Tom used to do the same thing," he went on. "He got into fistfights more than once from fighting my battles."

"You did the same."

"He carried me all the way to his house on his back once when I sprained my ankle. It wasn't easy, since I was bigger."

"I know." Rip had been so pale when she saw him that for a terrifying instant she'd thought he was dead. "I also recall the time you waded in when Tom and I were in the middle of a brawl with a bunch of bullies over school lunch money."

"You jumped in to help him. I couldn't let you get hurt."

She'd suspected that was it, but hadn't known until

now, so many years later. Her Galahad in torn jeans. He'd gotten a cracked rib, Tom had sported a shiner for a week and she'd been the proud owner of a split lip, but they had kept their lunch money.

"I was grounded for a month over that little fracas because my mother thought girls shouldn't fight. What it taught me was that girls shouldn't get caught at it."

He laughed, a pained sound. "We used to come to the lake to clean up before going to your house."

"Among other things," she said, allowing her voice to relax into amusement. They'd also gone swimming, cavorting in the water like puppies, or matching movements and strokes like a precision team as they pretended to be a school of fish numbering three. Then there had been the other times, before she turned into a young lady and become much too aware of the differences between herself and her two best friends, Rip and Tom.

"You're thinking about our swimming parties? I'd have worn trunks if I'd had any."

"You set a style in your blue jean shorts haggled off with a knife, just as you did with your Levi's and white T-shirts when everyone else was wearing designer names on their backsides. But that isn't exactly what was on my mind." She sent him a quick, amused glance.

"What? You going in starkers, all by yourself?" He turned his head, a corner of his mouth tipped in a grin, but his gaze was so steady she could see the moonlight off the water reflected in the dark surfaces of his eyes.

"You saw me?"

"Watched you as long as I dared, then stood guard so nobody else could get a peek."

"You didn't!" the breeze off the dark lake lifted her hair, so she could feel its coolness on her hot face.

"You have a mole, just here."

He reached out to touch her rib cage beneath her right breast, putting his fingertip unerringly on the small spot he mentioned. She drew a quick, startled breath.

"I have a good memory," he said dryly, before he took his hand away and pushed it into his pants pocket. "Anyway, don't sound so shocked. You did the same thing."

She had. The thrill of it was one of her most vivid memories. If she closed her eyes, she could still see him like some young god, cleaving the water with strong, sure strokes while sunlight glistened on his dark head and along the muscled length of his arms and shoulders. Her vision of what a man should look like had been forever shaped by his taut, hard grace, the clean, powerful lines of his chest and thighs, the length and shape of him.

He would have filled out more now, she was sure, gaining strength and brawn. Becoming bolder. Harder.

She dragged her thoughts back under control. With a quick, wondering shake of her head, she said, "You knew all the time and never said a word. I don't know how you can still think I'm any kind of lady."

"Well," he drawled, "you were quiet enough about it."

"That's supposed to be the difference," she asked with a slow grin, "A lady doesn't make noise about...things?"

"So I figured. Or a gentleman. I'm good at learning by example, see."

His smile wiped the strain from his features, took

the stiffness from his voice. Anna felt her heart lift at that evidence that he was no longer brooding on the evening just past. In an effort to keep thoughts of it at bay, she said, "My mother wouldn't agree with you. She heard Tom teasing me about seeing you, you know. That time, I had to stay in my room for two solid days. It was weeks before I heard the end of it."

"She cured you of the habit, did she? I wondered why you suddenly stopped."

"She made me feel wicked, if that's what you mean, but I don't know about the rest. Being contrary in all things, I think she may have just made wet, naked men irresistible for me."

He laughed, a soft chuckle deep in his throat. "Now why is it, do you suppose, that I have this sudden urge to go swimming."

"I can't imagine."

"We're two grown people. There's nothing to keep us from it." The words were edged with laughter, yet backed by equal parts of daring and persuasion.

She tilted her head, watching him closely. "You don't mean it."

"You don't think so?"

"We'd get caught. It's crazy."

"So be crazy for a change."

"We—we couldn't." The protest in her voice was no longer as strong.

"Why not?" he asked simply.

The temptation was incredibly strong. Just thinking of it made her skin feel parched and in need of the wet caress of sun-warmed water, made her heart lurch into a faster, more primitive rhythm. Longing began in the center of her stomach and spread outward in a tingling tide. It would be like returning to the past, to a more basic, better time when her affection for the man at her side had been as strong and deep as that for her brother, an immutable part of her life that she'd thought would never change.

Perhaps it hadn't.

Rip watched the indecision and longing mirrored in Anna's face and felt his insides draw with a painful intensity. She was so alluring there in the darkness with the moonlight highlighting the bones of her face and the mystery in her eyes. The need to have this moment with her was an ache with such bite and power that he thought it might stop his heart.

It wasn't the urge to see her naked, or even to lead her into some more risqué watery adventure, though he wouldn't mind those things. Rather, it was the need to have her abandon all her hard-learned precepts and inhibitions, to cast off the strictures and rules that circumscribed her life and join him in his element, his life on the outer fringe of acceptance. He wanted her to choose him over her upbringing, over the hide-bound, narrow-minded types like her mother and King Beecroft. He tried to think of some argument that might convince her, but could come up with only one.

"I won't touch you. That's a promise."

Her lashes flickered, but she didn't look away from him. She hesitated, moistening her lips with her tongue.

Then with slow deliberation, she reached up to unfasten the back of her polished cotton sundress. The deep neckline gaped, exposing more of the creamy skin that had been driving him half nuts all evening.

He glanced around, then gestured toward the beach area and deeper shadows of the trees above it. For himself, it didn't matter, but he wanted no unpleasant repercussions for Anna, in spite of his challenge.

He shed his clothes in a few quick moves, keeping his back turned for the most part, though his peripheral vision took in mind-blowing glimpses of enticing curves, inviting shadows. Then he took a few running strides and hit the water in a shallow dive, swimming submerged for long seconds to give Anna a chance to join him without embarrassment.

The gliding water cooled his hot skin, soothed his tried temper. The feel of it triggered brief memories of other days, of Tom. Anna's brother had been so full of life and devilment, clever and clownish by turns, quick to anger but just as quick to get over it. He and Rip had played and fought, shared clothes and food and chewing gum, BB guns and bandages for their injuries. Conscientious, afraid of nothing except the disapproval of his mother and father, Tom had been a real friend and a brother in all but name. There had been times when Rip wished with desperate fervor that Tom could really be his brother, and Anna his little sister.

He'd changed his mind about the last toward the end.

Surfacing with a quick upward stroke, Rip turned to his back and glanced toward the shoreline. Anna was just wading into the water, moving with unconscious grace while the moonlight turned her body into pale marble, like a living, breathing statue: gently rounded breasts, not large but beautifully proportioned to the smooth flare of her hips; flat belly with delineating shadows arrowing toward the shimmering, gold-touched triangle of fleece at the apex of her slender thighs; face sublime, upturned to the bathing light of the moon and eyes closed to savor the lake's wet, lapping caress.

He hadn't promised not to look.

Forgetting to tread water, he submerged and came up again with a soundless sputter. When he spotted Anna once more, she was swimming toward him, flowing with the water in near silent movement. It was as if her molecules were as fluid as the elements around her and she'd become a part of it, merged with it.

The need to meet her, to take her here, now, in a surging, liquid plunge, hit him so fast he felt the blood rush from his head to coalesce, hot and driving, in the lower part of his body. He gasped with it, fought it. Won, by the hardest.

No, she must come to him. That was the only way it was going to work. Now or ever.

As she neared him, she swirled to a stop with at least six feet of water separating them. Her gray gaze held glints of silver; her smile was tentative. He angled away from her, easing into a slow crawl. After an instant, she joined him on a parallel course. They matched stroke for stroke, breath for breath, reaching, pulling in concert down the shining path of the moonlight. The water coursed along their bodies, glided over sensitive nipples, sucked at their armpits, passed between their legs in a swelling current. They turned to their backs, breathing fast and deep so their chests rose and fell and their hearts raced, throbbing in their ears. The night air kissed their wet skin with coolness, shivered along their nerve endings so that goose bumps pebbled the surface. Turning once more, they reached, again and again, for the distant, retreating moon.

They didn't gain it. Turning, empty-handed and

tired, they swam back toward the shore. Silently, without looking at each other, they left the water, dried as best they could and donned their clothes over their clinging skin.

Rip stood for a moment, staring at nothing while he waited for Anna to finish putting herself back together. This had been a bad idea, he thought. Sublime in its way, yes, but dumb overall.

He wouldn't take anything for the last half hour, but he wouldn't be doing it again. It strained impulses that were already stretched, made them extra dangerous. Too much was at stake to take such chances, no matter how gratifying the experience.

A stir beside him signaled that Anna was ready. He reached to put a hand on her arm as support in case she stumbled in the dark. As she flinched, he drew back and curled his fingers into a fist.

Together, they walked the few steps to the car. As he moved at her side, a single, endless refrain pounded in his brain like a vow.

No more promises. No more promises...

7

Anna didn't mention the barbecue to her mother the next morning, certainly didn't breathe a word about the evening swim. The civic club luncheon date was her secret also, though she was well aware that news of it would be all over town by nightfall. What Matilda Montrose didn't know about, she couldn't forbid or work to prevent. She could rant and rave, of course. But Anna would only have to listen to it afterward, not before as well.

It felt terrible, not being able to discuss the situation with her mother in a quiet, reasonable fashion. As strong as the impulse might be, however, it was impossible. If her mother was left in the dark, she had no one to blame but herself. Which was all very rational, but didn't keep Anna from regretting it.

The luncheon was to be held, as usual, in the private dining room of the cafeteria-style restaurant. Service would be extremely informal; members simply served themselves from the buffet line. The arrangement nicely accommodated the members who couldn't arrive on time. Many of the group ran their own businesses, and weren't able to get away until there was no one in need of their services. Civic affairs had to be squeezed in around making a living.

If Rip was at all nervous, he hid it well. He greeted her with a smile and a compliment for her yellow linen suit as they met outside the restaurant across the street from the courthouse. Once inside, he seemed to radiate confidence, while his manner was politely cordial without being either stiff or outgoing. He let her take the lead, since it was her territory, but followed with a noticeable presence that made heads turn and left the whispers of hurried consultation in their wake.

She assumed she'd be the only person on hand he knew. She was wrong. The president of the largest bank in town greeted him on sight with a hearty welcome and a strong handshake, which was logical when she thought of it. No doubt Rip had made a sizable deposit on his arrival, and been in and out of that establishment many times over the course of his purchase of Blest. The lawyer who'd handled the sale was also extremely pleased to see him, as was the real estate agent who had represented the long distance owner.

Rip's popularity didn't end there. The head of the local lumberyard craved an introduction, as did an insurance agent who had heard Mr. Peterson was going to renovate and felt sure Rip would need an interim liability policy. The woman in charge of the art festival wanted to discuss something with him also, though actually standing next to Rip flustered the elderly lady so badly that she never quite pulled herself together enough to explain what it was.

Anna sympathized. She had thought she would be able to be with him today and still keep at least a small amount of her usual sangfroid, in spite of what they had done the night before. It didn't happen.

Every time she looked at Rip, her mind filled with visions of wet skin and raw masculinity. The sound of his voice, perversely enough, submerged her once more in that silent, mystic swim. She felt hot and cold by turns, spoke to people without consciously recognizing who they were and answered questions without knowing what she'd said bare seconds later. She ate without having the slightest idea what she was eating or how it tasted.

The problem, she thought, was her nunlike life-style of the last few years. It had been so long since she'd made love that her hormones had gone a little crazy under the influence of moonlight and close proximity to an oversupply of testosterone. She was still a little off balance from its effects, but she would recover. All that was required was self-discipline and getting as far away as possible from the source of the trouble. Which she would do as soon as the luncheon was over.

It was a relief when the remnants of the meal were cleared away and the meeting called to order. The usual business took a short while, then members were invited to introduce their guests. By that time everyone present was aware of who they had among them, and attention was riveted on what she had to say about him.

Anna kept it concise, glossing over Rip's history, outlining his business experience in California, but concentrating on what he proposed to do with Blest and the cultural and monetary benefits Montrose would derive from it. When she finished, the applause was adequate, if not overwhelming.

Rip stood and thanked her for inviting him and the

gathering for their welcome, said how happy he was to be back home, then sat down. If his hand was not quite rock steady as he lifted his water glass afterward, she was the only one who noticed.

The first person to reach them as the meeting broke up was Carrie DeBlanc, owner of the Kitchen Cupboard, a gift and gourmet food shop across from the courthouse. A tall woman, well-padded with compact muscle, she had straight silver-blond hair cut short for practicality, and warm Mediterranean blue eyes set in a mobile face that always wore a smile. Her voice was like a love-smitten bullfrog's, her laugh contagious and her sense of humor outrageous. She was also one of the best cooks in the country.

Reaching out to Rip, she said, "I want to shake your hand, Rip Peterson. I don't think we've ever met, but I have to tell you, right off, you're high on my list of favorite people, and climbing. Hell, after seeing how drop-dead gorgeous you are, honey buns, I may put you at the top!"

"I'm honored," he said with laughter in his eyes, "I think."

"And so you should be, so you should be. I'll flirt with anything in pants, I give you fair warning, but there's not many I'd take home. But you, sir, have won my heart, my hand, my first-born grandchild— hey, I'll throw in my new chef's cookware if you say the word. I'm grateful, I'm awed, I'm ecstatic. Would you like me to wash your socks, iron your shirts, bear your children? I'm a bit past the last, but never let it be said that Carrie DeBlanc wasn't game to the end, not to mention preg—"

"What did he do?" Anna demanded, smacking her hand down on Carrie's wrist to get her attention.

"Don't interrupt me, pet. I was just getting to the good part."

"Careful, Carrie, Rip doesn't know you're kidding."

Carrie sent him a roguish glance from the corners of her eyes. "You think maybe he'll take me seriously, take me to the Casbah, take me madly, passionately and as often as a hero in a romance novel? And I'm supposed to be careful? Foolish girl! I live for danger."

"You live to make men blush," Anna informed her. "Come on, don't keep us in suspense. Give with whatever it is that's gained your undying gratitude and other assorted favors."

"Only if you promise to bring this gorgeous hunk of manly magnificence to dinner at the first opportunity."

"You've got it," Anna promised. "Now, give."

"All right. He made King Beecroft play crawfish. How I would have *loved* to have been there to see it! Though I can get off, easy, on the very idea."

"Who told you that?" Anna met Rip's quizzical look with a helpless shrug.

"Well, let me see," Carrie said, putting a finger to her chin as she pretended to ponder. "I heard it from Beth Anne, who heard it at the bank from a cashier who had just been to the beauty shop. Now, I can't swear to it, but I think the same woman does Sally Jo's mother on Friday mornings. On the other hand, it could have been Sally Jo's sister who was having a new curl, or maybe it was…"

"I get the picture," Anna said hurriedly. "What I don't get is why you're so excited."

"Honey pie, sugar baby. Let me tell you." The

other woman lowered her voice to a dull roar and looked around as if scouting for spies among the civic club's distinguished membership. Leaning closer, she said, "King comes in the gift shop and orders a birthday gift for Patty, right? We're not talking the Hope diamond here. Between you and me, the Beecrofts still have money problems—you know King took bankruptcy a couple of years ago. The ceramic hummingbird he ordered Patty is nice, a little different, but not much more expensive than a box of chocolate truffles—which I could have told him Patty would have enjoyed a lot more."

"So?" Anna inquired in the vain hope of urging Carrie to the point a bit sooner.

"So, as is the nature of things, this hummingbird doesn't come in on time. It's back-ordered. But does Mr. It, the All-American, understand? Does he realize I can't manufacture a ceramic bird out of thin air? No, indeedy. He calls up the girl who works for me and demands that she drive a hundred miles to the nearest gift shop to buy a replacement at retail. Honestly. And when she said she couldn't do that, guess what he said? You'll never guess. He utters those immortal words, 'Do you know who I am?'"

"He didn't!" Anna exclaimed.

"He did, I wouldn't kid you. *What* an arrogant asshole. What a jerk, a noxious nincompoop with grandiose delusions. It is to laugh. Or spit. *Do you know who I am?*"

Rip frowned as he watched them choking on smothered laughter. Then he asked, "Well? Did she?"

Carrie fell abruptly silent, staring at Rip with her mouth open. Then she caught the glint in his eye, and whooped loud enough to be heard clear across town.

"Lord, I love this guy," she confided to Anna before answering him. "No, the girl actually didn't know him. She was completely clueless, being no more than seventeen and having just moved into town. And that's the best part of all!"

Carrie's partisanship and ability to draw a crowd broke the ice. A number of others stepped up to take Rip's hand and say a few words. Some remembered him and said so. Others seemed oblivious of the fact he was a prodigal son with a prison record. Several came forward out of simple decency, while a few hoped to increase their chances for future profit.

Why they approached made no difference; that they came at all was what mattered. She and Rip had stuck their toes into the water of Montrose community favor and found it not quite as chilly as it could have been. They had made progress toward easing him into some kind of place. The venture was a success.

"I'm hungry," Rip said as they walked back toward where he had parked his car.

She gave him an incredulous look. "You just ate."

"Enigma meat, wallpaper paste mashed potatoes, mush that might have been cabbage in another life? I couldn't have eaten if I'd been able to unclench my teeth."

"I know what you mean," she said in wry agreement.

"I've presided over meetings of rabid stockholders that were less nerve-racking."

"Now, how did I get the idea that you were tough?" she marveled to no one in particular.

"Because I am with everyone except you."

The smile that curved his mouth didn't quite reach his eyes. She wondered briefly if what he'd said was just banter, or if there was some truth, however minor, to it. She was given no chance to decide, however, for he went on at once.

"We were talking about food, weren't we? What happened to that subject?"

"Sorry. What did you have in mind?"

"An ice-cream cone?"

With a rueful smile and the lingering effect of being around Carrie, she said, "Milk and eggs—sounds like good, wholesome food. Why not?"

To Rip, the ice cream was ambrosia. He'd always had a fondness for it, probably because it had been one of the major treats of his boyhood. He took it straight, too. Plain vanilla, the soft kind, with no chocolate or strawberries, crushed cookies or heaven forbid, bits of candy. No, just the endless glide of rich flavor on the back of his tongue and the occasional crunchy bite of cone.

They ate while sitting in a booth in the back of the Dairy Queen. It was like a homecoming, the same sticky floors and red vinyl seats split from tools carried in the back pockets of farm boys and construction workers, the same smell of grilling beef, onions, mustard and milky concoctions, the same air-conditioned chill. The place had been the teenager's hangout when he was in high school. A lot of horseplay, flirting and courtship had gone on behind the high-backed booths. Significant moments of his life had taken place here, moments in the time he thought of as the Great Before—before the robbery, before the trial, before he had been carted off to prison in handcuffs in the back of a police van.

He knew he had missed it. He just hadn't realized how much.

Overlaying his pleasure was his gratitude for getting through the luncheon and having everything turn out all right. He hadn't been sure it would, by any means. But they had carried it off, he and Anna. She had stood beside him and made it work. It was a harbinger for the future, one he intended to savor.

"You bought me an ice cream once," Anna said, a faint smile curving her lips as she concentrated on methodically devouring the cone in her hand.

"I'm surprised you remember."

Rip, however, recalled it well. It was one of the few times they had been there alone instead of going Dutch treat with Tom, or with Tom shelling out for what they ate.

She caught an impending drip as she answered. "It was a special occasion."

Rip almost groaned aloud as he watched the slow, sinuous movement of her pink tongue, thinking of how cool and sweet it would taste. Voice suddenly husky, he said, "I wanted to buy you a hamburger and shake, but didn't have the money."

"I didn't want a hamburger and shake."

Her level gray glance sought and held his. He thought there was a message in it, if only he could decipher it. He tried, turning over that long ago day in his mind, searching for clues.

It had been a summer day, like this. He'd met Anna and Tom and King Beecroft on the road at the edge of town, and they had all pulled over to talk. He thought Anna had been annoyed with the other two over something, for she asked where he was going. When he'd said the Dairy Queen, she simply announced she was going with him and climbed into his truck. That was the same afternoon the two of them had wound up lying in the grass at Blest.

Was she saying, just possibly, that she had gotten exactly what she wanted that day? That to be with him, to take what he had been able to give her, to lie, finally, in his arms, was enough? He'd like to think so, but wasn't quite so egotistical. Unlike some.

As if picking up on his train of thought, she asked, "What did you think of King last night?"

"He's the same as ever," Rip answered with inflection.

"Unfortunately." A wry smile flitted across her face. "I was surprised that he mentioned Tom. It's the first time he's spoken his name, to my knowledge, since he disappeared."

"Too far removed from his favorite subject?"

"Himself, you mean? Maybe. But I was wondering if he could have a guilty conscience."

"You think he might've had a hand in what became of Tom?"

"Or knows something he isn't telling. Tom did run around a lot with him and his crowd that last summer, after you started working so much at the service station. It would make sense."

Rip thought of agreeing with her, of letting someone else carry part of the load of suspicion that had burdened him so long. But he couldn't do it. "King wasn't one of my favorite people, but I don't know that he was ever crooked."

"He was strapped for cash pretty often."

"So was I."

"Yes, but he had expensive tastes in cars, girls and other toys. You didn't. He was in the crowd that did drugs, too. I seem to remember he was in rehab during the trial."

Rip hadn't known that, but even if it was true, he couldn't see that it made a real difference to Tom or him.

"I can't prove it, but I always suspected King of getting Tom hooked. What do you think?"

He remained silent. He'd been fairly certain of it back then, still was, but the final choice had been Tom's.

"You aren't going to say, are you? Just as you never said a word to explain or protect yourself during the trial. Why, Rip? What are you hiding?"

"Do I have to be hiding something?"

"You don't have to be, but what else is there? Talk to me. Tell me what you did, who you saw, exactly what took place."

"You know all that, you were there in court when it came out."

"I know what was said, which was precious little. Sometimes my brain goes round and round with it until I feel sick. First, I think maybe you took the money for Tom but he wouldn't accept it. Then I think maybe King took it, but Tom found out and asked you for help putting it back. Or I wonder if it was Tom and King together, but something went wrong. The two of them ran, in their different ways, leaving you to pick up the pieces. Sometimes I picture Tom living on the streets somewhere, a shuffling, worn-out drug addict too ashamed to come home. Or I wonder if maybe he quarreled with King, was killed somehow, and now has turned to dust and bones in a shallow grave somewhere."

"And sometimes," he said softly, "you put my

name in all the places you just gave King, and wonder if I'm guilty as sin.''

She rubbed between her eyes with two fingers, as if she was getting a headache. ''I tried that, but it doesn't make sense. Why wouldn't you have concocted an alibi if you were going to rob the place where you worked? You're too intelligent not to have planned better than that. And why wouldn't you have arranged somewhere to go and a safe place to leave the money until it could be used? Then there was another thing. The station was robbed around eleven in the evening, but you weren't arrested until after 2:00 a.m. Surely you didn't drive around in your truck all that time. So what happened in between? What?''

He searched her face, seeing the frustration mirrored there and, beneath it, the doubt. ''What are you doing, Anna?'' he asked softly.

''Looking for answers, what else?''

''Right. That's the reason you're here with me, isn't it? Not faith or trust, nor even what's best for Blest, though it's important to you. It's about Tom and where he is now. You think I can somehow lead you to him.''

''I only want answers,'' she cried. ''The not-knowing is like an open cesspool poisoning the air. I have to discover the truth before the ugliness of it can be covered over and the space reclaimed. I need that, my mother needs that, so we can stop wondering, wishing, hoping, and finally move on. Let it go, you said, but we can't. We're not holding it. It's holding us.''

For a single instant, Rip felt the twisted jealousy of Cain, as if Tom were really the brother he used to pretend when they were kids, the beloved Abel who could do no wrong and was treasured by all. Then the feeling faded, melting away as if it had never been.

There was no blood bond. What's more, Cain had at least been due the same affection as his brother, whether he received it or not, while he himself had no such claim.

"Don't let your imagination run away with you," he said evenly. "What happened is no lurid mystery, nor even particularly interesting. It's just a sordid episode of a kind that's happened a thousand times before and will happen a thousand times again. I paid the price for it. It's over and done. If you can't accept that, I'm sorry, but there it is. If I could take you to where Tom is, I would do it in a minute. If I could produce him for you, I would. I can't do either one. End of story."

"Not in my book, it isn't." Anna's face had not a glimmer of a smile for the neat riposte. They stared at each other across the table for endless seconds.

Abruptly, she glanced down at her watch. "I should be going. I've been away from work long enough."

Before he could form a protest, she slid from her seat and turned toward the door. He rose to follow her. He saw her pause at the trash receptacle just outside the door to discard what was left of her cone. It felt like a rejection, not only of the treat, but of him.

Catching up with her in a few steps, he reached for her arm and pulled her to a halt. Ignoring the scandalized look from an older woman with crimped white curls covered by a purple hat to match her jogging suit, he said, "Don't forget we have a date to find a bed tomorrow."

"I offered to help you find your antique bed, and I'll do just that," Anna returned with emphasis as she spun to face him. "When I start something, I see it through to the end."

"I'm depending on it, since I have your word."

"So you do. But if you expect me to abide by it, then I think I have the right to look for the same from you."

"Fine, though it sounds to me like an amendment to our agreement. Shall we seal it the way we did last time?"

"I don't think that's necessary."

The chill in her voice did nothing to cool his irritation. "What about expedient, if not necessary? There's no telling what you might learn with the proper incentive. And if a mere kiss has so much influence, just think of the possibilities next time we get naked together."

A flush bloomed across her cheekbones. "That will happen," she said in incensed precision, "when the ice cream melting all over your shoes freezes again."

She pulled her arm from his grasp, turned sharply, then walked away. Rip stared after her a long moment, watching the proud tilt of her head, the determined set of her shoulders and the length of her strides that took her away from him.

Then he cursed in soft virulence and dumped his dripping cone in the receptacle. He thumped his fist down on top of the red plastic lid.

Ice cream was off his list. For good.

8

When Anna arrived at Blest on Saturday morning, a motor home as long as a city block was sitting on the lawn. She stood staring at it with her fists on her hips. It didn't take a genius to figure out what it meant: Rip was in residence.

As if to prove the point, he stepped out of the big vehicle and sauntered toward her. His hair was still damp from his morning shower, and the clean scent of a citrus-based aftershave drifted around him on the warm summer air. A species of hunger moved through her that had nothing to do with the fact she had skipped breakfast. She forced it down immediately, but annoyance for the necessity was strong in her voice when she spoke. "You don't waste any time, do you?"

"I've lost all I want and more," he came back with at once, his eyes narrowing a fraction.

Her face grew hot as she recalled, abruptly, the note on which they'd parted the day before. That embarrassment hurried her into speech with her next waspish thought. "I'm sure it will be more convenient, not to mention more comfortable, when your decorator comes calling.''

A corner of his mouth lifted and his dark gaze grew warmer. ''We can find out, if you'd like.''

''I didn't mean me!''

''Funny, because you're the only decorator I've got.'' His gaze slid over her, from the ponytail that hung down her back, to her legs exposed in natural linen shorts. ''Not that anybody would guess this morning. You don't look a day over fifteen.''

The memory in his eyes was one she had tried so hard and often to erase that her brain felt as if it had calluses. She drew a strangled breath. ''I think we were supposed to look for a bed?''

''Any time.''

''I meant the one in the attic!''

He lifted an innocent brow. ''So did I.''

He hadn't and she knew it. He stood there, so assured in his physical strength and the power of his hold over her through ownership of Blest. He seemed invincible, nothing at all like the frowning, self-effacing boy she had once known. She mourned that boy, with his tender touch and unshakable loyalties.

''You don't need me to make you over, and never did,'' she said against the pain of loss. ''You've already done that job extremely well.''

''I need you,'' he answered, the words as stark as the expression that closed over his face.

''Oh, yes, for respectability.'' She shoved her hands into the back pockets of her shorts, a movement that made her breasts strain against her red T-shirt. ''You'll be happy to hear we've made a start. Apparently some of the people we met yesterday, not to mention the cleanup crew you've hired, have been talking about what's going on out here. I had a call from the president of the chamber of commerce wanting to know if it was true you're going to revive the old art festival."

"What did you tell him?"

"Her," she corrected him, hastily shifting position as she realized where his gaze was centered. "I said I was sure you would, that it was your fullest intention to preserve and protect Papa Vidal's legacy and encourage the growth of the arts in this area. I also said you would be happy to open the house to the public for the Fall Pilgrimage of Homes, once the restoration was complete."

"Did you, now?" he demanded as his brows snapped together over his nose.

"It seemed the best way to make sure people remain interested, by giving them reason to believe they'll benefit."

"I don't want people tromping through my home, pointing and staring."

"You should have thought of that before you decided to live in an historical monument."

He gave a stubborn shake of his head. "Blest isn't that important."

"Don't be ridiculous. It qualifies to be registered with the National Trust for Historical Preservation. All that's needed is verification of its background."

"I looked at all that before I signed the deed," he answered impatiently. "If it's registered, it means I have to follow specific guidelines for restoration, but there's no obligation to open the place to John Q. Public."

"You didn't buy a house, you bought an idea. To make the best use of it, you'll have to convince people your motives spring from something more than self-interest. It's going to take a clean start to wipe out the past.''

The words were hard, but she did nothing to soften them. There were some things that couldn't be helped.

He lifted a hand to massage the back of his neck as he looked away through the oaks with their leaves shining in the morning sun. After a moment, he sighed, then gave an abrupt nod. ''You're right. So what's first on the agenda?''

''Crawling through a dusty attic that's getting hotter every minute.''

His glance returned to her. ''Since you're dressed for the job, we may as well get at it.''

Finding the bed was like a scavenger hunt. They were seduced from their quest by a thousand other discoveries: a washstand topped by a broken mirror, picture frames whose faded prints were protected by concave glass, a windup Victrola with the original wax recordings stored inside, a rocking horse shedding its moth-eaten wool mane. They poked through cartons of old Christmas ornaments, boxes of musty dress goods, crumpled frocks from the flapper era and ancient uniforms from World War I. They stepped around empty china barrels filled with yellowed wood straw and peeked into boxes of crumbling wax candles.

It was a mission into another dimension where they fought spiderwebs, endured stifling heat and inhaled nose-tickling shreds of disintegrating paper plus the lingering smells of ancient camphor, lavender, mildew and sweat. Bumping their heads and scraping their knees, they crawled over the accumulated trash and treasure of ages. The dust they stirred hung in the air, turning like golden veils in the shafts of light slanting through the gable vents.

The bed was in a corner, behind one of Blest's six chimneys. It had been dismantled, of course; there was no other way it could have been carried up the steep attic stairs. Anna and Rip stood looking at it, at the graceful curves of the head and footboards, the gold leaf that still embellished its carving, its massive strength that had survived nearly two centuries of use and abuse. It would have to be taken downstairs and put together again, piece by piece, like a puzzle. But when it was done, it would be a prize.

She reached out to smooth a hand over the heavy curves of a side rail. "They don't make things like this anymore," she said reverently.

"Think of the workmanship, the time and effort that went into it," Rip said.

"Think of the men and the women who slept in it," Anna added, "who were born and died in it."

"Who made love in it..."

She looked up at him in the dimness, caught by the vibrant huskiness and longing in his voice. They were both hot and dirty, but triumphant. Their hearts pumped living blood through their veins and they breathed, felt, were sentient with life as they stood there among the litter of distant, long-vanished souls. The moment of recognition stretched, becoming anticipation. Requiring affirmation.

Anna could not sustain the heat of his gaze. She lowered her lashes, staring instead at the warm, firmly molded contours of his mouth. His lips parted on a hissing intake of breath.

Did he move first, or did she? And did it really matter?

They came together, hot flesh against hot flesh with the grittiness of dust under their hands as they caught and held each other. His mouth was hot and devouring on hers, yet achingly sweet. His hard strength surrounded her; his arms and his hands molded her to him, matching contours and hollows. Their heartbeats thudded in their chests while their breathing was loud, near-desperate in the silence.

He traced her lips with his tongue, lapping her taste, urging her participation. She opened to him, welcoming him in as she twined her tongue around his, abrading, remembering. She couldn't get close enough, couldn't take him deep enough inside her. The scent and feel of him were inflaming; she wanted more. The ache for the swift, fast surge of completion flooded her so suddenly that she felt dizzy with it.

It was so right, so perfectly familiar that the anguish of it caught in her heart. Her soft murmur of old pain and new need trailed off with the ache of a sob. Tears pressed upward, wetting her lashes. She glided her open palms over the taut muscles of his shoulders, clutching handfuls of his shirt as she burrowed into him, slanting her mouth to allow him greater access.

It had been so long. So eternally long.

He spread his hands over her waist and down to her hips, dragging her closer. His mouth, hot and demanding, clung to hers while a shiver ran over him, leaving goose bumps behind. He shifted his hold, smoothing one hand upward and sliding it under her shirt to explore bare skin. He cupped her breast in the hot cage of his fingers, testing its resiliency. Bending his head, he laved the mole beneath it with his tongue in careful salute before shifting to attend to the tight bud of her nipple.

Her knees gave a little and she swayed under the onslaught of piercing sensation. He spread his legs, holding her even as the movement brought their lower bodies into greater, better, alignment. Heavy and heated, he pressed against her.

He broke for breath, chest heaving, as he glanced around in the semidarkness. Anna guessed what he was looking for, understood what he wanted: a clear space on the floor, protection, perhaps, against the chafing of bare, tender skin. Was it what she wanted also?

She wasn't sure, couldn't put two coherent thoughts together for the race of blood in her veins, the haze of arousal in her brain. Yet she must decide. Now, before it was too late—if it wasn't too late already.

An ancient feather mattress lay draped across a pile of old rugs some yards back along the way they had come. Rip turned toward it with her held close against him. He took an unsteady step.

It was then that they heard the slow shuffling on the steep access stairs. The sound was followed by the creak of a floorboard.

"Mist' Rip?" Papa Vidal called, his voice quavering in the wide emptiness of the attic. "You and Miss Anna up here?"

Anna was grateful to Papa Vidal for saving her from a grave mistake. Of course, she was. Not that his intervention had been necessary. She would have broken away from Rip's sensual spell, she really would. It had only been a matter of finding a way.

She should never have let it go so far. She wasn't an innocent; she knew the effect that kind of cooperation had on a man. It hadn't been something she'd intended; it had just happened.

She was afraid Rip had the wrong idea, that he

would expect to take up where they had left off at the first opportunity. It wouldn't work. The mood was gone; it would be all wrong. She would make that clear at the first opportunity.

In the meantime, Papa Vidal, lonely old soul that he was, stuck to her and Rip like a cocklebur. His presence encouraged attending to business, so they went through the house with pad and pen in hand, making notes on all that must be done. He was handy to have along since he remembered the house the way it was before it went out of the Montrose family. He knew what it had been like before the parlor and upstairs rooms were redone, and before the kitchen was brought inside from its separate, outdoor location and installed in the smoking parlor.

Since this last renovation had taken place in the early 1950s, and Rip planned to return the house to its 1850s decor, there was little from that more modern time worth saving. He wanted to add an extension on the back in the style of a *garçonniere*, one which would blend with the main house but include a modern kitchen and breakfast room. It sounded both convenient and architecturally pleasing. Talking, planning and reminiscing, the three of them rambled from room to room, winding up finally on the upper front gallery.

Rip left Anna and Papa Vidal while he ran down to the motor home for cold drinks to revive them from their hot, dusty morning's work. Anna moved to the railing, where she stood staring out at the massive oaks on the lawn and beyond to the tumbled headstones of the overgrown cemetery under its ancient cedars.

"Best take care, Miss Anna," Papa Vidal said as he came to stand beside her. "That old railin's none too steady."

He was right; the railing wobbled under her experimental touch. She gave him a quick smile as she stepped back a pace. "I'll have to be more careful."

"Yes, ma'am," he said, nodding. "You was thinkin' deep thoughts, I reckon. Don't suppose it'd be anything you want to talk about?"

Papa Vidal's faded gaze was entirely too keen. She suspected he knew what he had interrupted in the attic. He had always known what was happening at Blest, always kept everybody's secrets.

Anna looked away. As her gaze rested on the cemetery once more, she seized on it as a distraction. "Strange isn't it, how people used to bury their dead so close by? Though it must have been comforting to be able to visit any time they liked."

"Real cozy, it was," he agreed. "Now they got regulations about everything. Got to crowd everybody into special graveyards where hardly anybody goes once the funeral's over. Such a shame."

It was indeed. Anna's father had wanted to be buried at Blest. It would have been possible, since it was an established cemetery. Matilda Montrose had vetoed the idea after her husband's death. It was too old-fashioned, she declared, too eccentric. Instead, he had been installed in a neat and featureless Garden of Memories.

"We need to put cleaning and restoring the cemetery on our list," she mused. "Even the old fence is falling down."

"Oh, no, Miss Anna," the old man exclaimed. "Can't do that. No, ma'am."

"I don't mean we should change anything," she answered in response to his vehemence, "but I'd like to at least be able to get inside the gate. Anyway, it'll be an eyesore in contrast to the rest of the lawn once that's back in shape again.''

"It can wait a bit, can't it?" he persisted, an anxious look on his face.

"I suppose so, since it's not a pressing part of the restoration. Still, I don't see why—"

"I'm paintin' it, Miss Anna. Just like it is right now, briars and all. Got to catch the ghosts before they get away.''

Her smile was warm as she reached out to touch his bent shoulder. "Why didn't you say so? But I didn't realize you were working again.''

"Started a week ago. Been a while since I tried my hand. First time since…well, you know.''

She did indeed. Papa Vidal hadn't picked up a paintbrush since Rip went to jail and her brother disappeared. "It's another mural then? Where are you doing it?''

"Out to the old schoolhouse.''

"That Rip means to fix up for a guest house?''

The old man nodded. "It's a present, like, just for him. Don't suppose he'll mind me messin' up one wall.''

"He'll be honored," she said with assurance. "And just as glad as I am that you're back at your painting.''

"Mood was on me. Feels good, as I'd about decided it never would be again." He made a vague, painterly gesture with a hand stained with ultramarine blue.

"That's great," Anna said, rubbing his bony shoulder blade under his multicolored vest in sympathy and affection. "It's about time.''

Rip returned and they all rested on the antique church pew that sat against the shaded inside wall of the gallery, while they talked and sipped cold pineapple juice. Papa Vidal took Henrietta from his pocket and let her stalk around, pecking at the pill bugs and spiders that had made their home in the rotted canvas covering the floor.

As they watched the Silky hen, they discussed the possibility of replacing the cypress shutters that had once hung as sunscreens at the west end of the open space. Papa Vidal was reminded of a tale told about one of the previous owners. Back in the late forties, the elderly lady had enjoyed taking her morning bath in a washtub secreted behind the original screens. That was until she was surprised one day by the arrival of the meter reader, a new man who couldn't find the meter and was in search of someone to ask for directions.

As if on cue, a utility truck drove up just then. Rip had arranged for power to be brought to the house for use by the crew who would soon be working there. He went down to confer with the driver, taking Papa Vidal with him to help find that old, well-hidden meter.

Anna, left to her own devices, wandered back into the house. She made her way to one of the back bedrooms and slipped inside, walking up to another of Papa Vidal's murals that covered the interior wall where there were no windows. It was the last thing he had completed years ago, the mural he had been working on that fateful summer before everything changed.

The colors were muted, soft and serene. The composition was dominated by a huge oak that stood so stalwart and tall that its upper branches slid onto the ceiling, giving a sense of sheltering protection. Its shade pooled a darker blue-green than the sunny lawn that surrounded it, while Blest, in the background, was so bright with glassy-hot sunshine reflection that it seemed to shimmer like a mirage. And on the upper gallery of the house could be seen the silvery shades of a couple in Victorian dress, standing arm in arm, watching with loving approval some encounter that was taking place in the oak's shade.

A boy and girl, teenagers, lay in the warm grass beneath the great oak. The blue of his jeans was a slash of pure color; the pink of her sundress had all the shades of a wild rose. His hair was dark, hers silken pale. They held each other close, the boy hovering just above the girl in his protective clasp, the girl touching his lean cheek in a gentle caress. And in their faces was such wonder, such glory in the discovery of young love, that it suffused the painting. Its brilliant glow added so much depth and vitality that it seemed possible to step into the mural, to live, once more, in that shining and tender moment.

The couple were Anna and Rip.

Moving closer to the wall, she put out her hand and brushed Rip's painted face with her fingertips. If she closed her eyes, she could sense again the warmth of his skin, also the prickly cushion of the grass at her back. She could hear the sigh of the breeze in the leaves, know the welcome weight of the boy who lay with her and the gentle, untried magic of his kiss. Somewhere there, crickets and cicadas sang of heat and love. Somewhere a bird trilled, bees hummed and a hawk sailed on warm air currents, calling in plaintive hunger for its mate.

They'd thought they were alone, those two in the painting. Matters between them would quickly progress beyond tender touches and gentle kisses. As they had in the attic just two hours ago.

But soon Tom would appear from behind the big, shimmering house. With his face twisted in outrage, he would call his friend a bastard and a snake-in-the-grass, and tell him to get his dirty hands off his little sister. Rip would scramble up, wiping his palms on the sides of his jeans. Then they would fight, Rip and Tom, rolling in the sweet green grass. Only Rip would do no more than protect himself against Tom's flailing fists, and when Anna pulled Tom away, there would be blood in Rip's face and intolerable pain in his eyes.

So much pain.

Thinking, remembering, Anna squeezed her eyes shut and rested her forehead against the cool, dry painted wall. No, she didn't want that moment back after all. It hurt too much, even now.

A quiet footfall came from behind her. She stiffened, then straightened. Even as she turned, however, she knew who was there.

"So you do remember?" Rip's voice was soft with satisfaction from where he stood with one shoulder propped against the door facing. "I wondered."

"I remember," she whispered, blinking the haze of tears from her eyes.

"Then you'll know why I intend to hold you to your pledge to marry me."

"For revenge," she said, the words a little stronger. "Because of all the things Tom said to you that day."

It was a moment before he answered, a moment in which he turned his back to the door frame and crossed his arms over his chest. "One thing you can be sure of. It isn't for the sake of a virgin kiss."

"I never thought it was," she returned, putting as much scorn and courage as she could find behind the lie. "But it will only happen if I fail to give you what you want."

"If," he repeated. Then he added more quietly, "I'll have what I want, one way or another."

Her glance was scathing. "For what good it will do you."

"Oh, it will do me fine. I intend to see to it."

"You would." He meant, she thought, that he would take her as well as the house, and see that she enjoyed it. The terrible thing about it was she easily might. At least as long as the pleasure lasted.

He hesitated, then tipped his head toward the ceiling over their heads. "About what almost happened up there a little while ago—"

"Nothing did," she said with some force.

"Wrong. You almost got carried away, a little like sixteen years ago. Except this time you're the one remembering that I'm not on your level."

"I don't care about levels," she said in stringent denial. "What I care about is being used."

"My worry exactly."

It took her a second to figure that one out. "If you're suggesting I might've thrown myself at you to find out what you know, after all, then I feel sorry for you!"

"You always did, didn't you. But I guess that's honest enough, which is all I want. That, and to regain what was taken from me."

"Oh, and to be a Bon Vivant member, we mustn't forget that. Well, heaven forbid I should stand in the way. Maybe we should speed up this program. Maybe you should give a reception, an open house to kick off the restoration of Blest."

"A reception?" His brows drew together over his

nose as if she had suggested setting a bomb under the house.

"Why not?" she inquired, improvising rapidly under the spur of angry grief. "People have been anxious to get inside this place for years. You can impress them with all its decadent splendor, then present your plans for how it's going to look when you're done."

"What if nobody comes?"

The stark question, and the insecurity it revealed, touched her briefly before she pushed it aside. "They'll come," she said. "Curiosity will bring them, if nothing else."

"They'll come for you." His gaze was almost hostile.

"Possibly. Isn't that what you've been counting on?"

"It's entirely possible," he said in tight disdain, "that what I was counting on isn't available, may never have been there at all."

Without waiting for a reply, he pushed away from the door frame and walked away down the hall without looking back.

"People are talking about how much time you're spending with that man," Anna's mother said, her mouth set in a straight line as she stared across the breakfast table. "Going over there every day, taking him to things like Sally Jo's barbecue and the civic club luncheon. It's disgusting."

"Mother—"

"I've told everyone I know that it's merely on account of Blest, that you want the restoration done right for the sake of the community. But now I hear there's to be a party with you as his hostess." She slapped the table with the flat of her hand. "That's carrying things too far."

"He wants to be reestablished, I told you that. It can't happen unless he gets out and meets people." Anna kept her attention on the coffee she was swirling in her cup. It and a piece of toast were all she felt able to face. Her stomach was tied in a permanent knot these days.

"Let him meet them by himself!" The words were venomous.

"I promised to help," she answered as patiently as she could. "This open house seems a good way to let more people know what he has planned. There's a lot of interest among the businesses in town."

"All our friends are going to think your interest is personal," her mother returned with acid emphasis.

"They'll be wrong." Anna wasn't sure of that, but had no reason to think her mother would understand, much less sympathize, with the confusion in her mind.

"You'll be embarrassed. No one of any importance will show up."

Anna put down her coffee cup and pushed it back. Without looking at her mother, she said, "You had better hope they do, and are extremely nice to Rip as well."

"What do you mean?"

"If they don't, and aren't, you may find yourself with John "Rip" Peterson as a son-in-law."

"Of all the preposterous—" Her mother stopped and sat forward, her gaze sharpening. "How can you say such a thing when you have just told me there's nothing between you?"

"I said nothing personal." Anna used a fingertip to follow the warp of the linen tablecloth. "I suppose I should have mentioned it before, but I didn't really think Rip would go through with it."

"What are you trying to say?" her mother demanded with alarm threading her voice.

Anna told her, sparing no details.

"Oh, dear Lord." The older woman fell back limply in her chair. "You couldn't, you can't. It isn't possible."

"I gave my word."

"It's insane. People don't do things like that, not in this day and age."

"*I gave my word,*" Anna repeated. "The word of a Montrose."

Her mother stared at her with stricken eyes, as if absorbing the finality in her voice, the determination in her face. "We have to do something. The Bon Vivant midsummer dance is less than two weeks away."

"We?" Anna inquired in sardonic disbelief.

"I won't have you sacrificing yourself!" Matilda Montrose put shaking hands to her face, wiping at the pudgy flesh. "If only I'd known, I would never..."

"Never what, Mother?" Anna asked.

"Nothing, nothing."

"What have you done?"

"Oh, all right!" the older woman cried. "I told everyone I know just how underhanded and pretentious Rip Peterson is for wanting to own Blest, how like him to try to buy a heritage since he has none of his own. I told them the only way he could have gained a fortune was through some kind of dirty dealing—drugs, money laundering, or some illegal scheme cooked up while he was in prison. I told them—"

"I get the picture," Anna cut her off with a swift gesture as sick dismay flooded through her. "How could you do it? Why would you be so hateful and vindictive toward someone who is trying to put his life back together?''

"That man ruined my life!'' her mother declared in choked tones. ''He led my son into criminal ways, then destroyed him. He killed your father as surely as if he had shot him dead. If it wasn't for Rip, I would still have a decent house, nice friends, still be someone.'' Her mouth worked a moment longer, but sobs robbed her of words. She put her head down on the table, crying in despair.

"Rip paid for what he did,'' Anna said quietly as she took a fresh napkin from the holder on the table and reached to press it into her mother's hand. ''More than that, he says he's innocent.''

"Of course he does,'' her mother said, the words sarcastic in spite of being muffled as she wiped her face.

"What if it's true? I've been thinking—''

"Don't!'' Her mother jerked up her head. ''Don't you dare say it! Your brother was the sweetest, most gentle boy who ever walked this earth. I won't have his memory defiled in this house, do you hear me?''

Anna stared across the table with a frown between her eyes. "I didn't mention Tom.''

"But you were going to.''

She was right. "Tom was my brother, and I loved him, but he was hardly a saint. Besides, he was running with a bunch that—''

"No, I won't listen, I won't! I'll help you do what you must, but I never, ever want to hear you suggest that my son had anything to do with what happened to that—that felon!''

The vehemence in those words sent an extra niggling doubt through Anna's mind, but she had more important things to think about. "What can you do for Rip?"

"It won't be for him," her mother returned with loathing. "It'll be for you, to keep him from putting his filthy hands on my daughter."

Anna wondered what the reaction would be if she knew he had done that already, and that her daughter had returned the favor. But Matilda Montrose had never been the kind of mother who would understand the urgency of physical attraction, and it was too late to expect her to start now. With a small frown between her eyes, she said, "What do you intend to do?"

Her mother flung out a hand in irritation. "I don't know yet, but something. I still have connections, influence."

"Just be careful you don't make matters worse," Anna warned.

There was no answer.

9

It rained in late afternoon the evening of the open house, a cloudburst that washed the dust from the grass and leaves and left a measure of coolness in its wake. It was just as well; Blest had no air-conditioning.

There was also no electric light in the cavernous rooms, since the utility company had declared the old wiring in the house unsafe. Anna had ordered hundreds of candles and filled the chandeliers, then brought in every candelabra and candlestick she could beg or borrow. She had envisioned the house in the blaze of candle glow, but discovered that there was a vast difference between her modern conception of such a thing and what might have been considered bright light in the old days. At least the gentle flames concealed the worst of the dust, and cast a romantic sheen across the age-speckled mirrors and cracked plaster of the walls.

Rip's fear and Anna's secret nightmare, that no one would come, was laid to rest within the first half hour. The cars began arriving while the long summer twilight still lingered, and continued until well after it was dark. How much of the attention was due to rampant nosiness and how much due to Anna's efforts and her mother's intervention, she neither knew nor cared.

She stood beside Rip in the receiving line, introducing people and whispering names he should know. She also passed tidbits of information in a steady stream, such as who was married to whom, who lived where and did what, who had children and who didn't.

Several familiar faces appeared as the evening advanced: Sally Jo and Billy Holmes with their two children, many of the business people they had met at the civic club luncheon, even King Beecroft and his wife Patty. Carrie DeBlanc, magnificent in an animal print caftan, was one of the later arrivals. She slinked toward them like a two-hundred-pound femme fatale, her appraisal as blatant as Mae West at her most incredible.

"Honey, honey," she moaned to Anna as she gave her a big hug, "you're killing me with this man. Hide him quick, before I'm tempted to grab something to squeeze."

Anna laughed as she emerged from acres of silk folds. "I'd be careful if I were you."

"You mean he's liable to grab back? Be still my heart!" Releasing herself and turning to Rip, she spread her arms. "Hello, gorgeous. Where would you like to start?"

"I don't quite know," Rip answered, pretending to study the situation in spite of a heightened shade of red under his bronze-tinted skin. "I'm overwhelmed."

"And meant to be, sugar," Carrie crowed as she folded him into the silken tent of her embrace.

After that icebreaker of a greeting, the evening took on a momentum of its own. Rip greeted everyone who passed before him with an unaffected naturalness that made Anna's heart swell with pride. If he was at all nervous, there was no way to tell. He smiled and shook hands, made inquiries and wry observations with people who had been school friends or to whom he had spoken lately about the house. To the occasional question, he made easy answers without a trace of hesitation or suggestion of arrogance. For all that anyone could tell, he might have been born at Blest and lived there all his life; he was every inch the successful and urbane gentleman-owner.

Anna took little credit. She might have fed Rip history and statistics on Blest at every opportunity, but much of what he knew was due to long hours spent with Papa Vidal and to his affection for the place which sparked his interest.

He had dressed for the evening without advice from her, wearing a new gray suit paired with a cream shirt and a silk tie in a subdued pattern of dark gray, brown and cream. His cuff links were simple gold buttons, his shoes butter-soft black loafers. He had asked her to be certain his tie was straight, but that was all.

He should have looked like a banker, subdued and uniform, but the simple attire set off his dark hair and coppery bronze skin to such perfection, and he wore it with such confidence, that he stood out as a presence, someone of intrinsic importance. It didn't hurt, either, Anna thought, that he was easily the most handsome man in the room.

It was astonishing how proud she was to stand beside him in her rose chiffon and antique garnets, to be the one to lean close with a low comment or touch his arm to gain his attention for yet another introduction. She was aware of the murmur of conjecture about them but recognized, too, the glances of rueful envy that were cast her way by the female guests. It almost seemed Rip's past gave him an unexpected attraction, like a reformed pirate appearing in polite company.

On Rip's other side was Papa Vidal, dressed up in his Sunday-go-to-meeting suit, one of such vintage that it had a Zoot-suit stylishness of its own. It had been a struggle to get him to agree to stand with them to greet the guests; Anna had only managed it by suggesting privately that it would be a fine gesture of support for Rip. Actually, it had been Rip's idea to include him. One of the main reasons for restoring the house was the murals, he had said, and what better way to make that plain than to have Papa Vidal as a star attraction.

The maneuver turned out to be a master stroke. Papa Vidal knew everyone who was anyone and was easily able to put names to people when Anna failed. Better than that, it was the elderly painter whom the media zeroed in on when they appeared.

Where the television crew came from or who had called them, Anna didn't know. They seemed on the trail of a human interest story, perhaps the perennial favorite of the prodigal son. It didn't matter, for Rip turned their attention almost immediately toward Papa Vidal.

The elderly painter played it up like a pro, too, ignoring the cameras as he smiled and nodded with courtly aplomb, speaking to friends and neighbors who passed in front of him. Part shy artist, part sly showman, he seemed to revel in the attention.

Once Anna caught a glimpse of something white peeping from the elderly man's suit coat pocket. It was Henrietta, poking her head out for a quick look. She put a hand on Rip's arm, indicating the Silky chicken with a discreet nod. He glanced in that direction, then gave her a conspiratorial grin and wink. The warmth and secret pleasure of it, there in the middle of everything, sent heat spiraling through her body. The dark gold of his eyes deepened, growing more intense. The muscles of his forearm tightened under her fingers. She drew a swift breath through parted lips.

Then someone just stepping through the front door spoke to her and took her free hand. She turned reluctantly to greet the guest and the moment vanished as if it had never been.

It was a short time later that Anna glanced through the wide-open door and saw her mother coming up the front steps. She was wearing black lace and a militant expression. At her heels was Judge Benson.

Anna felt Rip stiffen beside her. Turning slightly, she took his arm, tucking her hand into the crook of his elbow in a casual gesture of solidarity. Then she waited for her mother to reach them with all the fatalism of a general watching an opposing army take the field. It could have been her imagination, but it seemed the noise level of the crowd lowered to an expectant hush.

Matilda Montrose crossed the threshold, glanced around at the milling guests, the subdued lighting and the camera crew filming the huge mural that dominated the hall. Her gaze rested on Rip, standing steadfast in the entrance as master of Blest. Then she fastened her attention on Anna and moved toward her with heavy steps.

"Congratulations," she said in brittle approbation. "It appears your little party is a success."

It was a valiant effort, even if somewhat less than

gracious. Anna felt the rise of compassion as she realized how much effort it had taken for her mother to make it. What had prompted her to come, she wasn't sure—whether curiosity to see what had been done to Blest thus far, dislike for being left out of what might be the social event of the summer, the need to see if anyone really would show up, or an impulse to support her daughter. It didn't matter. She was there and that was enough.

"Thank you so much," Anna said simply as she reached out to her.

A spasm crossed Matilda Montrose's face as she drew back from the swift hug. She turned toward Rip, and for an instant, it seemed she might say something cutting, might yet make a scene of the kind she had enacted at the steak house. Then Judge Benson was beside her, urging her along out of the way of the next arrivals coming up behind them. Anna's mother gave her hand to Rip, briefly touching his fingers before moving quickly past him. She summoned a neutral smile and greeting for Papa Vidal, then she moved on.

It was done, over. Anna released the breath she was holding. Beside her, Rip did the same. He covered her hand with his for an instant, then released her. And the evening went on.

The stream of guests finally dwindled to a few stragglers. Anna, Rip and the man of the hour, Papa Vidal, were able to abandon their posts. With that, the affair picked up speed.

Champagne disappeared in astonishing quantities due to the warm evening. The boiled potatoes topped with sour cream and caviar, the smoked oysters in bacon, the crab rolls, honey chicken on skewers and a half dozen other delicacies provided by the caterer were well received.

Clusters of people crowded around the different murals, exclaiming and making knowing comments about perspective and shading, whether they knew anything about them or not. Papa Vidal, standing before his hall mural, faced the bright television lights and gave an interview as if he had been doing it all his life.

A short time later, Rip mounted the first step of the stairs, using this vantage point for a small speech of welcome. With one hand in his pocket and the other holding a champagne glass, he stood at ease while he outlined what he hoped to accomplish with the restoration of Blest, and how he expected it to benefit Montrose and the business community. He saluted Papa Vidal and his work, and spoke of the artistic heritage of the region. He thanked the firms and individuals who had signed on as part of the project. Finally, he gave special credit to Anna for her encouragement, expertise and continuing aid in re-creating Blest as it had once been. He ended in a graceful toast to Montrose and the future.

Anna led the applause; she couldn't help it. She knew how much those few words had cost Rip, knew what it meant to him to stand there in the midst of so many of the people who had once condemned him and receive their approbation. Her smile was a little misty as he descended the step and came toward her.

"God, but I'm glad that's over," he said in heartfelt thankfulness. He tipped back his glass of champagne and downed at least half of it in a single swallow.

"You were wonderful," she said sincerely. "I think you impressed them."

"The house impressed them, also the champagne,

and maybe the money.'' The derision was plain in his voice. ''Because of all that, they're willing to tolerate me.''

''Don't sell yourself short, or the people in this town,'' she said, holding his gaze. ''They know where you came from, so they understand what you've done, what you've overcome. You were so young when it all took place and it was long ago. A few may not be able to get it out of their heads, but most of them genuinely honor your courage and hard work and wish you well.''

As Anna said those words, she found she really believed them. A part of it came from what she felt inside, but a lot of it was picked up from the attitudes of those milling around them.

''Anna,'' he said in some urgency, ''about our agreement—''

''Not now,'' she murmured, though reluctantly. With a nod, she indicated the television reporter approaching from behind him, cameraman in tow.

''Mr. Peterson,'' the woman said briskly, her eyes bright and her smile a cover for the avid interest in her eyes. ''This is quite a story, your rise from prison inmate to plantation owner, one I'd like to develop further. I wonder if we could get you to repeat your remarks for the camera? And also answer a few questions?''

Anna could feel Rip tense, then he relaxed again as if at some silent command. His dark gaze commanding, he mouthed a silent pledge to her. ''Later.''

''Later,'' she repeated, though her smile was strained. She was worried about him, about what he would say and how it would be interpreted, but there was nothing she could do.

"Don't fret," a deep voice spoke up from behind her. "He'll have them eating out of his hand, including that young woman with the microphone."

It was Judge Benson who had walked up to join her. She turned to answer him. "I hope you're right."

He gave a comfortable nod. "No doubt about it. He has backbone and style. Charm, too, and he's not afraid to use it."

Yes, Rip certainly had charm. She had succumbed to it, hadn't she? Anna murmured something politely appropriate.

The judge gazed at his drink a second before he went on. "Matilda was afraid she'd done the wrong thing, calling the manager at the TV station to alert him to this turnout of yours, but I told her not to worry, it would be fine. I think she sees that now."

She met his gaze in a long moment of understanding before she said, "I think you may be right."

"He'll go far, mark my words." The judge reached into his pocket and took out an envelope. "Here's a little something to help him on his way. Not much, but I think he'll see the value. You give it to him and tell him to come see me when he gets the chance."

"Yes," she said, her voice tight as she stared down at the heavy square of cream paper she held in her hand. "Yes, I'll do that."

The judge patted her hand, then walked off. She let him go without a word. The envelope was heavy with import. She knew exactly what it was without looking. It was her release, her salvation, her freedom.

It was Rip's invitation to join the Bon Vivants.

"Don't give it to him, Miss Anna. Just don't do it."

That advice, spoken with quiet urgency, came from

Papa Vidal on the morning after the open house. Not that Anna needed it. The temptation to get rid of the invitation had been with her since the night before, when the judge had put it in her hand. She had tucked it away, waiting for a good time to tell Rip. None had presented itself, or at least none she wanted to take. She'd carried the envelope home with her for the night, telling herself she would return to Blest first thing this morning and hand it over in a more private setting. Then she'd run into Papa Vidal on the drive.

"He'll find out," she said in tentative tones. "Somebody will mention it to him—Judge Benson or maybe Mother, since she arranged it. Then what?"

"Be too late," the elderly man said promptly.

"He would know I tricked him. It wouldn't be right."

"Yes, ma'am, it would be, Miss Anna. Make everything right for the first time in a long, long while."

Was it sadness and remorse she saw in his fading eyes, or just recognition of the world's basic unfairness? Did he know something about the situation, or only feel for Rip? Tilting her head, she asked, "Why do you say that, Papa Vidal? What's so wrong?"

"Lots of things," he answered, looking away with a vague air. "Lots of things in this life are all mixed up. Some can be put right, some can't. This one now, it preys on my mind. I'd like to rest easy about it. You know the way—it's all in your hands, Miss Anna."

Age and a tendency to melodrama—that was all there was behind Papa Vidal's urgings. If only it was as simple as he seemed to think. Her smile was wistful as she said, "Rip might hate me."

"If you think so, you don't know Mist' Rip. Could

be he'd be glad. Could be he's hopin' no invitation ever comes his way."

If she kept the news of his acceptance in the Bon Vivants from Rip, he would hold her to her word. She could allow herself to be pressured into marriage.

It would all be so easy. Rip would have what he wanted, and she would have, just possibly, what she had always needed.

"Oh, Papa Vidal, I don't know."

The old man sighed and scratched his head, then reached into his pocket to soothe Henrietta as if petting the chicken might quiet his doubts. "You'll do what you think best, I guess. But first—first I got something I want you to see."

He turned and walked away along the drive, back toward the outbuildings behind Blest. Anna watched his retreating back. What was he up to now? There was only one way to find out.

She glanced toward the motor home that still sat on the lawn, but there was no sign of movement. It seemed Rip might still be sleeping after his late night and the work of cleaning up after the party. It was Sunday morning, after all, and no workmen would be showing up. With reluctant footsteps, she followed Papa Vidal.

He was headed toward the schoolhouse, she saw after a moment. By the time she reached it, he was already inside.

The schoolhouse had one main, open room where classes had once been held. Beyond that was a pair of cloakrooms and a storeroom, while in the back was a sitting room and bedroom where the teacher had been housed in the old days. Everything had been torn apart for the refurbishing. The laths of the walls were exposed where plaster was being replaced, grit crunched underfoot from the sanding of the ancient oak floor and antique desks were stacked haphazardly in one corner. Papa Vidal ignored the clutter and debris, heading for the blackboard that stretched across the rear wall of the big room.

Installed some time after the turn of the century, when the schoolhouse had been part of the local school system, the blackboard was made of real slate and stretched from a level low enough to be reached by elementary children to the high ceiling. It made a fine surface for the mural Papa Vidal was in the process of painting.

The subject was the family cemetery, as he had told Anna earlier. Its image, sun-glazed and serene, lay on the smooth slate, capturing the weeds and fresh green grass waving over the graves, headstones leaning and covered with lichen in the shade of the cedar and the iron fence lurching in drunken dignity around it. Ghostly figures played there: a mother nursing a newborn while seated on a raised tomb, an elderly couple rocking side by side, a pair of children that Anna recognized as twins who had died of diphtheria some time in the late 1890s. It was perfect—a rich representation so uncannily lifelike it seemed to catch and hold the spirit and heart of eternal rest.

It was also disturbing, however. Then she saw why.

Rip stood outside the fence, gripping the iron railing. His figure was not quite finished; his expression had been left blank. Nevertheless, he seemed to be staring into the cemetery's far corner. Something was there, an ethereal mist that slowly evolved into a figure, a ghost leaning against a plain marble marker with the figure of a white, semitransparent deer at his side.

Tom.

The ghost was Tom, nonchalant and faintly defensive. He watched Rip with friendship and gratitude in his face. Regret was also imprinted there, and distant sorrow that his friend could not enter this place of peace and freedom from care that he had found. On the marker where Tom stood was his name and a date traced in delicate, shaded strokes of paint as if chiseled into the marble.

Anna wasn't aware of moving, hardly knew what she did or intended until she stood before the mural and reached out with trembling fingers to touch the lines of that fatal date. It was that day, sixteen years ago, when Rip had robbed a service station and her brother had disappeared. As she lifted her hand again, her fingers were wet. The lettering was fresh, as if that portion of the mural had just been completed that morning.

Anguish began in her mind and spread, achingly, to her heart. She closed her eyes tight against the press of tears, clenching her hand into a slow fist at the same time. Papa Vidal moved to her side, touched her shoulder with a shaking hand. She felt its frail weight, his intent to offer comfort. But there was none to be found, nothing that would ever take away the ravaging grief that tore at her.

Opening her eyes, she turned a blind and wavering stare to the elderly painter. "He's dead, isn't he?" she whispered. "Tom's dead, has been all these years. And Rip killed him."

A short sound came from behind her. It was a sudden exhalation, as if from a blow. She turned though she knew what she would find.

Rip stood in the doorway. His hair was tousled, as

if he had run his fingers through it in lieu of combing it. He had obviously dressed in a hurry for he wore jeans but no shirt and sneakers without socks. His face was white as death.

He had heard her, knew she thought him capable of murder. The knowledge lay in the pain-scourged darkness of his eyes. Still, he did not move, said not a word in defense. He simply watched her as if memorizing every line and plane of her face, every flicker of emotion that marked it. The sunbeams that fell through the windows so she could feel them dancing in her hair. Every breath she took.

"No, ma'am," Papa Vidal answered in a positive quaver. "Mist' Rip never killed him. Mist' Tom, he shot his own self out of shame for taking the money. He shot himself right here in the graveyard, here at Blest where he'd been happy. Left a note, he did, asking me and Mist' Rip to see him buried and not tell a soul how or why he died. Put the money back where it came from, he said—he didn't mean to take it. Don't never let anybody know, he said. And we did it. We did it 'cause we loved him and didn't want to shame him. But the price was high. It was sure enough high."

It was long seconds before the gentle words the old man spoke formed themselves into images that had meaning. Anna turned her gaze to Papa Vidal's ancient, wrinkled face. Tears tracked down the grooves in his cheeks like the slow trickle of water along a dry branch after a drought.

"Oh, Papa Vidal," she said, as her own eyes filled. Reaching out, she put her arms around him, holding him close.

"Wasn't me who was hurt the worst," he said, patting her back in an awkward attempt at reassurance and comfort. "Mist' Rip, he was the one they caught tryin' to do what was right, tryin' to put that money back. They caught him, but he never told. I would have, but he said not. So I did my best for him. I testified how I'd seen Mist' Tom driving past when I never seen a thing, told how I thought Rip was a good boy who made a bad mistake and meant to undo it."

She drew back, searching his face since she couldn't bring herself to look at Rip. "Surely he didn't have to take it so far, didn't have to go to prison? There was the note, wasn't there? You could have shown it to the judge."

"The note was there all right," the elderly black man said with pained scorn. "I took it to Tom's mama, and I told her the truth. She took that note and torn it up, then she called me a lyin', senile old fool."

Her mother. Her mother had known, but had refused to believe. Matilda Montrose preferred to have people think her son had mysteriously vanished rather than confess what he had done. She refused to accept that he was imperfect, that he had died rather than face his parents with his weakness and faults.

But that wasn't all. Anna's mother had chosen to allow an innocent boy to go to prison rather than besmirch the name of her precious son or her family.

She should have guessed, Anna thought. She knew what Rip was like, how he had been with Tom and with her. She knew his loyalty and his need to prove it, understood the streak of nobility that made him put friendship and honor before himself. She, of all people, should have guessed what he was capable of doing. Also what he could never have done.

Anna had shown better judgment as a child. She had recognized the warmth and generosity of spirit that he hid beneath the faded clothes and hands made greasy by honest work. She had seen, and been drawn to them.

Anna didn't want to face Rip, couldn't bear to see the condemnation in his face. She was no better than her mother. For a brief moment, she had believed he killed Tom.

She had failed him. She had also failed herself, failed to understand her own heart and mind, to recognize that she had loved him years ago and still did. More than that, she had failed Tom, who never would have wanted Rip to take the blame that had been his alone.

She had to acknowledge her guilt, had to let him know how sorry she was for doubting him, how much she regretted everything that had been done to him. With her heart in her eyes and bitter grief in her heart, Anna forced herself to turn.

Rip wasn't there. The doorway was empty of everything except the bright, unrelenting sun which shone where he had stood.

"Go find him, Miss Anna," Papa Vidal said as he stepped away from her and bent to pick up a paintbrush lying across a bucket. "I got me a paintin' to finish."

It was all the urging she needed. She left the old schoolhouse and walked back toward Blest, though she didn't go inside. Skirting the bulk of the main house, she reached the front drive. She paused a moment, glancing toward the cemetery. A movement under the big oak just this side of it caught her attention. She set off in that direction with sure, steady steps.

Rip was sitting against the huge tree trunk with his knees drawn up and his wrists resting on them. She stopped in front of him, studying the taut lines of his face, the stiff set of his shoulders. Then she knelt beside him. Moistening her lips in a nervous gesture, she sought for the right thing to say. Nothing seemed to fit, nothing was ever going to be enough.

This time, she had no candy bar to ease his hurt. She had only herself.

"I'm sorry," she whispered, since that was all that was left.

10

Rip rested his gaze on Anna's mouth for endless seconds before he allowed himself to meet her eyes. There was no accusation there, but only sorrow overlaid by a humility he had never expected to see and didn't particularly like. So Papa Vidal had told her everything. He had known it was preying on the older man's mind.

"I'm sorry, too," he said abruptly. "I'd just as soon you hadn't found out, not after all this time."

"I needed to know." She shielded her eyes with her lashes. "But I think I always suspected. It was so like—both of you."

"It won't bring Tom back."

"No." She pushed a hand through her hair, sighing a little as she let the breeze filter through the long, silken strands. "Nothing ever will."

He looked away, trying to ignore the tightening in his groin. In moody explanation, he said, "It was the drugs. He enjoyed getting high, thought he could control it. Though I tried—" He stopped.

"Was King Beecroft involved at all?"

"Tom never said so. He may or may not have put

him up to it, but it was Tom who knew my boss at the service station kept cash on hand in an old office safe. I told him myself, laughing at how the old man didn't trust banks, never dreaming Tom would..."

"So it was Tom who broke in, jimmied the safe's lock."

"He wouldn't have, if I hadn't put temptation in his way. I was responsible."

"No, you weren't. It was Tom's choice. Then he couldn't stand what he had done once he came down from the drug high. I understand. At least I'm glad it's over at last."

"Even the way it turned out?" Rip allowed his skepticism to creep into his voice.

"Even so. The wondering, thinking no one might ever know, was far worse."

"I doubt your mother will feel the same."

"She has a great deal to answer for," Anna said quietly. "I never knew about Tom's note. She never said a word, I swear."

"I realized that, after a while."

"Still, she knew you had seen it. She's been so on edge, waiting, I think, for you to do something, say something to show everyone what she'd done. It should be a great relief to her to know you have no intention of doing that."

"Don't I?" he asked tightly. "What makes you think so?"

She looked at him, her gaze clear to the bottom of her soul. "Because," she said unsteadily, "I know you."

He was lost in that moment. He stared at her with hot eyes, fighting a yearning that went back years. Her eyes shimmered in a mist of tears and her silk blouse rippled gently in the breeze, conforming to her warm curves. Her long legs, exposed as her short white skirt fell back from her knee, were golden and just right for wrapping around him. The moment was there, and might never come again.

He reached for her, drawing her against him, into his lap, tucking her head into his shoulder. All he meant to do, or so he tried to tell himself, was offer comfort and shared consolation for old pain, for lost youth and vanished dreams. Still, she came so willingly, fitted herself against him so easily. He needed her, needed the comfort she could give, far more than she needed him. Or ever would.

"Anna," he said on a stifled groan.

"Yes," she answered, and lifted her mouth to his.

She was sweetness and light and beguiling glory, and he had to taste those things at least once more before he left Blest. He took her lips, blindly questing, savoring their softness, their gentle curves and tender surfaces. He inhaled her scent that had haunted his nights for an endless time, been the constant companion of his desperately slow days.

She opened to him as naturally as a flower opening to the sun. He gave her his heat, his limitless need, half expecting her to shrink from it. Instead, she met it, matched it, twining her tongue with his in a sinuous dance of endless giving.

They had been here before beneath this oak. Then, as now, he held her close, loved her in the dappled, moving sunlight. She had pressed her hands upward over his chest to clasp them around his neck. He had taken advantage of that movement to brush his hand over her rib cage, then close his fingers gently over her breast. The soft moan she made had been incredibly sweet, but he had gone no further.

Now he would, must, or he would die. As he had died a thousand deaths in prison while thinking of the past that had been and the future that would never come.

Anna would die if he stopped. The heat of his body, the sure clasp of his hand on her breast and gentle abrasion of his thumb across her nipple mounted to her head until she felt dizzy with need. She murmured wordless encouragement while she memorized the firm molding of his mouth, tasted the corner with her tongue, then dipped deep inside, searching for greater depths, closer adhesion.

He gave it to her, following her lead in a smooth plunge as she retreated. He wanted what she wanted, needed as she needed, and he would deny neither of them.

The buttons of her blouse parted under his quick fingers. She felt the sun's warmth on her skin. Then came the heat of his mouth, the wet glide and swirl of his tongue, the abrupt capture and suction at her breast that beaded her skin with a shiver of erotic gratification. She threaded her fingers through his hair, holding him closer, tilting her head back so the sun made shimmering patterns of exquisite colors against her closed eyelids.

He shifted with her, stretching full length on the ground. His face blotted out the sun as he took her mouth once more. With her hands freed by the movement, she spread her palms over the firm muscles of his shoulders, enjoying their latent power. Letting the fingers of one hand drift down the ridges of his bare back, she pressed her palm closer to absorb the heat of his skin.

So intent was she on her explorations that it was an instant before she felt the waft of air under her lifted skirt, the pressure and sureness of his hand at the juncture of her thighs. The careful friction he created made her gasp and surge against him. He dragged her underwear down and off, then returned to his ministrations. His lips curved in the most tender of smiles as, a moment later, he sent her spinning into the vortex of arousal.

She was on fire, simmering with moist heat and urgency. She pressed against him in wordless need, trembling as she sought his belt buckle, lowered the zipper of his jeans. She wanted to touch him, and did, inhaling in sharp pleasure at the silken, turgid thickness, the weight and springing power of him. With a tried whisper, he gave her access, permission, showing her his shuddering pleasure as he bent his head to trail hot, wet kisses along her forehead, her hairline, into the spiral of her ear. He nipped her earlobe delicately, soothed it with his tongue, then sought and found her mouth to thrust deep inside.

At the same time, he covered her, settling between her thighs. He guided himself to the hot, wet core of her, then entered in a swift, desperate plunge. She took him with internal pulsing, clutched with urgent hands to draw him deeper. And held him while her being stretched, relaxed, then reshaped itself, tightly and forever, to fit his hard length, his savagely tender need.

Shared delirium. Sun-spangled wonder. Timeless magic that blended past and present. It met in their bodies and in their eyes. Holding her gaze, he withdrew until she refused to let him go further, then sank into her until she sighed and her lashes fluttered with strained repletion. Again. And yet again. Over and over until their breaths came in hard gasps, their muscles quivered and perspiration dewed their skins. She took him and clung, clasping him internally while turning her head from side to side with the amazing, near-intolerable pleasure of it. He took her and filled her, driving for her heart, embedding himself there in luxurious wonder.

Blending, striving, they moved against each other until, only half-conscious, Anna sensed her hold on reality slip, felt herself spinning, falling into the heated magic. She whispered his name as the dark contractions of her body took him with her, beyond earthly orbit, into oblivion.

They lay for long moments, gasping for breath and sanity. Rip reached it first. He sat up, lowered her skirt, found her panties and drew the edges of her blouse together.

Anna did not want to be sane. Didn't care if she could no longer breathe. She had felt the finality of the love he had made to her, knew its fierce magic had been designed to last for long years, a lifetime, if need be. It had been a goodbye—unless she could find some way to stop him.

Without opening her eyes, she said, "Marry me. Please."

Rip heard the entreaty in her voice and steeled himself against it. Zipping his jeans with an abrupt gesture, he said, "One sacrifice between us should be enough."

"Sacrifice?" She lifted her lashes, and the dazed vestiges of surfeited passion cleared from her eyes like fog from a mirror. "Who is sacrificing what?"

He said plainly, "I have no use for a pity marriage."

"Certainly not," she said in quiet assurance, "though not so long ago you were willing to take one based on duty."

He watched her sit up and rise to her knees, fastening her clothes with the dignity of a duchess. "I thought I would take you any way I could get you. I was wrong."

"I see. It was revenge after all."

"No!"

"No? It was all right, then, as long as there was no emotion involved. But you can't stomach the idea if it comes with love attached."

He hesitated, then said with choked finality, "You don't love me. What you feel is compassion and gratitude, and damned Montrose notions of honor. You think I should be repaid for what I've lost. Fine. Consider what just happened repayment."

Tears rimmed her lashes, but she wiped them away with a furtive gesture. "It was more than that and you know it."

"Was it? Did I presume too much, take more than you wanted to give? Don't give it a thought. I'll deed Blest to you. You can do whatever you like with it. That should make us even."

"Blest? But you can't!"

"I think I can," he said grimly. "The main reason I wanted it was as a way to get close to you. So maybe it was revenge. Who knows? But now it's done. I'll get out of your life."

"Oh, Rip, you've come so close to winning."

Her eyes were so dark, so liquid with dread that he felt his insides twist in pain and desire. He shook his head as much to dislodge that weakness as in negation. "The people, the media, the whole thing last night—it was all for you. They didn't care two cents about me, and they'll care even less when I'm history."

She settled back on her heels. Without looking at him, she said, "You've got it all figured out, haven't you."

"I think so." The urge to fling her over his shoulder and take her into the house, make love to her on the hard floor of Blest until they had splinters in uncomfortable places, was so strong he could barely force words past the clamped ache in his throat.

"For your information," she said, her eyes sparkling with anger, "I might have made love to you once out of gratitude and compassion if I had thought of it, which I didn't. But promise or no promise, I would never tie myself to you for life for such a stupid reason. I'm sorry if that makes me less ladylike and honorable than you seem to think, but I consider it makes me less of an idiot. There's nothing on God's green earth that would force me to marry you, including all your threats, if I didn't want to be your wife. And just so you'll understand exactly what I mean, here's something for you. For what good it will do you!"

Scrambling to her feet, she dug an engraved envelope from her skirt pocket. She flung it in his lap, then swung around and walked away.

Rip knew what it was the minute he saw his name in calligraphy across the front. Still, he ripped it open, tore out the card.

The damn invitation. Who would ever have dreamed?

It was the last thing he expected, the very last thing

he wanted. Tearing it in half, he threw the pieces as far as they would go and watched them flutter down to lie scattered in the grass.

Then it struck him like a blow to the heart.

Anna had known about the invitation *before* she had made love to him, *before* she had spoken a word about how she felt. She had already known she was home free.

He surged to his feet and ran after her, catching her in ten good strides. Swinging her around, he demanded through his teeth, "Why? Give it to me again, the part about wanting to be my wife."

"Go to hell," she said, each syllable precise and deliciously prissy, and her eyes blazing.

"There was something about love. Yours for me."

"In your dreams."

She tried to twist free of his grasp, but he wasn't allowing it. Closing his hands on her upper arms, he said, "You want to marry me. You were going to sacrifice yourself, after all, because that was the fastest way to go about it. Isn't that it?"

She stared at him, her lips set in a firm line. With tremendous effort, he resisted the impulse to kiss her senseless, opening her mouth one way or another. Giving her a small shake, he said, "Ask me again. See what I say this time."

"If you were half the gentleman you should be, you wouldn't even think of making me do such a thing," she said in accusation.

She was right. Which proved exactly what he had known all along. He was hopeless. Folding her in his arms, he sighed, then breathed in the sweet scent of her. "Do I have to get down on my knees?"

Her answer was muffled, though the shake of her head was plain enough.

"Wait until I can find candy and flowers?"

She drew back a little. "What for?"

"I'm trying to get this right," he explained, aggrieved, "but I need cooperation. You're supposed to be all flattered and fluttery."

"That's if I don't know what I want," she informed him with a jaundiced, upward glance.

"And what do you want?" he asked, his hands straying down her back, holding her against him.

"A man, not a gentleman, or at least one not quite so noble."

"That's easy," he said in choked gratitude.

"Yes, and no. You were always a natural, you know, always had the right instincts. Being a gentleman takes more than clothes and manners."

"Anna, no, I..."

"Trust me on this, I know what I'm talking about." Her smile twitched and he felt it just above his heart. She added, "Other than that, I want the same thing you want."

"I somehow doubt it. As I told you once before, I want you. Any way I can get you."

"You never told me that exactly. Why didn't you?" It was a complaint.

"I thought it," he said with some difficulty. "Isn't that enough?"

"No. Are you going to say the words now or not?"

He chuckled, a low sound of surrender. "I love you, Anna. Marry me, and live with me at Blest. I can promise plaster dust in your hair and paint between your toes, and a bevy of restoration experts looking over your shoulder every time you take a bath. And me. I'll be there, holding you, loving you, always and forever. We'll name our first boy Tom and our first girl Tildy for your mother, and maybe one day she'll forget and forgive the fact that I lived and her son didn't, that I am the trash who dared love her daughter all my life, and tried to marry her for spite, because living without her was no life at all."

Anna nestled close, holding tight as she nuzzled into his neck. "That was much better."

"And?" He couldn't keep the anxiety out of his voice.

"Don't be silly," she murmured. "I asked you first, didn't I?"

His first impulse was the best, after all. He bent and picked her up. Swinging around, he carried her up the steps of Blest and kicked the door shut behind him.

BILLY RAY WAINWRIGHT
by Emilie Richards

1

The north Florida air was as thick and wet as the sweat pouring down the backs of the men tearing up the asphalt on Route 194. On a hill one mile outside of Moss Bend, Billy Ray Wainwright waited at the head of the line of stalled motorists, too depleted by the May heat to feel more than a trace of impatience. The air conditioner on his Taurus had gone to its final reward that morning, and so far he hadn't had time to do anything except mourn its passing.

The male road crew, stripped to their waists and glistening in the late afternoon sun, worked with the enthusiasm and speed of men mired in a tar pit. The flagger, a buxom young woman in shorts, halter top and feed store cap, let a dozen cars and half a dozen pickups sail down the hill in the opposite lane before waving him past.

"What do you think you're looking at, Billy Ray?" she yelled as he stuck his head out the window and favored her with a lazy grin.

"Just the prettiest sight in River County, Gracie."

"Save your sweet-talking for the judge, counselor." She grinned back as she motioned him forward. Gracie

Burnette was happily married and the mother of the cutest baby boy for a hundred miles. Billy Ray had successfully defended her husband when a neighbor had accused him of stealing his bird dog.

Of course, it hadn't hurt that the dog had grown tired of a bitch in heat in the next county and found his way home on the day of the hearing.

Billy Ray Wainwright, defender of dognappers, barroom brawlers and alligator poachers. Billy Ray Wainwright, who had served as editor in chief for the *University of Miami Law Review*, ranked first in his law school class and turned down an associate position in that city's most prestigious law firm so that he could come back to the Florida Panhandle and take over his father's defunct law office.

Don Quixote had nothing on Billy Ray Wainwright.

"You come for supper someday soon, you hear?" Gracie yelled as he passed.

He waved and finished the hill, a meandering slope that was as undemanding as River County itself. The views of live oaks and pines were pleasantly rural, but the only impression he registered was of roasting flesh and overwhelming thirst. When he crested the hill and started down the other side, he gratefully pulled into the first parking lot on his right and turned off his engine.

An old frame building with air conditioners jutting from every window sat at the back of the lot. Once upon a time the wood siding had been painted the blue of a robin's egg, but the Florida sun had faded it to the washed-out hue of a cloudy sky. As a kid Billy Ray had spent a lot of hours at the Blue Bayou Tavern. To his knowledge there wasn't a real bayou for hundreds of miles, and the creek that sometimes trickled behind the tavern was mud brown. But folks in River County liked to tweak the truth. It was easier than trying to change things, and a whole lot more colorful.

The gravel in the parking lot crunched under the soles of his new loafers, and once he had stepped inside the tavern, discarded peanut shells took up the chorus. He was blasted with frosty air and the wail of Willie Nelson, and six feet into the room he was hammered with greetings.

"Hey, Billy Ray, how's it going?" As he walked by, an attractive middle-aged brunette in jeans and a skintight Blue Bayou T-shirt leaned over to kiss his cheek.

"Not a thing to complain about, Maggie." He slung his arm over her shoulder and gave her a quick hug. Maggie Deveraux was the owner, and in the years before Billy Ray's father transformed himself into a hopeless drunk, Maggie had been Yancy Wainwright's lover.

"Doug's over in the corner." She hiked her thumb over her shoulder, and through a haze of cigarette smoke Billy Ray saw the khaki-colored uniform of the county sheriff, Doug Fletcher. "He told me you were meeting him."

"You ought to charge him rent for that table."

"Can't hurt the place to have the sheriff put down roots in a corner. Fewer fights—"

"Except for the ones he starts."

Maggie winked as she started across the room. "Those? I don't pay no mind if Doug's involved. I just call 'em disagreements."

Billy Ray ambled toward the corner, exchanging greetings along the way. Considering that it wasn't quite five o'clock, the bar was crowded, but it was a

Friday night—and payday. And no one in Moss Bend paid attention to clocks, anyway.

By the time he made it across the room, Doug Fletcher was leaning back in his chair, his arms crossed over his chest and his long legs extended across the floor as if he were just daring someone to trip over them.

"About time you got over here." Doug waved a hand in the general direction of the seat across from him. "You friends with every dumb-ass redneck in the county, Billy Ray?"

Billy Ray lowered himself to the chair and loosened his tie. "Even you. And that's a stretch."

Doug held up his hand to get Maggie's attention. "You want the usual?"

"She's probably already bringing it."

"That's right. As far as Maggie's concerned, you piss holy water, don't you?"

Billy Ray favored him with a grin. "Why not? She's the closest thing to a mother I ever had."

"I don't know about that. My old lady fussed over you all the time. Little Billy Ray Wainwright could do no wrong."

"Your mama always was a good judge of character."

"My mama always was a pushover for a pretty face. You still got a pretty face, Billy Ray. How come you don't have it between the legs of some big-breasted woman these days?"

"That your tactful way of asking about my love life?"

Doug grinned. When he wasn't smiling he might pass for a pit bull, but Doug's grin altered his face. Like Billy Ray, he was thirty, tall and wide-shouldered, although the resemblance stopped there. Billy Ray's hair was light brown, his eyes were blue, and his features sharp and well-defined, from the straight slope of his nose to the square thrust of his chin. Doug was beetle-browed and pug-nosed, and his curly dark hair was beginning to part company with a forehead that had been too high to begin with.

"The way I hear it," Doug said, "you've got half the single women in Moss Bend panting over you, but you're not giving a one of them what she wants most."

Billy Ray leaned back in his chair and folded his arms. He still didn't know why Doug had insisted he meet him at the Blue Bayou, but clearly it was going to take some time to find out. "Just half?"

"You like living alone, taking cold showers?"

"Not as much as I like explaining my personal life to a no 'count county sheriff."

Doug barked an appreciative laugh. "I've got your best interests in mind, son."

Billy Ray realized he was still thirsty, and Maggie had not approached with the soft drink she knew he preferred. He was mulling over that strange turn of events as he looked up to see where she'd disappeared to. Immediately he noticed that the roar of the jukebox had halted and the room had grown suspiciously quiet, an ominous "calm before the storm" occurrence in a dive like the Blue Bayou.

His gaze snapped back to the man in front of him. "What's going on? Damn it to hell, Doug, you remembered, didn't you?"

"Me? I never forget a thing. And neither does Maggie."

As if on cue, Maggie appeared behind the bar with

a cake as wide as Doug's grin. A blazing forest of candles lit the tavern gloom. Exactly thirty, he guessed.

"Happy birthday, Billy Ray," Doug shouted as the crowd of patrons started to sing in off-key harmony. "And you'd better wish for a woman when you blow out those candles, 'cause I'm sure getting tired of being the one to make a fuss over you."

"Kitten, do you remember what I told you?" Carolina Grayson squatted on the floor in front of her five-year-old daughter and rested trembling hands on the little girl's shoulders. "Do you remember everything?"

Kitten was wearing one of the hand-smocked dresses that her grandmother, Gloria Grayson, had bought for her. Her lace-trimmed ankle socks were pristine, despite an entire day of wearing them, and the straps of both shoes were buckled exactly three punches from the end. The only thing to mar the perfect picture was the frown on her freckled face.

"We have to be quiet," Kitten recited. "We can't let anyone know we're leaving."

"That's right. We have to tiptoe." Carolina managed a smile. "Just the way you do when you sneak into my room at night to check on me."

"I don't."

She did, but this was no time to argue about it. Kitten did a number of things that most little girls didn't have to. At five, she was more mature than most teenagers.

"I'll carry Chris," Carolina said. "All you have to do is take care of yourself."

"But you're not supposed to lift him. You're sick."

"I'm fine. Really. And once we're in the car, all I have to do is drive. Okay? Promise me you'll try as hard as you can?"

Kitten gave a reluctant nod.

Carolina got to her feet. The room spun, and for a moment she was afraid she was going to pass out. But as she stood still and forced herself to breathe slowly, the dizziness passed. "Okay," she said in a low voice. "Pick out one toy, your favorite, to carry with you. Once we're settled, Grandma and Grandpa will send everything else."

"No they won't."

There was no time to argue about that, either, and besides, Kitten was undoubtedly right.

"I'll take Boom Boom," Kitten said. Boom was the stuffed panda that Kitten had slept with every night since infancy.

"I packed Boom. He's already in the car."

"Then I'll take Lizzie."

Lizzie was a fashion doll, the last toy that Kitten's father had given her before his death. Carolina tried not to think about what the doll meant to her daughter. "That's a good idea. She'll be easy to carry. I packed Chris's blankie, his dump truck..."

"Did you pack his stuffed horse?"

"Sweetheart, Grandpa threw the horse away because it got dirty, remember?"

"I got it out of the trash can. It's under his bed, in the bottom of that box with his sweaters. I let him play with it when nobody else is around."

Carolina stared at her young daughter. Tears sprang to her eyes. For a moment she didn't know what to say.

One step at a time. Someday soon Kitten would have a chance to be a little girl again.

"Will you get the horse while I get Chris?" Carolina asked softly. "Then we have to go. We have a long walk ahead of us."

"I'll get it. I can carry it. I don't mind."

Carolina bent and kissed the soft blond hair curling over Kitten's forehead.

By the time he left the Blue Bayou, Billy Ray's head was spinning. Normally he didn't drink, and when he did, he limited himself to one beer, which he could nurse until it had gone flat. Tonight he'd had two to wash down the birthday cake, the catfish sandwich and the heaping platter of fries that Maggie had hand-cut just for him. But he was still a mile from drunk. Mostly he was deaf from too much country music and camaraderie, and black and blue from a long series of slaps on the back.

Doug joined him in the parking lot, a toothpick jutting from the corner of his lips. Nadine, Doug's wife, had come and gone an hour ago. In fact, it seemed as if most of Moss Bend had put in an appearance sometime during the evening. "Got any plans for the rest of the night? It's not over yet." Doug gave a broad wink.

Billy Ray ignored the innuendo. "I've got to check out the garage for Joel. Cal's off on vacation somewhere. Then I'm going home."

"Too bad there's nobody at home waiting for you."

"Got a three-legged tomcat who lives in the barn. You probably told him it was my birthday, too."

"I can send somebody over to check Joel's place. You don't have to bother."

Billy Ray's grandfather owned the most successful garage in town, successful enough to need a watchman on the premises at night. Joel Wainwright serviced the sheriff department's fleet as well as half the cars in the county. At seventy-five, and after two heart attacks, he no longer did much of the repair work himself, but he was still a presence. His mechanics had a healthy respect for the old man's temper, and their work was as good as his had been.

Billy Ray slapped lazily at a mosquito. "Don't worry about it. I need to stretch my legs a little."

"I'm surprised Joel's not sleeping over the garage himself, with Cal gone."

"He would be, but he's been sleeping poorly lately. He does better in his own bed. And Cal's oldest boy is staying there after he gets off the late shift over at the tool and die, so we've got it covered."

"Well, if you check the place now, I'll send a man by around midnight, just to look it over till Cal's boy gets there." Doug punched Billy Ray on the shoulder; then he strolled toward his car.

"Hey, Doug."

Doug turned his head. "Yeah?"

"It was a good party."

In the rapidly dimming twilight Doug looked embarrassed. "Don't get sentimental on me, Billy Ray." He slid behind the steering wheel of one of the county fleet that was so well serviced by Joel Wainwright and gunned the engine. As he pulled out of the lot he serenaded Billy Ray with two blasts of the siren. Billy Ray knew he was lucky he hadn't gotten a full thirty.

The stars were coming out by the time Billy Ray got back out on the open road. The temperature still hovered around eighty-five, but something about the disappearance of the sun made it easier to bear. The change in shift from day to night birds hadn't gone smoothly, and the air was filled with song as they competed for dominance. Crickets chirped and whirred in harmony, and as the road wound by the Sassafras River, frogs joined in the symphony.

Billy Ray had come this way often as a boy. He and Doug had caught bass and trout in the river, and camped on its shores overnight. They had built rafts and floated them downstream into Moss Bend, and once, at thirteen, they had followed the river into the next county in hopes of running away.

He had never expected to spend his thirtieth birthday in the place where he'd grown up. Even at thirteen, he had believed that his destiny lay somewhere else.

But here he was. Still. Again. Perhaps always.

By the time he pulled into his grandfather's lot on the outskirts of Moss Bend, he was more than ready to make the trip across town to his own house, where he could take off the shoes sadistically pinching his toes and strip down to his boxer shorts. But he had promised Joel he would check the garage. After law school he had come back to River County to be near his grandfather, and he was determined to stay until Joel met his Maker. The least he could do was make sure that everything was secure.

The garage took up the equivalent of three city lots. A boxy white office building sat at one end, with an attached wing extending along the roadside, where the cars were serviced. Cars and trucks filled the surrounding parking lot, which was shaded in places by gnarled old trees that Joel steadfastly refused to cut down.

Toward the back of the complex the trees were

thicker, and because of the distance from the road and the small forest, security was sometimes a problem. Several weeks ago someone had crept on to the property when Cal was sleeping and stripped a Chevrolet of its hubcaps and hood ornament. Joel suspected a neighborhood teenager with the same model Chevy, but so far, the boy hadn't admitted a thing.

Billy Ray parked on the roadside directly in front of the office and closed his door quietly. If any of the locals were up to mischief, he had probably already scared them away, but now he played the game by the rules, prowling silently through the lot, peering into windows and around the sides of cars, even lifting the corner of a canvas tarp covering the bed of a pickup truck to peek inside.

He made a systematic sweep until he came to the area behind the buildings. Here only one dim security light shone, in deference to the neighbors, who had complained when Joel tried to install floodlights. This was the drop-off area for cars to be serviced the next day. Owners parked their cars and deposited their keys in a slot in the office door.

Billy Ray spent enough time at the garage to recognize some of the cars. Right now there was a beat-up station wagon that belonged to a waitress at the Peabody Luncheonette, and a 1970 VW van that was the pride and joy of an honor student over at the high school. There were three nondescript sedans that were too ordinary to identify at first glance, and one silver BMW that was the only one of its kind in the county.

Carolina Grayson's car.

Billy Ray carefully passed his gaze over all the cars, but his eyes stopped again at Carolina's. The Beamer had cost more than most county residents earned in a year. It was an exact replica of the one Carolina had demolished last winter when she ran off the highway after a Christmas party. Her husband Champ hadn't survived the accident to help her choose a replacement.

Joel didn't like to service certain models, and this one was among them. But nobody said no to a Grayson, not even someone as ornery as Billy Ray's grandfather. If Judge Grayson showed up at the garage with a team of Clydesdales and demanded a tune-up, Joel would adjust their oats and braid their manes. A Grayson had always been in charge in River County, and some things never changed.

Billy Ray was at the garage to check for intruders, not to think about Carolina Grayson. But Carolina was a hard woman to just file away. They had graduated from high school together, and although their paths hadn't often crossed in the years after River County High, she had remained in Moss Bend.

In high school Carolina had been a beautiful girl, a leggy blond vision with a million-dollar smile who had grown into a beautiful woman. She was one of God's chosen, blessed with beauty, poise, wit and wealth. She had sailed effortlessly from childhood in one prominent River County family to marriage into another.

Until the accident that had claimed her husband's life, her existence had been charmed—or at least it had appeared that way on the surface. She'd had a son and a daughter who were said to be as beautiful as she was, the affections of the Grayson family, and a husband who had distinguished himself in high school and college sports—which was better than graduating with honors in rural Florida. Champ had gone on to make a good living as the manager of a real estate development firm owned by the Grayson family. On the surface Carolina seemed to have it all, until the night she drove a car exactly like this one off the road and wrapped it around a tree.

Even then, she had been spared some of the problems of widowhood. After a month in the hospital she had moved in with the Graysons, and with their support and help, she seemed to be rebuilding her life. She did not have creditors at her door. She had household staff to see to her children's every need. She had been guaranteed the best medical care and rehabilitation. Carolina would get through this bad patch in an otherwise perfect life, and someday she would find another man like Champ Grayson to take care of her.

"Still hurting, Billy boy?" Billy Ray asked the question out loud, and the sound brought him back to his surroundings. He was standing in the drop-off lot of Joel's garage, thinking about a woman who had never been his. If once upon a time he'd had an adolescent crush on Carolina, he had been set straight by everyone who suspected it. Particularly her.

He started to move on. No one was on the premises, and now that he'd done his duty, he could go home for a cool shower. He had turned thirty today, and the least he should do was sit on his front porch, sip a glass of iced tea and think about the years ahead.

He would have done exactly that if he hadn't noticed a wavering shadow behind Carolina's car as he was turning to go. For a moment he thought he'd imagined it. The light was so dim that the shadows were deceptive. He wanted to believe he had fantasized what had looked like a hand extending from behind the car, the shifting of a body crouching beside the trunk.

He wanted to go home.

Billy Ray heaved a sigh as deep as the Sassafras River. "Somebody back there?" he called. "Because, if you are, you're trespassing."

He wasn't surprised that the night only grew quieter. Even the crickets seemed to be listening.

"Look, come on out," he said in a reasonable tone. "If you don't, I'll have to call the sheriff, and there's nothing Doug Fletcher likes better than cracking a few teenage heads together."

As he'd predicted, there was no answer. Billy Ray gave the intruder thirty seconds; then he made his decision. "Okay, I'll knock a few heads together without Doug. See if I don't."

He started forward. He had no intention of making good on his threat. He wanted to give the kid or kids who were probably hiding behind Carolina's car a good scare, nothing more. He suspected they would take off as he approached, and now that they knew the place was being watched, they would either be more careful or abandon the auto parts business.

When Billy Ray was five feet from the car, the shadow wavered again. A slender figure rose above the car trunk and skirted the side of the car. In the darkness Billy Ray couldn't see clearly, but the intruder looked to be medium height, of slight build and dressed in dark clothing.

"Look, let's not play games here." Billy Ray stopped, and the figure stopped, too. "I'm damned sure I'll win, unless you've got a gun. And if you do, blowing my brains out over hubcaps doesn't make a whole lot of sense."

"Billy Ray..."

For a moment the voice tickled the borders of Billy Ray's imagination. Then he realized why. It was a woman's voice, as sultry and soft as the north Florida breeze. A familiar voice.

"Billy Ray, I..."

The figure slouched against the car. He was rooted to the spot, still trying to take in the fact that the voice belonged to Carolina Grayson. Then, as she started sliding to the ground on the other side of the car, he surged forward, clearing the BMW in seconds. Just in time to catch Carolina in his arms.

She was unconscious by the time he was on the ground with her body slumped over his legs. The night was hot, but she was hotter. In fact, she seemed to be burning with fever, and when he patted her cheeks, she didn't wake up. Everything had happened so fast that he hadn't had time to figure out what was going on. Now, before he could begin to put the pieces together, the car door flew open and a little girl pounded her fists against his back.

"Leave my mommy alone!"

At least the child's identity wasn't a mystery. Billy Ray reached up and grabbed her by one wrist, holding it as gently as he could. "Stop it now! Your mama's sick, and I'm trying to help her."

"I heard what you said! You said you were going to knock her in the head!"

"Hush, honey. I didn't know it was your mama back there. I thought somebody was trying to steal her car." When the little girl stopped twisting and trying to punch him, he released her wrists. "What's your name?"

"My name is Catherine Waverly Grayson. Who the hell are you?"

If he hadn't been so taken aback, he might have laughed. But as it was, there was nothing funny about the situation. "I'm Billy Ray. Billy Ray Wainwright. Your mama and I went to school together."

"What's wrong with Mommy? What did you do to her?"

"Not one blessed thing. Has she been sick?"

Catherine Waverly Grayson knelt beside him and began to smooth her mother's hair back from her forehead. "She's been coughing a lot, and she's been in bed for days and days."

"Why isn't she home in bed right now?"

The little girl didn't answer. Billy Ray knew that if he were looking at her, her lips would be sealed tight.

He leaned forward, pulling Carolina closer to his chest. "Carolina, can you hear me?"

The answer was a moan. As he watched, Carolina's eyelids fluttered open and her eyes began to focus.

He hadn't been this close to her for years. As she began to take stock of her surroundings, he assessed the changes. The years had been good to her, but they often were to wealthy women with time on their hands and money to spare. Her heart-shaped face was unlined; her shoulder-length hair was expertly layered, so that even now it swirled artfully against her neck and ears. Her eyes were the same deep green, but they were clouded by shadows that hadn't been there twelve years ago.

"Can you sit up?" he asked, once she seemed fully conscious. "You can lean against me."

She managed a nod, and he helped her into a more

comfortable position. He didn't let her go. Any moment, he expected her to slump against him again.

He waited until she was settled before he spoke. "You're sick. You need a doctor."

"I saw…a doctor yesterday. I just have a cold. I'll be fine."

"You don't look so fine to me, Carolina. Matter of fact, you look like a woman with a full set of problems. And one of them knocked you to the ground a few minutes ago."

"Billy, I…"

He heard the tears in her voice, and he knew what they cost her. Carolina was eternally poised. He had never seen her show her feelings.

"Mommy, is he hurting you?"

Billy Ray had nearly forgotten the child standing at his elbow, the child who looked so much like her mother. He glanced at her and saw the naked fear on her face.

Carolina answered. "No, Kitten. No! Billy Ray's…an old friend."

"Told you," he said, giving the child a reassuring smile.

"I don't believe everything I hear!"

"Smart girl." He nodded. "Neither do I." He looked back down at Carolina. "For instance, I don't think the doctor told you this was a cold, did he?"

Carolina didn't answer. When it was clear she didn't intend to, he went on. "Look, let me get you home. You have to get back to bed. What on earth were you doing here, anyway? Checking on your car? They're pretty conscientious at Joel's, but they don't work after dark."

"I…can't go home, Billy Ray."

For a moment he didn't think he'd heard her right. Then he saw from her expression that he had. "You have to, honey. You're sick. It's either home or the hospital, take your choice."

"I *can't* go back. Please!"

Billy Ray knew desperation when he heard it. Now Carolina's eyes had filled with tears. He found it discouraging that even with her cheeks flushed with fever and tears clouding her eyes, she was still a beautiful woman.

"Mind telling me why?" He edged away from her.

Kitten answered. "We're running away."

"I see." Billy Ray didn't take his eyes off Carolina. "Mind telling me why?"

Carolina's voice was hoarse. "I tried to get the car started. Gabe brought it in…this afternoon. There wasn't anything wrong with it. Not really."

"Slow down." Billy Ray tried to put her words together in a reasonable order. "I don't understand."

"There wasn't anything…wrong with the car. Gabe brought it in for a tune-up, that's all. They weren't…supposed to get to it until tomorrow! But it won't start."

He thought he was beginning to see. "Gabe?"

"Gabe works for my grandfather," Kitten said.

Billy Ray nodded as if he understood. "Okay. Gabe brought it in and left it for a tune-up. Why are you here now trying to get it started?"

Carolina didn't answer.

Billy Ray continued. "Sometimes, if somebody leaves a valuable car in the lot, Joel removes a part or two. Just as a precaution. Your distributor cap is probably inside the shop somewhere."

"Oh, God…"

"Carolina, what's going on?" he demanded with a new note of steel in his voice.

"I have to get out of here. Can you find…the cap?"

"What have you done?"

"Done?" She looked confused.

"Honey, have you done something wrong? Is that why you're trying to get out of here when you ought to be home in bed?"

Kitten socked him in the shoulder. Hard. "My mommy's the best mommy in the world!"

He grabbed Kitten's hand. "You're sure not raising another little Southern belle here, are you, Carolina."

Carolina began to cry in earnest. Billy Ray knew the tears weren't for effect. He realized with surprise that, despite all the years that had passed, he still knew this woman. She was the natural extension of the girl she had been, a girl he had ceased to believe in a long time ago.

But here she was again. Carolina Waverly. Alias Carolina Grayson.

He shook his head. He didn't need this. He had made peace with his presence in Moss Bend, with his life, his status, his aborted dreams. He was thirty years old today, and he did not need round two with Carolina Waverly Grayson.

But even as he told himself to be careful, he gathered her closer. "Come on, Carolina. Tell me what you want me to do."

"Fix the car. Please. I have to get out of here."

"I can't do that, honey. You're in no shape to drive. You've got to think about your little girl." A wail started from inside the car as he finished his sentence. He shook his head. "Your kids."

"Kitten…?"

"I'll get him," Kitten said.

"I can't go back." Tears were sliding down Carolina's face, but she plunged on. "I can't, Billy Ray."

Kitten opened the car door, and in a moment a toddler, hair curling in disarray, was wailing on the ground beside them.

Billy Ray knew a crisis when he saw one. He had one distraught female in front of him and another who would punch the life out of him if he let her. And now there was a screaming baby boy to add to the mix. "Is there someplace I can take you?"

"The judge..."

He knew the rest of the sentence. If the judge was looking for her, he would try her friends first.

Billy Ray had two choices, and they were as clear to him as every moment of the thirty years he had celebrated today. He could take Carolina to the Graysons' house, despite her protests. Or he could take her to his place.

"Just tell me you haven't done anything that could get me in trouble for helping you." He leaned forward as he said the words. They were for her ears only.

She looked up at him. Only inches separated them, and for a moment his heart seemed to pause mid-beat. She took a deep, hiccuping breath. "It doesn't matter...if I've done anything. If you help me, you know he'll come after you...."

"The judge?"

She gave the faintest of nods.

"Have you done anything wrong, Carolina?"

"Is it wrong...to want to raise my own children, Billy Ray?"

He didn't know what was happening here, but he knew he wasn't going to find out anything else right now. He had to choose, and he had to do it right away. If he helped Carolina, he was siding with her against the most powerful man in River County, a man who could destroy him without even working up a sweat.

"Help me, Billy Ray. Please…"

He realized there was no choice to be made. He was Billy Ray Wainwright, a man who'd been born to tilt at windmills.

He wiped a tear off her cheek with his thumb. Her skin was too warm, and much, much too soft. "We'll go to my place, in my car. I'll call Joel and get yours delivered to my house tonight. We'll store it in my barn until you're well. Then you can decide what to do."

"I can't pay you back. I have nothing… *I'm* nothing. Not anymore."

"It's not about paying me back." He turned and searched for Kitten. She was comforting her brother. "Kitten, can you watch your mother while I get my car?"

"You're not going to call the cops, are you?"

"You watch too much television." He helped Carolina into a sitting position and settled her comfortably against the door of the BMW.

She touched his chest as he started to rise. "Please, Billy Ray. Don't tell anyone. I'll lose my children if you do. Please…"

He nodded. Then he started his jog to the roadside.

2

In the service lot, Billy Ray had mulled over the general facts of Carolina's life, but he hadn't considered the finer points. Now, as he drove home with Carolina beside him and her children drowsing in the back seat, the rest of the story came back to him.

Rumors had circulated after Champ's death, and time had only increased their number. Carolina had been at the wheel the night Champ died, and most of Moss Bend believed that the only reason she hadn't been prosecuted was the identity of her father-in-law.

Right after the accident, Billy Ray had grilled Doug for details, but Doug had been uncharacteristically silent. Billy Ray had been left to wonder, like everyone else, whether pressure had been applied by the Grayson family to keep the sheriff's findings a secret. Although Carolina had been well liked in Moss Bend, after the crash her popularity had taken a serious tumble. Many of the locals believed she had been drinking on the night of the accident, and many more believed that she had been drunk.

Champ's loss was a serious blow for the town. The young man had been everything the South believed about itself. Refined, chivalrous, and a success at everything he touched, Champion Collier Grayson had been Moss Bend's golden boy. He had charmed the hearts of even those ill-tempered residents who believed it was time for the Grayson family to loosen its hold on the county's politics and purse strings.

Billy Ray didn't know what to believe about the accident, but he certainly had reasons to be cautious. Despite them, tonight he had let the feelings of an adolescent boy intrude on the decisions of a man. He had sided with Carolina without having any good reasons to do so. All he really knew was that she was burning with fever, but she had been trying to leave town with her children, anyway. What did that say about her emotional state?

"Billy, I...I can't thank you enough."

Carolina spoke softly, as if she couldn't summon the effort to speak louder. He didn't know how to answer her. Doubt poured through him, and if there hadn't been two small children riding in the back seat, he would have pulled over to discuss his fears.

"I can't believe I've involved you in this." Carolina rested her head against the back of her seat. Her eyes were open, but she wasn't looking at him. She was staring straight ahead at the dimly lit downtown of Moss Bend.

Billy Ray stared straight ahead, too. He had chosen the fastest way home because he had to call Joel immediately. Only a small window of opportunity existed between the time that Doug sent someone to check the garage and Cal's son arrived to settle in for the night. Joel had to get to the garage during that time, reassemble Carolina's car and drive it to Billy Ray's. And it would take some time to wake him up and convince him to help, which was why Billy Ray hadn't tried to use his cellular phone in the parking lot.

"What's really wrong with you, Carolina?" Downtown was nearly empty, and the picturesque storefronts with their clapboard siding and country curtains had only security lights shining in their windows. Most of downtown, a six-block square of brick and frame buildings, closed down at eight. "And don't tell me it's a cold," he added.

She hesitated; then she sighed. "I have pneumonia."

He almost ran off the side of the road. "What?"

"Billy, I'm on antibiotics. I have them with me, and I can take them anywhere. I...I'm not sick enough to be in a hospital. Really."

"You picked a hell of a time to run away."

"It must look...that way." She began to cough, and for a moment she couldn't seem to catch her breath.

He waited until she was silent. "It sure does."

"It was the best time. For once, no one was... watching me. I was sick.... My car was in the shop...."

"Did you plan it that way?"

"I asked Gabe to take the car in. I told him I wouldn't be needing it...while I was sick."

He shot her a quick glance. "And all the time you were planning to leave?"

She nodded.

He realized that she had made her plans carefully, and he felt better. This was not the spur-of-the-moment action of a mentally unstable woman. Despite her illness, she had used logic and executed her plan with precision.

"I...I packed the trunk with a few things before Gabe took the car. I made...them look like bags for the women's shelter...in case anyone noticed."

"So you've been planning for a while?"

"Yes."

He drove on. He was out of town now, and he breathed a sigh of relief. Hardly anyone had been out on the streets. He had planned his route carefully, avoiding the one block with a bar and restaurant that stayed open late. His windows were tinted, and despite the heat, he had closed them so no one would be able to tell who was inside.

"You still live at the farm, don't you?" Carolina shifted in her seat.

"That's right." For generations his ancestors had supported themselves on fifty acres on Hitchcock Road south of town. They hadn't supported themselves well. No River County Wainwrights had ever been rich, but they had eked a living from the sandy soil, cultivating soybeans and corn and alfalfa. The land was still farmed by a neighbor, who also ran cattle in Billy Ray's pastures. Someday, if Moss Bend grew and spilled over the city limits, the land would be worth money. But now it was rich only in family sentiment.

"I've always liked that house," she said.

He was intrigued. He wondered if Carolina was just trying to curry favor, or if she really had a taste for simple white farmhouses, for wide front porches and ancient live oaks dripping enough Spanish moss to single-handedly give the town its name.

"I liked the garden," she added. "When I was a little girl...my mother told me it was the Garden of Eden."

Billy Ray's father had created the garden, insisting that despite his professional status, he had been genetically programmed to work the soil. Yancy had planted half an acre of camellias, azaleas and brightly colored perennial flowers along the roadside. The garden had declined as his father had. Billy Ray had done little to restore it.

"You won't like it now," he said.

"I know...it's overgrown. I've driven by."

That surprised him. Hitchcock was a rural road, paved only in the last decade. Basically, it led nowhere—which was a fitting symbol for the lives of generations of Wainwrights. "Well, if you were still expecting the Garden of Eden, you were disappointed."

"I like wild things. No one can control them."

He had never thought of the garden that way, but she was right. Birds nested in the locust trees that had sprung up in garden pathways; rabbits huddled under shrubs; squirrels fought battles with marauding raccoons. And sometimes, in the hours near dawn, deer came to prune the plants they loved the best. Billy Ray had no heart for controlling them or the jungle bequeathed him by his father.

Carolina turned to look at him. "He'll find us, you know."

"The judge?"

"If we leave town we have a chance. Here..." She shook her head. "I shouldn't involve you."

Billy Ray kept his voice low, but frustration sounded, anyway. "How in the hell did you think you'd make it *anywhere* in the shape you're in? What if you'd fainted behind the wheel, Carolina? You have two children to think about."

"I've never fainted before in my life. I've never considered...I might." She began to cough again.

He waited until she finished. "Seems to me that might not be the only thing you didn't consider. If you were trying to escape without being noticed, a silver BMW wasn't your best choice."

"I didn't have a choice. Do you think...I wanted that car? *He* chose it for me. He wants me to remember...every time I look at it. He wants me...to remember the other one."

Billy Ray's hands locked tight on the wheel as he considered that. He was not an admirer of Judge Whittier Grayson. The judge was a remnant of another time in history when powerful Southern aristocrats ran counties like this one with an iron hand.

That phenomenon still occurred frequently, of course, all over the country, but not with the same sense of noblesse oblige. Ruthless men and women clawed their way to power, but few of them felt they'd been born to it. Judge Grayson believed that River County was his birthright. From all appearances it was a birthright he had intended to pass on to his son.

Until Champ's death in a car driven by this woman.

After another fit of coughing, Carolina continued. "I was going to drive to Atlanta tonight...and sell the car. Go to another lot... Buy an ordinary used car. Move on from there."

He shook his head. "You would have left a trail a mile long and wide."

"I know...how to be careful."

"Do you?" His question hung in the air between them. One night last December she had not been careful enough.

Her eyes widened with hurt, and she turned away

from him. "My children's future…depended on not…taking chances."

She began to cough again, and Billy Ray knew better than to continue this way. He had to get Carolina home. Until she was settled and feeling stronger, she wasn't going to give him the answers he needed.

They made the rest of the trip in silence. Even when they turned onto Hitchcock Road, she didn't speak. Not until they'd gone half a mile and he'd slowed to turn into his property did she face him again.

"I'm at your mercy. I can't…drive anywhere. I'm weaker than I thought. I'd be lying…if I pretended…" She shrugged. "But if you let me rest here…until I'm better, I'll leave as soon as—"

"Carolina, by tomorrow morning, every cop in the county—hell, in north Florida—will be looking for you. You're going to have to come up with a new plan. But you're too sick to be worrying about this right now. Come inside. We'll work out something once you're feeling better."

Her expression reminded him of an animal caught in a snare. She hadn't given up, but she knew better than to hope for much.

He parked beside the house instead of the barn. He needed the barn for her BMW, and besides, he didn't want her walking farther than necessary. "Hattie came today. At least the house is clean and so are the sheets."

"Hattie McFerguson?"

"You know Hattie?"

"She cleaned for me. She's the best.…"

He tried to make conversation, as if this situation was somehow normal and the social graces applied. "I defended her son last year. He paid me what he owed, but for some reason Hattie thinks she owes me something, too. She sneaks in here every Thursday to clean and do my laundry, whether I want her to or not.''

"Hattie was..." Her voice drifted off. She shook her head.

"Was what?"

"One of the few people who believed...in me."

"That's all the recommendation I need."

Her eyes were sad. "Did you need one at all, Billy? Has it come to that?"

He thought about her words as he went around the car to open her door. By the time he got there, Kitten was awake, staring sleepily around her, and Chris was beginning to wail.

"Come on, little 'uns." He opened their door next, letting the night breeze cool them. "We've got real beds inside."

Carolina let Billy Ray get the children out of the car; then she got slowly to her feet. In the moonlight her face was pale, and despite having a suspiciously wet toddler weighing down one arm, he took her arm with his other. "Lean on me. Once we get into the house we'll get some cool liquids down you and some aspirin for the fever." He looked down at Kitten. "Can you make it?"

"I'll help my mommy."

"Great. Get on the other side. It might take two of us."

With nothing to argue about, she did as he'd suggested.

Carolina sighed. "When this is over...I will never ask anyone for another blessed thing."

Billy Ray didn't know what he'd expected from her.

He didn't pretend to understand this woman. He wasn't even sure he had ever understood the girl. But this display of backbone, this distaste for her own helplessness, was reassuring, somehow. She might have been pampered and protected until the accident that took her husband's life, but now she wanted to take care of herself.

He unlocked his front door and pushed it open. The house smelled of lemon oil and pine-scented cleaner. A light burned on a table in the corner, compliments of Hattie, who hated the thought that he came home every night to an empty house. Most likely he would find a pie in his refrigerator, too, one she had baked herself, and maybe a dinner to warm in his microwave.

Tonight, he would have to share.

"Let's get you to the sofa." He led them all into the living room on the right of the narrow hallway. The room was small, and furnished much the way it had been when his grandfather and grandmother, Edna, had lived here. Billy Ray hadn't had the heart to replace the old horsehair-stuffed chair that his grandmother had kept carefully covered in plastic, or to give away the rosewood piano with half a dozen keys missing. These had been Edna's treasures, and when Joel hadn't had room for them in his apartment in town, Billy Ray had promised to leave them where they were.

The navy blue velvet sofa was the only concession to the nineties. A grateful client—charged with setting up a pleasure palace on a side street in town—had given it to Billy Ray in lieu of cash. Billy Ray had never wanted to know exactly where the sofa had come from, but it was a substantial piece of furniture, no matter its origins.

He led Carolina there now and settled her against the cushions. Chris wiggled to get down and join Kitten, who had already made herself at home beside her mother.

"This guy's wet," Billy Ray said. "I hope you're not going to tell me all the diapers are in your car."

She opened a large purse and began to move things around. "I have one here. I'll change him."

He held out his hand for the diaper. "Rest. I've changed diapers before. But first I've got to call Joel, so we'll be gone a few minutes. Kitten, can you come with me? Your mom needs something to drink and some medicine."

Kitten, her eyelids heavy, looked from Billy Ray back to her mother, as if she were assessing the situation.

He raised a brow in question. "Do you need a character reference?"

"Go with Billy," Carolina said.

"She likes juice." Kitten stuck out her lower lip. "And not apple."

"I'll keep that in mind."

Carolina closed her eyes, obviously too exhausted to do anything else.

Billy Ray started through the house with the wiggling toddler on his hip. He didn't look at the little boy, afraid if he examined him too closely he might see a miniature Champ Grayson staring back up at him. "Does the wiggler talk?" he asked Kitten.

"Not much. Everybody talks for him."

"Uh-huh. You, too?"

"No. Mommy told me not to."

"His name is Chris?"

"Christopher Collier Grayson."

"And you're Catherine Waverly Grayson, but your mama calls you Kitten?"

"When I'm older I'll be Cat."

"Makes sense to me."

Kitten looked around. "Does anybody else live here?"

"Nope. Just me."

"Where's your family?"

"I have a grandfather, but he lives in town now."

"No, I mean your kids and stuff."

"I don't have children."

"Why not? Don't you like kids?" she asked suspiciously.

"I've never thought a lot about it." They had reached the kitchen, after winding their way through small rooms built one after another by successive generations with no talent for architecture. He liked the random placement of rooms, the way that connecting hallways narrowed or widened according to the builder's whim. The house had been built for living, not entertaining, and definitely not for show.

He liked the kitchen best of all. The house had no dining room. Meals had always been taken here or in the room that had served as a kitchen when the house was first built. This room was wide and long, with windows looking over the back acres. Sometimes he imagined the Wainwright women standing at the windows waiting for their men to come back to the house after a long day of chores, biscuits baking in the oven and pork sizzling on the stove.

At the sink he turned to Kitten. "I'm going to put Chris on the floor for a minute. Will you watch him while I get the juice for your mama?"

"I can take care of him."

He guessed that Kitten was only five or maybe six, but he was sure that if she said she could take care of her brother, she could. "Great. I've probably got orange juice. Will that do?"

"She likes orange juice."

"What about you? What do you like?"

"I like it, too."

"And can Chris drink some?"

"If you don't give him a lot."

"Kitten, do you know everything?"

"Just about."

He opened the refrigerator and found the juice. Also what looked like a chicken casserole, a fresh green salad and a blackberry pie. On top of the pie was a white envelope with his name on it. Hattie hadn't forgotten his birthday, either.

He bet she hadn't imagined it would end like this.

Carolina knew she had to rest, but she couldn't keep herself from studying Billy Ray's house. She had always pictured the inside much this way, simple and homey, the kind of place that grown children visited on holidays to relive childhood memories. It was a house where there would always be a bed if one was needed, a place at the table, a hug, a listening ear.

She knew, of course, that what she'd imagined had not been Billy Ray's experience. Like everyone else in Moss Bend, she had watched Yancy Wainwright deteriorate from a brilliant attorney into a belligerent alcoholic. Yancy hadn't been a storybook father, and Billy Ray hadn't had a mother at all. His had died bearing a brother who hadn't lived, either. His grandmother had died soon afterward, and Billy Ray had been raised in a house of men, with Joel Wainwright firmly at the head.

But the house... The house cried out for better times. For a family who loved it, for children to play in the fields and down beside the creek. In the years of her marriage to Champ, she had been told repeatedly that she imagined things she shouldn't, that she was too old for fairy tales, and that her delusion that life could be one big happily-ever-after made her unfit to be a wife and mother. But old habits died hard, and despite everything, she heard the house cry out for better times at the same time she heard Whittier Grayson's accusations.

The room began to recede, then to spin, gathering speed until she closed her eyes to shut it out. She wondered how high her temperature had climbed. She had been running a fever for days, but this morning she had awakened with a normal temperature. She had been on antibiotics long enough that she had believed herself to be past the crisis.

She supposed exertion and stress had brought on the relapse. The Graysons' house was nearly two miles from Joel's garage. She had carried Chris and her largest purse, stuffed with supplies, the entire way. Since the accident, she hadn't even been allowed to lift her son, but tonight, despite pneumonia, she had toted him the entire distance. And she had made it, too. Despite every obstacle, she had made it.

Just in time to collapse into the arms of Billy Ray Wainwright.

She supposed it was fitting that Billy Ray had been there to catch her. So often in the years of her marriage she had seen Billy from a distance and remembered the sweet innocence of their adolescence, the hours of passionate conversation, the pleasure of stolen kisses. Billy's attractions had been doubly evident when viewed from her position as Champ's wife. By then she knew only too well what integrity looked like. She knew how it felt to be seduced by power and prestige, and how little it meant to have the admiration of people she couldn't admire herself.

The distant Billy Ray had become the symbol of all the parts of herself that she had given up to marry Champion Grayson. But she had always known that if the distance narrowed between them, that if somehow Billy stepped back into her life and they were face-to-face again, he might swiftly become more than a symbol.

"Mommy?"

Carolina opened her eyes to find her daughter standing before her with a plastic tumbler of orange juice. She took it with unsteady hands, and Kitten held out a fist containing two white tablets. Carolina took those gratefully, too, and swallowed them with her juice.

Kitten snuggled beside her, and although a warm little body was the last thing she needed, she put her arm around her daughter and pulled her even closer.

"Tell me about the new house," Kitten said.

Carolina didn't have the heart to tell Kitten she was too sick for the game. Her daughter was already too responsible, too grown-up. She closed her eyes and gave it her best shot. "There will be children in the...neighborhood." She coughed, then went on. "You'll ride bikes on the sidewalk and climb trees. Big trees...with lots of branches."

"Will I have to wear a bike helmet?"

"I'm afraid so."

"Too bad."

Carolina gave her a quick squeeze. "We'll have sleepovers with pizza and video games...and all the little girls you want to invite."

"Ten?"

"If that's what you want...and in the morning..."

"Blueberry pancakes!"

"Exactly." Carolina rested her head on the back of the sofa. "You'll ride...a bus to school, or maybe you can walk or even ride your bike if we live close enough. I'll take you...and Chris swimming every single day in the summer."

"In a lake. A real lake," Kitten reminded her. "Not a pool like Grandpa's, where I have to stay in the shallow end."

"And we'll bring a picnic to eat...under the trees."

"I wish we were there right now!"

Tears filled Carolina's eyes, and she squeezed her eyelids tight. "I'm so sorry, Kitten. I guess...I just didn't know how sick I was."

"Are we still running away?"

"We're trying...."

"I don't think we're very good at it."

Carolina's next breath sounded like a sob, even to her. "I'll get you to that house.... I swear I will, sweetheart."

"Carolina?"

She opened her eyes at the sound of Billy's voice, and the jig was up. The tears slid down her hot cheeks. Some leftover feminine instinct made her wonder what she looked like, flushed and tearstained, but she didn't really have the strength to care.

"Joel's agreed to get your car and bring it here."

"Thank you," she whispered.

He frowned, turning what had always been a solemn

face into a somber one. "I'm going to take the kids upstairs and see if I can get them settled. Then I'm going to come down so we can talk. Will you be all right till then?"

She nodded, because she didn't trust herself to speak.

"I don't have a crib. Will Chris be all right on a bed against the wall if Kitten sleeps beside him?"

"He'll be fine. Kitten, you won't mind, will you?"

Kitten was frowning, too. "Where will you be?" she asked Carolina.

"Your mama will be in the next bed," Billy said.

Kitten looked unhappy, but she followed Billy out of the room. She was too responsible not to.

Carolina was surprised at how quickly Billy accomplished putting her children to bed. Or maybe she fell asleep while he was doing it. When she opened her eyes again, he was standing in front of her, and his face was still somber.

"If there was anything else I could do..." She let her voice drift away. She felt marginally better, as if whatever he had given her had nibbled away at the fever. But inside, where it really mattered, she just felt devastated that she had failed. Again.

"It should still be a little while before Joel gets here. I know how bad you feel. But I'd like a better explanation of what's going on before he arrives."

She studied him. This was the closest they had been in a dozen years. He was the same man, yet so very different. Champ had been beautiful in his youth, but as he matured, marks of the man inside had surfaced. He had grown fleshy because he was unable to deny himself anything. His boyish smile had given way to a cynical smirk that hardened into something more sinister in the final year of his life.

Billy had never been beautiful. As a boy he had been tall and lean, even-featured, but so serious that his face seldom lit with a smile. And that had been much too bad, because Billy had a fine smile indeed.

He had been well liked in high school, but he'd never called attention to himself. In those days Billy Ray could fade into the background whenever the situation called for it. And it often did. He was adept at working behind the scenes. He had learned to bail his father out of jail or avert yet another family disaster with calm logic, a steady gaze, a sincere handshake. She remembered that Joel had tried to protect his grandson from the worst of Yancy's exploits, but Billy had been forced to deal with many of them, anyway.

Now Billy's integrity and maturity were evident in his face. He was a man who would grow more handsome as he aged and Mother Nature stripped away all artifice. He had blue eyes that saw clear through to tomorrow. A chin that said everything about how stubbornly dedicated he was to anything he believed in. A mouth that knew how to smile, but also how to speak plainly.

If she could trust anyone, she could trust this man.

"What have you heard about me?" Carolina asked, her voice carefully low so that the children wouldn't hear. She supposed her pain showed through. She knew exactly what Billy had heard. She knew what everyone in River County believed about her, and she knew why.

"There's talk that you were drinking the night Champ was killed."

"There's talk...I was drunk."

He didn't nod, but the acknowledgment was in his eyes.

"I can't tell you I wasn't." She forced herself to keep her eyes locked with his. "I remember...getting ready for the party that night. And nothing more."

"Nothing?"

She shook her head. "I've learned it's...not uncommon. I suffered a severe concussion. And sometimes our bodies shield us from remembering...."

He moved to sit beside her. She turned so that they were face-to-face. "Do you drink, Carolina?"

"Socially. It's never...been a problem." She saw that he didn't believe her. And who could blame him? His father had probably said the same thing. Didn't alcoholics usually deny that they drank too much?

"What does this have to do with you leaving tonight?" he said.

"Has anyone told you...how unstable I am?"

He frowned. Billy would not be the kind of man who listened to idle gossip, but Moss Bend was a small town. She was surprised that this particular rumor hadn't caught his attention. After all, when the judge talked, people repeated his words as if they'd fallen off a page of the Good Book.

"I'm supposed to be an...emotional basket case. I'm supposed...to be incapable of caring for my children." Despite her hesitation, her voice had risen. She swallowed, and that provoked a coughing spasm. For a moment she couldn't suck enough oxygen into her lungs, and fear filled her.

"Calm down, Carolina." Billy took her hand. "You're all right. Try for a little breath, not a big one."

She managed after a moment to begin breathing normally again.

"You're upset." He didn't drop her hand.

"I have a right to be."

"I don't want to tire you. This is hard. I can see—"

"Whittier wants my children!" The words exploded from deep inside her. "He wants them, particularly Chris. And if...I don't cooperate with his plans, he'll put me...out of the picture! And I can't let that happen."

He covered her hand so that it was enclosed in his. He rubbed it, and only then did she realize how cold it was. She was burning with fever, but her hand was like ice.

"They're his grandchildren, Carolina. Are you sure he's not just looking out for their best interest? You've been ill. First you were injured, and now this...."

"He's blackmailing me, Billy." She looked down at their hands. "He's spreading rumors that aren't true. And if...I don't go along with whatever he wants, he'll...have me declared an unfit parent. And he'll take the children away. He's told me so."

"But rumors are rumors, Carolina. He would need proof."

"Billy, what county...have you been living in?"

She saw recognition in his eyes, and for the first time since this conversation had begun, she saw understanding.

"Yes," she said. "He would lie. He would pass out favors. He wouldn't...think twice. He never has. He wants his grandchildren. Nothing...will stand in his way."

"You know this for a fact? Or you're guessing?"

"He has...a piece of paper damning me!"

He didn't ask what it was. He waited.

She debated what to tell him, but in the end she could only tell the truth. She'd lived with enough lies in her marriage to last a lifetime.

"The judge has the results of my blood alcohol test...on the night of the accident." She made herself take a breath, then another. Then she delivered the bad news. "According to the test...I was legally drunk."

She looked up at him. "How can I prove it's a lie, Billy? I can't...remember the accident. I can't remember the party. And no one...will stand up to the judge. They know what could happen. So...they make themselves believe what they hear about me. And one lie turns into another. I was drunk that night. I killed my own husband. I can't...take care of my children. I'm imagining things...about the people who've tried so hard to help me."

She realized she was crying, but she didn't care. "These tears...could be used against me. I'm crying to get my way. Or I'm crying...because I can't control myself. Don't you see how it works? Running away will just be another sign that I'm unstable and unfit."

"Carolina..."

"All I'm asking...is that you not tell anyone I'm here. Please, Billy. I'm not asking you to believe me. Just give me...the benefit of the doubt. Please."

He was weighing her words. She envisioned the scale of justice, but it wasn't tipping in her favor. And why should it? What proof did she have?

"The judge and I have an uneasy truce," he said at last. "But I believe he's capable of the things you say. My father hated him. I don't know why, but I know he did."

"I'm still the girl you knew." She touched her

chest. "Deep inside. I'm still that girl. Please, Billy, believe in that girl, even...if you can't believe anything the woman has told you."

He brushed her hair away from her forehead. "I want you to go up to bed now. I'll be sure Joel doesn't tell anyone you're here. We'll take this a step at a time. But I won't betray you, Carolina."

He touched his chest, then he smiled a little, but it was a sad smile. "I guess the boy you knew is still here, too."

3

Hattie McFerguson was big-boned and big-hearted, a strong woman with strong opinions about everyone she encountered. She was the perfect choice to come to Billy Ray's to take care of Carolina, and she agreed without hesitation as soon as he phoned her the next morning.

Hattie, in jeans big enough for a stevedore and a bright yellow River County Road Race T-shirt, arrived before Carolina woke up. But Kitten and Chris were sitting at the kitchen table sampling Billy Ray's selection of cereals, and Kitten, at least, was giving a spoon-by-spoon critique.

"I'm not supposed to have sweet cereal."

"If you think that's sweet, try this." He poured his final option into the last clean bowl and pushed it across the table. "Marshmallows and chocolate chips."

She looked at it longingly. "Pretty teeth make a pretty smile."

"Did your mama tell you that?"

"My grandpa."

"Ah. The judge."

Kitten took a big bite. "I'm not supposed to talk when I chew, either."

"I guess you might lose a marshmallow or two."

She giggled, a sound he hadn't heard before. He was admiring the effect when Hattie marched in.

"You feeding these children your trashy cereal, Billy Ray?"

"I'm trying to. They've been taught better, but I'm making headway."

"Hi, Kitten." Hattie strode across the room and swept the little girl into her arms. "And Mr. Christopher." She put an arm around the toddler, too. "Where's your mama, Kitty Cat?"

"She's sleeping."

Hattie looked up at Billy Ray. She had a plain square face and golden-brown skin bequeathed her by a mixture of ancestors. Elaborate cornrows peeked from under a colorful African print scarf, and handmade turquoise earrings hung past her chin. "How's she doing?"

"She coughed through the night, but it seemed to ease early this morning. I think she wore herself out yesterday and relapsed."

"That would be like Carolina."

"She said you were a friend."

"She doesn't have enough." Hattie glanced at the children, and Billy Ray knew that more revelations would have to wait.

"She doesn't want anyone to know where she is, Hattie. Can you keep this a secret?"

"You don't work in the houses of *this* town without knowing how to keep secrets, Billy Ray. Some I've kept forever. Some I've saved until..."

He knew he had chosen the right person to help.

"Hattie?"

Everyone turned toward the doorway. A wan Carolina entered the room. Billy Ray started toward her, but she waved him away. "I feel better. You shouldn't have let me sleep so late."

"You shouldn't be up at all. I was going to bring you breakfast," Billy Ray said. "And Hattie's here to watch the children for the day. All you have to do is rest."

She looked as if she had something to say about that but would save it until later.

"I'm eating cereal," Kitten said. "It's like candy."

"I'm ruining their smiles." Casually Billy Ray took Carolina by the arm and steered her toward a chair at the head of the table. "Watch them, would you? They may go into insulin shock."

She settled herself with obvious gratitude and returned Hattie's gigantic hug. She was wearing pale blue shorts and a coordinating T-shirt, and her hair was neatly combed. But if she normally made more elaborate preparations to greet the day, she hadn't made them this morning. She looked washed-out and unsteady.

Much the way Yancy had looked on the morning after a bender.

"Juice to start?" Billy Ray asked.

"I'd love some."

He strolled to the cabinet and got a glass. "Coffee or tea to go with it?"

"Tea," Hattie said firmly, before Carolina could respond. "With lots of honey and lemon in it. Carolina, you're going right straight back to bed after breakfast, if I have to carry you myself."

Carolina looked sheepish. "I've imposed on Billy Ray way too much as it is."

"I'm done!" Kitten held up her bowl. "Chris is done, too. I want to go outside."

"You're going upstairs to take a bath and get some clothes on first, and so is that baby. Come on now. Let's see what we can find." Hattie ushered both children out of the kitchen.

Carolina waited until they were gone. "Does she know she can't tell—"

"She knows."

"Did Joel bring the car last night?"

"It's in my barn." Billy Ray set the juice in front of her. "I'll make you some tea."

"Thank you, Billy Ray."

He guessed she wasn't talking about the tea. "Are you going to call the Graysons?"

"Gloria has a guild meeting this morning at ten. She won't miss it, because if she does, there'll be talk. And she hates gossip about the family worse than anything. The housekeeper always drives her. I'll call when they're gone and leave a message on her machine."

Gloria was Carolina's mother-in-law. Billy Ray had never had much contact with her, but she had always seemed unemotional to a fault, a woman who lived to do her duty and not one thing more.

"What will you tell her?" he asked.

"That we're fine, and that when we're settled, we'll get back in touch."

"And you think that will take care of the problem?"

"No, but I think I owe Gloria that much."

"Not the judge?"

She seemed to think carefully about her answer. "After the accident...Gloria helped me because it was expected. The judge helped so I would be under his control." She sipped her juice. "I...I don't expect you to understand. It's all right."

"I had to tell Joel some of what you told me. I got him out of bed and made him reassemble your car. Considering, I had to tell him something."

"Billy, will he tell...anyone?"

Billy Ray thought about his encounter with his grandfather. Joel had stood quietly in Billy Ray's barn and listened to his explanation. Then, without a word, he had started toward an old Chevy jalopy of Billy Ray's that he planned to drive back to the shop where he had parked his own car.

"Joel, Carolina asked me to keep this a secret. Can you do that?" Billy Ray called after him.

Joel didn't speak until he reached the Chevy's door. "Your father knew a thing or two about the judge. More than he ever told me. But I always thought the judge was the one..." He shook his head and reached for the handle.

"The one what?"

"The one who turned your father into the man he was when he died."

"Billy?" Carolina repeated in a worried tone. "Will Joel tell the judge I'm here?"

"You couldn't beat it out of him," Billy Ray said. "Not in this lifetime."

She sighed, and with it, she began to cough again.

"You're welcome to stay here as long as you need to," Billy Ray said. "Hattie will take care of the kids while I'm at work. You're going to need time to get well and make some hard decisions."

She sipped her juice until she was able to talk. "The decisions were all made. But they won't do me any good now, will they. Last night, I had a shot at leaving town, but not anymore. He'll have the roads watched.''

"Has the judge attempted to get legal custody?''

She shook her head. "He didn't need to, since the children were right there, anyway. But when I told him I was ready to move out…he told me I wasn't ready, and that if I tried to leave before he thought the time was right, he'd take me to court to protect them.''

"He can't stop you if you have custody. You're their mother.''

She shook her head again, but this time sadly. "Billy, the judge and Doug Fletcher are thick as thieves. Doug would have me picked up for… something else. Running a stop sign or driving in a suspicious manner. You know how it works.''

He did know, but he didn't like Doug's name being dragged into the conversation. Worst of all, he couldn't defend his friend, because he knew Doug was perfectly capable of twisting the law to suit his own purposes. He wasn't a bad man, but he was an ambitious one.

He changed the subject. "Let me get you some toast. Then I have to get to the office. Have Hattie call me if you need anything. But don't go anywhere, Carolina. Don't try a run to Georgia in broad daylight. Rest and take care of yourself. When I get home, we'll talk some more.''

"Do you remember the conversations we used to have?''

He reached for a loaf of bread and took his time unwrapping it and retrieving two slices. He dusted off the toaster, although it was already crumb free. He didn't face her until the bread was nearly done.

"I remember." He leaned against the counter and folded his arms. "But I'm surprised you still do."

"I think it was the last time I really talked to anybody." She smiled sadly. "I missed you...after we stopped being friends."

"After you decided to marry Champ," he corrected her. It was more accurate. She had become engaged to Champ at the end of their senior year of high school, and although she and Champ hadn't married until they nearly completed college, the engagement had served to isolate her from everyone, but particularly from Billy Ray.

"It was the worst decision in a life filled with bad ones." She didn't look up from her mug of tea. "I've wanted to tell you that...forever."

"You weren't happy, Carolina?"

"Remember all those tent revival meetings that used to come through here in the summers and set up over at the fairgrounds? The ones where the preachers screamed and shouted about how awful hell was going to be?"

"I remember. I got dragged to my share."

She looked up, and her eyes were filled with pain. "Well, I've been to hell, Billy. And I can tell you, those preachers knew exactly what they were talking about."

Billy Ray's office consisted of three rooms on a side street in Moss Bend. He had a reception area, a conference room, and a private office that was just big enough for a desk and three bookcases. The front of the building was leased by the town's most popular florist, and even though Billy Ray had a reserved parking spot beside his office, most of the time he had to park on the street.

Today was one of those days. A Cadillac nestled comfortably where his Taurus belonged. Giggling young ladies in pastel sundresses streamed in and out of the florist's door, chaperoned by mothers wearing slightly more conservative adaptations. He supposed that Gabriel, the proprietor, was in the midst of another society wedding. Gabriel was an honorary member of the town's first families.

Billy Ray parked halfway down the block, smiling as one of the girls, a tanned brunette, winked as she passed. He didn't have the heart to point out that even though he wasn't quite old enough to be her father, he could be a beloved uncle. He supposed he was still young enough to be attractive to young women, but old enough to find maturity more appealing.

He thought of Carolina, who hadn't really been out of his mind since he'd encountered her last night. Even sick and discouraged, she was more appealing to him than the pretty brunette. But Carolina Waverly had captivated him from the time he first walked through the door of River County High and saw her giggling with her girlfriends beside her locker.

Billy Ray and Carolina had both lived their entire lives in River County, but because he lived so far out in the country, they had attended different elementary and junior high schools. Even so, that morning he had recognized her. He lived outside of town, but he had spent much of his short life in Moss Bend, at the garage with Joel or hiking from bar to bar looking for Yancy. He knew that Carolina's father had retired from the state senate to take over the family savings and loan in Moss Bend, where, despite being a widower in his late fifties, he'd quickly married a twenty-five-year-old debutante and fathered Carolina. Billy Ray knew that Carolina lived on Old Waverly Lane, which said everything about the length of the family's taproot in Moss Bend society.

He had recognized her, but he had never really *seen* her. Not until that moment. Carolina looked up from the gaggle of giggling girls and favored him with a smile. And somehow, he knew that he'd made a friend.

In the years that followed, their friendship had grown and deepened. Carolina had a whirlwind social life that revolved around the Moss Bend Country Club, but she had another, more serious side, too. In the classes that they shared she was always the one who asked the most probing questions, who wrote the most thoughtful papers. Whenever there was a chance to collaborate on a project, she always chose Billy Ray. They were intellectual equals, and they could sit for hours discussing ideas—and often did.

By their junior year their friendship had progressed beyond ideas to feelings. They sought out each other when times were rough. If they didn't share everything, they did share the small problems of their lives, commiserating when a teacher gave an unfair grade or when an honor went to someone less deserving.

When Carolina wasn't required at a party or at drill team practice, they sometimes hung out together after school. By unspoken consent, they never went to each other's homes. They studied at the library or took long, lazy walks through the woods bordering the old town dairy.

He had first kissed her under a tree beside a crumbling silo. They had paused there to rest after a particularly long walk. For the first time, Billy Ray had opened up a little about his father. Yancy had been admitted to the hospital two nights before, after a fall from the footbridge behind the Blue Bayou. Broken bones and a concussion were nothing to Yancy compared to his sudden separation from cheap whiskey. That morning Billy Ray had visited his father in the hospital on the way to school and found him in restraints because he had pitched his bedpan at a nurse.

Billy Ray didn't tell Carolina that story, but he did express his frustration. "I'm leaving this town the minute I'm out of high school," he told her. "And I'm never, never coming back."

She slipped her arms around his waist in comfort. He looked down at her, at the soft blond hair that fell to her shoulders and the sympathetic green eyes that told him she understood, and he was lost.

He knew better than to fall in love with Carolina Waverly, and he knew better than to kiss her. But he had done both that afternoon.

Now, just outside his office door, Billy Ray heard a shrill whistle that cut off the parade of memories. He turned to find Doug, in full uniform, cutting across the parking lot. Doug lifted his hat to the last of the women exiting the shop, then joined Billy Ray at the door to his office.

"Don't you have somebody to arrest?" Billy Ray asked him.

"Want me to ticket that car?" Doug inclined his head toward the Cadillac.

"Nah, it'd be just my luck if it belonged to the wife of somebody over at the courthouse. I'll just have Fran put a polite note on the windshield telling them to park somewhere else next time. Not that it'll do any good."

Billy Ray opened the door and let Doug pass in front of him. Fran, his secretary, had the air conditioner turned too high, but considering that the mercury had already shot up past ninety, he didn't have the heart to complain.

"Hey, Franny," Doug greeted her. Fran was an older woman, with frizzy gray hair and deep lines engraved between perpetually narrowed eyes. She disapproved of most things and of even more people. Luckily she didn't disapprove of Billy Ray.

"Bad pennies always turn up," she said, her eyes narrowing even more at the sight of Doug.

"Now, come on, Franny. You love me," Doug said. "You always have."

"The way I love rutabaga and horsemeat."

"Um-um! You cooking up some for lunch?"

"You get out of here, Doug Fletcher." She switched her gaze to Billy Ray. "You're late."

"Sorry. I got held up. Any calls?"

"I put a fax on your desk. And Mrs. Balou wants you to call her when you have the chance. She says somebody was out on her patio last night, staring in her windows."

"Call the men with the butterfly nets," Doug said. "We're out there two, three times a week checking her place. If you ask me, the old bat's *hoping* somebody'll stare in her windows."

Fran sighed heavily. "I don't believe anyone asked you."

"Doug's the sheriff now," Billy Ray reminded her. "Be nice to him or he won't fix your parking tickets."

She lifted her chin. "Some people park where they're supposed to."

"Got any coffee?" Doug asked her.

"We have coffee. We have filters. We have water."
She began to type.

"I'll get you some," Billy Ray told him. "Go on
in my office. I'll be there in a minute."

He found a fresh pot of coffee in the conference
room and filled two mugs, adding sugar to Doug's. In
his office he set it in front of his friend before he took
his own seat. "What brings you here so early?" he
asked casually, although he had a pretty good idea
what Doug was going to say.

"Did you check the garage last night, the way you
said you planned to?"

"Uh-huh. Why?"

"And you didn't notice anything special?"

"The place was secure. I checked it, then I went
home." He wondered how long he could evade the
truth without telling a lie. "Did you send somebody
around at midnight?"

"Yeah, and he didn't see anything, either."

"Then what's the problem?"

"Well, it seems a car disappeared out of the service
lot last night. Carolina Grayson's car."

"Is that so?"

"What do you know about it, Billy Ray? Your
grandfather's not saying much. How about you?"

Billy Ray sipped his coffee. Fran liked it as strong
as battery acid, but the jolt of caffeine was exactly
what he needed. "Did somebody report the car stolen?"

"Judge Grayson."

"Oh. It's his car?"

"It's Carolina's car. And she's missing, too."

"It sounds like you have your answer, then. She's

gone. The car's gone.'' Billy Ray shrugged. ''It doesn't sound like a crime's been committed.''

''You know more about this than you're saying.''

''I know when I should stay out of a situation that's none of my business.''

Doug sat back and worked on his coffee, too. The two men had been friends for too many years to fool each other. Billy Ray just hoped that because of that friendship, Doug would back off.

''You and Carolina were friends in high school,'' Doug said when his mug was significantly lighter. ''Seen much of her lately?''

''I stopped seeing her when she got engaged to Champ.''

''You never much liked him, did you?''

''We didn't travel in the same circles. I barely knew him.''

''You know, Billy Ray, old Champ wasn't everything he appeared to be.''

Billy Ray waited. Doug might look like a good old boy on the surface, but even when it seemed as if he was just passing time, he was usually working on something.

''Neither was Carolina,'' Doug added, when his coffee was gone and the mug was perched on the edge of Billy Ray's desk. ''Some people look good on the outside, you know, Billy Ray? But when you peek underneath, it's like one of those fire ant hills on a winter day. Nothing seems to be going on, but you stir 'em up?'' He shook his head. ''Trouble for everybody.''

''You want to stop talking around the subject, Barney Fife, and get right to it? You're warning me about something, but I don't know what.''

"Carolina's in plenty of trouble. She took off with the judge's grandkids last night."

"Wait a minute. They're Carolina's kids, aren't they? I hadn't heard that the judge has any particular right to decide when and where she goes. Am I wrong about that?"

"She's not a well woman, if you know what I mean."

"I don't."

"She's not stable. She drinks. She forgets she's supposed to be watching her babies. She's...what's that word? Paranoid. That's it. She imagines things. The judge doesn't want her left alone with them. He's worried."

"I can understand that. But none of that sounds like the Carolina I used to know."

Doug stood and stretched. "People change, Billy Ray. You know that. Keep an eye out, would you? And if you hear something..."

"If I hear anything worth repeating, I'll give you a call."

"You do that." Doug touched his hat in farewell.

Billy Ray watched his friend disappear through the door. Doug was suspicious that Billy Ray knew more than he was telling. It was too bad Doug knew he'd been on his way to Joel's last night after the party. Now, before he did anything else, he was going to have to call home and tell Carolina to keep the children inside for the rest of the day. He might live in the middle of nowhere, but he was pretty sure a sheriff's car would find its way past his house today.

And more than once.

Carolina knew she was a good mother. But over the years, Champ and Whittier had chipped away at her ego so that little of her confidence remained. Her husband had accused her of being a terrible wife, and eventually she'd begun to believe him. Her father-in-law had told her repeatedly that nothing she did was good enough for a Grayson, and eventually she'd succumbed to that belief, too.

But no one had ever convinced her that she wasn't good with her children. She was patient, concerned, strict when she had to be, but always loving. Despite the personal cost, she had protected Kitten and Chris from the influences surrounding them, carefully steering a path through the worst of her husband's problems so that the children wouldn't be touched by them.

Now she lay on Billy's living room sofa and watched as they sat entranced in front of a Disney video that Hattie had rented for them that afternoon. They were tired and uncharacteristically quiet. Even Chris, who wasn't old enough to understand what was going on, sensed the tension in the air, and he had worn himself out whining for most of the afternoon.

"You doing okay, Carolina?"

She smiled up at Hattie, who had just come in from making dinner in the kitchen. "You've been so good to me. I can't thank you enough."

"Nobody's been good to you in a long, long time."

Carolina didn't know what to say, but Hattie didn't give her a chance to speak, anyway. "Billy Ray called. He's on his way home. I ought to take off now and do some errands. You'll be all right until he gets here?"

"I'll be just fine."

Hattie rested her hand against Carolina's forehead;

then she nodded, satisfied. "Fever's gone. I'll see you tomorrow, and I'll bring some toys for Chris."

"Thanks, Hattie. For everything."

Hattie said goodbye to the children, who were so engrossed in their show that they hugged her without taking their eyes off the screen. Carolina felt her own eyes growing heavy. She had napped in the early afternoon, but she was still sleepy. She let her eyelids drift shut for a moment.

When she opened them, Billy Ray was standing in front of her. She drew a sharp breath and began to cough. "I'm sorry. I didn't mean to startle you," he said.

She sat up, and he sat down beside her. "I didn't hear you come in."

"You were sleeping."

"I guess I was, but I'm always at least half awake, listening for the children."

"Next time I'll make children noises when I come home."

She saw with relief that Kitten and Chris were still watching their video. "I don't seem to do much of anything right, do I? What if Chris had gotten into something?"

"Carolina, Hattie told you I was on my way home, didn't she? So you knew I'd be only a few minutes. And Kitten's sitting right there. If you didn't hear Chris, I'm sure she would have gotten you up. Go easy on yourself. You're sick. You're supposed to rest."

She thought about how different his reaction was from the reaction Champ would have had, or the judge. Both of them would have used this as an excuse to point out her failings.

She wondered if Billy even knew he was being

kind. She doubted it. To him, his words were simply reasonable. To her, they were like a fresh breeze making headway on a decade of emotional cobwebs.

He rose. "Hattie said she made supper. I'll go see what I have to do to get it on the table."

She rose, too. "Kitten, can you keep an eye on Chris? Give a yell if you need me."

Kitten nodded without turning.

"Where are you going?" Billy Ray frowned.

"To help you."

"Don't be silly. I—"

"I'd like to talk to you. I'll just sit and watch, if that makes you happier."

"It will."

She followed him into the kitchen. She could hear the television and probably any signs of life from the living room. She took a seat at the end of the table, which Hattie had already set for their meal.

"The kids been okay today? I'm sorry they had to stay cooped up."

"So were they. Hattie did take them out to the barn for a while. We watched to be sure there weren't any cars on the road first. They played with your cat."

"He's not my cat. He just lives there."

"*He* is going to have kittens."

"Damn." Billy Ray shook his head. "He—she showed up one day a couple of weeks ago and stayed. I guess she lives on mice and rats. She's so big and ugly, I thought she was a tom."

Carolina laughed, and it felt surprisingly different and good. "You're sure it's not just that you don't know how to tell?"

He looked up from his search through the refrigerator and smiled. Her laughter caught in her throat, and something she hadn't felt for a long time thrummed inside her. Despite her illness. Despite the crisis in her life. Despite a million fears for the future.

"I can tell the difference," he said. "At least in humans."

A few seconds passed before she was able to pull herself together and move on. "The cat doesn't just live on mice and rats. Hattie says she leaves food for her when she comes to clean your house."

"Did Hattie name her, too?"

"Kitten named her."

"Let's see, a little girl named Kitten named my cat. What did she call her? Mary Sue Watkins?"

"Three Legs."

"Well, it's descriptive."

"Kitten's good at cutting to the chase."

"What about her mother? Is she good at it, too?"

"Not nearly good enough. But I'm about to try."

"I'm listening."

Carolina took a deep breath. "Billy, I want you to know some things. I don't know why exactly. But I do."

He looked as if he wasn't sure he wanted to know them, but he didn't stop her. He pulled a salad out of the refrigerator and set it on the counter; then he began to fill glasses with ice.

"I...I know what you went through with your father. I've been through it, too."

He stopped what he was doing and cocked his head. "What are you saying, exactly?"

"Champ was an alcoholic." She shook her head. Even now, she was downplaying it. "No, it was worse than that. He abused drugs, too. He abused anything he could get his hands on." She looked up at him and said the words it had been so hard to admit even to herself. "He abused me."

He was silent, but a muscle jumped in his clenched jaw. "For how long, Carolina?"

"I can't even tell you when it started." She shook her head. "It was so subtle at first. I bet you can't understand that. I can't even understand it, though I've been getting some help from a counselor recently. At first...I thought it was just because he loved me and wanted me to reach my potential. He would criticize little things. I'd try to do better. He'd be pleased. Then he'd find something else."

"Did it get...?" He set down the glass he'd been filling, as if he was afraid to hold something so fragile in his hands. "Did it get worse than criticism?"

She looked away. "Yes." The word was barely audible. "It got worse."

His tone was sharp. "Why did you stay with him, then? You had other places to go, didn't you? You had money to get away."

"This is so hard to explain. I'm only beginning to understand it myself. I..." She looked down at the table, at the wood surface that had seen a thousand family dinners, a hundred spilled glasses of milk. "I was raised to please. My father was nearly sixty when I was born. He didn't like noise, and he didn't like trouble. So I had to be quiet, and I had to be good. My mother was always busy with other things, and the only time I got to spend with her was when I was doing exactly what she told me to."

"Okay. But I knew you then, remember? Despite all that you had ideas. You had strong opinions. You were the girl who was going to do things and be somebody."

"And I was the girl who gave up that dream to do exactly what everyone expected." She was humiliated that her voice caught on the last word. "Champ was the prize catch in River County. I didn't even know I wanted him, but once he let me know I could be Mrs. Champion Grayson if I set my mind to it, I couldn't resist the temptation."

She turned up her hands in defeat. "I was so young. So silly. Everyone envied me. He was handsome, rich. And he treated me like a princess. Once I said yes, I made him my life. And I didn't want to fail. So every time he told me I was failing, I just tried harder. And I believed...I believed he was right."

"I'm a general practice attorney. I handle divorces. I know the psychology of this. But you let him..." He shook his head, as if he couldn't say the words.

"He slapped me more than a few times, but he only beat me twice." She swallowed. "I left him after the first time, but he came after me, promising to reform. Now that my father's dead, my mother lives in Palm Beach. She's hoping to find another rich husband. I went to stay with her, but she sided with Champ. I told you, she only wanted to be with me if I was doing what she told me to." She managed a wan smile. "She hasn't changed."

"Did you need her permission to change your life?"

It was a hard question, but a fair one. "No. I went back to Champ because I believed he would change. I also believed if I didn't go back to him, his addictions would get worse, not better."

"So you thought you could save him?"

"Yes. And instead I killed him."

He didn't even blink. "That's a little harsh, don't you think?"

"I don't know. I can't remember. I just know what I've been told."

"You said Champ beat you twice."

"I bet you're good in the courtroom, Billy."

His eyes were serious, and he didn't smile.

She finished her story. "After I went back to him, things got better for a while. Then I got pregnant again. It wasn't planned. I wasn't secure enough to bring another child into our marriage. I was using birth control religiously, but I ran out of luck. When I told Champ, his drinking got heavier, and I found he was making regular trips out of town to buy drugs.

"I confronted him one night, just after Chris was born, when I couldn't stand any more. I told him I was going to take both children and leave him. He came after me. He shoved me against a wall, and I lost consciousness. Kitten wasn't quite three. When I woke up, he and Kitten were gone, and they stayed gone for three days. The Graysons knew where Champ had taken her, but they refused to tell me. I was frantic. Finally he brought her back, and, of course, he promised to reform again. But at the same time, he warned me that if I left him, he'd find me and disappear with Kitten *and* the baby next time, and I'd never see either of them again."

"And that's why you stayed with him?"

"It was a mixture of things. Fear. Self-disgust. Some flicker of hope that he would really change. Mostly it was inertia. I didn't know what to do or where to go to protect the children. There was nobody to turn to."

"He drained you dry, one drop at a time. The bastard!"

She looked up. She had been staring at her hands, hands that hadn't been able to set her life in order. "I let him."

Billy Ray came to the table and squatted in front of her so they were face-to-face. "You were young and insecure. And from what you've told me, he had no scruples about destroying you. Don't blame yourself. Look at what happened and learn from it, but don't waste your time wishing you'd acted differently."

"Sometimes I wonder if I drank too much that night on purpose, Billy. Maybe I planned to run off the road and kill Champ, or kill myself. Because I hated him. By the end of our marriage, I hated him!"

"You had reason to hate him."

"But did I have reason enough to kill him? To get behind that wheel and run the car into a tree? I'm telling you this because you're going to have to ask yourself that question. By sheltering me here, you may be protecting a murderer, Billy. It's entirely possible I set out that night in December to kill my own husband."

4

"**Y**our lungs sound clear, but pneumonia's nothing to fool with. You still need to take it easy for a while. Don't overdo. Otherwise, as far as I can tell, you're on the road to recovery." Garth Brodie, a young physician who was paying off substantial medical school debts by practicing in a public health clinic in lower River County, removed his stethoscope and got to his feet.

Carolina adjusted her blouse. "I told Billy I was practically well. But he insisted. I'm sorry he dragged you here. When you took this job, I bet you never expected to make house calls."

"Billy Ray's helped a couple of my patients get disability benefits when nobody else would take their cases. I figure I owe him more than a house call."

Garth, dark-haired and baby-faced, was regarding her with veiled curiosity. Carolina knew that Billy Ray must have told him something about her situation to get him to come. His arrival, on this the fourth day of her stay at the old farmhouse, had been a surprise to her.

"I hope Billy told you that nobody's supposed to know you saw me today," she said.

"He did." He hesitated. "Is there anything...you want to talk about?"

"Thanks. But no."

"Well, if you need anything else, just let me know." He finished packing up his bag.

"Garth, there is...one thing."

He nodded, like an old country doctor with all the time in the world.

"I was in an accident in December. I suffered a pretty serious concussion as a result. I...I can't remember anything that happened in the hours before it. Do you think I ever will?"

She listened as he listed the expected disclaimers. He hadn't seen her records. All cases differed in outcome. But at her disappointed expression he added, "Do you have glimmers? Little slivers of memory that come and go?"

"Sometimes I think I do. Then, before I can grab and examine them...they disappear."

"That's probably a good sign. You may not be ready to remember yet. Sometimes we block out traumatic events until we're ready to accept the memories. But sometimes it's purely physical. There just aren't any guarantees."

A knock sounded on the bedroom door. "Come in. We're finished here," Garth called.

Billy Ray entered with Chris in his arms. "Special delivery," he said, setting Chris on the bed beside his mother. "How's she doing, Garth?"

"Fine. The antibiotics did their job. And she's young and healthy enough to fight off a recurrence if she just takes care of herself." He turned to Carolina. "Hear that?"

"Vitamins, sunshine, bed rest and a healthy diet," she recited.

"I wish all my patients had the drill down." He smiled. "I wouldn't be surprised if the accident you mentioned lowered your resistance, and that's why you fell prey to pneumonia. Stress plays a big part in how well we fight off disease."

"I'm working on that, too." She smiled, and his face changed subtly, as if for the first time he was seeing her as a woman.

He turned away. "Billy?" He nodded to Billy Ray. "I'll see you soon."

"I'll show you out."

The two men disappeared. Chris climbed into Carolina's lap, and she fell back on the mattress, taking him with her. He giggled and she turned him to his back, tickling him while he giggled, louder.

"Mommy?"

Carolina looked up to see Kitten standing in the doorway. "Come here, sweetie. Help me wrestle your brother."

The three of them were giggling and roughhousing when Billy Ray returned. She didn't even know he was watching until Kitten spotted him. "Stop!" She grabbed her mother's arm. "Stop!"

Carolina realized that Billy Ray was smiling at them, and she grinned in response as she straightened her clothes. "Whoops. I'm afraid you caught us laughing."

"I'm appalled."

Kitten jumped off the bed and ran past him out into the hallway. Chris wrapped his arms around her neck and held on for dear life. Carolina's smile died, and she shook her head.

"What's going on?" he asked. His smile died, too.

"You caught us in behavior unbecoming to a Grayson."

A look of utter disbelief settled on his features.

"I know. It's hard to believe, isn't it?"

"Children aren't supposed to laugh?"

"The Grayson household is very dignified, very quiet. The children were expected to be the same way." She knew she sounded bitter, but she couldn't help herself. "Of course they could laugh, but only when it was appropriate and subdued. If I made them laugh too loud or too long, I was accused of provoking hysteria and upsetting them. If they didn't sleep well that night or eat everything on their plates, it was my fault."

"You make the Graysons sound like monsters."

She shook her head. "I don't mean to. They aren't." A small smile escaped. "Not precisely."

His expression softened. "I'll talk to Kitten. I'll tell her laughter's encouraged here."

"Don't, Billy. Let her discover that for herself. It will make more of an impression." She changed the subject. "Listen, why did you bring Garth home with you? I told you I was almost well. Didn't you trust me?"

"Not where your health is concerned. You're so desperate to feel better, I was afraid you were exaggerating."

"Actually, I'm relieved to have my own diagnosis confirmed." She rose, carrying the clinging Chris with her. "And now I have the final proof."

He looked wary. "You're still weak in the knees.

You're not well enough to move out. I hope that's not what this is about.''

"Not yet. No. But I am well enough to pull some weight around here. I made dinner today while you were at the office. I can finish it now, then we can eat.''

"You were supposed to rest. This was your first day without Hattie to take care of the kids.''

"I love to cook. It was relaxing. And the only thing you're supposed to say is thank you.''

He hesitated for a moment. "I'm sorry. Maybe I like taking care of you.''

For a moment she couldn't move. He was close enough to touch. He had changed from his suit into a soft green polo shirt and jeans. His hair was freshly combed. He had beautiful hair, thick, shiny and bone-straight. No matter what he did to it, it always fell down over his forehead. She liked the effect, because it softened his serious demeanor and made him more touchable.

And she wanted to touch him now.

She didn't, although she was surprised by how un-natural it felt to restrain herself. "I'd like you to think of me in a different way. Not as somebody you have to take care of, but somebody who can pull her own weight. I know that hasn't been true—''

"Carolina.'' *He* touched *her.* Just the briefest pressure of his fingertips against her shoulder. "Of course it hasn't been true so far. But fact is, I guess I've enjoyed doing things for you and watching you get better. We were friends a long time ago. It's good to be friends again.''

"Is it? Despite all the trouble we've caused you?''

"Whatever trouble you've caused is nothing compared to what you've been through. Okay?" His fingertips moved up to her cheek. He stroked it gently. "Stop worrying."

She wanted to close her eyes, to let her eyelids drift slowly shut so that she could relish the delicious feel of his fingertips against her skin. But she hadn't been married to Champ Grayson for nothing. She knew how to control her feelings and, most of all, how to avoid expressing them.

"I'd better get dinner on the table," she said.

He dropped his hand. "I'll help, if you'd like."

"I'd like." She preceded him into the hall before she let the moment dictate a more intimate response.

Downstairs, she settled Chris in the corner of the kitchen with some of the toys Hattie had brought for him to play with. Kitten was drawing pictures in the living room, one of the activities she'd been praised for at her grandparents' house. Carolina didn't expect that to last long, since Kitten was an active, verbal child with little interest in sitting quietly, but she didn't encourage her to join them. Kitten would discover on her own that here at Billy Ray's house, she was welcome to be herself.

"What can I do?" Billy Ray asked when Carolina began to remove covered dishes from the refrigerator.

"You can toss the salad. Just leave a little portion plain for Kitten, please."

"Italian all right for you?"

"Perfect."

Carolina had decided on stew because she'd found a small chuck roast in Billy's freezer, and stew was something she could work on in stages without getting tired. Now she poured it into a large saucepan to reheat and turned on the stove. "You know what, Billy? I could use some red wine. I couldn't find it earlier. Do you have any in the house?''

The silence that followed didn't disturb her at first. She assumed he was trying to remember. But when it extended too long, she turned to see if he had heard her. He was watching her, his expression troubled.

For a moment she couldn't figure out what she'd said to provoke that reaction. Then she knew. She shook her head. "You know, I thought we'd gotten beyond that.''

He didn't answer her directly. "I'm not much of a drinker. I don't keep liquor on hand. Just a few beers, in case I have company.''

"I wanted wine for the stew. Not so I could slug down the entire bottle before you got home. I just thought it would improve the flavor.'' She could feel her face tightening into a grimace. She forced herself to relax. Billy only knew what he'd been told about her. She couldn't expect him to believe everything she'd told him. Not without a shred of proof.

"I'm sorry,'' he said.

"For the record, I rarely drink wine. It gives me a headache. I never drink beer, because I don't like the taste. My favorite drink is a gin and tonic, heavy on the tonic and light on the gin. My limit is two, over a long evening, but my real preference is to sip plain old ginger ale with a cherry in it. I like to remain stone cold sober. Somebody at our house had to.''

"You took me by surprise.''

"Well, if my asking for liquor surprised you, I guess we're making headway,'' she said lightly, even though her heart was heavy.

"I lived with an alcoholic, Carolina. And I know the lengths my father went to for a drink. He's been dead for years, but last summer, when I was doing some remodeling upstairs, I found a half-filled bottle of whiskey behind the paneling in his bedroom. I guess the only surprise is that it was half full. His memory got bad at the end, or that bottle would have been empty.''

She didn't look at him. She didn't trust herself to. ''I can't tell you if I was drinking on the night Champ died. But I can tell you I wasn't drinking seriously on the nights leading up to that one. Or the years. I'm not an alcoholic.''

He was silent as she turned up the heat on the stove. She stirred the stew too hard and too fast, scraping the sides of a pan that had nothing sticking to them.

''I trust you,'' he said at last.

''Do you?''

''I'd better. Or we're going to have metal filings in our supper.''

She didn't know he was behind her until she felt his hands close over her shoulders and squeeze. She set down the spoon and turned. His hands settled in the same place once she was facing him.

''You've told me a story anyone might have trouble with,'' he said. ''But I want you to know I believe you, Carolina. Maybe I'll have a few moments of doubt here and there. That can't be helped. But I'm on your side.''

She swallowed tears and nodded. ''I know.''

He paused, as if he were wrestling with himself; then he pulled her closer and kissed her hair. He released her without a word and went back to the table, where he had been tossing the salad.

She didn't know what to say. There was nothing to

say. She turned back to the stew and began to stir it again. But slowly, this time.

Kitten liked red. The crayons Hattie had brought for her had three different reds. A bright one, a dark one, and one that was almost orange. She had used every one of them, scribbling up and down on the coloring book picture of a puppy running through flowers.

She wasn't staying in the lines. She didn't care who told her she had to. She was going to color the whole picture so dark that the lines wouldn't matter, anyway.

Halfway across the page the almost-orange crayon snapped in half. She giggled. She liked the noise it had made. And now there were two crayons where there had been one before.

"Four red crayons," she sang under her breath. "Four, four, four..."

From the kitchen, over her song, she could hear the murmur of voices. She held her breath for a moment and sat perfectly still. No one was shouting. Billy Ray never seemed to shout.

Her father had shouted. She remembered that, although she didn't really want to. Mostly he had shouted at her mother, but he'd shouted at Kitten, too, if she got in his way. Finally she had invented a game, the invisible game. If she moved around the corners of a room as quietly as a whisper, then she was practically invisible. And if her father couldn't see her, there was no one to shout at.

At first she had been surprised when she went to live with her grandparents after her father was killed in the accident. Nobody shouted at her grandfather's house. But it wasn't exactly the same as here, at Billy Ray's. Nobody shouted at her grandfather's house, but sometimes she had almost wished they would. Sometimes silence and low voices were worse. At least when somebody shouted, you knew why they were mad at you.

She pressed down on the crayon again, scrubbing it across the page, and the crayon snapped once more.

"Five crayons," she crooned.

The crayon's snapping sounded a little like a shout. But Kitten didn't know why she was mad.

On his way home from work the next day, Billy Ray thought about his encounter with Carolina during the dinner preparations the previous evening. The time had come for him to make a choice. Either he believed her story and was willing to go the extra mile to help her, or he pulled back now. Because he was fast becoming immersed in her life.

Even as he thought about that choice, he knew it had already been made. If he'd had any lingering doubts, they had been allayed as he watched Carolina put the children to bed last night. As sick as she had been, as pressured by her situation, she had never spoken a harsh word to either of them since coming to live at his house. But now that she was regaining her strength and vitality, the full measure of her love was apparent.

The children adored her, too. They knew when they talked to Carolina that they had her full attention. They could count on her to keep them safe, but also to keep their happiness in mind. She was creative in the way she dealt with their problems, encouraging them to think of their own solutions or giving them appealing choices. And she was never afraid to show her affection.

He had watched her carefully tuck each child into bed, making sure Kitten had her panda bear and Christopher an old stuffed horse that looked as if it belonged in a landfill, and he'd realized that no matter what had happened one night last December, this woman should never be separated from her children. She was not unstable; she was not a threat in any way. The only threat to the children was the possibility that they might be taken from her.

Now that she was nearly well enough to travel, the time had come for Carolina to plan her next step. He was certain she had been giving it a lot of thought, but she hadn't shared any decisions with him. He half expected to come home one evening and find her gone. Carolina might think that was best for all of them, but she was wrong. He was already involved; he wanted to be sure she was safe and in a good position to care for herself and the children when she left.

He slapped his palm against the steering wheel. "You're full of shit, Billy."

He'd never been very good at lying to himself. Sure, he wanted her to be safe and happy. But he was beginning to think that was only a part of what he wanted.

The other part was a whole lot more complicated.

He was still debating what he would say to her when he turned off Hitchcock Road to his house. He was so deep in thought that seconds passed before he noticed the cars parked in his driveway.

One of them was the sheriff's car, and beside it was a late-model Lincoln. Exactly like the one that Judge Whittier Grayson parked in the courthouse lot.

Billy Ray's first thought was for Carolina, his second for Kitten and Christopher. He didn't spare his own situation more than a mutter. By taking in Carolina, he had already pitted himself against the judge. He had known that from the beginning, and he had done it with a certain amount of satisfaction. Now the die was cast. And he wasn't even sorry.

He took the front steps two at a time and opened the door to find Carolina in the living room, perched on the blue velvet sofa with a protective arm around each of her children. He had expected to find her distressed, but he had misjudged her.

She didn't even look up when he walked in. She was speaking calmly, her eyes riveted on Judge Grayson. "I'm well, and I'm perfectly capable of caring for the children. Thank you for your concern, but we won't be moving back to your house. It's time for us to manage on our own."

By anybody's standards, Judge Whittier Grayson was an imposing man. He was tall and gaunt, with the gray-tinged complexion of a man who had smoked heavily most of his life. But it wasn't his physical build or his face that made him such a force to reckon with. His silvering dark hair and nondescript features were a perfect background for eyes of such a piercing blue that they seemed to consume whatever they were fixed on. Billy Ray had seen this work to his advantage in a courtroom. The judge could silence the most recalcitrant witness with nothing more than his stern gaze.

Now Billy Ray was the focus of that gaze. The judge turned and fixed him with a stare that would have made a weaker man feel like a stranger in his own home.

"It seems to me, Billy Ray, that you might have had the decency to tell me that Carolina was staying with you." The judge's voice was cultured, a soft Southern drawl that owed more to Georgia's aristocracy than to Florida's melting pot of snowbirds and crackers.

Billy Ray lifted a brow. "Whatever passes between you and Carolina has nothing to do with me, sir. She's a responsible adult."

"She's certainly an adult, but stealing my grandchildren from my home is hardly the act of a responsible one."

"The children are mine, and they are mine to take care of as I see fit," Carolina said calmly. "I made the best decision under the circumstances. And that's what I'll continue to do until they're grown and able to make decisions for themselves. Billy gave me a place to finish getting well. As he said, this has nothing to do with him."

"Nothing, Carolina? You bring my grandchildren along while you live and consort with another man? And with your own husband hardly cold in his grave?"

She lifted her chin. "I will not debate ethics or morals with *you*. Billy is simply a friend who lent me a helping hand. Luckily he hasn't been poisoned by the lies you've told about me."

"Do you see?" Judge Grayson turned to Doug and lifted his shoulders in distress.

For the first time, Billy Ray glanced at his friend and wondered what Doug was making of all this. Doug didn't respond, since the judge's question had really been a comment. But he was staring at Carolina, as if he, too, was judging her harshly.

"If you've said what you came to say, perhaps now

would be a good time to leave," Billy Ray said. "I'm sure Carolina's tired, and the children are hungry."

"I intend to leave with my grandchildren."

Billy Ray watched Carolina's face. Not an emotion flicked over it. "Have I misunderstood the situation? Do you have legal custody?" he asked the judge.

"No, but I intend to begin the process. And I intend to be certain she doesn't move them out of the state while I'm fighting for it. I want those children with me now, so I can watch over them. Surely you can see that's best?"

"I can see that until the court gives you custody, the children are Carolina's to bring up as and where she chooses."

"Are you my daughter-in-law's attorney as well as her lover?"

Billy Ray shot her a questioning glance. She gave the slightest nod. "I *am* her attorney," he said, switching his gaze back to the judge. "As for what else I am, let me remind you that when Carolina came here she was recovering from a serious illness. And, as you've pointed out, her children were with her. Give both of us credit for a little good sense."

"Give you credit?" The judge's laugh was devoid of mirth. "I thought you'd moved up the evolutionary scale, Billy Ray. I thought quite possibly you were going to make something of yourself, despite the sorry drunk who fathered you. Now I can see that neither you nor my daughter-in-law deserves credit for anything except hiding my grandchildren. But the game's over, boy. I know where they are, and until the law gives them to me, I'll be watching you both."

He turned his penetrating gaze to Carolina. "Take them anywhere outside the limits of this county and

I'll come after you. Do you understand? I'll know where, and I'll know when to steal them back. And you'll never find them again, missy. Not in a million years.''

Kitten began to cry. She was old enough to understand what was happening, even if she didn't understand why. Carolina stroked Kitten's hair gently, but her eyes blazed. "Get out," she said quietly. "I won't have you upsetting my children for another minute. Get out, and don't come back."

"Doug, get him out of here," Billy Ray said, stepping forward. "Right now."

Doug hesitated, but clearly nothing else could be done at this time. He started toward the judge, but the judge, his lapse in dignity repaired, was already on his feet. The two men left together, but Billy Ray noted the way that Doug stepped back deferentially to let the judge go first.

And he noted the way that Doug refused to meet his eyes.

The silence was broken by the soft sound of Kitten's weeping, but neither Billy Ray nor Carolina said a word until they heard the sound of cars disappearing in the distance.

"How did he find you?" Billy Ray asked, scooping up Christopher, who had finally left the sanctuary of his mother's arms.

"He didn't say. I've been careful, but I couldn't keep the children cooped up forever. We've been outside to play. Maybe someone saw us from the road."

Billy Ray deposited the little boy in the corner with his toys. "Someone sent to find you, probably."

"It can't be helped now." She smoothed Kitten's hair back from her forehead. "It's all right," she told the little girl. "Grandpa's mad because we left. We knew he would be. But he won't do anything to hurt us. He's just upset."

"He said he'd steal us! He said you would never find us!"

"He's angry. But I won't let him take you. Not ever." Carolina kept her own anger out of her voice, but Billy Ray could see it in the way she held herself and in her eyes.

Kitten clung to her for another minute; then Carolina sent her upstairs to wipe her nose. Carolina stood, but she was staring off into space, not at Billy Ray. "I made dinner."

"Are you in the mood to eat?"

"The children need to. You need to."

"We have to talk."

She finally looked at him. "I'm so sorry about the things he said. About you being my lover. About your father." She shook her head, and her eyes filled with tears.

"Hey, I was only sorry that the first didn't happen to be true."

She nearly choked; then she gave him a blinding smile, even though her eyes continued to fill. "You always did think fast on your feet."

"I always told the truth, too. Still do. If I'm going to be accused, anyway…" He smiled.

"Are you really willing to be my attorney?"

"If the son of the town drunk's good enough for you."

"He's too good for me. He's too good for everyone in this godforsaken town!"

"Hey, let's not overdo." But Billy Ray let her see that he was grateful for the praise. He was too old to be hurt by Yancy's reputation, but her good opinion of him mattered. More than it should.

"Are you going to need an attorney, Carolina? Are you going to stay around long enough to need one? Or are you going to find a way to start over somewhere else?"

"I'm staying."

He was more than surprised. "You're sure?"

"You heard him, Billy. He'll search, and he'll find me. Wherever I go, whatever I do. I've given this a lot of thought. I lost the element of surprise when I collapsed that night. Now he has time to prepare, to get a network in place. Even if we escape from town undetected, we'll never be safe. We'll always be looking over our shoulders. Here I have you, I have a few friends who'll support me. And Judge Sawyer has never been fond of my father-in-law. If such a thing as a fair hearing exists in this county, I'll get one."

Judge Sawyer was the judge who would probably hear the case if it went to court. He and Whittier Grayson had butted heads more than once. He wasn't as powerful as Whittier, but this time the final decision would be his. Obviously Carolina really had considered her situation carefully. And she was making an informed choice.

"He threatened to steal my children. Can we use that?" she asked.

"It would be your word against his. I don't think we can count on Doug to testify. I'm your attorney, and they'll say Kitten was coached. But if he said it once, he might say it again with other witnesses."

"What do you think my chances are of keeping the children? As my attorney, not my friend."

"I don't know. I don't want to mislead you, because

there aren't any guarantees. Frank Sawyer and your father-in-law may not like each other, but they're both old-style Southern gentlemen. And in the end, they may stick together.''

She moved a little closer, close enough to touch him, in fact. For a moment he thought she was going to, but she didn't.

She cocked her head, but the expression in her eyes was as vulnerable as one of her children's. ''You may be right about everything else, but you're wrong about that. There was only one gentleman in this room tonight, Billy Ray, and it wasn't my father-in-law.''

5

Maggie Deveraux, the owner of the Blue Bayou Tavern, had an old house on the edge of Moss Bend, complete with a front yard full of moss-draped live oaks, and pines that spread a thick carpet of needles on the ground below them. In the fall she gathered pecans from a grove that flanked the borders of her property, and in the summer she harvested blackberries from a wild thicket in the woods behind her house.

Maggie had a tire swing and sandbox for her grandchildren, who visited infrequently from California. But most of the time the big house was nearly empty, and the yard, perfect for children to play in, was much too silent.

Maggie was only too glad to say yes when Billy Ray asked if Carolina could move into the upstairs bedrooms with her children. She named a nominal rent, promised complete use of the kitchen and living areas, and asked Kitten her favorite color so she could quickly repaint the small bedroom that would be hers. Kitten chose red, and without a blink, Maggie proceeded to paint the room the vibrant red of spring tulips. Carolina threatened to provide sunglasses to any-one viewing the room, but Kitten was entranced.

After Champ's death, Carolina had asked Judge Grayson to sell the house she and Champ had owned together. All the furniture and almost everything else she owned was in storage, but the money realized from the sale had been carefully invested, along with what she'd received from Champ's insurance policy and so-cial security, so that now she had a monthly income that just paid the rent and minimal living expenses.

"I have to get a job." Carolina finished packing the few things she had smuggled out of the Grayson house on the night she left. Kitten and Chris were with Mag-gie, who had volunteered to keep them while Carolina made the move.

Billy Ray watched Carolina sort items to place in plastic grocery bags. "A job? You're sure?"

She nodded without turning. "And I have to get one fast."

A week had passed since the judge's visit, an om-inously quiet week. Doug had ignored all of Billy Ray's telephone messages, and Billy Ray had only seen the judge in court—where he had handed down a particularly harsh judgment against one of Billy Ray's clients. Billy Ray was just counting the hours until all hell broke loose.

"Are you really ready to work?" Billy Ray held open a bag so Carolina could stuff Christopher's horse inside. "You know, you have a lot of adjustments coming up."

She straightened. "The day care center at the Meth-odist church will have openings for both kids starting next month, and I registered them this morning. I have to work. I have to prove I can provide for the children.

Champ and I had no savings. He drank or snorted every penny he made. I didn't know how bad it was until after the accident, when I had recovered enough to go through his papers. He lied to me about our investments. He even drained the trust fund my father set up for the children. I'm lucky the premium on his insurance policy came right out of his salary, or we wouldn't have had that, either.''

He didn't remind her that the Graysons, millionaires many times over, would certainly leave their estate to Kitten and Christopher and could easily spare a portion of it now. He knew that it would be snowing in hell before Carolina asked the judge and his wife for more help.

He took the bags out of her arms to carry them downstairs. ''What kind of job are you planning to look for?''

''As a matter of fact, I already have an interview.''

He realized she was struggling to sound nonchalant, but clearly this job, whatever it was, meant the world to her.

''Oh?'' He struggled to sound nonchalant, too.

''One of my sorority sisters from college is Jen Wilton, of Wilton Mills in Georgia. I called her to see if they had any openings in personnel. They're looking for a personnel manager in their facility in Cairo. I majored in business and psychology, so I know I can do the job. And I'd be good at it. I did a six-month internship before I graduated. I love working with people, fitting employees to the right job, helping them iron out their problems. I'll do anything to support my children, but this would be more than just a way of making money.''

This job would be a way of boosting her self-esteem. He could see that plainly. He wished that he could hand it to her on a silver platter—although he knew that if he did, it would completely destroy her joy in it.

"What are your chances?" He started for the door, and she picked up two more bags and followed him.

"I don't know. Jen's putting in a good word for me. She knows what kind of person I am, and she knows I was an A student. But, of course, she won't be doing the hiring. She got me the interview, but I'll be on my own once I'm there."

"And when do you go?"

"Friday morning at ten."

"What are you going to do with the kids?"

"I'm going to see if any of my former friends will help. But most of them disappeared from my life after the accident."

She didn't sound bitter, although he thought she had a right to. "What time will you need to leave?"

"Nine. Eight-thirty to be safe. It'll take most of an hour to get there, if Doug Fletcher or his boys don't stop me at the county line."

"If I don't have any appointments, you can bring the kids to my office."

She smiled her gratitude.

Billy Ray realized he would do a lot for another one of those smiles. "I'll have Joel fix up a car for you. That might throw the sheriff's department off the track. But even if a deputy stops you, if you don't have Kitten and Chris along, he should let you go."

"That would be the judge's fondest wish, wouldn't it? For me to leave River County for good without them. He'd get custody by default."

Outside, he dropped the bags in her trunk. "Are you going to keep this car?"

"Temporarily. I'm not going to antagonize the Graysons further by selling it now, not with everything else at stake. I'm sure Judge Sawyer would think I was just being vindictive."

"Do you really think your father-in-law gave you this car as a reminder of the accident?"

"I'm sure. Champ drove a company car, but he was the one who chose the BMW for me, against my wishes. Then Champ died in a model just like this one, and the judge couldn't miss a chance to remind me of that every time I get behind the wheel. I'm in no position to buy another without selling this one. Champ let our car insurance lapse, so there was no reimbursement."

"We need to document all Champ's frailties, Carolina. We can start with that one."

"Can we really use it if I have to fight for custody? He's not on trial."

"We'll have to see how things develop. If we can show enough proof that Champ wasn't what he appeared to be, then we can show how much stress you were under in the marriage. That way, no matter what they try to prove about you, Judge Sawyer will look at your situation more kindly."

"He was the children's father. I don't want him dragged through the mud."

"All well and good if the Graysons don't drag the children's mother through it."

She winced. "I hate this. Why does it have to be this way? I'd allow them to visit the children. Kitten and Chris are their grandchildren, and I could respect that as long as they weren't abusive. Why do they have to demand custody?"

"Why *do* they?"

"Because Whittier Grayson has to control everything and everyone in his world! He destroyed his son by turning him into a puppet. The only way Champ could rebel was by living a secret life."

"That's something we won't be able to use in court."

"I know. But it's true."

"I know."

She closed the trunk before she turned. "Do you?"

"I'm sorry it took me some time to believe everything you've told me, but I'm a lawyer, Carolina. A good one hears all the facts before he comes to a conclusion. Then he goes all out to defend what he knows is right."

"That's a pretty idealistic take on it, don't you think? I'll bet you defend people all the time who are as guilty as hell."

He grinned. "I prefer it the other way though."

She relaxed visibly. "Your whole face changes when you smile. Did you know that?"

He crossed his arms, enjoying this. "Does it? How?"

"Well, you're a pleasure to look at any old time. But even better when you smile. Some woman must have told you that by now."

"Are you fishing for a head count?"

If anything, she looked more intrigued. "Why didn't you ever marry, Billy? You're great with kids. And I know for a fact there are single women all over town who'd pick out a veil and a preacher in an instant, if you just gave the word."

"How do you know that? Is there a secret network of single women in Moss Bend?"

"I just know."

"I almost got married once."

An interesting but unchartable array of emotions crossed her face. "Really? Who was the lucky woman?"

"Nobody you'd know. In the end she decided she wasn't so lucky after all. When I decided I had to move back here to watch out for Joel, she refused to come with me. And she was right. She was a big-city girl. She would have hated Moss Bend."

"I'm sorry."

"I'm not. We weren't right for each other."

"Who *would* be right for you?"

He wasn't sure he could answer that. At least not when it was this particular woman asking the question.

"Someone I could talk to," he said at last. "About everything and nothing. About the conflict in the Middle East and why Mrs. Balou keeps imagining men are peering in her patio windows. About why the Braves traded Dave Justice to the Indians and whether our kids ought to attend Stetson or Florida State."

"So it just takes a conversationalist? That's hard to believe. Lots of women like to talk, Billy."

He wondered if she knew she was one step away from flirting with him. Her eyes were shining, and just the hint of a dimple flashed in one cheek. He remembered that dimple from their adolescence. In those days he had very nearly lived for the moment Carolina smiled at him.

He tilted his head, eyes focused on her lips. "You know, I've always wondered..."

The dimple deepened. "About what?"

"Whether you knew just how serious I was about you back in high school."

She leaned back against her car. "Serious?"

"First love is powerful stuff. I guess I loved you about as much as I've ever loved anybody, Carolina."

"Oh, Billy…"

"You didn't know?"

"I wondered."

"Then you didn't care."

"I cared. More than I can tell you. But I was a product of the way I'd been raised. I thought life was a fairy tale. Your home situation was so difficult, I knew you couldn't offer me anything, not for a long, long time. And, Billy, you never told me you cared about me."

"What right did I have? I couldn't involve you in my life."

"Champ was offering the moon. The stars. Happily-ever-after. By saying yes to him, I thought I would please everybody."

"Thought?"

"I pleased everybody but me."

He moved a little closer. "You weren't happy, even then?"

"Every time I saw you after that, I went home and cried. I missed you so much. I told myself I didn't, that I'd get over it. But I never did. Not really. Because in all the years that followed, I still wanted to cry when I saw you. By then I understood what I'd given up. And I knew it was too late to get it back."

He was touched and, somehow, absolved for caring about her, even though he hadn't realized that he needed to be. He had not been a fool all those years ago; Carolina had cared about him, too.

His arms dropped to his sides, as if a barrier between them had disappeared. "I guess it's stupid to bring this up. We're twelve years older. You've been married. I've had lovers. We've both changed."

She nodded. "I have children and a reputation that can only hurt you now."

"You're vulnerable and scared. You're waiting for your future to be decided by other people."

"Actually, I'm waiting for you to kiss me."

He didn't. Not yet, anyway, but he moved a little closer. "This is going to complicate everything, Carolina."

"Kissing me?"

"The things that go with it."

"Then maybe we could take it one small step at a time. You kiss me now, and we can discuss step two some other time. We can have a real conversation about it, if that would please you."

He laughed, low in his throat. Her dimple deepened, but her eyes betrayed feelings that weren't so easy to pretend away. She *was* scared and vulnerable, and there was worse. She wasn't sure she could please him. Carolina had a darker side she hadn't had as a girl. She was unsure of herself, confused and wary. For years a man had told her she wasn't good enough.

If Champ Grayson weren't dead already, Billy Ray would gladly have wrapped his hands around the golden boy's throat.

"Billy..." Her voice was tentative, although her smile was still in place. "I want you to know... Champ and I didn't have a real marriage. Not after I discovered I was pregnant with Chris, and hardly before that. I don't know if that matters. But he's been gone from my life for a lot longer than six months. I know this looks bad..."

"Not after everything you've told me." He put his arms around her and pulled her the short distance to his chest. "And he *is* dead. You're still very much alive."

He lowered his face to hers, not the boy who had kissed her once upon a time, but the man who wanted her now. A man who wanted the taste and feel of her, the warmth and, most of all, the inner woman. Both the girl he had loved so long ago and the woman she had become.

Her lips were as soft as he remembered, as giving and sweet. Memories rushed through him, sensory memories of scents and texture and flavor. The memories had hidden all these years but now instantly rekindled, and although neither of them was the same, the memories were still intact.

He felt the bare expanse of her leg move between his and her hips press against him. Her breasts sank against his chest, and she wrapped her arms around him as if she was afraid he might pull away. Her lips parted for his tongue, and each pressure was answered, as if their needs were perfectly in tune.

They had agreed to take this one step at a time, but Billy had advanced a mile when the sound of a car engine penetrated the thick fog of desire. He pulled away, and Carolina didn't resist. They turned as one to see Doug Fletcher's car sitting in the driveway. As they watched, arms and legs still entangled, Doug backed out and sped down Hitchcock Road.

Kitten didn't want to visit Billy Ray's office, and she made sure he realized it. On Friday morning, ten minutes after Carolina had gone to her job interview, Billy Ray realized that keeping Kitten and Chris busy was going to be tough.

"I don't suppose you'd want to make a fort under the conference room table?" Much to Billy's surprise, Fran, who had sternly reminded him that she had not been hired to baby-sit, was trying her best to entertain the children.

"With what?" Kitten demanded.

"We'll throw a blanket over it. You and Chris can have a snack in there. Pretend you're bears in a cave."

Chris pulled yet another volume off the conference room bookshelf.

"I could be a bear, but Chris won't stay. He hates the dark." Kitten grabbed his hand, and he began to scream.

"Can you think of something else you'd like to do?" Billy Ray picked up Chris, who stopped immediately.

"No. It smells in here."

"Old books. Old building."

"I hate it."

"Now that you mention it, so do I. Fran, find us another office, will you?"

"This was good enough for your father."

As a matter of fact, the office had been too good for Yancy, who at the end of his life had depended on Joel to pay the mortgage. After Yancy's death, Joel had kept the building as an investment for Billy Ray, renting the front to Gabriel, the florist. But it was still hard for Billy Ray to imagine the day when Yancy had been a prospering attorney who had needed the entire space.

Now he looked around with new eyes. "Maybe it's

time we freshened it up a little, then. Will you call the painters?"

"How about a new carpet?" Fran said, getting into the spirit.

"That's a good idea."

"And how about some new clients to pay for the renovation?"

"I have plenty of clients."

"Not clients who pay their bills."

"Can I help it if I'm a nice guy?"

"Nice guys don't practice law. And Mrs. Balou called again. Now she thinks it might be aliens at her patio door, and she wants you to sue them."

"If we win, it might pay for the renovation...."

"Take these children somewhere, Billy Ray. They don't need to be cooped up on a beautiful morning. Your first appointment isn't until three, and I happen to know you worked late last night. So you're allowed some time off."

"Hear that, kids? We've been set free."

Kitten wrinkled her nose, a perfect replica of Carolina's. "Where are we going?"

"Do you like getting dirty?"

She cocked her head as Chris socked him in the shoulder enthusiastically.

"Do you like grease and grime and loud noises?" Billy Ray continued.

Kitten's eyes shone like stars. "Where are we going?"

"We're going to fix cars."

"Really?"

As they made a hasty exit, Fran's "harrumph" was still echoing through the building.

* * *

Joel Wainwright was closer to eighty than seventy, stoop-shouldered, wrinkled and liver-spotted from too many years in the Florida sunshine. Billy Ray had watched his grandfather age in proportion to his only son's exploits, so that even at sixty, Joel had looked like a much older man.

At sixteen Joel had run off to see the world, and he hadn't returned to Moss Bend for ten years. Along the way he had learned that he didn't have to be a poor dirt farmer like his ancestors. By the time he came home to stay, he had honed his talent as a mechanic into considerable skill. By the time he was thirty, Joel owned his own garage, and by the time he was thirty-five, Joel's Garage had the best reputation in River County.

Although Joel could still clean a carburetor at lightning speed, most days he chose not to. He had never been a talkative man, but now he seemed to enjoy passing the time with his customers more than their cars. His staff was knowledgeable and talented, and he kept a close eye on their work. But most of the time he could be found behind the counter in the waiting room checking accounts with an old adding machine manufactured twenty years before the advent of the home computer.

Today, when Billy Ray and the children arrived, Dahlia, Joel's office manager, was behind the counter, chatting with a customer. Dahlia, a dark-skinned wraith of a woman, had been with Joel as long as Billy Ray remembered. Next winter, when her husband Pete retired from his job as a janitor at the courthouse, they planned to move south to be closer to their children in Orlando. She would be sorely missed, but Billy Ray suspected that Joel might outlast several managers before he finally sold the garage.

Kitten immediately headed for a lamp in the corner. It was a pink Cadillac with a gilded shade, the most ridiculous accessory in the world, which was why Dahlia had presented it to Joel on his last birthday. Now Kitten, with Chris at her heels, began to turn it on and off, watching the gold shade shimmer.

The customer left, most likely prompted by the light show, and Dahlia gave Billy Ray a broad smile. "You ought to have a couple of kids of your own by now."

"Well, this morning these two belong to me. I thought I'd give them the garage tour. Is Joel around?"

"He's fiddling with a car. Bay one."

"Why?"

"Grady's sick. Jimmy's at a funeral. Mabel Groves was his aunt. They're burying her this morning over at First Baptist."

Like everybody in town, Billy Ray knew who Mabel Groves was. Like everybody in town, he knew *everybody* else.

"What's Joel working on?" he asked.

"Something with brakes. One of the sheriff's cars."

"Oh?" He wasn't excited about being at the garage when one of Doug's deputies came by to get the car. "When are they coming by to pick it up?"

"Joel's promised to get somebody to drop it off at the station." She grimaced. "Probably me. The things I do for that man."

"I don't know what he'll do when you leave."

"He'll keep right on going." She hiked a thumb at

Kitten and Chris. "I know those two. They're the judge's grandkids."

"That they are."

She lowered her voice. "What are they doing with you?"

Billy Ray was surprised Dahlia hadn't heard the gossip. "Their mother and I are friends. She has an appointment this morning."

"And you're watching them? With all the folks who work for the judge?"

"Carolina prefers to have someone else taking care of her children."

"Uh-huh."

Dahlia was a savvy woman. Billy Ray knew she now understood the basics, if not the details. Joel chose that moment to come into the waiting room, wiping his hands on a grease-stained rag.

"What are you doing here?" he asked gruffly. His brown eyes flicked to the children in the corner. "You kids got nothing better to do than play with my lamp?"

"What else can we do?" Kitten asked. She glared at Billy Ray. "It's not dirty in here. You said it would be." She glared at Billy Ray.

"I promised them grease and grime." Billy Ray winked at his grandfather.

"Got plenty of that. Got something to cover up their clothes?"

"Chris still stuffs things in his mouth. We'll have to keep a good eye on him."

"Dahlia, think you can keep an eye on the kids while Billy Ray and I get under that car?"

"You need some help?" Billy Ray said.

"Yeah, a stronger arm than I've got. Got a stuck bleeder valve, and my arms ain't what they used to be. Step into some coveralls, boy, and do some real work."

A few minutes later, to Kitten's delight, Billy Ray was wearing grease-stained coveralls. Dahlia had found a man's shirt with Joel's Garage stitched on the pocket for Kitten, rolling up the arms so that the little girl looked like a miniature pigtailed mechanic. Chris's green playsuit was covered by a man's ragged T-shirt.

Billy Ray appraised Kitten, who looked for all the world like a five-year-old Carolina. "Now, look, we're going to need your help. These are the tools I'm going to use." Billy Ray laid out an assortment, naming each one and pointing as he did. "Do you think you can remember?"

"Can I get under the car?"

Billy Ray thought about Joel's insurance, about lawsuits and liability. "Just for a moment. Once we're finished."

"Can I fix something?" She was so excited she couldn't stand still. She delivered the question as she hopped from one foot to the other.

"I'll definitely find something for you to fix. But not this car. This car's just for looking. Okay?"

"I like the way it smells here!"

Bay one smelled like gas and oil, like tires and sweat-stained upholstery. This kid was definitely not going to be the next Judge Grayson.

Billy Ray circled the car, which Joel had driven up

on a low ramp, since the repair had appeared to be minor. But when Joel pointed to the valve that just wouldn't give, he snorted in disgust. "Guess I really am getting old if I can't get one of these unstuck. Took a torch to it, too."

"I'll see what I can do. You probably loosened it enough for a fresh arm to get it."

"*Young* arm. Mine's old and tired."

"Okay, Kitten," Billy Ray called. "Get me the box wrench."

"I've got a hammer socket right there," Joel said.

"Yeah, but she doesn't know that."

Joel came as close to laughing as he ever did, gurgling deep in his throat.

Billy Ray heard tools dropping on the concrete floor on the other side of the car, then the box wrench slid around the corner, propelled by a tiny hand. "Good job," he called. "Exactly what I needed. Now hand me the hammer." He waited until he had that in his grasp, too.

"Just fix the darn valve," Joel said, 'so I can bleed the line and get rid of the oil I put around this thing."

"I'm getting to it." The valve was every bit as stuck as Joel had promised. Billy Ray squatted, carefully using his weight to help loosen it. Repairing a broken valve was no fun.

The valve came unfrozen at last, and he tightened it so that the leak Joel had noted would be sealed. "There you go."

"Damn old age, anyway."

"Anything else you need?"

"Oil filter needs changing. I'm too creaky to be scooting underneath these things."

Billy Ray suspected Joel just liked having him and the kids around. Billy Ray had spent most afternoons here as a boy, handing his grandfather tools, learning simple, then complex, repairs. If he hadn't passed the bar, he could have made a good living as a mechanic.

"I'll do it," he told his grandfather.

"I've got to make a call. I'll be back to help you finish up."

"Go ahead."

Billy straightened; then he beckoned Kitten closer, so he could show her exactly what he'd done. She was fascinated. Chris, in Dahlia's arms, seemed perfectly happy, too.

"Next I'm going under the car to change an oil filter." He gave a primitive explanation of what that meant and had the feeling that Kitten would greatly have preferred a lecture on the differences between on-line and V-type engines and cubic-inch displacements.

"Can I come, too?"

"You can take a peek first. I'll show you what I'm going to do."

Her eyes lit up the way most little girls' probably did when they'd just been presented with a Barbie Dream House. He donned goggles for the job ahead and slid under the car. Then he made room for her. She joined him, lying on her back beside him. He pointed out the vital parts, giving a quick automobile anatomy lesson along the way.

"The filter's like the strainer Mommy uses when she drains spaghetti."

"Same principle. Now scoot, short stuff, because this gets messy."

"I don't mind."

"Well, your mommy would if she had to wash motor oil out of those pretty pigtails."

Kitten grumbled, but she did as she was told.

Billy Ray worked as quickly as he could, but the filter, like the bleeder valve, was stuck, and he had to try a cold chisel and ball peen hammer to loosen it. The sheriff's department cars were roughly used, and they frequently created problems for Joel's mechanics.

He was grunting with the effort and concentrating all his energy on the filter when he heard what seemed to be a scuffle above him. Dahlia sounded as if she'd moved away, but her voice was raised.

"I can't let you do that."

A man's voice responded in a quieter tone, but it wasn't Joel's.

Customers came and went at the garage, and old friends often dropped by just to chew the fat. Billy Ray wouldn't have thought twice about what he'd heard except for the tone of Dahlia's voice. Usually she was unflappable, but now she sounded distressed.

He scooted out and peered around. When he didn't see her, he pushed himself to his feet and circled the car.

She stood in front of the garage. Facing her was the judge, who had Kitten by the hand. Dahlia was grasping Chris tightly, as if the judge, or the young sheriff's deputy beside him, had tried to take him from her arms.

"What's going on?" Billy Ray advanced to Dahlia's side.

"Billy Ray, the judge here says these children are supposed to go with him."

Billy Ray realized poor Dahlia had been thrust in the middle of the battle between Carolina and her in-laws. Dahlia's husband had worked at the courthouse for more than thirty years, and he was about to retire. He needed the judge's goodwill to make sure he was allowed to finish the months necessary to receive full benefits.

Billy Ray reached for Christopher, despite his own oily coveralls. "You can go answer the phones, Dahlia. I know you're needed inside."

He waited until she was gone. "I thought we'd settled this, Judge," he said calmly. "Carolina is the children's mother. Carolina asked me to watch them this morning. That puts me in charge. I can't let you take either of the children without her permission."

"For a smart boy, you're not acting so smart." Judge Grayson didn't relinquish his granddaughter's hand.

"Smart and reliable," Billy Ray said. "And Carolina's relying on me to make sure these children are returned to her this afternoon."

"This is a small town. A small county. I'm not an ambitious man. I figured out a long time ago that I didn't need anything more than what I had right here. I settled for circuit court judge when I could have had more. I never ran for the senate, like Carolina's daddy. I just stayed here and made this part of Florida mine." The judge looked down at his granddaughter. Kitten looked confused; she began to bite her lip. "I'm not going to let anybody take what's mine," he added.

"The children belong to Carolina."

"How's your practice getting on?" Judge Grayson asked in an apparent change of subject. "I don't see as much of you as I might in my courtroom."

Billy Ray knew the subject hadn't been changed at all. "Shall we cut straight to the point? Make your threats right out in the open. I've got work to do."

"Threats?" The judge chortled. "I wouldn't lower myself to threaten you, Billy Ray. I save my threats for people who might really do me some harm. But I'll tell you how it's going to be. You're nobody. Your law practice is nothing. This garage is nothing. And after the people of River County realize that you've sided with the woman who killed my son and kept these innocent children from living under my protection, then they'll realize that you and everything you love are less than nothing, too. You won't want to live here anymore when that happens. And I won't blame you one bit."

Billy felt fury rising inside him, but he kept his voice calm. "You know, Judge, for all your ambition, you don't own this county. Wainwrights have lived here just as long as Graysons have. With or without your approval, we intend to stay." Billy Ray stooped and swept Kitten toward him, lifting her into his arms along with her brother. She began to cry softly.

The judge's hand fell away. Despite his arrogance, in a physical struggle, he knew he would lose. The deputy, Al Cranston, who had grown up trailing along behind Billy Ray and Doug, stepped forward, but he stopped when Billy Ray narrowed his eyes.

"The law says that these children are my responsibility today," he told Al.

"I've filed for custody," Judge Grayson said. "On the grounds that my daughter-in-law is unfit. And I'll win."

"We'll see."

"I'll get visiting rights first. You might as well let me have the children right here and now."

"I'll let you have them when I see a piece of paper telling me I have to."

"You've made a bad choice, Billy Ray. More than one. Choices often come back to haunt us."

"Unfortunately, not always. Some people continue to prosper, anyway."

The judge studied him silently, a slight smile on his face. Billy Ray didn't blink. Finally the judge turned, with Al at his heel, and walked away.

6

"Billie Ray?"

Billy Ray looked up from the papers he'd been working on since his three o'clock appointment. Fran was standing in his doorway, hands on her ample hips.

He put down his pen. "Why aren't you gone?"

"Because you aren't. And I'm getting real tired."

"I'm sorry, Fran. Go on home. I've still got work to finish."

Fran marched over and took the papers from his hands, tapping them into a neat pile. "Not anymore. Touch these again tonight and I'll make confetti out of them."

Billy Ray leaned back in his chair. For the first time he noticed it was growing dark outside, which meant it was probably sometime after seven. He had promised Carolina he would stop by on his way home from work to give her the details about what had occurred at the garage that morning.

Carolina had picked up the children from his office just after noon, and although he hadn't had a chance to tell her everything, he had managed the basics. He had also warned her not to let Kitten and Chris out of her sight.

He had no illusions that anything that had transpired at Joel's had changed Judge Grayson's mind. The man still wanted his grandchildren, and he had proved he would go to almost any lengths to get them. He had proved he was perfectly capable of snatching them right out of Carolina's arms, as long as his own reputation didn't suffer accordingly.

He stretched and looked his most repentant. "You're right. I'm beat. I'll leave."

"You'll leave one step ahead of me, young man. Don't think you're getting me out of here till you go, too."

He grinned, but her expression didn't change. Billy Ray knew when he'd lost. "Give Carolina a quick call for me, would you, while I get my stuff together? Tell her I'll be right over." He gave Fran Maggie's phone number.

Somewhere deep inside him, anticipation began to build. He hadn't been alone with Carolina since he had kissed her in his driveway. He had tried to put that kiss out of his mind, but it had grown into something of magnificent proportions. Kissing Carolina had been like coming home. He had walked around for days in a state of acute arousal, and the only woman he wanted was her.

Outside in the lot, he waited until Fran got into her own car before he got into his. Safety was rarely a problem in Moss Bend, but like anywhere else, there were occasional car thefts and muggings. With all the other businesses on the street closed for the night, the block was eerily empty. He waved her on, then turned to his own car. Fran dawdled in the lot, and he realized she was waiting for him to get in and drive away.

He laughed, gave her a mock salute and got behind the wheel of his Taurus. Only then did she head for home.

A thunderstorm had come through the county that afternoon, and now, with the sun setting and the temperature cooling, the earth smelled fresh and new. He elected to roll down his windows, even though Joel had temporarily resurrected his air conditioner, and he drove that way nearly as far as Maggie's house before a new idea struck him.

That morning he had promised Kitten that she could repair something when he finished changing the oil filter, but the incident with the judge had chased everything else from both their minds. Not until they got back to his office had the little girl expressed her disappointment. The whole day had gone sour for her, and that had bothered Billy Ray ever since.

Joel always had extra tools lying around the garage, along with old auto parts he saved for that one-in-a-million chance he might need them. Billy Ray could easily put together a few things for Kitten to play auto repair with. He would clean out a box and load it. When Kitten tired of the game, he would return the tools, and if she didn't, he would replace them with new ones.

He called Joel on his cell phone, just to be sure he didn't object. Joel didn't. In fact, he told Billy Ray where to find a brand new red toolbox one of his distributors had sent as a sample. "Fill it up, I don't care," Joel said. "That's a cute little gal."

Billy Ray kept a key to the garage on his chain, a talisman against the day when he would find his grandfather slumped peacefully between cars, a vacuum gauge in one hand and a hydrometer in the other. Joel had already put in an order for his epitaph: "If Joel couldn't fix it, it hadn't been built."

No one was around when he parked behind the garage and got out to unlock the door. Joel usually closed right at five on Fridays, and today had been no exception. A security light burned inside, but all was quiet. Billy Ray found the toolbox exactly where Joel had promised it would be; then he went out to the bays and flicked on the lights to find what he needed.

For company he flipped on the radio Grady and Jimmy always played at top volume and listened to Dwight Yoakam and Clint Black as he gathered tools.

The first blow caught him completely by surprise. One moment he was bending over to examine an old set of spark plugs, the next he was sprawled on the concrete floor. Before he could recover, something or someone landed on his back.

He kicked out, squirming and fighting to get to his knees, but the man on top grabbed him in a fierce bear hug. Before Billy Ray could dislodge him, something rough and foul-smelling slid over his head and the world went suddenly black. He hadn't had time to see anything except the scuffed toe of a boot. Now he couldn't see anything at all.

He struggled, trying desperately to free his hands, but whoever had attacked him had already prevented that. As he struggled, he felt rope twisting around his wrists, and when he tried to slam his bound hands into his attacker's stomach, he felt the scuffed boot connect with his leg.

"You're gonna git beat. And you're gonna git beat harder if you fight!"

Some part of his mind tried to put a face to the gravelly voice and failed. His feet were the only weapons left, and Billy Ray twisted hard, landing on his back and kicking out again and again, once contacting a soft body part with a satisfying thud.

"Jay-zus! Get him, you idiot! Get his feet!"

This was a different voice, affirming his foggy conviction that at least two men had teamed up to beat him. He continued to writhe and kick, but with his hands tied and his head covered, it was only a matter of time until his feet, too, were immobilized.

He quickly lost track of what the men were using to beat him. Feet, fists. Once, from a distance, he thought one of them had picked up something from the shop to use as a weapon. Before he could decide what it might be, the world went black.

"Are you sure you don't want to eat something, Carolina? There'll be plenty of chicken left for Billy Ray when he gets here."

Carolina smiled her thanks at Maggie, but she shook her head. "I hate to eat without him, in case he hasn't had supper. But you're a sweetie to be worried."

"Then I'm just going to clean up a little. You sit and finish your tea."

Carolina had wondered how living with Maggie would work out, but after a few days she already knew things were going to be fine. Better than fine. The Blue Bayou took most of Maggie's time, but when she was home she was giving and friendly without being pushy. She genuinely enjoyed the children, and they responded to her with an open warmth that was sadly different from the guarded good manners with which they treated Gloria Grayson and Carolina's own mother.

"You know, I could try Joel." Maggie dried her hands on a dish towel. "Billy Ray might have decided to go there first. I could tell him we're holding dinner, if Billy Ray wants some."

Carolina considered. She had already tried Billy at the office and gotten a recording. "Maybe that's a good idea. Otherwise he might stop for fast food on the way over."

"I won't be a minute."

Carolina went to the sink and rinsed out her glass. Maggie had made iced tea with extra slices of lemon and fresh mint sprigs. After years at the Blue Bayou she was the consummate hostess.

Maggie bustled back in. "Okay. I got Joel. He says Billy Ray was going over to the garage before coming here. But that was about an hour ago, about the time Fran called you, so I called his house. Nobody's there."

"Did he say why Billy was going over there?" Carolina listened as Maggie explained about the toolbox. "But the garage is only five minutes away. I wonder what happened?"

"Maybe it took him a while to find things."

Carolina wanted to believe that was the case, but nothing really added up. If Billy had made a side trip to the garage, he must have expected it to be a short one. Otherwise, he would have called her to explain he was going to be late.

She tried to reassure Maggie. "Well, I didn't say anything about dinner when we talked this afternoon. He probably stopped somewhere." But that didn't seem to be enough of an explanation. Even if he'd been starving, Billy still wouldn't have kept her waiting this long without a phone call.

Maggie wasn't reassured. Her attractive face was screwed up in a frown. "We could call the garage, but I doubt he'd answer. I'm sure their machine is on."

"You know what? I think I'll just go over there. It'll only take a few minutes. Will you keep an eye on the kids?" At the moment, Chris and Kitten, who'd had their supper and bedtime baths hours ago, were visible through the doorway watching a television special about African elephants.

"Sure. I'd just as soon you'd find out what's happening."

Outside, Carolina climbed into the BMW and started toward the center of town, veering at the first traffic light toward Joel's Garage. She supposed her concern for Billy Ray stemmed from her own situation. Anyone who lived with as much uncertainty as she did often saw problems where none existed. Billy had probably gotten into a conversation with someone and forgotten about the time.

But Billy wasn't Champ Grayson. He wasn't the kind of man who would easily forget his obligations.

The garage was dark except for a security light inside and one in the drop-off area. She circled the lot, looking for Billy's car, but even so, she nearly missed it. Billy had parked beside the back door, in a narrow slot between two larger cars that had blocked her view.

Her heart began to beat faster. Billy's car was here, but there were no regular lights on inside the garage. She wished there was someone she could call, but the law in River County was joined at the hip to Whittier Grayson. And without proof that something was wrong at Joel's, no one would listen to her.

Carolina parked behind Billy's car and got out. She rattled the back door, calling his name. To her surprise, it opened in her hand.

She entered the dark garage. "Billy? Are you here?"

The garage was silent. After a lot of fumbling she found a light switch and flicked it on. She was in the reception area, which was awash in scattered papers. The furniture was overturned; a lamp was smashed, but as far as she could tell, she was alone.

Carolina put her hand over her mouth. Someone had been here, someone with no scruples. And Billy's car was still parked in the lot.

Was the intruder still here? Was he lurking close by in the shadows? For a moment she wanted to run, but the thought of Billy lying somewhere in the building stopped her. She stood without breathing and listened. The garage was silent.

She knew better than to continue on without something to protect herself. Whoever had been here had emptied the reception desk drawers on the floor before flipping the desk on its back like a beached turtle. Scissors glinted in a corner, and she bent and snatched them from the floor, grasping them with the point out, the way she had cautioned Kitten never to carry them.

The building sprawled out on both sides of her. She tried to remember the layout. To her left was the divided area where the repairs were carried out. To her right were storerooms, or maybe offices, she thought. Which direction would Billy have gone?

"Billy?" This time she shouted, but still no one answered.

She chose the repair area first, creeping on trembling legs down a narrow unlit corridor to the swinging door at the end. She pushed it open, and the repair area stretched out in front of her, divided into sections so that multiple repairs could be carried out at once.

"Billy?"

The security light shone dimly in the corner, illuminating only a minimal area surrounding it. She couldn't make out much. Heavy equipment, lifts, a car parked on a ramp. She placed her hand against the wall and began to feel for a light switch. She moved farther left, groping unsteadily, until at last a switch materialized under her fingers. She flipped it, and the room lit up.

Billy Ray lay trussed and unmoving on the floor in the second cubicle.

In Maggie's extra bedroom, Garth cleaned a cut on the side of Billy Ray's face and taped it. "You could have been killed."

"Nobody intended to kill me. Just to put the fear of God in—" He looked up and saw Carolina watching him. She could see him visibly repress whatever he had been about to say.

Carolina wanted to weep. She had managed to cut the ropes binding his hands and feet and revive him. Then, somehow, she had gotten him out to her car for the trip back to Maggie's. The burlap sack the intruders had fastened over his head had afforded his face a little protection, but he was still a mass of bruises and abrasions. He had refused to go to the emergency room, but he *had* allowed Maggie to call Garth.

"You're going to report this, aren't you?" Garth demanded.

"Joel's at the garage reporting the break-in to the sheriff right now," Carolina said.

Garth wasn't satisfied. "What about the attack?"

"Tomorrow I'm going to track down Doug Fletcher and have a little talk with him." Billy Ray winced as Garth probed his shoulder.

"I don't think anything's broken, but I can't be sure about this shoulder without X rays. You come in tomorrow. No excuses."

"Yeah. Thanks."

"Carolina?" Garth looked to her for support.

"He'll be there, if I have to tie him back up again and drag him in."

"I'm going to leave him in your care. Wake him up every couple of hours through the night and check his pupils." He explained how to be certain the concussion Billy Ray had suffered wasn't more serious than it seemed. "Call me if there's any change." Garth turned back to Billy Ray. "You're going to need to take it easy while you heal. You'll be sore for a long time. Whoever did this was thorough."

Maggie had been putting together ice packs. Now she came into the room with one in each hand. "I don't even know which bruise to start with," she said. "Billy Ray, you look like you just barely survived the worst fight in the history of the Bayou."

"At least there...I could have seen who I was punching."

Garth took Maggie aside to give her more instructions.

Carolina lifted Billy Ray's hand to her lips and kissed it. "We both know who did this. You didn't have to see."

"I didn't see anybody. I didn't recognize the voices."

"This was my father-in-law's doing. They aren't

going to find anything much missing at Joel's. Those bastards the judge hired trailed you there, then set out to beat you senseless.''

Maggie joined her at his side. "I'm going to put these on his shoulder first. And Garth told me what to give him for the pain."

Carolina stood. "I'm going to check on the kids." She lowered her voice. "Then I'm going out for a little while."

"The kids are sleeping. I checked before I got the ice packs. I'm glad I got them to bed before you and Billy Ray showed up." Then, as if Carolina's words had finally sunk in, she frowned. "Did you say you were going out?"

Carolina put her finger to her lips. Both women went to stand in the doorway. "I have an errand."

"Carolina, don't…" Maggie seemed to balance her words. "Oh, darn it girl, don't do anything stupid. Okay?"

Carolina hugged her hard. "Don't worry. I'm just going to do something I should have done a long time ago."

Outside, the moon was up, and the sky was dotted with stars. She climbed into her car and backed down Maggie's drive at full throttle, screeching tires as she turned on to the road.

She reached the Grayson house in a matter of minutes. Her in-laws had never moved to the fashionable suburb on the west side of town, where young professionals built replicas of Tara on quarter-acre lots. Their own Greek Revival plantation house stood in the town's oldest neighborhood, surrounded by similar stately homes and century-old plantings. Carolina's childhood home had been in this neighborhood, too.

On the trip over, she had realized what night it was. The Graysons participated in a bridge group with five other couples from the country club. The group met on the third Friday of every month, and Carolina knew that Gloria and Whittier were hosting tonight. She remembered that when she had still been living with them, Gloria had warned her that the children would need to be particularly well behaved this night. As if Kitten and Chris could possibly be quieter or more subdued without being drugged.

She didn't care if her in-laws had company. She was so angry that she didn't care about much of anything except speaking her piece. If she spoke it in front of half the town, so much the better. She had been silent much too long.

She was wearing a blue chambray shirt, striped shorts and sandals. Everyone inside would be dressed in casual party clothes. No one was going to mistake her for a guest, even if her mother-in-law tried to introduce her that way.

The woman who opened the door was the real reason that Gloria's parties received such acclaim. Tonight Inez was wearing a black uniform with a crisp white collar and her most solemn expression. Carolina knew that when Inez had finished greeting guests she would go back to the kitchen to make certain the dinner buffet was perfect.

"Miss Carolina?" Inez looked her up and down. "We've got a party going on tonight...."

"I can see that." Carolina stepped inside, pushing past Inez. She could see that the party hadn't progressed to the dining room. The guests were mingling and drinking cocktails at the end of the large hallway, in the room Gloria liked to call the "family" room. But there had never been a place in this house for family. Everything here was designed for show. The crystal chandelier hanging in sparkling tiers from the high ceiling, the carefully selected French antiques, the exotically beautiful Persian carpets.

"Wait here. I'll get Mrs. Grayson," Inez said.

"Don't bother. I'll find her." Carolina started down the hallway.

"Miss Carolina, I don't think—"

"Inez, please *don't* think. This has nothing to do with you."

Carolina could hear Inez's disapproving murmurs as she stalked into the family room. The guests were gathered in small knots throughout, all with drinks in their hands, all with tight, polite smiles. One by one the conversational knots untied, and the room grew silent. Carolina ignored her mother-in-law, who started toward her from a far corner. Instead she wound her way through the partygoers, who moved aside to give her a wide berth, and headed straight for the judge.

He was among the last to stop speaking. He was immersed in what looked like a heated debate with a man whom she recognized as the new president of her family's savings and loan. The appropriateness of that wasn't lost on her. Her family and what they had accomplished in Moss Bend were still an important part of the town history and society structure. She hoped these people would remember that and give her the benefit of the doubt.

As she drew nearer, the judge seemed to realize that the room had grown quiet. He turned, and without a change of expression, he watched her approach.

"I would like to talk to you, sir."

He lifted one brow. "I'm afraid your timing isn't the best, Carolina." His tone made it perfectly clear that he thought that was too often the case.

She advanced on him until they were only a foot apart. "As a matter of fact, my timing is perfect. Because I'd like these good people, friends of my family as well as yours, to hear what I have to say."

"Haven't you made enough scenes in this community without adding another to your repertoire?"

"I don't believe anyone here has witnessed those so-called scenes. I believe they've only heard about them from you and Mrs. Grayson, who have every reason to paint me as unstable."

"And what reason would that be?"

"That you want my children. You want to raise them according to your dictates. You want to destroy them the way you destroyed your own son!"

The gasps behind her were audible. Gloria reached her husband's side and put her hand on Carolina's arm. She was a small woman who disappeared to Atlanta every five years and returned weeks later looking like a much younger woman. In addition to face-lifts, she pursued a rigid diet and had her hair colored an attractive ash blond. Only the expression in her eyes gave away the fact that she was nearing sixty-five.

"You're not well," Gloria said. "I believe you need to rest awhile, dear. Why don't we go back to the—"

Carolina shook off her hand. "I am perfectly well. But Billy Ray Wainwright isn't. Tonight someone followed him to his grandfather's garage and beat him senseless. The same garage where you tried to take custody of my children this morning, Judge. Without a court order. Without my permission. Doesn't that seem like an odd coincidence?''

"I don't patrol the streets of Moss Bend, Carolina. I try criminals, I don't arrest them. I'm sorry if your boyfriend was attacked, but the fact that you think it had anything to do with me is proof that your children need someone else to care for them.''

"Billy Ray gave me shelter when I took my children and escaped from this house, and now he's acting as my attorney. Today he stood up to you and refused to let you steal my children. Even your most ardent supporters will have trouble discounting the possibility that you were behind the beating, Judge.''

He laughed. "My most ardent supporters know I'm not a thug.''

"But you're a powerful man who is not above hiring thugs to do your dirty work. Power has a funny way of corrupting people. They begin to believe they have a right to make the world work the way they want it to. They begin to believe they have a right to control everyone who steps into their path. Their wives, their children, their in-laws.''

She switched her gaze to Gloria. "Gloria, this man destroyed your son. Champ was an alcoholic and a drug abuser when he died, a violent man with no self-control and no morals. Will you allow your husband to destroy your grandchildren, too?''

"You've said enough!'' The judge grabbed her by the arm. "You may say whatever you like about me, but I won't have you talk about my son this way!''

"If you take me to court and try to get custody of my children, I'll say a lot more, and I will back up every word of it.'' She shook off his hand, but she knew he only let her go because the room was filled with people.

She turned, but she didn't leave. "Please don't be embarrassed that you were forced to witness this," she told the gaping guests. "I'm here right now *because* I need witnesses. You've watched me grow up. You know who I am. I'm not the person the Graysons are claiming I've become. I'm the woman you've always believed me to be. But I'm a woman who will not let these people steal her children or destroy the people I care about. Not anymore."

She sighed and shook her head. "That's it. And now you'll have something really interesting to talk about tonight, won't you."

She headed for the door, and the guests parted nervously to give her a clear path.

She was almost there when she heard a rapid click of heels behind her. She turned to see her mother-in-law bearing down on her. Carolina stepped out onto the porch and Gloria followed her, closing the door behind them.

"Just what are you trying to do to us?" Gloria demanded.

"I believe that's perfectly clear."

"Must you destroy us all?"

Carolina searched her mother-in-law's artificially young face. "Gloria," she said at last, "you and I have had our differences, but I know you're a better person than he is. And you know it, too. Don't let him do this. We both know what Champ had become by the time he died. We both know why. You can't do anything about Champ. But you can be sure the same fate doesn't await Kitten and Chris. That can be your redemption."

"Who are you to speak of redemption? You killed my son!"

Tears sprang to Carolina's eyes, but she shook her head. "I was at the wheel of the car that night. That's all I know. But I can tell you this. Sometimes I think Champ is better off dead. He was in hell while he was living here on earth. Whatever was waiting for him on the other side couldn't have been worse than that."

7

Billy Ray lowered himself to his desk chair and turned it sideways so he could stretch out his legs. It had taken a week before he could sit comfortably at all, but now, two weeks after the beating, his bruises were fading. Yesterday he had discarded the sling Garth had given him to immobilize his shoulder.

"What do you want first? The morning's faxes, the mail or the phone messages?" Fran had followed him to his desk; now she stood over him like a mother who was determined to make her teenage son clean his room.

"Give me the most important of each."

"We're still not caught up. Next time you get beat up, do it on vacation."

"Good idea. Next time I'll ask for a rain check."

Her voice didn't soften, but her expression did. "You look a little better today."

"No place to go but up."

"I'd like to wring that Doug Fletcher's neck. If he wanted to, he could find out who did this!"

But, of course, Doug didn't want to find out. Billy Ray had limped into Doug's office the morning after the attack, only to find Doug unavailable to him. Doug had taken three days to get around to talking to him, and nothing good had come from their conversation.

Doug hadn't bothered to ask Billy Ray how he was doing. He'd sat at his desk with his feet propped high, and he'd shrugged after listening to Billy Ray's account.

"If you didn't see anybody, I can't help you much. We didn't get any leads worth following from evidence at the scene. Most likely somebody was looking for cash or parts to sell, and you got in the way. But I'm sending a patrol by the garage a couple of times a night for a week. That ought to keep vandals away." Doug didn't look at Billy Ray as he delivered that message. He looked just past Billy Ray's injured shoulder.

Billy Ray wasn't quite speechless with anger. "It went beyond vandalism, Doug, and you damned well know it! Somebody beat me but good. And they did it because I'm involved with Carolina Grayson."

"Why *are* you involved with that woman, Billy Ray? Back in high school she threw you over 'cause you weren't worth a plugged nickel to her. She'll do it again the minute she doesn't need you anymore. Now, I'm not saying what happened to you had anything to do with that. I'm not saying that at all. But I am telling you, friend to friend, that you'd be a whole hell of a lot better off without her."

"Friend? What kind of friend, Doug? It's been three days since the attack, and you're just getting around to an interview."

"Joel told me you didn't see anybody that night. I was busy trying to figure out who might have done it."

"You were busy losing the trail." Billy Ray lowered his voice and advanced on the desk. "You were busy letting Judge Whittier Grayson tell you when to piss and when to grin, you lowlife Judas!"

Doug got to his feet. "Get out of my office, or you'll wish you hadn't come in the first place!"

And because, and *only* because, there was no reason to stay, Billy Ray had left.

He hadn't heard from Doug again, but he hadn't expected to. Doug had declared his allegiances.

Now Billy Ray looked down at the papers covering his desk and grimaced. "If Carolina calls, or my grandfather, put them through. Otherwise, hold all my calls. I'm going to try to make some headway."

Fran left, and an hour passed. He was just taking a break when his intercom buzzed. "Carolina's here. Do you want me to send her in?"

Billy Ray got to his feet as Carolina opened the door.

"Billy…" She smiled with her lips, but her eyes were sad. Something had happened. Something more than just seeing him bruised and battered.

"Close the door."

She did. He came around his desk and perched on the edge. "What's going on?"

"You want the good news first?" Before he could answer, she went on. "Sure you do. Because once I tell you the bad, the good's going to get lost."

"Let's hear it, then." He held out his hands.

She took them in her own, but she didn't move closer. "I got the job."

"Carolina…" He pulled her between his legs until they were face-to-face. He smiled at her. She had applied for half a dozen jobs in town, but he knew she was talking about the job at Wilton Mills. "I'm so glad. That's wonderful. When do you start?"

"I go in next week to fill out forms and have the company nurse do a physical. I can take the rest of the week to settle the kids into their day-care classes. Then I start the following week."

"When did you find out?"

"Just about fifteen minutes before I got these." She dropped his hands and reached inside the purse slung over her shoulder. She presented him with a sheaf of legal documents.

He scanned them. As expected, the Graysons were petitioning the court for custody of their grandchildren.

"We knew." He handed the papers back to her. "Now the fight's out in the open."

"I'm scared."

"You don't have to be. We'll win."

"Will we?"

"We're going to pull out all the stops." He took her hands again. "Look, I've been thinking about something. Hear me out."

"What's that?"

"I want to give the Graysons visiting rights in the meantime. Now that they've begun this thing, they'll petition Judge Sawyer to let them visit, anyway. If you fight, it will make you look bad. If you let them visit without dragging it through the court, you'll be in a position of strength. We'll have them sign a document promising they'll abide by your terms. Time, place, frequency. If they don't sign, that will make them look like *they* don't want to cooperate."

"I don't want the kids in the middle of this."

He squeezed her hands. "They already are. I'm trying to make sure they aren't torn apart in the tug-of-war.''

She didn't look convinced, but she nodded. "I trust your judgment."

He pulled her hands to his chest, cupping them against his tie. "Why don't you let them take the children late Wednesday, from say, four to seven?"

"The judge won't even be home until six or so."

He grinned. "That occurred to me."

"You think this will appease them?"

"It's a start. But if you have any reason not to let the children go, anything you haven't told me before, now's the time. Will they be safe?"

She nodded reluctantly. "Safe, but not happy."

"You'll have to prepare them well."

She sighed and nodded again.

He didn't say anything else. Carolina had waited on him hand and foot during his recovery, but they hadn't been this close since the day he had kissed her.

"I'm proud of you." He brought her hands to his lips and kissed them. "You'll get through this."

"Billy..."

He smiled at her with his eyes.

"Does it hurt when I touch you now?"

"We could see."

She slid her arms around his waist, but she didn't squeeze. "What will I do Wednesday? I'll go crazy."

"Have an early dinner with me."

"The last time I tried to have dinner with you, somebody beat you senseless."

"Come to my house after you drop off the children."

She leaned forward and gently kissed his lips. The kiss was achingly sweet, and much too short. She stepped away. "Maggie has the children over at the drugstore. I have to go."

"Guess what?"

She smiled. "What?"

"That didn't hurt."

She touched his cheek tenderly.

Kitten didn't want to see her grandparents. She liked Maggie's house better. Maggie's house smelled like blackberry pie, like jasmine flowers and the cool, wide hallways of the old town library, where Kitten went for story hour. At Maggie's house her bedroom was painted as red as the hibiscus in Maggie's yard. Maggie took Kitten to pick hibiscus each morning, along with the other flowers that grew in her garden.

The flowers reminded Kitten of Billy Ray's house, where flowers grew as wild as weeds. She missed Billy Ray's house and Three Legs the cat. Billy Ray had promised her she could see Three Legs soon, and she wanted to go there real bad.

But she didn't want to go to her grandparents' house.

"Kitten, are you listening?"

Kitten faced her mother. Her mother was wearing a yellow sundress with little purple flowers scattered like polka dots all over it. Her mother was pretty when she smiled, but even now, with a frown on her face, she still looked nice. "I don't want to go!" Kitten bit her bottom lip.

"Kitten, it's only for a little while. I promise. We have a piece of paper that says they can't make you stay. I know that's what's worrying you."

Kitten didn't think a piece of paper could make her grandfather do anything. Once, in Sunday School, her teacher had asked what God looked like, and Kitten had said her grandfather. The teacher hadn't seemed surprised.

But God was supposed to be good, and Kitten didn't think her grandfather was. Not really. He made people do things. He punished people, the way God had punished people by sending a flood to cover the earth. But she didn't think he loved people, the way God was supposed to love everybody.

She didn't think he loved her.

"I don't want to go!" She stopped biting her lip. She stuck it out instead.

"Well, you're going to. And this will be easier on Chris if you cooperate. I'll take you there, and I'll pick you up. Billy Ray will come with me to get you afterward. Please?"

Kitten knew that when her mother got that certain look on her face, nothing anyone could do would change her mind. That happened more and more now. Since they had come to live at Maggie's house, her mother seemed very sure about a lot of things.

Kitten tried again. "They'll make me be polite."

"Being polite is important. Please remember your manners."

Kitten rolled her eyes. "*They* won't let me forget."

"I'll get Chris up from his nap, then we'll go." Carolina left Kitten's room. Kitten knew she had little choice but to follow.

In the car, she sat with her arms crossed and her lip down to her chin, but her mother didn't waver.

"You don't love me!" Kitten said at last. "Or you wouldn't make me go!"

"I love you. You still have to go."

When they pulled up in front of her grandparents'

house, Kitten considered a struggle. But already she could feel herself turning into the little girl her grandparents wanted her to be. That little girl seemed like a stranger. That little girl always had to color in the lines and speak softly. That little girl ate everything on her plate and sipped her drink without slurping.

Kitten hated that little girl.

Her mother looked determined, but not one bit happy. Still, she got out of the car and came around to open Kitten's door before she reached for Chris in the car seat.

She set Chris on the ground and took his hand before she spoke again. "Kitten, try to be on your good behavior. But you're allowed to be yourself. You don't have to pretend to be somebody else."

Kitten frowned. She was surprised her mother knew about the other little girl, the good one who wasn't really Kitten at all.

She looked up and saw her grandmother waiting, arms crossed over her chest just the way Kitten's were. Her grandmother was smiling, but she didn't look happy. She never played with Kitten or Chris. She just told them what to do. Kitten didn't think that her grandmother really loved her, either.

"If I'm me, she's not going to be happy," Kitten warned.

Carolina squatted in front of her so that she could look straight into her eyes. "Nobody can make you something you aren't, not unless you let them. Do you understand?"

Kitten wasn't sure.

"You don't have to be somebody else to make people love you. Because then they don't love *you*. They love somebody you aren't."

Kitten nodded, because in a funny way, that made sense to her.

"You're a wonderful little girl. And I love you very much just the way you are. Remember that, sweetheart. No matter what." Carolina got to her feet and turned to face her mother-in-law.

Kitten slipped her hand inside her mother's and walked up the sidewalk.

Billy Ray had planned to be home by the time Carolina got there, but a long-distance telephone call kept him at the office later than he'd expected. When he arrived, Carolina's car was already parked in front of his house, but she was nowhere in sight.

"Carolina?"

"I'm over here."

He faced the direction her voice had come from, but no one was in sight. "Send up a signal," he called. "I can't see you."

"Left at the camellias, right at the azaleas." She appeared behind a thicket of overgrown shrubbery in his father's garden.

He picked his way through the tangle of vegetation, along what had once been a path. Carolina had made a home for herself right in the center of it with a basket of rusting garden tools from the barn.

She wiped her forehead with the back of her hand. "I hope you don't mind."

"Mind?" He was puzzled. "Are you kidding? But what are you trying to do?"

"I'm going to restore the Garden of Eden."

"I believe you might need the Lord's help for that."

Her face had been painfully serious, but her expression lightened. She nearly smiled. "I don't think He'll mind. I'm just pulling a few weeds."

He didn't touch her. She didn't look like a woman who wanted to be touched. "Why?"

"Therapy. I just want to set something to rights. And I can't tell you how good it feels to jerk weeds out of the ground and banish them to the compost pile."

"Honey, I don't have a compost pile."

"You will by the time I'm finished. A big sucker of a compost pile. Barn-sized."

"Um... Are you going to leave a plant or two?"

"You'll love it." She cocked her head. "Tell me you don't mind?"

Mind? Did he mind Carolina using his front garden as a pressure valve for more stress than anyone deserved? Did he mind Carolina at his house, pursuing a project that could take years? Decades?

"You do whatever you want, any time you want to. My neighbor up the road wants to bushhog the whole thing and plant corn."

She slapped her hands on her hips. "He'll have to answer to me!"

"My daddy used to come out here every night when he wasn't off drinking. I'd find him on his hands and knees talking to the plants. The garden was always more than he could handle, but I think it kept him from taking his own life." He shook his head. "Taking it all at once, anyway."

"He must have been quite a man. He had a vision. I can see it, even if he never quite achieved what he wanted here."

"Do you want me to stay and help?"

"Honestly? No. I'd like to be alone."

He understood perfectly. "Good, then I'll make dinner."

"Please, don't go to much trouble. I'm not really very hungry."

"I promise."

She flashed him a grateful smile; then she lowered herself to the blanket she'd spread to protect her dress and returned to pulling weeds.

Half an hour later she appeared at his front door, hot and bedraggled, but still incredibly lovely. "Can I come in?"

"You'd better believe it." He swung open the screen door, and she brushed past him, the hem of her skirt tickling his knees provocatively. "Doing better?"

"There aren't enough weeds in the world to cure what's wrong with me, but that helped." She headed straight for the downstairs bathroom. "I'm going to freshen up, then I'll help with supper."

"Don't worry about it. It's almost finished."

"I'm impressed."

"You haven't seen it yet."

She gave him the first real smile of the day.

Back in the kitchen, he put the finishing touches on their omelet and slid it under the broiler to brown. Then he ladled fruit cocktail into bowls and popped the handle on the toaster.

By the time Carolina joined him, the meal was on the table.

"This looks great." She brought the coffeepot to the table, as casually as if they'd been fixing meals together forever. "Cream but no sugar, right?"

He felt a surge of warmth that she'd noticed. Sometimes the small details were the ones that seemed most important. The unconscious intimacies. The unspoken affirmations.

He watched her pour. "And you take toast with no butter. Only a little jam," he said.

She set the pot on the table. "That's Gloria's doing. She's conscientious, if nothing else. When I lived with the Graysons, she made sure I never had to wrestle with demon fat grams."

"I'll bet she didn't serve omelets."

"I wonder what the children will have for supper tonight? She'll let them have a little fat, of course. She understands they need it. But she'll be certain it's carefully measured. Champ couldn't control his diet after he left home. I guess he was making up for all the things his mother never let him have—" She bit off the last word. "I don't want to talk about Champ or Gloria. I'm sorry."

"They're on your mind tonight. Understandably."

"Kitten didn't want to go." Carolina looked up from her plate. She still hadn't taken a bite. "I had to force her, Billy. When she's with them, she has to be someone she's not. The pressure's too much."

"Kids can handle a lot of pressure. And at the evening's end, she comes home to you."

"For how long?"

He put his napkin back beside his plate and rose. Then he circled the table and held out his arms. "Come here."

She was against his chest in seconds. "I'm sorry!"

He stroked her hair. It was fine and soft under his fingertips, and even though he was there to comfort her, something altogether male and sexual engaged inside him. "It's all right. If you need to cry, cry."

"I need to scream!"

"You can do that, too. Just give me a chance to plug my ears."

"You're so good to me!"

He wanted that to be enough, but it wasn't. He wanted to believe he was a better man than he was, because being needed by Carolina was more than he'd ever expected. But his body was coming to life against hers. In a moment his reaction would be no secret.

He moved away and held her at arm's length, as if he needed to see her face. "Being good to you is no hardship."

"Do you know what bothers me?"

He told himself to be patient, that she needed a friend tonight. "What?"

"That I've found you again, but our time together revolves around my situation." She said the words forcefully, as if she was expelling them from deep inside her.

"Your situation is very complicated."

"Billy, I don't want the custody issue to be all there is between us. But that's the way it is. You've been beaten within an inch of your life. You've lost your best friend. Your practice is going to suffer—we both know the judge will see to that. I'm just somebody who's making your life harder. I'm a burden, when I want to be more."

His heart was beating faster. He told himself that Carolina was so badly in need of support that she was interpreting her own gratitude as something else.

He spoke slowly, carefully. "You're not a burden. I want to help you. As for the rest of it, we can take everything a step at a time." He was being reasonable, responsible. He was taking care of her, the way he had always taken care of the people in his life.

He wanted to sweep her into his arms and kiss away everything that lay between them.

"I've taken my whole life one step at a time, playing by everybody else's rules. Do you know where that's gotten me? One step closer to nowhere!" She shook off his hands, a gentle but uncompromising flick of her shoulders. "I'm sorry. I don't know what's wrong with me tonight. You're going to start believing everything the Graysons say about me."

"No chance of that."

"Just tell me this. Do you have any feelings for me? I know we're friends, and I know you're concerned. I even know that once upon a time you thought you loved me. But we were kids, Billy Ray. And we're not kids anymore."

"I don't think either of us can talk accurately about feelings right now, Carolina."

"Oh, I can. I want you. That's one of those feelings that just can't be denied. I look at you and I go all soft inside, like everything I am is melting and running together. Used to be I just wanted to be with you, that I felt whole when we were together, and I liked the way I felt when you kissed me. But that was a long time ago. And both of us are all grown up now, with grown-up needs."

He could think of a thousand reasons to speak, but none of them was as compelling as his need to kiss her. Before her last words died away, she was crushed against his battered chest, held securely in his black-and-blue arms. Her lips were soft against his and as familiar as a daydream.

She broke away just long enough to speak. "Don't do this because you think I need you."

"Feel how much I need you," he said, pressing his

hips against hers and holding her tightly against him. "I'm not a saint, Carolina. I couldn't make love to any woman as a public service."

Her answer lay somewhere between a laugh and a moan. He had remembered how it felt to kiss her, but he had never felt her body squirming unsatisfied against his. Sensations burst inside him like skyrockets. He silenced the inner voice that pointed out she was a passionate woman starved for love, that no one had touched her this way for a very long time. It was enough that she trusted and desired him.

Well, nearly enough.

"Will dinner keep?" She kissed him again before he could answer. She slanted her lips a different way and moaned softly when his opened under them.

"I don't care." He ground out the words like the final prayer of a dying man. A lifetime of restraint dissolved around him. He could no more turn away from her than he could turn back time. This was inevitable, and had been since the kiss they had shared in his driveway.

He found the zipper at the back of her dress and inched it down. Under his palm her skin was warm and smooth, and it seemed to heat as he touched it. His fingertips grazed the side of her breast under a satin bra. He lifted the bra higher, releasing her breast, and felt the warm soft mound tighten under his hand.

Her breath caught. She found the buttons of his shirt, as if to hurry him along, jerking them out of the buttonholes. She continued to kiss him all the while, as if she couldn't bear to end that intimacy. He had vague thoughts of sweeping her off her feet and carrying her upstairs, but he was still weak. And the bedroom seemed far away.

"I love your sofa." She whispered the words, a veiled plea, against his lips.

He knew what she wanted. In its last incarnation, the blue velvet sofa might very well have suffered the same fate.

"Carolina, this is happening so fast...."

"It's twelve years later than it should be."

His hand closed around her breast, and he couldn't be a good guy any longer. They were adults, and they wanted each other with a fierce hunger. They could deal with the results of this. They could work out anything.

The last button gave on his shirt. Her sundress slid down her arms and pooled on the floor at her feet. He reached for the clasp on her bra.

A knock at the front door rattled through the house.

Billy Ray closed his eyes, his breathing harsh and uneven. "Who in the hell?"

"Billy Ray? Are you in there?"

He recognized his grandfather's voice. Apparently so did Carolina. She made a sound like glass crashing to the floor.

"I'm sorry. I didn't know—"

She had already moved away and was bending to retrieve and zip the dress. "You don't have to tell me."

"I have to answer it."

"Of course you do."

"Maybe the Fates are trying to tell us something." He jerked his shirt closed and buttoned it with one hand as he tucked it into his pants with the other.

"Sure. Maybe we're supposed to wait another twelve years."

He called to Joel. "Come on in. I'll be right there."

Then he looked down at Carolina. "Are we going to listen to them?"

She lifted her chin resolutely. "I want you, Billy. I know you don't trust it yet. Not completely. But I want you. And I'm not going to let anybody, not the Graysons, not the Fates, tell me what's good for me! Never again. I'm a big girl. I know my own mind."

"It wasn't our minds talking just now, Carolina."

"No, it was every part of me talking." She touched his face. He was surprised to see that her eyes were filled with tears. "All of me, Billy. Please believe it."

8

With Billy Ray at her side, Carolina waited in the Graysons' hallway for Kitten and Chris. He had volunteered to get the children with her, and she had gratefully accepted, although she knew she shouldn't involve him any further in her struggle with her in-laws.

Gloria escorted the children through the family room and out to meet her. Carolina stooped, and Chris ran screeching delightedly into her arms. Kitten was more subdued, but she hugged Carolina hard, as if she really hadn't been sure her mother would return.

"What did you do today?" Carolina asked Kitten, trying for a semblance of normalcy. "Did you play with your dolls?"

"I don't like dolls."

"She refused to play with any of her toys."

Carolina rose with Chris in her arms to face her mother-in-law. "Did she?"

"I've bought lovely dolls for Catherine. Some of them are very expensive. Now she claims she doesn't like dolls."

Except for the fashion doll Champ had given her,

Kitten had never really liked dolls, a fact Gloria had refused to recognize. Carolina tried to smooth the waters. "Children go through phases, Gloria. I'm sure she'll enjoy them another time."

"I like running and jumping. I like putting stuff together!" Kitten launched herself at Billy Ray, who caught her just in time and swung her into his arms.

Gloria raised an eyebrow. "If you ask me, she's doing too much running and jumping. She hardly sat still for a moment."

"She's an active little girl." Carolina was about to turn away when she realized something she never had before. Her mother-in-law, the ice queen of Moss Bend, was hurt. She had bought Kitten expensive toys as a way to show her love, but Kitten had spurned them.

For the good of her children Carolina swallowed her own anger, reaching out to Gloria in the only way she could. "You know, Kitten loved that craft kit you bought for her last summer. Remember? The one with the beads and wire for stringing necklaces? She's wonderful with her hands. She had so much fun with it. Maybe next time they visit you could find something like that to do together."

For a moment Gloria looked as if she was going to decline the suggestion. But clearly Carolina had just traveled the extra mile, and the breeding Gloria was so proud of demanded that she be gracious in return. "Thank you," she said stiffly. "I'll think about it."

"Next time they visit?" Judge Grayson appeared in the family room doorway. "Do you think because of your...generosity today, we aren't going to pursue custody?"

Before Carolina could remind him that he was going

to upset the very children he claimed to be trying to protect, his wife turned to him. "We will not discuss this now, Whittier. Do you understand?"

In all the months she had lived in this house, in all the time she had been required to spend with her in-laws, Carolina had never heard her mother-in-law stand up to the judge.

Whittier's sunken eyes blazed, but he disappeared back into the family room. Gloria waited until he was gone. "Neither of the children ate a decent supper. You'll want to feed them again before bedtime. Something healthy."

Carolina didn't know what to say. Certainly not "thank you." She wasn't quite up to that; besides, it wouldn't be appreciated. She settled on the obvious. "I'll bring them at the same time next Wednesday."

Gloria nodded, then, without saying goodbye to anyone, she started off down the hall.

Outside, Billy Ray set Kitten on her feet, and she scampered toward his car. Chris struggled to get down, and Carolina put him on the ground to follow his sister. "You'll want to feed them again before bedtime," Billy said in a perfect, tongue-in-cheek imitation of Gloria. "Something heal-l-l-thy."

Carolina giggled. She was so relieved to be safely away from the Graysons that she felt twenty pounds lighter and twenty years younger. "Do you have any ideas?"

"I was thinking ice cream."

"Exactly!"

He took her hand, sliding it inside his with an ease and familiarity that sent warm shivers down her spine. She walked beside him to the car, basking in the glow of his unspoken support. They seemed like a real family, going out together for a treat.

But they weren't a real family. For a moment she could only think of the poor choices she'd made in her life. Then Billy Ray squeezed her hand, and she realized that the days of poor choices were over.

At the corner table in Moss Bend's newest ice-cream parlor, Billy Ray watched Kitten and Chris gobbling mounds of ice cream. Carolina had wisely insisted that theirs be put in bowls with the cones perched on top. He could just imagine Chris, cone in hand, ice cream all over the front of his playsuit.

The little boy grinned up at him, as if hoping for a grin in return. Chris looked a little like his father, a fact that had perturbed Billy Ray at first. But right now Chris looked more like his mother. He had Carolina's eyes and chin, as well as her smile. Above and beyond family resemblances, he was Chris, and Kitten was Kitten. Billy Ray was fast falling in love with them.

In the past few days he had admitted to himself that he had never fallen out of love with the children's mother. He could admit that to himself now, although the love had gone underground for more than a decade. He didn't believe in soul mates. Yet he didn't know how else to explain the connection he felt to Carolina, the sense of rightness when he was with her, the need to become part of her. The last went beyond sex. He wanted her. Oh, yes, he wanted her in every possible way, and tonight had proved it beyond a doubt. Sexual frustration had reached new and painful heights. But most of all, he wanted to be with Carolina forever.

"Grandpa got mad at me." Kitten waved her spoon,

ice cream dribbling down her chin. "He said I was bad. I told him I wasn't. Just a 'vidual."

"A 'vidual?" Billy Ray grinned. "Who told you you were a 'vidual, sugar?"

"Mommy says I'm a 'vidual."

"In-di-vidual. Close enough." Carolina reached over and wiped her daughter's chin. "And so you are."

"He was mad 'cause I didn't want peas."

"Peas..." Billy Ray made a face as if he were strangling. "Peas!" He wrapped his hands around his throat.

Kitten laughed out loud, banging her spoon on the table in emphasis.

"You two 'viduals are going to get us kicked out of here." But Carolina smiled. "Kitten, it's great to be an individual. Just be sure you know what's worth standing up for and what's not."

"Yeah. Peas are worth a fight," Billy Ray said when Kitten looked confused. "But chocolate cake, now. Fighting over chocolate cake's not worth the time of day."

"I like cake," Kitten said.

"See? What'd I tell you?"

The little girl giggled again and dove back into her ice cream.

"Carolina?"

Billy Ray looked up to see an attractive redhead with a toddler perched on her hip. He got to his feet in unconscious good manners, and Carolina looked up at the same moment. A few seconds passed before she responded.

"Taylor, I haven't seen you in a while."

"I know. I'm sorry."

Carolina nodded, but her expression didn't warm.

"I really *am* sorry. I deserted you when you needed me. It was unforgivable." Taylor's dark gaze traveled to Billy Ray. "Hello, Billy Ray. We were in high school together, remember?"

He only vaguely recognized her from high school, when he had been so involved in taking care of his father that he hadn't participated in many activities. Nowadays he knew Taylor as the wife of the River County state's attorney, John Betz.

"May we sit a moment?" Taylor said.

Billy Ray held out a chair, and she sat. He did, too.

"How are you?" Taylor asked Carolina. "You look wonderful."

"I'm feeling well, thank you."

"I understand you've moved?"

"News travels fast."

"Not fast enough sometimes." Taylor's gaze flicked to Kitten and Chris, who were just finishing their ice cream. "Kitten, my Mandy's over in the corner. Do you want to go say hi to her?"

"Can I?" Kitten asked her mother

"*May* I. You bet. Scoot."

Kitten got up, and Chris followed. Kitten grabbed his hand and pulled him behind her.

"I have something to say to Carolina," Taylor told Billy Ray.

He pushed back his chair, but Carolina put her hand on his arm to stop him from leaving. "There's nothing you could say that Billy won't hear straight from me, anyway," Carolina said.

"Fine. It's about the party, Carolina."

For a moment Carolina looked blank; then she paled before Billy Ray's eyes. "The party…in December?"

Taylor nodded. "Is it true you don't remember that night?"

"For what my word is worth? Yes, it's true."

"Your word is all I'll ever need."

Carolina leaned across the table. "What's this about, Taylor? I nearly died, but you didn't visit me in the hospital. You were my best friend, but you fell off the face of the earth."

"John wouldn't let me visit. He said Judge Grayson wanted everybody to stay away. And I was fool enough to do what he wanted. But that's not what this is about." She leaned across the table, too. "I hear the judge filed for custody of your kids."

"That's right."

"You're the best mother I know."

Carolina waited.

Taylor looked as if she was going to cry. "We were at the party that night with you and Champ. You and I spent a lot of time together. You were upset, although you wouldn't say why. But I stayed nearby most of the night, because I was worried about you. I never saw you take a drink. Not the whole time we were there. Not once."

Carolina didn't respond. Billy Ray could see her fighting for control of her emotions.

"I'm representing Carolina at the custody hearing," Billy Ray said, to give Carolina some time.

"John says you're the best attorney in town."

Billy Ray had been up against John Betz too many times to take the compliment at face value. John was firmly entrenched in the politics of Moss Bend, and a close friend of the Grayson family. If John was commenting on Billy Ray's prowess as an attorney, it was because he knew the judge intended to pull out all the stops at the hearing.

"Carolina is going to need character witnesses," he said. "Will you be willing to tell Judge Sawyer what you've told us tonight?"

"If I do, John will crucify me."

"Then it sounds as if you're going to have to choose between your husband and your best friend again, Taylor."

"Billy—" Carolina put her hand on his arm to stop him. "Don't worry about it," she told Taylor. "But thanks for telling me, even if you can't tell the court."

Taylor stared at her; then she nodded grimly. "Carolina, you go on and call me as a witness. I'll tell every little thing I know about that night and any other. John can be damned. I watched a bully named Champ Grayson tear my best friend apart bit by bit. I'm not going to let my husband do the same thing to me."

When the ice cream was finished Billy Ray took Carolina back to his house to get her car.

"Can we see Three Legs?" Kitten clasped her hands in supplication. "Please?"

"Sure. But she's not in the barn anymore." Billy Ray led them toward the house.

Carolina took his arm. "I didn't notice her earlier. Billy, have you gone all soft and squishy? Are you keeping that flea-bitten animal in your house?"

He tried not to squirm. "You were busy with other things, if I recall. And there's not a flea in sight. The vet says she's in perfect health. And with the kittens due..."

"Every mother-in-need in the state of Florida is going to be on your doorstep once the word gets out about you.''

He unlocked the door, doing a visual check first to be sure nothing was out of place. The locks were new, and so was the caution. After what had happened at Joel's, he knew better than to take chances.

Three Legs, a moth-eaten calico who was fast plumping up under Billy's care, had made herself at home on his infamous sofa. The children petted her carefully, and she preened at their attention.

''What do you think about the things Taylor said?'' Carolina spoke quietly as she watched Kitten and Chris from the doorway. ''If she testifies that I wasn't drinking that night, won't that go a long way toward destroying the judge's case against me?''

''Honey, she couldn't have been with you all night.''

''What do you mean?''

''I mean the Graysons' attorney will probably use Taylor's testimony against you. He'll say that since the court has in its possession a test that proves you *had* been drinking, then obviously you were very good at keeping your problem a secret. Which could explain why so many people were fooled.''

''I can't win, can I?''

''I didn't say that.''

''No, but you are saying that every good thing that's said about me can be turned around and used to take my children away.''

''What I'm saying is that we have to be realistic. One person won't make the difference. But half a dozen or more may very well. We have the right to hire an expert to examine you and the Graysons to determine your relative fitness to parent the children.

I know the woman who the court will most probably appoint to interview the kids. She can't be bought. I'm sure she'll recommend it's in their best interest to remain with you.''

"But the Graysons can hire an expert, too, can't they?"

"I'm afraid so."

"Billy Ray, I don't know what I'll do if I lose."

He tried not to imagine that possibility. In the days since he had taken Carolina as a client and pitted himself against the Grayson family, he'd been both warned and admonished by his colleagues in the local bar association. No one thought he had a chance. Everyone who had dared to discuss the case with him thought that his decision was professional suicide. Judge Grayson would destroy him. No client would dare ask Billy Ray for representation after this. When the smoke cleared, Judge Grayson would still be sitting on the bench. Judge Grayson would be ruling for or against Billy Ray's clients. Judge Grayson—no matter what the outcome of the custody hearing— would exact revenge on Billy Ray.

But his career was secondary to something even more important. If he wasn't able to secure custody for Carolina, how would she view him? Forever after, would he be the man who had failed her at the most important moment of her life?

She seemed to read his thoughts. "I trust you, Billy. I know you're doing all you can."

But was he? And even if he did everything humanly possible, was he going to win?

"So, Three Legs. It's just us." Billy Ray stretched out in an easy chair, since Three Legs was refusing to give up her sofa. Carolina and the children had gone home for the night and arrived safely. She had called to say good-night.

"I wish I were there with you," she'd said before hanging up. "I wish Joel hadn't come to your door, too."

Lord, he wished the very same thing.

"So, Three, what do you think? Maybe I ought to stuff all of you in one of my old junk cars and head for the border come midnight. Forget River County and everything that's ever gone with it."

Joel had told him as much earlier that night, when Billy Ray walked the old man out to his car after Joel had caught him with Carolina.

"Next time, I'll call ahead," Joel had said gruffly. "Your shirttail's still hanging out."

Billy Ray had given an embarrassed laugh but no denial.

Joel had clapped him on the back. "She's the best thing ever happened to you, boy. Take her and run. Start over somewheres else. Don't stay around this place on account of me."

Now Three Legs meowed and changed positions, as if she was trying to get comfortable. Billy Ray popped the tab on a can of Dixie beer. Joel wasn't the only reason he and Carolina had to stay here and meet their fate. Self-respect was another. And what kind of life would it be for the children if they were constantly on the run? The judge had all the resources that he and Carolina didn't.

He flipped on the television, but the Braves game had been rained out, and none of the sitcoms looked appealing. Even with a mountain of work to do, he couldn't seem to get out of the chair. He propped the beer between his legs and closed his eyes. Visions of a life with Carolina moved through his mind. Carolina waking up in the morning beside him. Carolina at night in his arms. Making love to her with nothing between them except heat and desire.

When he opened his eyes a few minutes later, Doug Fletcher was rapping on his window.

He let Doug in, although he checked the shadows first to make sure his boyhood friend was alone. "What's black and blue *and* black and blue?" he asked as Doug joined him in the narrow hall.

"Shit, I don't know, Billy Ray. You're the one with all the answers."

"Well, I don't know, either, but I can sure as hell tell you it's not going to be me."

"I didn't come here to fight with you."

"Good thing. The last time we went hand to hand, I knocked out one of your teeth."

"Shit, I was nine, and it was loose to start with. Goddamned Tooth Fairy gave me a nickel, and I was lucky to get that."

Billy Ray started back to the living room. "If you want a beer, you know where to find one."

Doug joined him a moment later, a Dixie clutched in his hand. He took a seat beside Three Legs, who was twisting again, trying to get comfortable.

"Whose no 'count cat is that?"

"I guess she's mine."

"She's about to have kittens. Did you know?"

Billy Ray took a long swallow before he spoke. "Why'd you come, Doug? I notice it's dark outside. Is this how we're going to meet from now on? So the judge won't know?"

Doug didn't deny it. "You've got a good thing here, Billy Ray. You know that, don't you?"

"What good thing are we talking about?"

"This house is yours. The office in town belongs to you, the flower shop, too. Lots of folks in River County look up to you. Maybe you'll never be on anybody's Dream Team or take big, important cases right on up to the Supreme Court, but you'll always have work here."

"So?"

"So what are you giving it all up for?"

Billy Ray considered, working on the beer a little at a time. "What makes you think I'm giving it up?"

"The judge is going to beat you to a bloody pulp."

"Hey, now, that's some fine police work, Doug. You finally figured out who was responsible for that little incident at Joel's."

"We both know who was behind it."

Billy Ray was surprised to hear Doug admit it. "Just tell me, were you in on it before it happened?"

Doug shook his head, and Billy Ray believed him. They had been friends too long for Doug to lie successfully.

"So...just after the fact," Billy Ray said, raising his can in toast.

"I don't even know who was there that night. I was just told it wouldn't be worth my while to look too hard."

"Since when did you ever do what you were told?"

"Since Judge Grayson got behind me in the last election."

"Interesting. If I'd had to make a guess, that's what I would have said, too."

"Do you know what it's like to go from being lower than dirt to being sheriff?"

"You were never lower than dirt. You come from good people. Honest, hardworking people."

"Who never had a nickel, never had a day's education beyond grammar school, never had any dreams except maybe selling the next litter of hogs for a little more money. I slept under flour sack quilts, got one new pair of shoes a year, even if my feet grew. Shit, Billy Ray. I'm the first River County Fletcher to make anything out of himself."

"Yeah, you've made something out of yourself, all right. You've made yourself the fall guy for a puffed-up, sadistic county judge with delusions of grandeur."

To his credit, Doug flinched. He finished half his beer before he spoke again. "Let somebody else defend Carolina Grayson. And leave her alone. If you don't, you're going to lose more than this case. You're going to lose everything."

"Not if the people of this town stand together and tell the truth about Carolina. The judge's day of reckoning has come. But it's going to take some cooperation to make it happen."

"He's got this town clutched tight in his fist. Nothing you can do will change a damned thing." Doug finished his beer.

Billy Ray figured that Doug had said what he'd come to say. He expected him to put down the can and head for his car. But Doug wasn't quite finished.

"Do you know why your father started drinking, Billy Ray?"

"Does this have something to do with what we've been talking about?"

Doug sat forward, dangling the can between his

knees. "Did Yancy ever tell you why he couldn't face himself every night? Why he had to drink himself into a stupor just to survive?"

"Nope, he never did. And I doubt that he told you, either, since you were a snot-nosed little kid. As far as I know, nobody knows. He was an alcoholic. He drank. That's it."

"Somebody knows. The judge knows."

Billy Ray let that wash over him. He knew that his father had nursed an abiding hatred of Judge Whittier Grayson, but he'd never wanted to think much about it. His memories of his father were painful, and he'd tried to bury them. Yancy was dead, and the old saw about sleeping dogs had always made sense to Billy Ray.

"Why don't you just get on with it?" he asked at last. "Say what you've come to say, then get out of my house."

"I don't know details, just a little the judge told me."

"Uh-huh. And that was...?"

"Your daddy tried to stand up to the Grayson family, but he wasn't strong enough. In the end he sold out, just like everybody else ever has. It didn't come out too badly. He made some real money off the deal, but he had nothing much to spend it on...."

"So he started drinking?"

"That's the story." Doug got to his feet. "That's all I know."

"Why did he hate the judge so much if he made good money off the deal, supposing that's really what happened?"

"Because he didn't make as much as he thought he should have. The judge said that Yancy thought his loyalty was worth more, and he carried a grudge to his dying day."

"This is just fascinating," Billy Ray said cynically. "Trouble is, without any details, it sounds like a pack of lies."

"Look, it had something to do with a case Yancy was working on, back in the seventies. You want to find out more, just figure out when your daddy started drinking and work back from there."

Billy Ray did have his father's records. The firm had been housed in the same office, and in the years between Yancy's death and Billy Ray's return to Moss Bend, the files had been stored in the office attic, where they still resided.

"Why'd you tell me this?"

"To show you that you can't win. Nobody ever wins against the Graysons. I don't want you getting hurt."

"I already got hurt. Remember that little case you forgot to investigate?"

"That was nothing."

"Just a warning?"

Doug shook his head and looked sincerely sad. "Not a warning, a reminder. This is Moss Bend, Billy Ray. This is River County. And when it comes right down to it, you forgot you were a nobody, just like me."

9

The weeks before the hearing passed too quickly. Billy Ray worked late every night to find more people who would testify on Carolina's behalf. The hours didn't really matter. Between Carolina's new job, the children, and interviews with both the psychologists she had hired and the psychiatrist hired by the Graysons, she had no free time to spend with him, anyway. They made do with telephone calls and an occasional hastily snatched meal with the children and sometimes even Maggie. Once she brought the children to his house after work to view Three Legs' lone new kitten, but Billy Ray could feel the tension building inside him. Despite all Carolina's reassurances, he knew that if he failed her, their chances of any kind of future together were nonexistent.

On the night before the hearing, he sat at his desk poring over his strategy. Never had he been so hampered by circumstances. Although it was unfair, he knew that the custody ruling would rest heavily on the events surrounding Champ's death. In the end, Judge Sawyer would base his decision on what sort of woman Carolina was. Had Carolina run her car off the road because she'd had too much to drink, as the Gray-sons claimed? Or, worse, had she, in retaliation for years of abuse, tried to kill her husband? The record showed that she had been wearing her seat belt, but Champ had not. In desperation, had she prayed that she might save her own life and kill her tormentor?

Billy Ray rested his head in his hands and closed his eyes. Without Carolina's memory of that night to guide him, he could only make assumptions. If she'd ever had a drinking problem, there were no signs she had one now. She had little taste for alcohol. He knew all the subtle signs of a secret drinker, and she had none of them.

But what had she been like before the accident? Not surprisingly, the psychiatrist hired by the Graysons claimed that Carolina was unstable, even dangerously paranoid at times. Translated into layman's terms, his report concluded that her ability to make decisions was impaired, that by refusing to admit that she had problems she hampered her own treatment. Her prognosis, in his opinion, was poor.

But Billy Ray had the reports of two psychologists who had examined her at his request. Both had spent considerable time interviewing Carolina and the children. Both felt she was particularly well adjusted, given her circumstances, and, if anything, too willing to admit her own faults. Each of them strongly recommended she retain custody.

The rest of the evidence was similar. For every witness, report and recommendation that the Graysons had against Carolina, Billy Ray had found two in her favor. Judge Sawyer would be faced with sifting through a ton of evidence, weighing the statements, predicting the future.

In the end, Judge Sawyer would have one event on which to hang his decision. A man had died, and Carolina had driven the car he died in. Would the children ever be safe in her custody? Or would they be safer in the custody of the town's most prominent family?

Had the case been tried anywhere else, or with anyone else, Billy Ray knew he could go to bed tonight reassured. Without irrefutable evidence that the children were in danger, the court always favored parents over grandparents. But this was River County, and the Graysons always had their way.

"Billy Ray?"

Billy Ray lifted his head and gazed bleakly at Fran. "Why are you still here?"

"Because you are."

"Fran, it's way past time for you to go home."

"Hush up, boy. I found something you ought to see."

For a moment he couldn't imagine what she was talking about. For weeks, one case and one alone had consumed him. He had done his best for his other clients, but his heart had been elsewhere.

The odor of mildew wafted toward him as Fran waved an old file folder she clutched in both hands. "I got to thinking about what you said, Billy Ray. About what that no-good Doug Fletcher told you about your daddy. You know, back in those days I was just a clerk. I didn't do much more than file and answer phones, and I didn't know one case from the other. But I remember gossip. This was a busy office, and there wasn't much time for it. Unless it was important."

Billy Ray was tempted to tell Fran he was too busy for this right now. Doug's nocturnal visit still weighed heavily on his mind, but this was not the time to think about his father. Whatever had transpired between Yancy and Judge Grayson had nothing to do with Billy Ray, and absolutely nothing to do with Carolina.

"I've been up in the attic most of the day. I think you should read this." Fran held out a thin, ordinary folder, which seemed to hold just a few sheets of paper.

If the file had been as thick as most files in the office, he would have simply waved her away. "Do I have to read it now? I'm pretty busy."

"I think you should know what kind of man you're going up against tomorrow."

He held out his hand, curiosity eating away at exhaustion. "I already know what kind of man Judge Grayson is."

"You know, Billy Ray, I grew up over on the river. There was a family just down the road with three sons. Gibb, the middle one, was a troublemaker from the get-go. Everybody knew Gibb was a bad seed. Something turned up missing from our yards, we knew who'd taken it. After a while we got sort of used to it and kept everything under lock and key. It was just Gibb, after all. Then, one day, old Gibb robbed a bank in Tallahassee, and when somebody tried to stop him, he shot that poor man point blank. We'd all kind of gotten used to him, you know? He was just Gibb. A troublemaker. A bad seed."

She shrugged. "Now Gibb's on his final appeal. Billy Ray, you listen to me. Sometimes thinking you know somebody is about as dangerous as that bank robbery."

She stepped forward and put the file in his hand.

"You read this. Then you tell me you know what kind of man the judge is and maybe I'll believe you."

The Blue Bayou was cranking up for a long night. Cigarette smoke battled the jukebox to see which could pollute the air more effectively. Both pool tables were surrounded by men making noisy bets on the games in progress, and at the bar, a young woman with tangerine-colored hair was doing a provocative bump and grind to loud applause.

"Already had one fight," Maggie told Billy Ray as she caught sight of him heading toward the back of the room.

"Just one?" Billy Ray dragged his shirt collar away from his neck and loosened his tie. Maggie's window air conditioners weren't making a dent in the late August heat.

"Tempers are short tonight. I might close early." She leaned over to kiss his cheek. "I'm getting too old for this. I'm thinking about selling and moving out west to be near my grandkids."

For a moment he wanted to ask Maggie to take Carolina and her kids and make the run for the border tonight. But it was too late now. Too late to run. Too late to start over somewhere else. Tomorrow was only hours away.

"Can I get you anything?" Maggie said.

"I'm just here to see Doug."

"He's been drinking steadily. You might want to drive him home once you're done talking." Maggie headed toward the bar, most likely to make sure that the voluptuous redhead kept her shorts and halter top firmly in place.

Doug was sitting by himself, at the same table

where Billy Ray's birthday celebration had been held. He didn't look up as Billy Ray approached, or even when he sat down.

"What are you doing here?" Doug stared into the dregs of a pitcher of beer. "I thought you'd be busy all night preparing for tomorrow."

"I am preparing for tomorrow."

Doug finally looked up. "Must be some defense, then, if you're looking for answers in a joint like this."

"I'm not looking for answers. I've a mind to tell a story. Thought you'd be a good audience."

Doug narrowed bloodshot eyes. "I'm surprised you think I'm good for anything."

"I don't know if you are, but the story will be good for you. If you listen."

Doug looked away, picking up the pitcher and pouring the rest of the beer into his glass. "I guess I'm as ready as I'll ever be."

Billy Ray folded his arms. He knew just where to begin. He'd had practice telling Joel about an hour ago. "About twenty-two years ago, more or less, my daddy was approached by some workers over at the old asbestos plant in Spring Creek. Seems they were all developing health problems of one kind or another, and they thought it was because of conditions at the plant. They'd tried a few other lawyers, but none of them were all that excited about taking the case."

"Let me guess. Your daddy was different," Doug said sarcastically. "Old Yancy Wainwright, knight in shining armor."

"Yancy agreed to look into the situation for them. In those days, nobody knew just how dangerous asbestos was. There were regulations, of course, but not near as many as there are now. The thing is, the plant over at Spring Creek didn't even follow the regulations that were in place. Someone had paid off inspectors, done favors, whatever, to avoid implementing the latest safety measures. My daddy figured that out, right along with something else. For all practical purposes, the Grayson family owned the plant. They'd set up a dummy corporation to manage it, but in reality, they were the ones who got the cash at the end. Lots of it. He figured out pretty easily who was making sure things weren't being done the way they ought to be."

Doug sat back with his beer. "So? The Graysons own half of north Florida. They can make their own rules."

"I'm going to make this simple, Doug. Real simple. Yancy went after the Graysons, evidence in hand, and threatened a huge lawsuit. At first he was sure he'd win. But the judge wasn't about to take his threats lying down. He met Yancy secretly a few nights later and told him that if Yancy came after his family, they'd destroy him. Then he produced a sheaf of forged documents linking Yancy to everything from illegal gambling to embezzlement."

Doug managed a sneer, but just barely. "And Yancy got scared off that easily?"

"There was more. The judge told Yancy that he'd make an out-of-court settlement with the victims, a settlement big enough to make them think they'd gotten a good deal, but not nearly what they could have gotten if the case went to court and they won. All Yancy had to do was recommend that they take the judge's offer and keep silent, and the judge would tear up what he had on Yancy."

Doug didn't say anything, but he didn't look surprised, either.

Billy Ray leaned forward. "So it came down to this for my daddy, Doug. He could risk his whole career and fight for what he knew was right, realizing the whole time that he was pissing in the wind. Because with all the Graysons' resources, he knew he'd probably lose everything he'd worked for *and* the case. Or he could recommend that the victims settle. And if they settled, they would get a little money, which would be more than they'd ever had before, and he'd be safe."

"I guess I don't have to ask which he did, huh?"

"I guess you don't." Billy Ray sat back. "He didn't even leave records, nothing except for a couple of pages he typed and filed away in the attic, just before he died. Maybe he wanted me to find it someday, I don't know. But I do know this. What Yancy did destroyed him. It ate him up. He couldn't live with himself."

"You're telling me that's why he started drinking?"

Billy Ray met Doug's eyes in an unflinching gaze; then he reached across the table to the empty pitcher. He turned it upside down and held it there.

A minute passed. Neither man said a word. "I'm telling you that's why he started drinking," Billy Ray said at last. "Don't tell me you can't understand it."

Doug didn't say a word. Billy Ray continued to hold the pitcher in front of him, his forearm tensed and bulging with the effort. Then, slowly, he righted the pitcher and set it closer to Doug. "You've got a choice, Doug. You can get Maggie to bring you another pitcher. Or you can go home to your wife and figure out what kind of a man you are. Whatever you do, don't try to drive. If the law picks you up for drunk driving in River County, there's no telling what sort of lies might be used against you.''

Billy Ray pulled into his driveway and cut his engine, but he was too tired to get out of the car. Through his windshield, he gazed at a festival of stars lighting the clear night sky. For a moment he wanted to back out of the driveway and head toward the farthest one, with no thought of tomorrow.

Instead he gathered what little energy he had left and got out, slamming the door behind him. He had done all he could to prepare for the hearing. By this time tomorrow, Judge Sawyer would be pondering all that had transpired in the courtroom, and Carolina would be praying steadily.

And what would he be doing?

On the porch, Billy Ray fished through his pockets for his key ring, but his front door opened as he pulled the keys from his pocket. Carolina stood on his threshold, a fresh white vision against the dim light in his hallway.

He rocked back on his heels and hooked his thumbs in his pockets. "What are you doing here?"

"I wanted to see you. I went to the office after I got the children in bed, but you weren't there. Then I came here to wait. Hattie gave me your key, just in case. She's watching Kitten and Chris tonight. I hope you don't mind."

"Mind?"

"Well, I as good as broke into your house."

"Make a copy before you give the key back to Hattie and keep it for yourself."

She stepped aside so he could come in. "Why would I need my own key?"

He was at a loss for words, desperate straits for an attorney.

She filled in the silence. "Unless you'd like to see more of me than you have in the past weeks?"

"Carolina, sure I want to see more of you. But I've been busy with the hearing. You've been busy with the children and work—"

"I can't imagine ever being too busy for you. So I guess it comes down to something else. And I need to know what that something is, Billy. Before I go into that courtroom tomorrow morning, I just need to know what's going on. Because I don't want my feelings about you mixing with what happens there."

He faced her, and she pulled the door closed behind him. "Do you really think this is the right moment to discuss this? You're frantic about tomorrow's outcome. I'm preoccupied. I'm exhausted."

"You may be both, but that's not what's been between us, is it?"

He supposed it wasn't. He supposed he'd been making excuses for weeks now, but the reality was something else again.

When he didn't speak, she started toward the living room. "Come in here and sit down. I made iced tea while I waited for you."

"Don't take care of me, Carolina. I don't want you waiting on me."

"Sit down," she said, with an edge to her voice. "I'll get tea for myself, then. Unless you want to wait on me?"

He expelled a harsh breath. "I'm sorry."

"Good. I'm not."

He watched her walk away, pale skirt caressing the backs of her calves as she moved. Carolina had always had the sexiest walk imaginable. She didn't strut or sway, but the sensuous rhythm of her hips always made him think of sultry Southern nights.

Nights like this one.

Just before the birth of her kitten, Three Legs had abandoned the sofa for the guest room closet, and now he didn't have to battle her for a place to sit. He stripped off his tie and undid the top buttons of his shirt. When Carolina returned with tea for both of them, she sat in the closest chair, setting his glass on the table in front of him.

"If I've misunderstood things, Billy, please tell me now."

He couldn't talk to her like this. Carolina sitting with a spine as straight as a fence post, he with hands clamped on his knees.

"Come here." He opened his arms. "Please."

She considered, then she moved over to sit beside him, her skirt brushing his pants leg, her hip brushing his.

"You've just come out of an abusive relationship, Carolina. And I came to your rescue when you desperately needed help. We were friends a long time ago, and—"

"I don't need a history lesson. I'm every bit as aware of our pasts as you are."

He tried a different tack. "You say you don't want your feelings about me to mix with what happens tomorrow. But how do you know your feelings haven't already mixed with everything that's happened so far? Can you separate your need for support and friendship from everything else?"

She seemed to consider his words. "We've covered this before. What you're saying is that I can't tell the difference between desire and gratitude. Or desire and a need for security."

Put that way, it sounded as if he were talking about a child. And Carolina was not a little girl.

"I suppose you don't have any reason to trust me," Carolina said. "I've made a mess out of my life. What proof can I offer that I know my own mind?" She moved away just a little. He missed the warm feel of her leg against his. "But if you don't trust me in this, Billy, then you don't trust me at all. If I'm lying about my feelings, even to myself, then what else am I lying about?"

"I don't think you're lying. Of course I don't think that."

"Then I'm not very bright?"

He pushed his hair back from his forehead. "Did you ever think about law as a career? You could give John Betz a run for his money."

"Well, if I'm not lying, and you're giving me credit for some intelligence, you must think I'm unstable. Lord knows, there are those who'd agree with you."

"Of course I don't think you're unstable!"

"Then here's the verdict." She didn't smile. "I've thrown myself at you, and you're not really interested. But you're too good a man to tell me. You don't want to hurt me—"

"Shut up, Carolina." He gave up the fight that had been wearing him down for weeks. He wanted her with a pure, hot passion that had burned so brightly that keeping it contained had cost him strength and energy. He pulled her into his arms, tugging her halfway across his lap in the process.

"Don't you do this if you don't really want me." She held him away, hands flat against his shirt. "I mean it, Billy. I won't let any man hurt me again. Not in any way."

"I would throw myself off the old water tower before I'd hurt you." He held her still against him for a moment, savoring the warm weight of her breasts against his chest when her arms finally crept around him. But this wasn't a time for savoring. The fire inside him had been set free, and now it blazed brightly. If there were reasons they shouldn't make love, the flames had turned them to cinder.

"We can do this here," he said, his voice curiously deep and unsteady. "Or we can go upstairs."

"If the doorbell rings tonight, I don't want you jumping up to answer it." She pushed herself away from him and got to her feet. Then she turned and started swiftly through the house and up the stairs. He followed, catching up with her outside his bedroom door.

"I hoped tonight would end this way." Carolina pushed open the door. Candles burned on his dresser and nightstand. The windows were open, and the fragrance of honeysuckle and late summer roses drifted through them. The faded quilt that covered his bed was turned down in invitation.

She had believed in him. More than he had believed in her. He felt as if he'd been given the most precious gift.

"I took a risk and trusted you." Carolina faced him. "Now you take one. Forget everything but this. There's nothing we can do about any of the rest of it tonight. Forget everything but me. Me, and what you want."

"You are what I want." For years, he realized—although he'd stopped admitting it to himself after her marriage.

"Maybe if you had told me that a long time ago, I wouldn't have married Champ. If you had told me you wanted me when we were kids, maybe I would have waited for you. Not that it's your fault. I was a fool then, a fool who needed pretty words, daydreams and reassurances. But I'm not a fool any longer."

She reached for his shirt, her long, slender fingers unhooking the buttons and pulling them loose, one by one. She trailed one of those fingers along the newly exposed ribbon of flesh. "They say some things are worth waiting for. Do you think this is one of them?"

He closed his eyes as regret washed over him. If he'd had the courage to tell her his feelings all those years ago, things might have been different. They might have grown together, learned together, and at the beginning of their adult lives, perhaps they might have married. Perhaps this old house would be filled now with the sounds of their life together.

But they were who they were, and they'd done what they'd done. He held her palms flat against his chest and opened his eyes and his heart. "I love you, Carolina. I think I always have."

Her eyes grew misty. "And I love you."

He took her lips; she moved closer, and with one kiss the protests and the reassurances disappeared. He found the zipper of her dress; she found the clasp of his belt. They undressed each other quickly, hungry to strip away everything that still separated them.

He was a thoughtful, steady man, a man who considered everything and took care of those around him. Now he was someone else, desperate for the solace and release he would find inside this one special woman. She was beautiful; he registered that much. As perfect, as wholly female, as he had known she would be.

Her skin whispered softly against his, warm and slightly damp in the summer heat. Her hair gleamed like silver in the moonlight and felt like silk against his shoulders and chest. On his bed, she moved against him, her legs tangling with his, her hands exploring greedily, as if she needed to claim all of him at once.

Time lost its meaning except as a way to measure the agony of unfulfillment. He knew how to pleasure a woman, but now knowledge and calculation defied him, and he could only take pleasure in her. He reveled in the exquisite climb toward release, tasting and touching and joyfully drinking in the soft sounds she made.

Then he was inside her, without thought, without plan, without permission. He paused in horror as he realized what he had done.

"Billy..." She lifted her hips in invitation, straining toward him. Her eyes were wide and fixed on his. He realized that by taking his own pleasure, he had brought her to hers.

She was more than ready for him, crying out his name euphorically as he withdrew, then thrust again.

Time lost *all* meaning then, and there was no longer any agony to measure. Ecstasy grew and exploded at the moment he realized Carolina had found her own ecstasy in his arms.

10

Carolina had not expected to sleep at all that night, but back at home, in the narrow single bed under Maggie's crocheted coverlet, she dozed fitfully. She had stayed with Billy Ray until after midnight, making slow, healing love again, after their first greedy race to fulfillment. But she had wished she could stay with him until dawn. Before tonight she had only guessed how much pleasure she would find in his arms. The reality had been far sweeter and more explosive than the most detailed fantasy.

She had spent her young adulthood with a man whose interest in sex depended solely on the quantity of drugs or alcohol circulating through his system. Too much or too little, and Champ had been unable or unwilling to make love. And after the first year of their marriage, love had had very little to do with it, anyway. At college, away from the influence of his parents, Champ had been a different man. In those early days she had been able to convince herself that she loved and needed him. But after their return to Moss Bend, those tender feelings had died slowly and painfully, no matter how hard she tried to sustain them.

Now, after just hours in Billy Ray's arms, she knew that what she had felt for Champ, even in those golden days of their sad relationship, had been nothing compared to what she *could* feel.

She closed her eyes and tried not to think about Billy Ray or what lay ahead of her. The hearing was set for ten o'clock, and because of the Graysons' status, it would probably last longer than most. Judge Sawyer would bend over backward to be certain there were no hints of impropriety; Billy Ray had warned her that he would probably allow the testimony to drag on for hours. He would not want to be accused of making a hasty decision.

Outside her window, she could hear crickets, a constant and somehow comforting drone that screened out more disturbing noises. When Champ had been at his most abusive, she had learned to concentrate on sounds, the whirring of a fan, the hum of a car engine, to remove herself from his grasp. He could scream or slap her, but the most essential part of herself she had kept from him.

Now she concentrated on the crickets, closing her mind to her fears for the children and her fierce desire for a life with Billy Ray. She would get through this night, as she had gotten through others.

The crickets receded as she began to relax. Drifting between wakefulness and sleep, she opened her mind and images paraded leisurely across it. She saw Kitten as an infant, a spunky, demanding baby who had refused all attempts at scheduled feedings and had only been happy when Carolina held her. Chris, in contrast, had slept through the night almost immediately. He had been placid and cheerful, nearly as contented watching the world go by from his infant seat as he was in his mother's arms.

She could never choose between her children. They had both brought so much into her life. But she was sure that if the Graysons were to choose, Chris was the one they would ask for. Chris, who would pass on the family name.

Chris, who would be easier to mold and easier to destroy.

She sat up, panicked, and for a moment she couldn't catch her breath. Then she forced herself to lie back down. Once more she concentrated on the crickets.

Time crept by until she was no longer aware of the passing minutes. Little by little she relaxed again until at last the crickets faded and sleep claimed her. She dreamed she was in a room with too many people. Someone had made a fire in a freestanding fireplace in the corner, and the temperature was well over eighty.

She didn't like the room. Even the Christmas tree by the front door failed to add a note of cheer. The house embodied the worst of modern architecture. Spaces so undefined that privacy was impossible. Low ceilings, cold tile floors, gray expanses of concrete broken by windows that no one ever opened. Because of the array of hard surfaces, the noise was as unbearable as the heat.

She wanted to go home, but she couldn't leave Champ. If she asked a friend to take her, Champ would drive himself later, and Champ was in no shape to drive. If she left in the BMW without him, he would take his revenge against her when he got home.

And Champ's considerable talent for revenge was

heightened by liquor, which had been flowing in abundance all night.

"You're going to leave him, aren't you?"

Carolina looked up and found that Taylor had joined her. They were standing near the punch bowl and a doorway into the hall, where the room seemed coolest. People came and went here, and Carolina had wedged herself behind the table to avoid conversation. "Heavens no. It's too early to leave," she said with a forced smile. "We haven't even sung Christmas carols."

"I wasn't talking about the party."

Carolina knew that, just as she knew it wasn't safe to tell Taylor or anyone the truth. She *was* going to leave Champ. She was going to take the children and run. She had decided that evening on the way to the party. Now it was simply a matter of waiting for the moment when their chances of escape were best.

"I think you should leave him." Taylor put her hand on Carolina's arm. "Your husband's a no-good bastard."

The sympathy on Taylor's face was fixed in Carolina's mind as she began to rise above the room. Even as she hovered above the house and drifted toward the clouds, she could still see it. Then, as she looked down at a familiar road below her where her own BMW crept toward the house she shared with Champ, Taylor's face disappeared, and Champ's, distorted by rage, took its place.

"I'll kill you, bitch, if you try to leave me! See if I don't!"

Carolina woke up with Champ's name on her lips and her head bursting with pain.

Carolina looked lovely, but somber. Her pale hair was pulled back from her face by a dark headband,

and she wore a navy suit brightened only by a pale yellow scarf and conservative gold pin. Billy Ray knew that she'd gotten to bed too late last night. After all, he had been the reason. But now, looking at her eyes, he knew that even after she'd returned home, she hadn't slept.

He took her arm, pulling her against the wall in front of the room in the county courthouse where the hearing was to be held. "Are you all right?"

She attempted a smile that died before it bloomed. "I just have a headache, that's all. I'm okay."

"You're sure?"

"I... Billy, I dreamed about the party last night."

For a moment he didn't understand. Then he realized what party she was talking about. "Have you done that before?"

"I think I have. The dream seemed..." She shrugged. "Familiar. But I was so upset last night that I woke up right afterward, and I held on to it." She had been staring at the floor, as if to focus her thoughts. Now she looked up at him. "Do memories return as dreams?"

"I don't know. But if they do, the court would consider them unreliable, at best." He was an attorney today. Only her attorney, because to be anything else would damn them both.

"I know. I wasn't planning to tell the judge, but, Billy, I think... I think I was planning to leave Champ, that I'd decided to do it and he realized it."

Something clenched inside him. "Do you remember more than that?"

"He was screaming at me.... Before the party or afterward. I don't know. Maybe both. That wouldn't be unusual." She paused. "And Taylor was in the dream. We were at the party, and she asked me if I was going to leave Champ, and I told her no, because I was afraid to tell anyone what I'd decided. She put her hand on my arm." Carolina put her hand on his arm in demonstration. "She said, 'I think you should leave him. Your husband's a no-good bastard.'"

"That's pretty specific."

"That's what she said."

"She'll be here later. I'll ask her if she remembers a conversation like that. If she does, it must mean your memories are beginning to return."

"I'd like to know what happened that night. Whatever the truth, I could live with it better than this uncertainty."

He wondered if she would be able to live with Judge Sawyer's final ruling better than she had lived with that uncertainty. What would Carolina do if Chris and Kitten were sent to live with their grandparents?

He hadn't slept last night, either.

She dropped her hand and straightened her shoulders to prepare herself. The hearing was due to begin in a few minutes, and some people were already inside, although the Graysons hadn't made their appearance.

"Should we go over the things I've discussed with you one more time?" Billy Ray asked.

"No. I'm going to be calm, no matter what's said about me. No scenes, no tantrums. And I need to make it perfectly clear that I'm willing to let the Graysons see the children, just as long as they understand that all final decisions about their upbringing are mine."

"No one will hold a few tears against you. But no outbursts, and no accusations you can't substantiate."

He squeezed her hand. "I trust you. You'll do fine. Just be the woman I love."

She smiled, and for a moment she looked like a woman flirting with her lover. Then she sobered. "I'm ready."

He took her elbow and guided her toward the doorway.

The first few minutes laid the groundwork for the battle. The Graysons had arrived exactly at ten, the judge in an expensive dark suit and Gloria in a matronly dress that had obviously been purchased off the rack for the occasion. For the first time in Billy's memory she looked like someone who would bake cookies or make doll clothes for her grandchildren.

Their attorney, Sam Franklin, was a senior partner at Moss Bend's largest firm, a hometown boy with chubby cheeks and thinning hair who might take Judge Grayson's place on the circuit court bench one day. Billy Ray had gone head to head with Sam often enough to know he was a worthy opponent.

Sam stated the nature of the Graysons' concerns about Carolina and their reasons for believing that Kitten and Chris would be better off under their supervision.

Since it was Sam's job to prove his clients were right, the morning belonged to him. As Billy Ray expected, the first person to testify was the psychiatrist, Dr. Jack Bellows, who had been hired by the Graysons to evaluate Carolina's fitness as a mother. Not coincidentally, he was the same man whom they had hired after the accident to counsel her. Legal wrangling before the hearing had not produced favorable results for Carolina. Because her mental stability was at issue,

Billy Ray had not been able to convince the court that anything that had transpired in their early sessions was covered by doctor-patient privilege. Carolina had effectively waived that right by declaring she was mentally fit to be a parent.

Dr. Bellows was a stern-looking, elderly man who glanced at his watch twice and was called to task for it the third time by Judge Sawyer. His testimony was as negative and damaging as Billy Ray and Carolina had known it would be. By the time Billy Ray had a chance to do nothing more than object to a few statements, the stage had been well set.

Billy Ray approached the front when it was his turn to cross-examine the man. "Dr. Bellows, your credentials are impressive. But have you had any experience treating post-traumatic stress syndrome?"

The man frowned. "That's not my expertise."

"And your expertise is?"

"Psychoanalysis."

Billy Ray nodded, as if he understood perfectly. "Could you describe your average patient? Is it someone you treat or evaluate after a serious accident, like the one my client suffered, someone with sudden memory loss, or someone trying to cope with the violent death of a spouse?"

"My average patient is someone who chooses to examine his or her life to discover who he or she is and why he or she behaves as he or she does." He leaned forward. "Someone who is willing to work with me for years. Psychoanalysis is a long-term proposition."

"I see. And in the days immediately following the accident, is that what Carolina Grayson told you that she wanted? To analyze the events of her life, starting, I suppose, in early childhood?''

"Carolina Grayson was evasive and angry. As I've stated, she refused to admit she had problems.''

"Then why was she seeing you?''

He paused as if he saw the trap. But he couldn't refuse to answer. "She was there because Judge and Mrs. Grayson believed that she needed help.''

"Let me make sure I understand. Carolina was there under duress. She did not want psychoanalysis, yet it was forced on her. In your professional opinion, wouldn't this explain her reluctance to talk to you about the things that really mattered to her? Or to feel comfortable sharing her feelings?''

"She was belligerent and uncooperative. When I questioned her about the accident and her part in it she—''

Billy Ray couldn't believe his luck. "Excuse me, but why would you question her directly about the accident, Dr. Bellows? If your expertise is psychoanalysis and that's what she was there for, why would you concentrate on one traumatic event in her recent past? Particularly when you say that's not your area of expertise?''

"I was doing my best to help her.''

"But not, by your own admission, in any way that you're truly qualified to help.''

The judge listened to Sam Franklin's objection and waited for him to spout off a list of Dr. Bellows' credentials, but Billy Ray guessed his point had been made.

He continued. "Before we finish, Doctor, will you please tell the court why you were chosen to evaluate

Carolina for the purposes of this hearing? Do you have any special relationship with the Grayson family?"

"I've spent time with them socially."

"I see. And did you discuss Carolina with them after any of your sessions?"

The doctor was silent.

"Dr. Bellows?"

"I couldn't discuss the case in any detail. I was bound by rules of confidentiality."

"Did you discuss Carolina's case with the Graysons at all?"

"In general terms," he said at last.

"I see. And why was that?"

"They were understandably worried."

"About Carolina? Or about their grandchildren?"

"I don't know."

"While you were still working with Carolina after the accident, did they discuss their desire to take custody of the children?"

"I really can't say."

"You have to say, Doctor."

Judge Sawyer affirmed Billy Ray's words.

The doctor sighed and looked at his watch again. "Yes, Whittier told me he was going to file for custody if Carolina tried to leave with his grandchildren."

"I see. So while you were working with her, you knew that the Graysons wanted custody."

He frowned. "Yes. But I don't see what difference that makes."

"Don't you? You were probing for information and making harsh judgments about my client when, to my knowledge, a psychoanalyst does neither. Were you looking for reasons that Carolina should be separated from her children to please your old friends, or were you sincerely trying to help her, Dr. Bellows?''

"Your Honor!" Sam Franklin leapt to his feet.

"I'll withdraw the question," Billy Ray said.

The witness was excused, and Billy Ray took his seat beside Carolina.

What gains he'd made seemed to trickle away in the next hour. Sam called one witness after another to testify to Carolina's lack of fitness for parenthood. A preschool teacher of Kitten's testified that the little girl had often been preoccupied and angry, and that conversations with Carolina about the problems had led nowhere. Carolina had missed appointments and made excuses, and more than once she had been late picking Kitten up after class. Billy Ray got the woman to admit that Kitten was always clean and well dressed, that she appeared to be well fed and never physically abused. She also admitted that many parents were late getting their children, and that the preschool had been forced to institute a policy to deal with the problem.

Carolina jotted Billy Ray a note. "I was only late twice, both times because Chris was sick. And the only time I missed an appointment was when Champ refused to let me out of the house."

But the vision of Carolina as a less-than-perfect mother was forming.

The pattern broadened. Sally Whitcomb, a former next-door neighbor, claimed that Carolina left the children in her care frequently, usually on short notice, and that they often seemed unhappy and tense.

Another neighbor testified that she had heard Carolina screaming late in the evenings, and that she had feared for the safety of her children.

"Was she screaming at the children?" Billy Ray asked when his turn came.

"That's certainly how it seemed to me."

"But you don't know for sure, correct? She could have been screaming for another reason. Perhaps because someone was hurting her?"

The woman drew herself up straighter. "We don't have that kind of neighborhood."

"No? I'm afraid everyone has that kind of neighborhood." Billy Ray stepped back. "You reported the screams to the police?"

"No."

"You didn't? And why not?"

She hesitated. Her eyes flicked past him. He was almost certain she was looking at Judge Grayson. She looked back at Billy Ray. "Because her husband took care of it."

"Her husband?"

"Champ would tell her to be quiet. The screams always stopped."

"He would tell her to be quiet?"

"That's right."

Billy Ray consulted his notes. "According to my records, the closest wall of your house to the house where Champ and Carolina Grayson lived is twenty-five yards away. Does that sound right to you?"

"I suppose."

"Did you often hear normal conversations from the Grayson home?"

"Of course not."

"Could you hear a conversation spoken in a normal tone of voice?"

"Not likely."

"Then when Champ *told* Carolina to be quiet, it

wasn't in a normal tone of voice. In fact, he was shouting at her, wasn't he?"

She glared at him. "I suppose he was."

"Now, you could hear what Champ said. You've told us he told Carolina to be quiet. Correct?"

"That's right."

"But when it was Carolina's turn you only heard screaming. You didn't hear words that you can report now? Just screams?"

She didn't answer right away. He had to prod her.

"I guess that's right," she said reluctantly.

"So you really have no way of determining who she was screaming at or why."

"No."

Billy Ray clenched his hands in his pockets, but he composed himself without betraying his feelings and took his seat as Sam, on his redirect examination, tried to clear up the doubts Billy Ray had raised. Carolina didn't look at him.

The neighbors and Kitten's teacher were only a warm-up, good people, probably, who believed they were doing their Christian duty. The next series of witnesses had even harsher testimony to give. One was a bartender at a local hotel who claimed that Carolina was a frequent customer and that he'd had to refuse her service more than once because she'd already had too much to drink.

Billy Ray had conferred with Carolina when the witness had been listed. "Have you ever seen him before?" he'd asked.

"The only time I ever saw him was when I went to the hotel to pick up Champ, who was usually in a back room passed out cold. The next day Champ always went back and paid this guy to keep quiet."

Billy Ray knew better than to spend much time on a witness who would lie so blatantly and blithely. He walked to the front. "Before this trial, I asked if you would be willing to give the court the names of customers who might have seen Carolina at the bar, just so we could corroborate your testimony. At that time, you refused. Would you mind explaining why?"

"I could get somebody in trouble like that. The guys who spend a lot of time at the bar aren't always supposed to be there. Maybe their old ladies think they're at church or something." He gave what passed for a grin and winked.

"Then perhaps now you'll give the court some dates and times when you claim to have seen my client drunk, so that my client has a chance to defend herself."

"I don't keep a guest book. I just know what I seen."

Billy Ray propped his hands on the railing outside the witness stand. "And all *we* know is what you *say* you've seen."

"I ain't lying. Why would I lie?"

"Why indeed?" Billy Ray said.

The lies continued until it was almost time to adjourn for lunch. Strangers who claimed they'd seen Carolina drinking alone in bars. A furnace repairman who claimed that Carolina had been disoriented on the morning in November when he went to service her furnace and that he had seen an open bottle of bourbon on her kitchen counter. A baby-sitter who insisted that she'd been forced to stay behind one evening after Carolina returned home in order to get her into bed because Carolina was too drunk to manage it herself.

Billy Ray knew the baby-sitter's story. He had

asked Carolina about the woman when her name turned up on the Graysons' list. "Did this woman ever really sit for you?"

"Once, a couple of years ago. She was working for a sitting service then, and she came highly recommended. I caught her leaving with a silver pencil case I kept on an upstairs bookshelf. Of course I never let her in the house again. But I told the Graysons the story."

"Was anyone with you when you caught her?"

"I think... You know what? Yes. My friend Eden Harper. We were in an evening exercise class together, and she'd come home with me to borrow something. She was there. She teased me about it for a long time afterward."

"Do the Graysons know she was there?"

"I don't remember telling them. But it was a long time ago."

Now Billy Ray stood and reserved the right to recall the witness later in the afternoon. He didn't add that Eden, who would appear later as a character witness for Carolina, would be refuting the woman's story and hopefully establishing a pattern of deceit among the Graysons' witnesses.

The judge conferred with the bailiff for a moment, giving Carolina time to whisper in his ear, "I don't know if I can stand much more of this."

Her voice wavered. He didn't look at her. He could only imagine how hearing these lies was affecting her. "You'll be all right. We'll break for lunch soon."

The last witness Sam Franklin called was Taylor Betz.

Billy Ray got to his feet and asked if he could approach the bench. "Your Honor, I don't know what kind of game's being played here, but Taylor Betz is our witness."

"Your Honor, Mrs. Betz has agreed to give testimony that affects Judge and Mrs. Graysons' case. Under the circumstances, I think she should be allowed to give it now."

They argued for a moment, but in the end Judge Sawyer ruled that Taylor could take the stand for the Graysons. With a knot in his stomach, Billy Ray sat down.

"What's going on?" Carolina touched his arm. "Why is Taylor testifying now? They aren't finished, are they? She's on our side."

"Apparently not anymore."

Taylor, wearing a simple green dress and a bleak expression, took the stand, and the preliminaries were finished quickly. "Mrs. Betz, what is your relationship to Mrs. Carolina Grayson?" Sam asked politely.

"We've been friends since high school."

"Would you say that you know her well?"

"Yes." Taylor's voice was soft.

"And were you approached by Mr. Wainwright and asked to testify as to her good character?"

"Yes." This time her voice was even softer.

"Instead you decided to testify for Mr. and Mrs. Whittier Grayson, correct? In fact, you asked for the opportunity to do so."

"Yes." Softer still.

"Let's go back in time a little. We've heard testimony today that Carolina Grayson has a problem with alcohol. Have you seen this demonstrated yourself?"

Billy Ray objected, pointing out that the witness was not an expert at determining whether someone had an alcohol problem.

"Then let's be more specific," Sam said. "On the night of December 20, which is the night that Champion Grayson died in an automobile accident with his wife at the wheel, did you see Carolina Grayson drinking too much?"

Taylor hesitated. "Carolina was upset that night, and she was acting strange. She didn't seem to want to talk to me or anyone. She spent the evening standing beside the punch bowl. The punch was strong, made with rum and red wine and some other liquor, I think. I had one cup and realized I couldn't handle any more. But Carolina stayed there the whole night, and afterward I realized why."

"Your Honor, Mrs. Betz is simply making a guess," Billy Ray said.

"I'm perfectly capable of telling what Mrs. Betz is doing," the judge said coldly, turning back to the witness to dismiss Billy Ray.

"What happened right before Carolina Grayson left the party?" Sam asked. "Take your time and tell it exactly the way it happened."

"Sometime just before midnight Champ decided it was time to go, and he took Carolina's arm in the hallway. I was the only one around. Everyone else was inside by the piano singing Christmas carols. Carolina shook off Champ's hand and told him not to touch her. I was worried about her. She hadn't been acting like herself at all that evening. So I asked if she wanted me to drive Champ home so she could stay a little longer." She hesitated. "Champ had been drinking. He...he wasn't in any shape to drive."

Sam waited, and when Taylor didn't go on, he prodded gently. "What happened next, Mrs. Betz?"

Taylor's voice was so low that Billy Ray had to

strain to hear her next words. "Carolina said no, that she would drive him. She said that she had business on the trip home that only she could take care of. And fifteen minutes later, Champ Grayson was dead."

11

Carolina faced Billy Ray. "Yes, sometimes I left the children with Sally on short notice. I was off trying to find Champ or trying to get him home without anyone else knowing. He would call me and threaten suicide, or his secretary would call and tell me he had passed out in his office. I never knew when or what I'd have to do to keep his double life a secret. Of course the children were fretful at Sally's house. They sensed something was wrong. It was!"

He put his arm around her and pulled her to rest against his chest. They had come back to his office for lunch just so that Carolina would have a place to discharge some emotion. The morning had been devastating.

He stroked her hair. "It's not Sally's testimony that's going to be our biggest hurdle."

She pulled away. "John made Taylor testify. She wouldn't have said those things about me if John hadn't forced her. The Graysons got to him, and he got to Taylor. No one's safe, Billy Ray. No one in this town except you and me will stand up to them! I'm going to lose my children!"

"We still have the two psychologists, your counselor and our character witnesses." He didn't tell her that Fran had just informed him that two of their witnesses—one of whom was Eden Harper—had decided not to testify. And what about those who were still going to speak for Carolina? Had Judge Grayson gotten hold of them, too? Would their testimony damage Carolina more than it would help her?

Carolina refused to be comforted. "They still have Doug Fletcher and the Graysons themselves. I know exactly what all of them will say!"

Fran appeared in the doorway. "There's a lowlife waiting in the library to see you."

By the expression on Fran's face, Billy Ray knew this was something he needed to take privately. Fran bustled into the room and told Carolina to sit down while she made her a sandwich and some tea.

"Just tell me this is going to be all right." Carolina grabbed his hand. "Tell me you can make magic, Billy."

"I'm going to try my damnedest." He squeezed her hand; then he excused himself, leaving Carolina in Fran's care.

Doug was waiting in the library. Billy Ray stepped inside and closed the door to face his boyhood friend. "I gather this isn't a social call?"

"I've got something for you." Doug pulled a slip of paper out of his back pocket and handed it to Billy Ray.

Billy Ray glanced at a series of digits, obviously a long-distance telephone number. "What's this?"

"Just call that number. Tell them who you are and ask about Francis Turner. You'll get an earful."

It took Billy Ray a moment to understand. "Francis

Turner, as in Frank Turner, the lab technician who performed the blood alcohol test on the night of the accident?''

"One and the same."

All Billy Ray's attempts to find Frank Turner and subpoena him to testify had met with failure. Turner had pulled up stakes in January, paid off the lease on his apartment, quit his job at the county hospital and disappeared without a trace. Billy Ray had planned to point out this strange turn of events to the judge as he presented Carolina's case and ask that the lab test be thrown out because of it. But his chances were only fifty-fifty of getting what he wanted.

Now he wove the piece of paper through his fingers. "You're testifying after lunch, aren't you?"

"Yep. That's the way things stand." Doug hooked his fingers through his belt. "You might want to ask me a few questions about the accident scene, Billy Ray."

"I intend to."

"Well, you might want to ask me exactly where I found Champ Grayson that night. I was in a hurry, you know. Trying to get Carolina to the hospital. Trying to see if anything could be done for Champ. Of course the poor bastard was as dead as he could be, but I didn't know that right away. I just might have left a few details out of my report, though. A few things the court might want to know."

"I'll remember that."

Doug looked away. "I've been remembering a few things myself this morning. Do you remember the time I crossed Old Man Roland's land to get to the river, and I left his gate open by mistake?"

Billy Ray played along. "Uh-huh. It was a good

year for catfish, and you had orders to bring a mess home or your mama would tan your hide.''

"Back in those days, if I didn't catch a catfish or two, we ate butter beans and corn bread for supper and called it a meal.''

"We had days like that at my house, too.''

"Well, Mr. Roland lost a cow out on the road, on account of my leaving the gate open.''

"I remember.''

"He was going to have me arrested for trespassing, do you remember that?''

Billy Ray didn't reply.

Doug shook his head, as if he still couldn't believe it. "You told him you'd help me work off the cost of that cow. You didn't have a thing to do with it, but you offered to help me out, anyway. You were twelve. We pulled weeds and picked fruit and cleaned manure out of his stinking old barn all summer long.''

"Is that why you gave me this?'' Billy Ray held up the slip of paper. "Old debts?''

"Nah. It's just that I've been living my life on old memories. Remembering what it was like to be no-body and poor and wanting what everybody had but me. I wanted to be a gentleman. I wanted what Champ Grayson was born to, but look where it got old Champ. I guess I'm going to settle for being a no 'count red-neck instead. But I'll be goddamned, Billy Ray, if I'll be a drunk along with it, or a double-crosser, either.''

Billy Ray put the paper in his pocket and stuck out his hand. And the weight of the world seemed to lift from his shoulders as Doug clasped it in his own.

Billy Ray came out of his meeting with Doug to find Carolina gone.

"She's over at the day care checking on the kids," Fran told him. "She was too nervous to eat. I tried my best."

He should have expected it. Carolina was sure she was going to lose her children. He couldn't blame her for wanting to be with them now, even if it was only for a little while.

"I've got to make a call. Don't put anyone through, but let Carolina into my office if she comes back."

"She said she'd meet you at the courthouse." Fran hesitated. "She was upset. It's not going well, is it?"

"It's not finished yet. But I'll walk over to the church after I'm off the phone and get her. She shouldn't be alone right now."

He made his call, and when he was finished, his body felt lighter still. He said goodbye to Fran and crossed the street. The Methodist church where the day care center was located was only two blocks away. He covered them quickly, but he didn't even have to go inside to find Carolina. She was standing beside a tree looking over the churchyard where Chris and the other two-year-olds were sliding and climbing over bright plastic play equipment.

Billy Ray came up beside her, but she didn't turn. "Does Chris know you're standing here?" he asked.

"He hasn't even looked up. He's having such a good time. He's so easily pleased, so happy to go along with everyone else's plans for his life."

Billy Ray thought about his talk with Doug, and about the phone call he'd just made. "You'll be the one making those plans for a long time to come, Carolina."

"If I'm not..." She faced him, placing her finger against his lips when he started to protest. "If I'm not,

I don't ever want you to blame yourself, Billy Ray. You've restored my soul by believing in me. You've fought for me when no one else would. You've stood up to the worst threats. Someday I'll tell the children about this, about what you did for all of us. Even if the Graysons get custody, I'll tell them what a gentleman you were to fight and to care. The children will need to know what a real gentleman looks like, and no matter what happens, that's something I can show them. I hope someday Chris will turn out to be just like you."

He gathered her into his arms. His heart beat so fast he felt dizzied by it. "You haven't given up, have you?"

"Not by a long shot. But, Billy, you have to know that no matter what happens in that courtroom this afternoon, I still love you. I still believe in you."

He didn't know how he could hold her closer, but he did.

Sam Franklin looked like a cat lapping away at a milk cow's titty. In a criminal trial, Taylor's testimony would not have been strong enough to carry any weight. But in a custody hearing, the judge had to consider many factors. And Taylor's words would affect Judge Sawyer deeply. She was Carolina's friend; she had even been asked to testify for Carolina. And nothing Billy Ray had asked her in his cross-examination could get her to admit that she had been coerced by her husband into testifying for the Graysons.

Billy Ray wanted to wipe the smug expression off Sam's face, but he knew exactly how to play his cards. He watched as Sam called Doug to the stand to talk about the night of the accident. Carolina fidgeted beside him, but she calmed after Doug was sworn in. She didn't know what was about to happen. Billy Ray had chosen not to tell her. As much as he hated to string her along, he wanted her reaction to Doug's testimony to be genuine.

Sam referred to his notes. "Sheriff Fletcher, will you tell us about the night of the accident that killed Champion Grayson?"

"Certainly. I got a telephone call at home from a woman who lived down the road from the accident site. She'd heard the crash. I called the paramedics and took off. I don't live far away. I got there in a few minutes, before the ambulance arrived."

"And what did you find?"

"Champion Grayson was dead, and Carolina Grayson was seriously injured."

"Who was driving the car?"

"Mrs. Grayson was at the wheel. She was still behind it when I arrived, and she was unconscious. Mr. Grayson was beside her."

"And was another car involved?"

"No, sir. She ran off the road and hit a tree. The car was demolished. We had to have it hauled to the junkyard."

"Tell us about the road conditions that night."

"The temperature was in the forties, but there hadn't been any rain. The roads were dry."

"In your expert opinion, did the roads seem hazardous?"

"Not at all. They were perfectly safe."

"And did you notice any reason why Carolina Grayson might have run off the road? A pothole, a barrier, debris? Any obstructions of that nature?"

"Nothing. And I looked carefully, too."

"Then, in your opinion, Sheriff, what was the reason for the accident?"

"Alcohol."

"And what made you think that was true?"

"The smell was unmistakable. The car smelled like a distillery."

Billy Ray didn't object, although clearly, by Sam's pause, he expected him to.

"So you ordered a blood alcohol test, Sheriff? To be done at the hospital?"

"It's pretty much routine in situations like this one."

"I see." Sam turned to the judge. "I have here the original blood test performed on Carolina Grayson that night. I'd like to enter it, if I may."

Billy Ray had talked to Carolina about the problems with tests of this nature and his plans to object strongly to this one, but now he did nothing. When she frowned at him, he just shook his head slightly, then turned his eyes back to the front.

"Do you have any objections?" Judge Sawyer asked him.

"I have no objections."

Sam turned back to Doug. "The test concludes that Carolina Grayson's blood alcohol level was three times as high as the law allows." He sounded like a young boy who had just been given a special birthday present. "Was this what you expected to find?"

Doug sat back a little and crossed his arms. "As a matter of fact, no."

Sam looked startled, but he recovered quickly and tried again. "Sheriff, you ordered the test. You must have expected to find her alcohol level was high."

"No, sir, I didn't. As I explained, the tests are routine in a case like this one. I make sure they're always performed. And I have a technician up at the hospital who I always use. A fellow named Greg Cameron. He's the best, and I can trust him. Unfortunately, he was out of town for the holidays."

Sam ignored the last part. "Sheriff, according to your own testimony, the car smelled like a distillery."

"But I didn't have any reason to think the smell was coming from Mrs. Grayson."

Sam didn't recover as quickly this time. "Still, the test was conclusive. So whether you were surprised or not, she was the driver, by your own testimony. And the test results stated that she was legally drunk."

"That's right. That's what the test said."

Sam seemed to consider where to go from there. Finally he stepped back. "No further questions, Your Honor."

Billy Ray stood and ambled toward the front. Doug met his eyes. And waited.

"Sheriff Fletcher," Billy Ray said, "you've described the accident scene for us. No water on the roads, no barriers, not even a pothole. You've said that you thought alcohol was involved, yet you've said that you didn't expect to find that Carolina had been drinking. I think we're all a little confused. Will you clarify a little, please? What exactly did you find when you arrived at the accident scene? Will you describe what you found inside the car?"

"Well, first, both Mr. and Mrs. Grayson were still inside, and she was unconscious. Mr. Grayson had been killed on impact—that was determined later by the coroner. Mrs. Grayson was slumped over the wheel. She'd hit her head on it, but she had her seat belt fastened, and that's what saved her in the end."

"No air bags?"

"No, it was an older model."

"Go on, please."

"Mrs. Grayson's arms were dangling at her sides, but Mr. Grayson's hands were still gripping the steering wheel. In fact, he had one arm threaded through it. He wasn't wearing a seat belt. Frankly, it looked to me like he had grabbed the wheel and forced the car off the road. And that's why I ordered a blood alcohol test for both of them, because it was clear to me that—"

"Objection!" Sam was on his feet, his cheeks bright red and his eyes wild. "This is opinion. This isn't fact."

"I believe you invited the sheriff here to tell us what he found," Billy Ray said. "And he is an expert witness, with opinions based on years of experience."

A chair screeched along the wood floor behind him. Billy Ray turned and saw that Carolina was standing, her hands resting on the counsel table as if to hold herself erect. Tears were streaming down her cheeks. "I told Champ I was going to leave him. I couldn't stand the abuse any longer. I couldn't stand living that way. He got drunk at the party, so drunk he started to scream at me on the way home. And for the first time I screamed back. I told him I was going to take the children and leave! I'd already decided earlier that night to leave him. That's what I meant when I told Taylor I had business to take care of with him. Champ told me he'd kill me if I left. He called me terrible names and threatened to kill me again. I was so tired of hearing that. So I dared him to try...."

She put her face in her hands and began to sob. "I remember...."

Billy Ray reached her side and took her in his arms. "Shh. Carolina..."

"He grabbed the steering wheel! When I fought him, he hooked his arm through it. I remember now! I saw the tree coming...." She was shaking uncontrollably.

"We'll have a recess," the judge ordered. "Sheriff Fletcher, you are excused for now. Mr. Wainwright, calm your client or she'll be required to spend the rest of these proceedings outside in the hall." Judge Sawyer rose and retired to his chambers.

Billy Ray eased Carolina into her seat; then he sat beside her, chafing her hands.

"I dared him, Billy," she said through her tears. "For the first time in years I felt powerful. I finally realized I had to leave him, no matter what, and I knew that no matter what he did, he couldn't hurt me anymore."

"He almost killed you."

"But he didn't!"

"Do you think anybody will believe these lies?" someone roared.

Billy Ray looked up to see Whittier Grayson towering above them, Sam Franklin hanging on to his arm.

"I believe her," Billy Ray told him. "And in what passes for your heart, so do you."

"Your client has just shown herself to be the unstable, paranoid woman I've claimed all along!"

Billy Ray got to his feet. "You know, you might have had a chance at pulling this off, Judge Grayson. Except for one small detail. When you pay off too many people, eventually someone does something foolish. And Francis Turner wasn't too bright to begin with. You should have known better than to trust him.''

He looked beyond Whittier to Gloria, who had joined Sam Franklin in the effort to get her husband to leave. "Mrs. Grayson, the man who performed the blood alcohol test on Carolina on the night of your son's death disappeared two weeks later. I couldn't find him to question him.''

The judge was sputtering with fury. "This has nothing to do with her, with this case, with—''

Billy Ray cut him off. "It has everything to do with her. Your wife can stop this farce before it goes any further, before I tell the court what I discovered this afternoon.''

Billy Ray turned his gaze back to Gloria. "Francis Turner, the technician who performed the test, is in jail in Minnesota right now, awaiting trial on a manslaughter charge. It seems he was busy spending some of the money your husband paid him for falsifying Carolina's lab test, and he got into a brawl. Somebody died. The Minnesota cops traced him back here after he told them where he'd gotten the money. They thought he'd stolen it. Doug Fletcher had a little talk with them yesterday.''

"I don't believe it. I—'' Gloria grabbed her husband's arm. "Did you do this, Whittier?''

"Of course I didn't! Who do you think you're talking to? I'm the circuit court judge! Nobody can prove I did anything wrong. There is no trail, nothing to lead anyone to me. I—''

She shoved him hard, both hands against his chest. He let out a gasp.

"You destroyed my son," she said in a low voice. "And I believed, deep in my heart, that we had another chance with Champ's children, a chance to do it right. But I was a fool. Worse than a fool. Carolina's none of the things you wanted me to believe, is she? She didn't kill Champ. I can see it clearly. You killed him!" She shoved him again. "*You* killed him."

Billy Ray came out from behind the table, and with Sam's help, he pulled Gloria from her husband. The bailiff and Doug materialized to lead Judge Grayson off to one side of the courtroom. Sam took Gloria off to the other.

Carolina rose and faced Billy Ray, the counsel table between them. "It's over, isn't it?"

"It's over," he confirmed.

"I'll keep the children?"

"I don't think there's any question about that now. We can probably prove that Turner's sudden wealth is due to your father-in-law, if it comes to that. But I don't think it will."

Sam approached them, more deferential than Billy Ray had ever seen him. He cleared his throat and addressed Billy Ray. "Gloria's willing to settle. She'll agree to Carolina having full custody, as long as she retains visiting rights."

Carolina answered for herself. "What if she changes her mind later? What if I have to go through this all over again?"

"We'll get Judge Sawyer to issue a consent order. It's as binding as a judgment," Billy Ray told her. "The children are yours. After this travesty, no court would even consider another suit." He reached for her hands. "The children are yours, Carolina. All yours. We won."

With tears streaming down her cheeks, she leaned over the table and kissed him.

They were separated then, by well-wishers who had come to testify for her, Hattie and the two psychologists who wouldn't be called on to testify now, as well as the old friends who hadn't deserted her. Billy Ray stepped back and watched Carolina basking in the warmth of her victory and her acceptance back into Moss Bend society.

More than a few feet seemed to separate them. As people crowded around her, he felt a gulf widening with every hug, every word of congratulations. Last night, when he had made love to Carolina, he had convinced himself—or so he'd thought—that she knew her own mind, that she was not simply grateful to him, that she had not come to him only out of a need for support and encouragement.

Last night he had confessed his love to Carolina, a love as deep and true as forever. And in return she had told him that she loved him. But now he remembered the day so many years before when he had discovered that Carolina was going to marry Champ Grayson. On that day he had seen her from a distance, too, surrounded by giggling high school girls and their envious mothers as she showed off her sparkling engagement ring.

On that day he had walked away—seemingly forever—because he had known, deep in his adolescent heart, that he had never had a chance with Carolina. They were different people from different worlds, and she needed something he could never give her.

More than a few years had passed, but for the first time in the weeks since he had taken Carolina into his home, Billy Ray saw himself without illusions. On the outside he was a successful adult with much to offer a woman, but on the inside he was still that adolescent boy, yearning for the girl he loved but unable, somehow, to claim her. Then Carolina had needed the acceptance of Moss Bend society. Now she needed time and space to find out exactly who she was. With no interference. With no demands.

Carolina looked up from her circle of admirers and sent him a smile of purest joy. He smiled back at her, but Billy Ray had already begun to protect his heart.

Doug came to stand beside him. "What'll she do now, do you suppose?"

"She has a thousand choices, doesn't she?"

"Son, if I'm not mistaken, you're choice number one."

"She's been through a lot. She needs time before she makes any decisions."

"You know, Billy Ray, there are some things about being a gentleman that just don't make any sense. Giving a woman too much time to make up her mind would be one of them."

Billy Ray picked up his briefcase and did what he'd done so many years ago. He took one last look at Carolina surrounded by her friends; then he walked away.

12

He wished he were a knight in shining armor. He wished that he had single-handedly slain all of Carolina's dragons. But he had only carried the standard.

Billy Ray stared over the hillside view just outside of town. Summer had just about come and gone, and Route 194 still wasn't fixed. Today Gracie Burnette, the flagger, was wearing cutoffs and a baggy T-shirt, sending traffic up and down the hill with the fancy waves and flourishes of an Olympic rhythmic gymnast.

"How're you doing, Billy Ray?" she called as he inched in her direction.

"No complaints." He wasn't about to tell her the truth, that he was tied up in a million and one knots, not to mention tired and hot. His air conditioner had stopped working again, and even Joel had given up on it. It was time to replace it or look for another car, but new carpet for his office had wiped out what little extra cash he had.

He was nobody's idea of a knight, nobody's hero. He was a backwoods lawyer, in debt up to his eyeballs, whose clients, like the Burnettes, would be grateful till the day they died but never finish paying off their bill. And most of *them* would stop using his services the minute they realized that from now on Judge Whittier Grayson wouldn't give them a fair hearing if Billy Ray represented them.

Gracie grinned. "You come see us now, you hear? You don't come 'round near often enough."

He leaned out the window and managed a grin himself. "I'll be over soon. Give that baby boy a hug for me."

She waved him past, and he started up the hill. When he reached the top, Moss Bend lay spread out in front of him, a lazy north Florida town fading and wilting in the afternoon sun. He had the craziest notion to turn his car around, sail past Gracie and keep right on going. A world existed beyond the boundaries of River County. A world where he could forget his roots and still make something of himself. Joel would understand. And there were roads and planes in and out of the area. He could be at Joel's side in a matter of hours whenever he was needed.

But it wasn't only Joel who was keeping him here.

The parking lot at the Blue Bayou was jammed with cars, and he frowned as he pulled into the last space at the very edge. He didn't know any reason why Maggie's place would be crowded this early. There were no important games on television, and Donny and the Moondogs, Maggie's house band, didn't start their gig until nine. But it was the end of a hot week, the end of a hot month, and he supposed that Maggie's was as good a place as any to keep cool.

Inside, Maggie greeted him with a warm hug as he adjusted to the air-conditioning and the old Reba Mc-Intire standard wailing from the jukebox. "I've hardly seen you, boy! What's keeping you so busy these days?''

''I just had a lot of catching up to do.'' As far as it went, it was the truth. After Carolina had won custody of her children, there had been a backlog of work waiting for his attention. Not that the work was going to continue.

''Well, don't you make yourself so scarce anymore. Those kids keep asking about you. They're wondering where you're keeping yourself.''

Regret was as sharp as a knife slicing through him. ''I miss them, too.''

Maggie looked like she didn't want to change the subject but knew better than to continue. ''Doug's at his table.''

''He tells me he might buy this place if he doesn't win reelection in the fall.''

''Oh, he'll win. People 'round here understand temptation, but they believe in redemption. Doug made sure the truth came out about Carolina. That's probably more than they'd get from the next guy. Besides, they got too many earthquakes out in California. Guess I'll be around the Bayou a few more years.''

She went off to insinuate herself between two young men who were arguing over a mousy woman in a denim jacket.

Doug was working on a pitcher of Coke. He poured a glass for Billy Ray as he made himself at home across the table.

''You're looking hot and horny, son,'' Doug said, pushing the glass toward him.

''Considering that I'm sitting down, I'd say you're just making a bad guess about the second part.''

"That hangdog expression's all the proof I need. You mooning over Carolina Waverly?"

Billy Ray found it interesting that every time he had heard Carolina's name since the hearing, she was Carolina Waverly. It was as if Carolina had never had the unfortunate luck to be connected to the Graysons.

The custody hearing and all that had gone on in the courtroom were supposed to be private, but people in town had discovered the most important parts. Moss Bend's golden boy Champ Grayson had abused his wife, and after his death Carolina had been framed by his father so that she would lose custody of her children. Even Taylor Betz, Carolina's closest friend, had twisted the truth to assure that her state's attorney husband stayed in Whittier Grayson's good graces.

John Betz had resigned last week to take a position down in Boca Raton. Taylor had left Moss Bend the next day, supposedly to look for a house and settle their children before the beginning of the school year. Judge Grayson, though, was still handing down rulings.

"I'm not mooning." Billy Ray downed his Coke in two long swallows.

"I remember you mooning over Carolina after she told everybody she was going to marry Champ. You were always quiet. You got quieter. Like now."

"That was a long time ago. Your memory doesn't go back that far."

"I remember things that really matter. Things that happened to you always mattered to me."

Billy Ray toyed with his empty glass. "Maggie doesn't think you'll lose the next election. Not that my support's worth much, since my career here in Moss

Bend is Southern-fried history, but just so you know, I'll stand up for you.''

Doug grinned. ''The devil you know's always better than the one you don't, huh?''

''You were never the devil. You were just running scared. But you stopped. It takes a big man to stop running, especially when the past is chasing him.''

''You never ran. Never in your whole life, and I've been there for most of it, so I know, Billy Ray.''

''Don't make me out to be a hero, Doug. I'm nobody special.''

''There's a lot of folks around here who think differently.''

Something about the way Doug said the words alerted Billy Ray. He looked up from his glass and saw most of the population of the Blue Bayou on their feet moving in his direction. Maggie was leading the way with a huge sheet cake blazing with sparklers.

''Damn it, Doug...''

Doug leaned back in his chair. ''It's a new day in Moss Bend, Billy Ray. A day when maybe we'll get on with being more of a town and less of a kingdom. Judge Grayson announced his retirement from the bench this afternoon. Rumor has it a delegation of the town's leading citizens forced him into it. You didn't know, did you?''

He hadn't known, but right now his attention was riveted on the events around him. ''What's going on here?''

''We're having a little celebration in your honor. See, lots of people think you ought to consider running for office yourself. A couple of important ones have sure come open recently, haven't they? But even if you don't run, we just want to say thanks. Thanks for standing tall.''

Embarrassed, Billy Ray closed his eyes as the crowd surrounding him began to sing ''For He's a Jolly Good Fellow.''

Kitten was looking forward to kindergarten. She had a bright yellow Hercules lunch box, a new dress with a sunflower on the pocket, white tennis shoes with real laces, and a backpack with one pouch for pencils and one for paper.

She found her mommy in the kitchen giving Chris the last of his supper. Chris always made a mess, but Mommy never seemed to care. Right now he was tearing up bits of bread on his high-chair tray and smashing them flat with his plastic cup.

''I want to show Billy Ray my lunch box.'' Kitten stood in the doorway and watched her mother washing dishes at the sink.

''Well, I'm sure he'll want to see it.'' Carolina said the words as if she meant them, but she didn't smile.

''How come he doesn't come and see us anymore?''

Carolina didn't answer for a moment. Then she turned, taking a dish towel from the rack beside the sink to wipe her hands. ''He's very busy, Kitten.''

''And I want to show him my room.'' Kitten's room was yellow now. The bright yellow of her lunch box. Maggie had helped her paint it again last weekend, and she hadn't even minded that Kitten had gotten paint in her hair.

Carolina continued to dry her hands. ''The next time he comes over, you can show him everything.''

Kitten was tired of waiting. She got tired easily. Her grandmother Grayson told her that she needed more patience, and maybe she did. But she hadn't gotten any yet—as a matter of fact, she was tired of waiting for patience, too.

"Well, I'm going to go and get him!" She stuck out her bottom lip as far as it would go. When she did that in front of Billy Ray he always told her that her lip was wide enough to serve a pizza on.

"Kitten, you're not going anywhere." Carolina threw the dish towel on the counter. "He lives miles away."

"I can walk! I walked miles and miles that night we went to Joel's Garage. You know I did!"

"Well, you're not walking to Billy Ray's. You'd get lost, and it's getting dark. That's final. Understand?"

"Then you do it!" Kitten heard her voice rising, but she didn't care. "You miss him, too. I know you do. And you're old enough to drive. I'm not!"

Carolina stared at her; then she began to laugh. "You're not old enough to baby-sit, either, pumpkin pie. I can't just go off and leave you and Chris alone."

"You don't have to. Hattie said she'd come."

"When did you talk to Hattie?"

"I called her. Her number's 555-2231. She told me and I remembered. 'Sides, it's written down by your phone. She's coming over. We talked about it. She said you ought to go to Billy Ray's house and shake some sense into him."

Carolina looked away. "Did she?"

"Can you really shake sense into people?"

"I'm afraid not."

"Can you try?"

"I'm afraid not."

"Well, why not?"

Carolina looked back at her. "What?"

Kitten raised her voice. "Why not? Is that one of those things my grandmas say?"

"Your grandmas?"

"They're always saying stuff like that. Girls can't do this. Girls can't do that. Girls are supposed to be pretty all the time. Girls are supposed to be quiet. Aren't girls supposed to tell boys when they're being stupid?"

"How old did you say you were, Kitten?"

"Silly! You know how old I am!"

Carolina opened her arms, and Kitten skipped into them to give her mother a hug.

"Girls are supposed to say whatever they have to say," Carolina told her, holding Kitten at arm's length so she could look into her eyes. "Whatever, whenever. And don't you forget it."

Kitten stuck her lip out again. "Are you going to call Hattie and tell her not to come?"

"No, I'm going to comb my hair and get my keys while we're waiting for her."

"I could give you the lunch box to show Billy Ray, case he doesn't want to come back with you."

Carolina hugged her hard again. "No, you save it. I'm going to make sure you have a chance to show it to him yourself."

Billy Ray knew that his friends had wanted to honor him. Some of them were sorry they'd judged Carolina harshly—and him right along with her. Some of them wished that they'd stood to be counted instead of giving in to old habits—and old Southern gentlemen. Some of them had just wanted him to know that a new era had arrived in River County, and they were glad it had.

But Billy Ray wasn't sure what the fuss was about. He had defended a woman who needed defending. And God and the State of Florida willing, he had won. What had he done that demanded celebration? Attorneys won cases every day. They employed brilliant defenses, did grueling detective work, negotiated creative settlements, and no one threw them a party.

He had done none of those things. He had simply defended Carolina. He had never asked to be in the limelight. He hadn't asked for the dawn of a new day in River County, either. He had only asked that people tell the truth. He wished with all his heart that his strategy had been brilliant or innovative, that he could take credit for the outcome of the hearing. But in the end, he had simply believed in a woman and fought for her.

The sun had gone down as the party at the Blue Bayou cranked to its highest level. He had sneaked out between one slap on the back and another, and now the air outside had cooled almost enough for him to draw a comfortable breath. He climbed into his car and pulled onto the highway before somebody realized he was missing.

All day he had been tempted to call Carolina and take her out to dinner. But he still didn't know what he should say to her. He had only seen her once in the days since the hearing. She had come by to sign some documents, but Fran had been scurrying in and out of the office, and he had received one telephone call right after the other. They'd hardly had time to exchange a personal word.

Which was just as well, since he hadn't known what

to say. Carolina's life had taken a new path. She was a free woman. She could move anywhere she wanted, do anything she wanted, be anything she wanted. She was no longer bound to River County, and she had shed the Grayson name as effortlessly as a butterfly shedding its cocoon. But Carolina was a good woman and a faithful one. She believed that he had worked miracles. She believed she would be forever in his debt.

He didn't want her in his debt. He wanted her in his life because that was where she wanted to be and for no other reason.

He was driving too fast, he realized. He slowed at the junction to Maggie's house, but he didn't turn. He continued on until the turnoff to Hitchcock Road.

He was going to have to talk to Carolina, but he still wasn't sure what to say. How did he tell the truth without telling her once more that he loved her? How did he set her free when, like every man in her life, he really wanted to bind her to him forever? He adored her, and he was one step from pulling out all the stops to keep her, even though he knew, deep in his heart, that she had to have time to heal, to find out who she was and what she wanted.

She had to have time without him.

By the time he pulled up in front of his house, he was too hot and tired to put the car in the barn. He parked in front and sat without moving; then he forced himself to get out and go inside.

Carolina was waiting in his hallway, iced tea for both of them in her hands, and Three Legs and Four, the new kitten, winding in and out of her ankles.

"I'm not waiting on you." She held up the glass.

"I don't wait on men anymore. I do favors for friends, though. Are we still friends?"

He wanted to take the tea out of her hands and kiss her until she was silent, but he just stood there staring at her.

She shook her head. "It got to be pretty clear you weren't coming to me. You know, I'm tired of being the one to do the work on this relationship, Billy, and someday soon that's going to have to end. But I thought I'd give this one more shot. Take your tea, come inside and sit down."

He held out his hand. The glass was slippery and ice cold.

She started toward his living room; then she stopped. "On second thought, I know a better place to have this conversation." She turned and started up the stairs.

He called after her. "Where are you going?"

She looked over her shoulder. "Where does it look like?"

He was afraid he knew—and afraid he might be wrong.

When he didn't answer, she smiled seductively. "It's hot as heck out there. You look like you could use a shower. I'm going to get one running for you while you take off your clothes. Then you'll be more in the mood for what I have in mind."

"And what exactly is that?"

She raised a brow. "You finishing your tea. And us finishing that conversation we never had."

He followed her up the stairs. "I don't need a shower."

"I know where you've been. I got the news about Whittier early this afternoon, and then Maggie told me about the party. I bet you smell like cigarette smoke. Come on up, you'll feel better."

He got close enough to take her arm. "Carolina, what's going on?"

She wrinkled her nose, and he gave up. "Fine. I'll hop in the shower."

"Sure you don't want me to run it for you?"

"I'll meet you downstairs."

But she wasn't downstairs when he emerged wearing clean boxer shorts, the only clothes left in the bathroom when he got out of the tub. She was waiting for him in his bedroom, her shoes kicked off, the jacket to her sundress hung neatly over a chair, and the dress itself unbuttoned clear down to the valley between her breasts. She was sprawled comfortably on his bed, holding his iced tea.

"Now, isn't that better?"

He had never seen her quite this way. She was smiling, as if she knew a joke that he didn't. The haunted look he had come to associate with her was gone. She was a woman who knew what she wanted, a woman who had figured out exactly how to get it.

He thought of all the things he needed to say, and he opened his mouth to let them pour out.

She shushed him with a wave of her hand. "Don't you dare waste my time on nonsense, Billy. I was a baby when I gave up on you and married Champ, but I grew up quicker than a June bug. You're dealing with a full-grown woman here. I know what I want. I know who I want. And I know everything that comes with the package."

She leaned toward him, moving as slowly as a summer afternoon. The tops of her breasts glistened in the mellow light of the rising moon. "Kitten pointed out something to me today. Want to know what it is?"

"Sounds like I'm going to, one way or the other."

"She wanted to know why women weren't supposed to tell men when they were acting stupid. And I realized that's exactly what I was doing."

"Have I been acting stupid?"

"As a matter of fact, you have, and for a little while there, I thought it was my fault. I got used to taking the blame for lots of things that weren't my fault when I was married to Champ, and sometimes I forget not to."

"Carolina—"

She shook her head. "I know you've been a bachelor for a long time, Billy Ray. I know it might take you a while to get used to having a ready-made family. So I'm willing to wait until you grow into it. I've got a place to live, a wonderful job and a town where I can hold up my head again. And you're worth waiting for. So I'll wait. I might even start school while I am. I'm thinking about getting a degree in counseling, so I can help women in the same trap I was in. Or even better, I might go to law school to do the same thing. Do you think you could stand another lawyer in the family?"

"You have a thousand alternatives." The words sounded as if he was choking. "After a life with almost none at all."

"Is that what's been worrying you?" She slid off the bed and started toward him. "Billy, can you even imagine that a life with you wouldn't be at the top of my list? Or that loving you would keep me from doing everything else I was meant to do?"

He realized that he had to name his greatest fear

now or forever keep silent. "Don't do this because you're grateful, Carolina."

She tipped her head, as if she needed a different view, but her expression softened. "You know, there are lots of reasons to love a man. Because he's smart, or good-looking, or knows how to kiss a girl silly. You're all those things, so you've got that part down pat. But the best reason is because he stands beside you when you need him most. I was raised to believe in Southern gentlemen. I know the real thing when he's right in front of me." She smiled just a little. "Especially when he's waiting there in his shorts and he's a fine, fine specimen indeed."

"You didn't come here just to have a conversation, did you?"

"Right from that first day in high school, you always did know what I was thinking." She unbuttoned the remaining three buttons of her dress and let it drift to her ankles. "Now, stop being a gentleman for just a moment. I've come this far. You have to cover the rest of the distance by yourself."

He did, without hesitation.

Hours later, she was asleep beside him, her head pillowed against his shoulder. Moonlight poured through the room, and he knew that soon he would have to take her home. But there would be other nights like this one, nights when Carolina slept beside him until morning and their children slept soundly in the other bedrooms.

As if she felt him watching her, she opened her eyes and her lips turned up in a soft smile. "I just had the nicest dream."

He stroked her cheek with the backs of his fingers. "What was it?"

"You were holding our first grandchild, a little boy Chris's age, and he looked just like you, even though he was Kitten's son. We were right here in this house. Somebody called out 'Judge Wainwright,' and I turned around, because they were talking to me."

He smiled. "Carolina Waverly Wainwright, circuit court judge. You'll get my vote."

She kissed his fingers. "The house looked just the way it does now, Billy. But it was filled with people and laughter."

"Were we rich and important?"

"I didn't think to look. But I doubt it. We were happy. That was all that mattered." She closed her eyes and snuggled closer.

Billy Ray was content to lie quietly for a few more precious minutes and watch her. He was nobody's knight, nobody's hero. But for the first time he was completely satisfied that Carolina Waverly knew exactly who he was.

He was the man she wanted beside her. Forever.

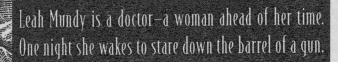

Take 2 of
"The Best of the Best™"
Novels FREE
Plus get a FREE surprise gift!

Special Limited-Time Offer

Mail to The Best of the Best™

3010 Walden Avenue
P.O. Box 1867
Buffalo, N.Y. 14240-1867

YES! Please send me 2 free novels and my free surprise gift. Then send me 3 of "The Best of the Best™" novels each month. I'll receive the best books by the world's hottest romance authors. Bill me at the low price of $4.24 each plus 25¢ delivery per book and applicable sales tax, if any.* That's the complete price, and a saving of over 20% off the cover prices—quite a bargain! I understand that accepting the books and gift places me under no obligation ever to buy any books. I can always return a shipment and cancel at any time. Even if I never buy another book, the 2 free books and the surprise gift are mine to keep forever.

183 MEN CH74

Name	(PLEASE PRINT)	
Address	Apt. No.	
City	State	Zip

This offer is limited to one order per household and not valid to current subscribers.
*Terms and prices are subject to change without notice. Sales tax applicable in N.Y.
All orders subject to approval.

UBOB-98   ©1996 MIRA BOOKS

One bold act—one sin—committed in an otherwise
blameless life begins a family's descent into darkness.
And this time there is no absolution....

Confession

THE TRUTH HAS THE POWER—
TO DESTROY EVERYTHING.

When Rebecca has an affair with her daughter's
boyfriend, all those close to her are forced to deal
with the fallout and forces everyone to reexamine
their own lives. CONFESSION is a poignant tale
chronicling the destructive path of a wife and
mother's confessed affair with a younger lover.

The newest blockbuster novel from the
New York Times bestselling author of
A Glimpse of Stocking

ELIZABETH GAGE

Available as a trade-size paperback in May 1998—
where books are sold.

MEG465

MIRA

Also available by
bestselling authors

Jennifer Blake and EMILIE RICHARDS

Don't miss the opportunity to receive these other romantic stories:

Jennifer Blake:
#66281	GARDEN OF SCANDAL	$5.99 U.S.☐ $6.99 CAN.☐
#66429	KANE	$5.99 U.S.☐ $6.99 CAN.☐

Emilie Richards:
#66152	IRON LACE	$5.99 U.S.☐ $6.99 CAN.☐
#66273	RISING TIDES	$5.99 U.S.☐ $6.99 CAN.☐

(quantities may be limited)

TOTAL AMOUNT	$
POSTAGE & HANDLING	$
($1.00 for one book, 50¢ for each additional)	
APPLICABLE TAXES*	$ _____
TOTAL PAYABLE	$ _____
(check or money order—please do not send cash)	

To order, complete this form and send it, along with a check or money order for the total above, payable to MIRA Books, to: **In the U.S.:** 3010 Walden Avenue, P.O. Box 9077, Buffalo, NY 14269-9077; **In Canada:** P.O. Box 636, Fort Erie, Ontario L2A 5X3.

Name: _____

Address: _____ City: _____

State/Prov.: _____ Zip/Postal Code: _____

Account: _____

*New York residents remit applicable sales taxes.
Canadian residents remit applicable GST and provincial taxes.